The Seventh Age

Titles by Scott Marcy

Novels

The Seventh Age
The Great Gate
Elven Born

Strange World Survivor Series

Surviving Eden: Episode 1
Game of Shadows: Surviving Eden – Episode 2
Into the Storm: Surviving Eden – Episode 3

The Seventh Age

By

Scott Marcy

Second Printing, 2017

www.ScottMarcy.net

ISBN: 0692216456

ISBN 13:9780692216453

To my mother, father, and God. Their love, patience, and guidance made this book possible.

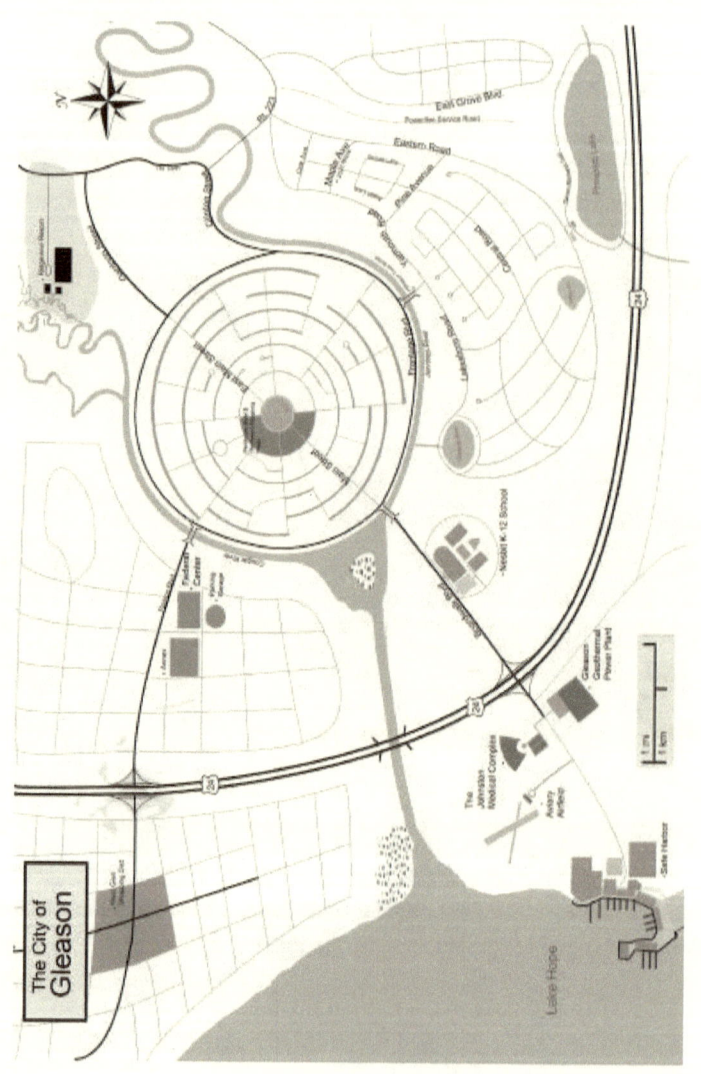

The City of Gleason

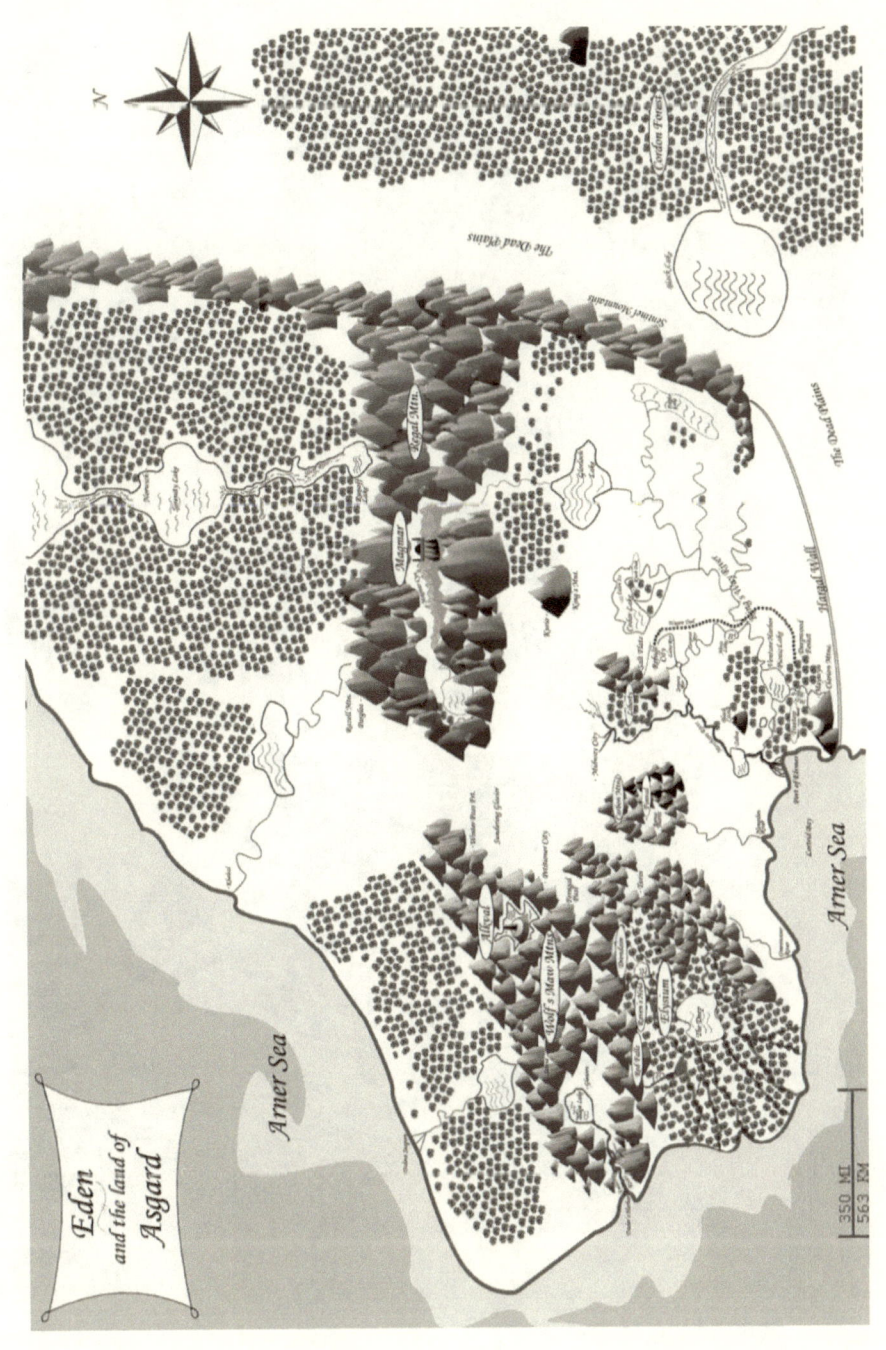

Eden
and the land of
Asgard

Arner Sea

N

The Dead Plains

Golden Forest

Sound Mountains

Arner Sea

350 MI
563 KM

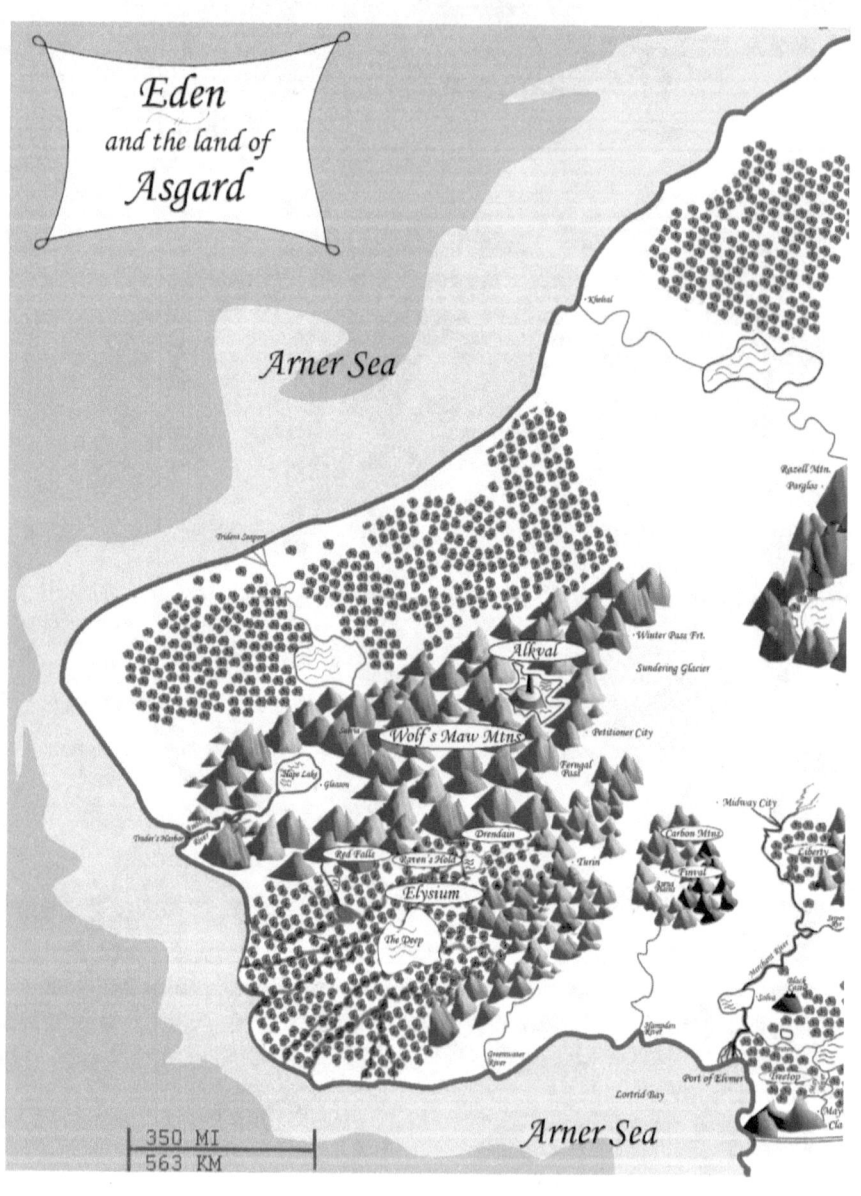

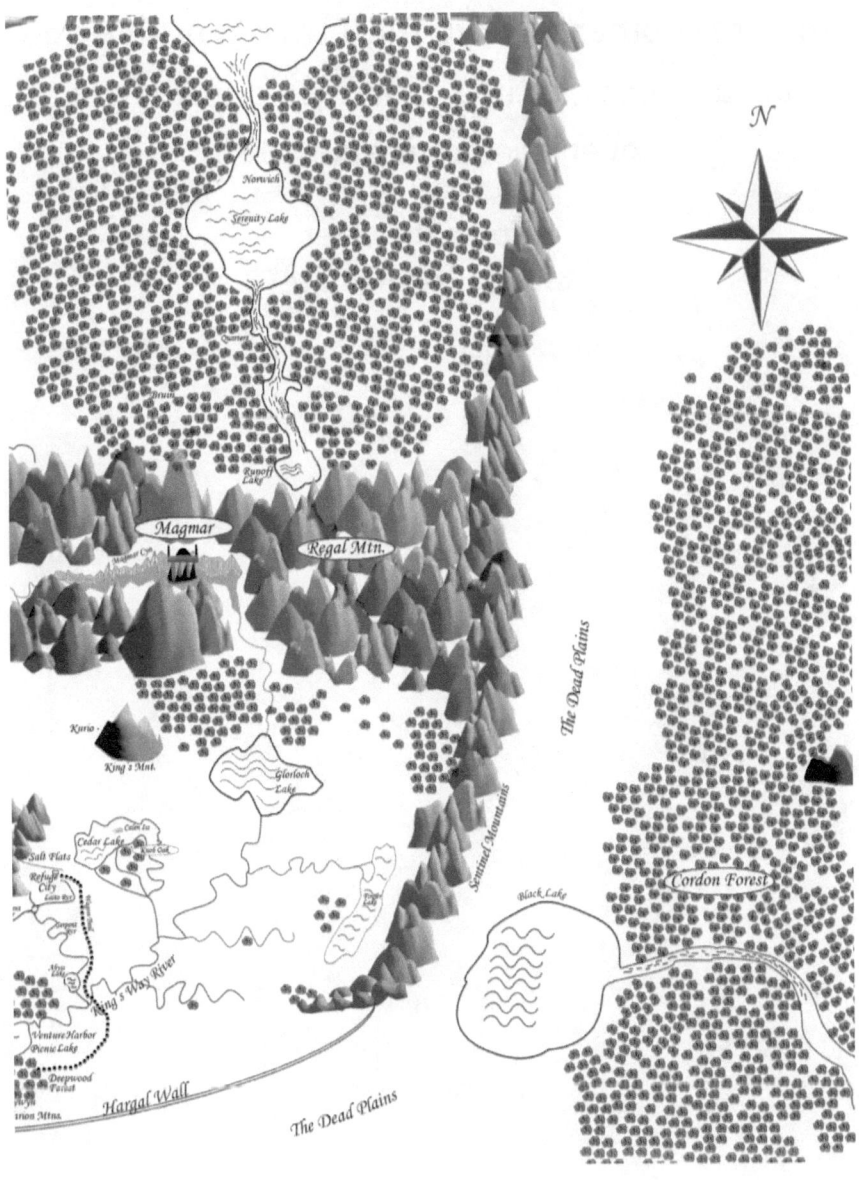

"Once in the lifespan of the universe, the element rhunite submerged into the 11th dimension and ceased to exist in time. Why? No one knew, not even the great elders ...."

– Tobin the Elder
"Lectures on Rhunite"

Introduction:

"The end of our world began like any other day, the end of the 'Sixth Age,' the age of man. We were unaware that we stood upon the precipice, an unknown land stretching out before us, the beginning of the 'Seventh Age.' We awoke to our mundane and burdensome lives, a day that would be the same as all others, a day of boredom and drudgery. Our minds could not conceive, and hearts could not accept that everything – our trivial lives, our unquenchable desires, our many loves, our vices, and our virtues – were about to end. It was impossible. Unthinkable. Ridiculous. Our perceptions were concrete, the sure bedrock of our lives, allowing no alteration. We peered into the depths of space and understood all of nature, from the infinitely small to the cosmically large; humanity was fated to rule the Earth and perhaps the universe."

"We were wrong."

Tarina paused a moment and brushed a golden tress behind her pointed ear. The elva, a female Elven, sat with an oracle scroll draped across her lap. A group of Elven children – who had recently taken part in the ceremony that marked the passage from child to adult, "The Ascension" – sat on the floor in a semi-circle before her, youthful faces looking up at her with expectation, jubilant to hear the sacred stories. These sacred tales were a sign of their ritual passage through the journey of life, an achievement, a watershed event, and they were eager to hear and understand this secret knowledge. The firelight in the hearth illuminated the room, casting long shadows upon the floor, making Trina appear ancient and storied. The hour was late, the time for tales.

"I am chronicling this tale for future generations, but none of these stories are mine. These tales belong to others, lives that eclipsed mine. It is their story that you must remember, and the one you must tell to your children. The day their age ended, it gave birth to our Age."

"Hear my tale, my children, and cherish my words. I will tell you humanity's faded dominion – that once held sway with ancient religions, powerful armies, and unquestioned authority – the glory of humanity burned bright, and holy men proclaimed the future with hubris, knowing the mind of God, knowing His hidden ways, and knowing His path through the wilderness. These celestial cartographers charted our course to the future, prophesying: peace, wonderment, abundance, and triumph; men with itching ears, men consumed with insatiable lust, devoured their words, but prosperity fled from them, as shadows from the rising sun. Hear my tale, and take heed to my warning. The future is uncertain; the path ends; the divine conceals; man searches: he searches without end. Embrace the moments of your life, because this is the Great Spirit's greatest gift."

"Thus we begin our tale ...."

Chapter 1

Underpaid and underappreciated, one of the faceless millions, Rory Vakhal was a mid-level government employee. Like most federal employees, the minutes passed with glacial speed. His thoughts coagulated, his body fossilized, and he watched the clock. It was late afternoon, and he was exhausted. A pile of documents, one more stack in an endless bureaucracy, was ready for storage. He slid them across his desk, the next pile awaiting his bloodshot eyes. Leaning back in his chair, he pinched the bridge of his nose, massaging away the eyestrain and trying to concentrate. He fought to begin. The engine that drove his ambition began to sputter, and his emotional fuel gauge read "empty." He raised his cup and swallowed the last dram of coffee, sour and bitter like his attitude. The morning was gone, and so was his coffee.

He picked up a folder and leafed through it. Months of tedious research, late nights pouring over records and storage facilities filled with documentation resulted in 12 indictments. Such was the life of a forensic CPA, his time divided between the FBI and the Treasury Department.

He rose up from his desk and stretched, elbows raised and back arched. Government jobs meant government desks and government chairs – chairs designed by the Marquis de Sade – or so it felt. He sat in the same chair 60 hours a week; the least they could do was buy him a comfortable chair, but expensive desks and plush chairs belonged to management: men and women measuring success by the opulence of their furnishings.

Far from the hallowed halls of Washington, his office lay on the eighth floor of the Government Services Building. He stood before a plate glass window and absorbed the beauty of Gleason, Kansas. The golden fields and green plains formed the tapestry that he called home.

Harvest was in full swing, which caused his mind to drift back in time. Long ago days filled with near endless labor still made his body ache. The

1

harvest would continue well into the night, and they were welcome to it. He enjoyed air conditioning and a comfortable office far too much to leave them. Yet a part of him felt trapped by these comforts, a gilded cage for the middle class.

Off in the distance, miles of circles – circular crops of wheat, sorghum, corn, and soybeans – stretched off into the horizon. The crops burst up from the soil with a promise of a bountiful harvest and a modest profit. However, farmers had to bring in the harvest before insects and drought withered them. Off to the west, ranchers guided their cattle to green pastures and fresh waters, lands fed by a complex network of rivers and streams.

When people thought of cowboys, they imagined horses instead of helicopters and all-terrain-vehicles. A few holdouts still ranched by horse, but most people had shifted to new technology, machines changing every facet of farm and ranch life. Old timers puzzled over computers, gave up in frustration, and drafted their children to implement the new technologies. It seemed as if nature and a simple way of life were bygone concepts.

Agriculture still reigned supreme in Gleason, but gnawing apprehension compelled the people to diversify. A fragment of Greenwich Village moved to Gleason, and Main Street received a facelift. National chains filled empty stores, and a small slice of New York City relocated to small town America. The marriage of big city and heartland USA was an unlikely combination but an apparent success. City weary business people, retired civil servants, and – most of all – *artists* moved to the area, fleeing urban claustrophobia, urban mania, and urban violence, their exodus bringing much-needed income.

Gleason was home. Rory was born there, and if God answered his prayers, he would die there. He loved the people, he loved the town, he loved the land, and he loved the way of life. But like most locals, he was unsure what to make of this refugee influx. Art studios and galleries outnumbered grocery stores, and the people who frequented them were peculiar. Benign, but strange in a city sort of way.

His cell phone chirped in his jacket pocket, and he retrieved it. Christy sent him another text message. "See you tonight, coming in late." Three long months had passed, but she was finally coming home. Parts of him were elated, creating an uncomfortable bulge in his trousers.

A second text arrived from Bill Kendal, "Meet me in the conference room." The tyranny of the urgent once again demanded his attention. He picked up the folder from off his desk and placed his coffee cup on a Disney coaster, a memento of better days and a forgotten vacation. And when he left his office, he locked the door behind him.

Various government agencies occupied the building and the annex across the street. One could find every federal agency represented within its walls. Most government agencies insisted upon hard-line phones even though everyone carried a cell phone. The office phones rang all day as if it was an emergency call center. Investigators labored at computer screens, and support staff scurried from meeting to meeting, pens clutched between their teeth, carrying yellow legal pads, coffee cups, and piles of resource materials. The scene repeated itself every day, Monday through Friday, nine to five – the machine never slept: its appetite was voracious, and it consumed information from around the globe. Gleason was but one small tributary feeding into the larger river of information that was the Federal Government, a government yearning to know every trivial detail, communication, and miscellaneous internet search made by its citizens.

Half the office workers were strangers. An endless stream of new employees took up residence in their office, rented banal homes, and complained about Gleason, regarding small town life as oppressive. Eager for the lie of success, petty bureaucrats on a relentless government treadmill, they soon departed without a "goodbye," eager for the bright city lights. Gleason was just a "whistle stop" in their larger career track, a place one would never list on a resume. Rory stopped learning their names and discounted them as tourists.

The other half of the office became his surrogate family. They celebrated holidays, danced at weddings, cried at funerals, played golf on weekends, and went out for drinks. He could not imagine working at any other office, even though Christy suggested transferring more than once. She worked for the State Department and often traveled to Washington D.C., a grueling commute by anyone's standards. Still, it was a safe environment for their 4-year-old son, Michael, and that pleased her.

Rory passed by the elevator bank, which ran slow and overfed occupants filled it. The stairs were faster and healthier and walking rewarded him with a smug feeling of superiority. He jogged up to the next floor, the tapping of his feet echoing off the concrete walls, and congratulated himself on raising his heartbeat. His boss, Bill Kendal, had an office at the end of the hall.

Federal managers measured their success by office placement and the opulence of their furnishings. They competed for softer carpeting, custom desks, costly art, and leather chairs. A private secretary and full staff also helped. No matter how high one rose within the department, there was always someone with more: more floor space, more furniture, and a reserved parking space. A new desk created a tumult and sent shockwaves through the building.

Rory made a quick right turn, and through a glass wall, he saw Bill. As was typical, Bill sat at the head of the table, in command, a captain at the helm, sailing into combat. Rashaan and Steve, yes-men and hangers-on, sat on either side of him. Sea lampreys of the bureaucratic ocean, they attached themselves to whatever predator appeared strongest and nourished their careers.

Rory combed his fingers through his short, russet locks, struggling to discern the reason for the meeting. Everyone appeared grim, as though on trial and listening to the prosecution. He submitted all of his expense

4

reports with receipts, and his progress was satisfactory – then why did his stomach hurt? When he approached the door, he took a deep breath and braced himself for the verbal assault. "Bill, what's up?"

"Close the door and take a seat." A deep frown marred Bill's typically jovial expression. He sifted through a stack of papers and spread them out before him, evidence for the prosecution. Feeling like a condemned prisoner, Rory sat beside Steve.

"What's up? You have me worried," Rory said.

"The Assistant Attorney General and the DEA – those bastards – are taking credit for the Miami Harbor Investigation. They made a deal with Loro Verde Import/Export without consulting us. In exchange for their testimony against the Rios Cartel, their CEO and CFO are getting amnesty." Bill rubbed the back of his neck and glared at the reports as if to set them on fire. "The case we worked on for six fucking months just got flushed. I can't believe this. We needed this touchdown."

Rory's lips formed many questions, but all of them went unexpressed. He poured a glass of water and took a sip. Bill continued his verbal temper tantrum. "… We do all the legwork, and they get all the credit. We have the lowest closure rate of any department. We could be looking at staff reductions."

"This is bullshit," Steve blurted.

"You're right," Rashaan agreed, feeling the need to be heard. "We need to pursue our own cases and stop cooperating with them. Otherwise, we will never get the spotlight."

"Alright," Bill said, leaned forward, and gripped the side of the tabletop, "we need a field goal. There has to be some way we can capitalize on our work."

Rory shrugged. "Loro Verde has over two billion in assets, most of them in the Port of Miami. Amnesty doesn't mean innocence, and they forfeit all of their assets under the Controlled Substances Act and under the Money Laundering Control Act. I know these amnesty plea deals. They have to acknowledge their guilt before a judge and the accuracy of the charges against them. If we act fast, we can file a motion in Federal and Florida courts to attach these assets. You know how much the Assistant Director Mason likes supplementing the Federal Government's budget with a convict's funds."

"That's good." Bill slid forward to the edge of his chair. "We will still get credit for our work. It's not as showy as a front page drug bust, but it works. The other agencies will go crazy trying to get a share of the credit. Steve and Rashaan, get on that right now. I want our legal counsel to submit papers in court by the end of the day."

"We got it," Steve said, and Rashaan reiterated the sentiment. Both wanted credit for completing the task, so they walked and then ran down the hallway. Rory moved his hand to pick up his glass of water, but he saw something strange: ripples emanated from the center of the water and flowed out to the rim of the glass. Many things could cause it, a faulty air conditioning compressor or an electric motor out of balance, yet something about it troubled him. He held the glass, which should have insulated it from vibrations. He took a sip and dismissed the observation.

Bill rose to his feet and grinned. "Keep this quiet until we get it locked down in court. I don't want anyone moving in on our action." Rory exited the room, chasing after Bill. Bill asked, "So when is Christy getting back?"

"Tonight," Rory said. A buxom blonde strode past them with a swish of her skirt, and both men watched her sashay past them. "I think I'm going crazy."

Chapter 2

President John F. Kennedy said, "Victory has a thousand fathers …." Both state and federal government authorities exemplified this sentiment, as evidenced by the conclusion of "The Miami Harbor Investigation." Fashionably clad law enforcement officials, government officials, politicians, and private contractors milled about the rooftop bar, drinks in hands and avarice in their souls. They sipped martinis and exaggerated their role in the investigation, celebrating the victory as if it was theirs. The interagency task force seized 1145 kilos of cocaine and arrested 31 individuals, allegedly affiliated with the Rios Drug Cartel.

Richard Drew raised his right eyebrow and cocked his head. "I find your conclusion that 'This is a major win …' hard to believe. The estimated annual consumption of cocaine in the United States is around 600 tons, worth an estimated 38 billion dollars. You confiscated almost 1150 kilos of low-grade product. According to my sources, it was of such low quality as to be worthless."

Assistant Director Greg Mason, of Homeland Security, grew red-faced and raged within his soul. He sipped his single malt whiskey, pausing to temper his response; words, like bullets, could never be undone. "The drugs were of adequate quality and had a street value over 27 million dollars. This hurt the Rios Cartel. They lost some of their best people, and we rescued two agents. Those men are home with their families thanks to our efforts."

"Yes, you covered the details at the press conference." Richard posted a quick update to his blog. "'Adequate quality' might suggest that you were appeased."

"'Appeased?'" Greg asked, his back becoming ramrod straight.

"Most drug cartels are international corporations. They understand their markets, and they know their business environment. A show bust is a part of doing business. It makes the law enforcement agencies happy and docile. It also gives the public the illusion of safety, so they supplied your agents with some low-grade product, a 'throw away load,' and sacrificed peripheral people that no one they would miss. These busts make a big splash across the headlines, and they distract everyone from their actual importation channels," Richard stated, searching the internet for the next distraction.

Greg took a swig of his scotch, choked down the venom that welled up from his soul, and he formulated a strategic response. It had to be firm; it had to be decisive, but it had to be tempered. Before he could reply, three other people barged into his interview. Mary led Richard by the arm and escorted him across the rooftop terrace, away from the bar and Greg.

When she looped her arm through his, he surveyed her body as any man might. Her steel blue, fitted blouse had one too many buttons opened, allowing him to see the swell of her breasts – breasts a bit larger than nature might allow, and she wore her black satin pencil skirt a bit too tight. The sum total effect of her attire enticed men. The smoldering, sultry scent of her "La Merque" perfume, intoxicated the male mind. It might have signaled danger if he was paying attention. Why would a woman dress in such a fashion? What did she want? He ignored the warning signs and gave into his desires.

I'd do her, he mused.

Mary asked, "I was wondering if you would like to meet some of my top agents? They were a part of the raid on the compound. Automatic weapons fire strafed their car. I can forward you a short video if you like. I'm sure your readers would like to see the carnage."

"Great," Richard said, hoping for an action packed video clip. His finger combed his curly brown locks from his angular face and looked at her expectantly. "The public loves action and blood. Was anyone injured?"

"Two agents were grazed, and one agent is in the hospital under observation. My man was hit in the chest by a 9mm round, but he was protected by his Kevlar vest."

"Oh, that's good," Richard replied with deflating interest and returned to idle internet searches. "I'm glad to hear it."

They hospitalized the agent despite his objections. Mary insisted that he spend the night. If he tried to exit the hospital, she would have shot him and then checked in his unconscious body. Gunplay added drama and excitement increased public interest. That meant a larger budget and promotion. She moved in close to him, entering his body space, her breasts nearly touching him and her hips jutted toward him, and she pulled up raw video footage. "It's really exciting." The footage came from the raid, and the agents fought in mortal combat: rounds punching holes in the cars, glass shattering, and the agent collapsing in agony.

"If the networks like it, I might be able to get you airtime on national news." Richard placed his right hand on the small of her black and then slid it down to the rising swell of her bottom and let it linger there. "We can talk about it back at my suite over drinks. It's just two floors down."

She bowed her head and lowered her gaze. "Okay," she said with a meek voice. "I don't mind."

"Great!" He guided her toward the elevator and ushered her inside it. As the doors slid shut, he said, "I'm sure we can work something out."

A middle-aged man, John Richmond, watched the drama and shook his head. Men were so arrogant. She was the real predator, and once she had him, when she really had him, he would live to regret the day they met.

"I'll have another." John leaned against the bar and held up his glass. The bartender eyed him as if a potted plant asked for a drink. To be fair, the man was invisible – round belly, graying mane, and world-weary eyes – or so it seemed when compared to the powerful and elegant revelers. His ill-fitting suit could belong to an insurance agent or perhaps a grocer. The truth was difficult, maybe impossible, to believe.

The bartender refilled the man's drink and said, "No problem," as though he did John a favor and returned to drying glasses. John sipped his drink and faded into the background. He was just another middle-aged man, looking for solace in a glass of cheap liquor.

John studied an advertisement, playing on the bar television. A woman clad in a glistening scarlet bikini wandered through a seaside villa and then passed through billowing white gauze curtains. Her lover, one assumed, a man with six-pack abs and a bronze suntan, lounged near the pool. He held up his right hand, and she placed a glass of scotch in it. She then sat next to him and stroked his chiseled chest, rippling with powerful muscles. Was it a liquor ad, a swimsuit ad, or a resort ad? A moment later a bottle of men's cologne appeared on the screen, wrong on all three counts. He tried the cologne: it smelled like cabbage.

The anonymous stranger turned and observed the beautiful people. They wandered about the terrace – gods of pop culture – and schmoozed with the Washington elite and boasted to reporters. They were winners of the genetic lottery: beautiful, handsome, ambitious, and arrogant. They embodied the public's perception of success, but this was deliberate: Hollywood created it, and marketers sold it. They were successful because society insisted upon it. It made sense, according to a vacuous and superficial logic.

The real powerbrokers, dark figures hidden from the public, knew this stranger, and they called him "Angel," short for "Angel of Death." He and his associates performed black bag operations, intelligence gathering, and assassinations for Homeland Security, saving the world while staying in the shadows. They paid him through the legitimate arm of his corporate empire, the TEBD International Consulting Group.

John smirked and shook his head. Politics was a drug the ambitious mainlined. Few suspected and no one admitted that he was the reason the raid succeeded. A law enforcement friend, Special Agent Justine Travis, begged him to help. Her brother was one of the kidnapped agents, and John owed her a favor.

John avoided recognition. This was – for more reasons than one might suspect – the required outcome. The name John Richmond, as well as his body, was a façade. They provided him with a human face, a generic face, that hid an inhuman creature; such anonymity would have been denied him if he exposed his true nature.

The weight of someone's stare interrupted John, so he glanced over his right shoulder. "My but this is an important event," he said to Christy Vakhal. "Our Dark Friends are sending everyone to this soiree." Assigned to Homeland Security by the US State Department, Washington assigned Christy to high priority events.

"I could say the same about you," Christy said and slipped onto a stool beside him. She flicked a golden blonde tress over her shoulder and set her empty glass down on the bar. "I'll have another," she said to the bartender.

Not even a gray skirt suit and ecru silk blouse could conceal her amazing figure. Between that and her Hollywood beauty, a group of men congregated behind her. Without looking back, John said, "She's married, and she outranks you. So move along, boys."

After the bartender set another glass of scotch on the rocks before her, she said, "You should get the award. Greg just showed up and took all the credit."

"That's Greg's job, and he's welcome to it. I'm very well paid for my efforts, and our employers fear exposure. They prefer us to remain in the shadows, so I'll stay in the shadows ...."

———

The Bonita Estrella Hotel lay just across Ruiz Boulevard. It housed tourists, businesspersons, and a medical convention. However, it was also an intersection that would change the course of humanity. If the politicians knew, if the intelligence community knew, if the authorities knew, if the public knew, or even if the cartels knew, they would have acted – but they did not know, and they did not act, and they did not care.

The hotel was a sensible compromise between luxury and economy, plain faced and functional. Its reinforced concrete and glass exterior resisted hurricanes, or whatever nature could throw at it. The 30-story building afforded tourists a prime view of both the City of Miami and the Atlantic Ocean. True, there were bigger and more beautiful accommodations. But it was a bargain, and bargains drew crowds.

Suite 2812 on the twenty-eighth floor contained the body of what had once been a husband and father. Four red holes, the size of a man's thumb, marked the back of the man's Hawaiian shirt. Blood splatter coated everything: the ceiling, the walls, and the furnishings – red droplets appearing like modern art.

The body of a woman lay face down on the balcony threshold, the result of a feeble attempt to flee. After repeated rape, the woman escaped her attacker and made a break for freedom, even if it was only onto the balcony. Three more shots cut her down and left her draped across the balcony threshold, blood flowing from the thumb size holes in her back and then congealed in the tropical sun.

The reason for their death was an accident, at least an accident on their part. The minimum wage security guard had no way of knowing that the

The Seventh Age

5 kilos cocaine was low grade. Otherwise, he would never have sold it to the drug dealer. The disgruntled dealer decided to make an example of them. The product – which they hoped would fund an upscale lifestyle – covered the beds, tables, and television with white powder; the white dust provided a stark contrast to the glistening red blood.

A ten-month-old baby, clad only in a diaper, crawled through the blood and gore. She grasped her mother's arm with a blood soaked hand and tried to rouse her. No matter how hard she tried, her mother would not stir. The baby girl laid her head on her mother's shoulder and waited to die.

Time passed, and despite the blistering sun, her mother's body grew cold. Death lingered, and the baby girl grew weary and hungry. She crawled through a pool of blood over to the edge of the balcony. The railing balusters were set too wide, a cost-cutting measure by a corrupt contractor, and the girl passed between them. The brilliant sunlight stung her brown eyes as she gazed down at city traffic. Cars and buses, appearing the size of toys, rushed from light to light, as if in some bizarre race. From the dizzying height, she wobbled on the ledge.

"… I'm flying out tonight," Christy said. "I'm going home early and surprising Rory."

"What was the name of that town you lived in?" John's face lit up, and he said, "Oh yes, it's Gleason, Kansas. I should visit you and meet your husband and little boy."

"I prefer to keep my two live separate," Christy said. "Rory would worry."

As it would happen, John glanced across the street and spotted the balcony – and the blood. His eyes were far sharper than that of any human. A moment later, he spotted the corpse of a woman, the open

13

glass door, and then the corpse of the man. When he spotted an infant tottering on the balcony's edge, he gasped.

The drink slipped from John's fingers, plummeted, and then shattered on the coral stone floor. He surged toward the edge of the terrace. Christy's head snapped to the right as he sprinted through the bureaucrats. John ripped away the façade. Golden wings grew from his back and golden locks cascaded over his shoulder. His skin turned to porcelain, and his eyes beamed like blazing sapphires. Breasts exploded from her chest, and narrow hips became wide. For you see, John was actually Sabrina, and Sabrina was an Elven Maige.

Sabrina streaked through the reveling crowd and hurtled over the edge. The astonished patrons gasped as Sabrina plunged out of sight. A woman screamed and pointed: "Look!" All eyes beheld the baby tottering on the edge of the balcony. The baby tumbled and plummeted toward the concrete.

Sabrina stretched her wings and swooped up underneath the infant. She reached out and caught the baby in midair. Clutching the bloody baby to her chest, she soared up from the city. Her wings flapped three times, and she rocketed into the Miami sky.

The baby reached out with a bloody hand and touched Sabrina's face, leaving a smear of blood across her cheek. Hovering with sweeping flaps of her wings, Sabrina examined the carnage and the corpses of the baby's parents. She then turned her attention to the child and looked into the baby's big brown eyes, and her heart broke – a dam collapsed in her soul as she cradled the new life.

Her right hand wiped the blood from the infant girl's face and caressed her cheek. "If you want me, I'll be your mother." The baby smiled and then pressed into her. "Very well then, we are a family. I think I'll call you Eliza. I loved Audrey Hepburn in 'My Fair Lady.' Do you like that?" The girl squealed her laughing approval.

14

The Seventh Age

Little Eliza buried her face into her new mother's neck, closed her eyes, and held on tight. Sabrina caressed Eliza and deliberated her next act. She spent 88 years on Earth, and her soul was weary; crime and injustice came as natural to humanity as breathing. They never had enough violence, hatred, or selfish ambition. One brutal man replaced another: governments rose and fell, yet the macabre parade continued.

Besides, they had witnessed her true form. She could never return. There would be too many questions, and they would try to take Eliza from her. No, they both needed a fresh start in a familiar place.

Sabrina rotated in the air toward the west, and she chanted in a low voice. The Elven words rumbled on her lips and cracked like thunder across the face of the deep. A great vortex rotated before her, and the blue sky swirled like flowing waters: it parted and ripped – a portal yawned and formed a wide circle.

The land of Asgard – the Wolf's Head Peninsula, surrounded by the Arner Sea on the planet Eden – lay beyond the portal. Astonished faces gazed up from the rooftop bar as the people pointed at her. She shook her head and sighed. The decision would set the course of their lives. She and Eliza flew toward the portal and home.

After they had passed through it, Sabrina closed the portal. Christy stood before a half-wall on the rooftop terrace. Eyes wide, mouth agape, and face ashen, she watched Sabrina disappear, and moments later, a thunderclap accompanied a percussion wave. It shattered every window on the strip and shook the building on which Christy stood. When brilliant white light blasted from a white star, hovering in the middle of the mid-day sky, Christy shielded her eyes with her hands. A throaty rumble arose from the Earth, and the planet awoke from its long slumber, a great beast shifting under the feet of men.

Chapter 3

"I told you. You need to start looking," Bill lectured Rory. "Christy's gone for months at a time, and you just wait for her, taking care of the kid. That's not right. Women are the ones who are supposed to take care of the children and change diapers." Bill shuddered and snarled at the thought.

Rory tried to ignore Bill's chauvinism. However, a growing part of his psyche found it soothing, and something within him longed to dominate her. Perhaps it was evolutionary instinct or a learned behavior. Whatever the source, it took root within him and grew each day, like a strangleweed coiling around its prey. He tried to argue it away — he tried to reason it away, but Christy's void strengthened it. She called it "caveman thinking," and went on the attack whenever he expressed it. He usually agreed with her to avoid conflict and retreated to the garage, pretending to work on a project until her temper cooled. When the argument ended, like a midday storm, he returned and spent the rest of the day trying to make her smile, a sign that she still loved him.

His heart grew weary from the routine and the crushing loneliness. Christy's trips came with greater frequency and duration. Further compounding his misery, her career progressed at an exponential rate, while his career languished. The tidal forces of life were pulling them apart, and all he could do was watch her drift away.

Qualifying for fieldwork with the FBI occupied his time and comforted him. He always envisioned himself a hero, kicking down doors and exchanging gunfire with dangerous criminals. Reality disillusioned him. The FBI was largely a bureaucratic organization, and only field agents, less than one percent of the total staff, discharged their weapons in the line of duty, and only then on an infrequent basis. Only a tiny fraction of the one percent shot a suspect.

"We need to go out for drinks and get you back in the game. Let Christy come home to an empty house," Bill said.

"You forget about my 4-year-old son, Michael. Mrs. Darby needs to be home by six to fix supper for her husband. I can't go out."

"Man, she *is* in control," Bill said. "Okay, here's what you do. You leave her with the kid tomorrow night and then go out. What is she going to say? No, you have to stay home? She's been away for three months."

Even though Bill neither was married nor had a steady girlfriend, he claimed to be an expert on affairs the heart. Rory decided long ago not to take marriage advice from such men. "No can do," Rory said. "I plan on sleeping with Christy all night long, all the next day, and then all night again. I'm going to be too exhausted to go out."

"Yeah, right," Bill laughed. "Tell me another lie. Once you make a commitment, they're too tired." Rory understood Bill's rage. He was balding, paunchy, abrasive, and opinionated – not the qualities most women looked for in men. Thus he migrated from one disastrous relationship to the next, love always out of reach.

The pair stepped into the elevator and headed down to the lobby. The sun fell behind the expansive horizon and shrouded the land in the darkness. Street lamps flickered to life and cast long shadows across the lobby. Bill wanted a celebratory drink, and he hated to drink alone. How could Rory say no? He called Mrs. Darby and begged her to watch Michael for a few more hours.

Bill continued his diatribe as they strolled along Pearce Boulevard toward the center of town. He began with women, switched to liberals, and then shifted back to female judges. According to Bill, they were all "lunatics." Rory wanted to run away screaming when Bill got like this, but Bill was the boss and Rory's best friend. They passed over the Ruben Goddard

Truss Bridge with Bill waging "the battle of the sexes." Rory ran his hand over the green painted steel and eyed the turbulent waters. He leaned over the side, looked past the bridge and studied the swiftly moving waters of Cougar Creek, contemplating a sailor's dive followed by a swimming escape. Rory resisted the urge to jump into the river and swim away.

He dodged traffic on Frontage Road, which was always heavy these days. Art galleries, clothing boutiques, and decorating shops rose up two stories surrounding him and replacing the small town he knew. The Amigos Bar was now a ballroom; Pearce Drugstore was a now yoga studio; Madison Furniture was now the Wildwood Emporium, and the Public Library was a private bookseller. These retailers and others purchased every bit of downtown retail space and, after filling it and every other resource, they reaped enormous profits, selling by day and night, paying only minimum wages to employees. The newly transplanted residents consumed these goods with endless appetite, and then these retailers transferred their profits out of the community. So how did Gleason really benefit? Although Rory hated the congestion and the pretentiousness, he did appreciate the new footbridges that spanned the busy streets, making it easy to avoid traffic.

Mayor Orville Gruber worked together with the city council to increase summer tourism and to keep the socialites, and their money, in Gleason. They devised a promotional, "The Spirits of Kansas," a wine and cheese festival. Crowds of artists, tourists, and socialites cascaded together and formed a torrent of nighttime revelry. Men and women milled from shop to shop, carrying plastic cups filled with boutique wine and paper plates covered with cheese — stinky cheese that made the town smell like dirty sweat socks. These shoppers wandered through the outdoor mall and perused the merchandise. Many enjoyed alfresco dining at outdoor cafes, and the rich aroma of gourmet dishes made Rory's stomach rumble.

Bill grumbled as he and Rory weaved through the crowd, not hiding his contempt for the interlopers that crowded their streets. When they passed by Sheriff Tom Hughes, they waved and smiled. Tom patted his large belly, offered them a snaggletooth grin, and then returned the wave.

Like most of the local officials, Tom was too old to change with the times, and he was too proud to admit that modern society left him behind. It was a bad time to be a relic, though. This was an election year. The new, unfamiliar face of Edwin Rojo appeared on every available billboard, and his promotional campaign signs stood in most yards. He even had a slick website and campaign commercial playing on television. Everyone but Sheriff Hughes assumed that Edwin Rojo would win. The sheriff handed out campaign fliers and shook hands. Although they assured him of victory on Election Day, a quiet sense of mourning settled upon his old friends and supporters.

The red brick face of "The Pembroke Hotel" connected to the fashionable "Northwest Shopping Plaza." Passing through the hotel's front doors spirited one back to the old west. Red mosaic tiles covered the floor and climbed halfway up the walls. Where the tile ended, tan stucco began, and tall, arched windows looked out upon the nighttime cityscape, a slice of New York in Kansas. Hanging brass lamps with opaque glass cast a gentle glow over the lobby. They weaved around the furniture, resisting the urge to rest in one of the semi-reclining chairs — chairs which always reminded Rory of a hammock — and climbed the grand staircase to the second floor.

Tourists packed the hotels and spilled out of the Northwest Shopping Plaza, which was fashioned after a high-end ski resort. Most locals found it enigmatic since they had neither mountains nor ski slopes — the nearest mountain was over 350 miles away —but that didn't seem to bother the architects.

A complex array of wooden beams supported a vaulted, circular roof and sheltered three stories of small shops and several towers. The upscale bar, which catered to tourists, resided in one of the towers and had a choice view of the entire town. When they exited the elevator, they passed by the restaurant, which Bill called "the dead zone." He strode past it without a second look and scanned the bar. "Can you believe all the women around here? I'll bet you twenty I can have sex on the premises."

"No bet. I've fallen for that trick too many times," Rory replied.

"Yeah, but no hookers this time," Bill replied. The pair took a seat at the bar and ordered martinis, dry. Gin was the new scotch. "Alright, who shall it be?" He scanned the assorted female patrons.

Rory sighed and took a swig. He hated this game. He wanted to return to work and then go home, but Bill insisted. Drinking and whoring were realities that took Rory by surprise. He always imagined FBI agents as clean cut and happily married: Eliot Ness wearing a crisp suit and a fedora. However, the debauchery of FBI Special Agents astonished him.

"What about that one over there in the black dress ... the blonde?" Bill nodded toward the woman. "She's great. Right?"

Rory searched the room and found Bill's target. A gorgeous blonde with a classically beautiful face lounged in the middle of the bar. Like a silk cloth draped over a magnificent sculpture, a black satin dress clung to her curvaceous body and advertised her services. She was just the way Bill preferred his women — wanton.

"Hooker," Rory declared. "I see her here all the time. You better have a grand in your pocket because she is expensive. The stockbrokers and financial planners use her a lot, or so I've heard."

Another text message arrived from Christy. "Flight delayed in transit, going to be in very late." "Don't wait up." For three long months, they communicated by video-call, texted, and even played chess on the internet. Christy always won. He labored to keep their relationship alive, and he wanted Michael to have time with his mother. Even if it was only simulated contact over the internet, Michael could still hear his mommy say, "I love you." He longed to hold Christy, to be with her, and to touch the face of the woman that held his heart. He gulped down the martini, extinguishing the pain, and ordered another.

Wearing a lopsided smile and clutching currency in his right hand, Bill slid off his stool and sashayed across the room. Leaving without carnal knowledge was not an option, and Rory had to witness it. Otherwise, what was the point? Bill chatted with her a few minutes, and the negotiations commenced. Bill winked at Rory as the pair left the bar.

Rory swiveled around to the bar and, leaning upon one elbow, he stabbed the olive in his martini, hoping the liquor would dissolve his loneliness. A frantic din blasted from the TV above the bar and gave Rory a headache, but the bartender raised the volume anyway. Set in downtown Miami, a blonde reporter, Kendra Smith, stood in the middle of an abandoned street, a shattered display window serving as a backdrop. She interviewed a Florida state official, who blamed the attack on a terrorist plot. The tall, square-jawed man said, "An electromagnetic pulse (EMP) bomb blast destroyed all the technology for 53 miles. It cost Miami-Dade over one billion dollars in damage to its infrastructure. President Townsend needs to act. We need federal disaster relief and military aid. We need transformers, generators, and fresh water …."

"Kendra, we need to interrupt. Whitehouse Press Secretary Stewart Childs is about to make a statement," said Frank Nesbit, news anchor.

"Greeting ladies and gentlemen, I just came from a meeting with President Townsend. He is in the war-room with his top military advisors. A panel of leading scientists blamed the destruction on a seismic event, measuring 4.0 on the Richter scale, a small quake by most standards. The epicenter of the quake was just off the Florida coast, and it, not terrorists, caused the EMP …."

Rory shook his head and rolled his eyes. It made no sense. The quake was so small that no tsunami and no aftershocks resulted. Besides, most experts he read disputed the electromagnetic earthquake theory. How could such a seismic event cause an EMP of that magnitude? They were grasping at straws to ease tensions and stabilize Wall Street.

"… The President met with a bipartisan panel of congressmen. Congress is going to pass a relief bill and have it on the president's desk by sundown. In the meantime, the Army is already on route with relief supplies. They are transporting generators, water, and food …."

When the anchor shifted back to Kendra in Miami, they saw a red pickup truck barreling down the street. It had silver stack exhausts, a chrome roll bar, knobby tires, and a lift kit – making it stand several feet off the pavement. It bellowed like a roaring beast, and its bed bristled with men holding shotguns and rifles. Kendra scurried onto the sidewalk just as the truck came to a stop.

The driver's side door flew open, and a portly man wearing camouflage clothing stepped down from the truck. His right palm rested on the butt of his sidearm, and his left hand held a rifle. Unshaven and bearing arms, a motley crew of eight men piled out of the back of the truck. They surrounded the reporter.

"My name is Phil Pope, and I am from the great state of Georgia." All of the men began to cheer. When a shot exploded from a rifle, they all ducked. "Travis, I told you to keep your finger off the trigger."

"Sorry Phil," Travis said.

"We are here to here to kill some terrorists. I plan to shoot them and tie them to the hood of my car." The men gave a deafening shout, and Travis accidentally fired his rifle again. A fierce glare from Phil made Travis cringe and hide behind the other men. "We don't need the military. We'll take care of it." He held up his rifle and said, "I've got all I need right here …."

The bartender turned the TV volume down, and the patrons returned to their festivity. Time passed, and Rory was lost in deep thought. Bill again slipped onto the stool beside Rory and straightened his tie. "Carnal knowledge on the premises," he said. "Pay up, $20."

"I said, 'No bet,'" Rory replied. "How much did she cost?"

"I got a working man special: it was only $300," Bill said, smug pride evident on his face. Rory wondered how much Bill earned. It had to be a lot more than him. "If you sleep with her too, we get a 2 for 1 special, $250 a piece. What do you think?"

"I'm not cheating on Christy," Rory said.

"Hey, I'm your boss and your best friend. We've known each other since we were 7-years-old. You know Christy is cheating on you. Don't you? Do really think she is celibate for three months? If you don't believe me, just ask her, and watch her eyes. She'll tell you 'no,' but you'll see the truth." Bill grew quiet for a moment. "Women, who the hell can figure them out?"

Rory preferred it when Bill talked about women; that way he wasn't slandering minorities or the poor. It struck Rory as strange that a man could be a jackass and a good man all at the same time – and Bill was a good man. He was a good uncle to his nieces and nephews, a good boss to his employees, and a good friend to Rory. He thought of Rory as a brother and supported him with unquestioning loyalty. When Christy had a miscarriage, Bill had wept and refused to leave.

"You know, Tim Easter only got the promotion because he was black," Bill said and slurped his gin. "If he were white, he would still be back at the bottom of the pile. The man is an idiot."

Rory looked about to see if any African Americans were nearby. Seeing none, he settled down and sipped his gin. By the third martini, Bill had shared his views on lesbians. He was a deacon in his church and, according to his minister, "All lesbians and fags were going to hell." Rory made the mistake of rolling his eyes. "… You don't agree?"

Perhaps it was the booze or a faint spark of courage, but he said, "No. I don't think they are going to hell for being gay. I think heaven and hell is a matter of attitude and relationship. Many animal species have gay populations, and that includes dogs. My dog, Sparky, was gay. He tried to hump every male dog in the park."

"I wonder if gay dogs go to hell?" Bill puzzled in all seriousness.

"You know Steve is gay, don't you?" asked Rory.

"The hell you say," Bill said. "He has a girlfriend. I've seen her photo on his desk."

"That's his cousin," Rory replied. "Steve is still in the closet."

"I can't believe it," Bill said. "Are there any others?"

"Mildred," Rory replied.

"What?" Bill exclaimed. "That sweet little old lady is gay? That's disturbing."

"The human heart is a strange thing. It wants what it wants. Christy had a lesbian fling during her sophomore year of college before we started dating her junior year," Rory said. "I never told you … well, because I knew what you would say." Rory always felt they were destined to be together. Now he wondered if that was a mistake.

"No way," Bill replied. "Christy?"

"Yeah, she confided in me that she had a fling when we went to Colorado State," Rory said and finished his drink. A familiar buzzing filled his brain and mired his thoughts. "I don't care. She is with me. That's all that counts."

"Is she? Then why is she going on all those trips? I know why she goes away on them," Bill said. "She's cheating on you with other women."

24

The Seventh Age

"She's not cheating. It was a fling, a mistake according to her. She never wants to talk about it." Rory rubbed his face and ordered another drink.

Bill searched his memory. Christy moved to Gleason when she was 14-years-old. They were friends in high school, college, and beyond. His heart ached for Rory, and he patted him on the back. "Believe what you want. But consider this, if you had sex with a man, would you call it a fling? Men are either gay or straight: there's no middle ground."

"Christy is straight. She prefers guys. We have a baby together. Remember?"

Bill shrugged. "You don't have to convince me. You're the one sleeping alone. By the way, I hope I'm wrong – for your sake."

Chapter 4

Businessmen exited the bar and walked through the front doors. A blonde beauty worthy of a Hollywood movie – Christy – slipped around them, and all eyes turned toward her. One of the men paused to hold the door for her. "Thank you," she said, avoiding eye contact, and entered the bar. The men hesitated a few seconds, wondering if they should reenter the bar and pursue her, but women of her beauty were seldom available. Fear of rejection urged them to leave, but shame dogged their steps when they trudged away.

She rose to her to the tiptoes, chewed on her index fingernail, and scanned the bar. It was Bill's favorite and the most likely place she would find her husband. Three months, three thousand miles of travel, ungrateful bosses, ridiculous demands, and bland hotel food lay behind her. She searched the crowd for the man she loved –Rory.

Christy pushed through the crowd and entered the club. Men and women, trying to close a last minute agreement for sexual favors, spilled out of the bar and lingered in the foyer, verbally dancing around spending the night together. Men pursued while women evaded in most cases, but some same-sex couples were performing the same dance, more than normal, which surprised her. She doubted that the fire code allowed so many occupants, but bribes solve many problems. She dragged a small suitcase behind her, carried a garment bag, and pushed her way through the crowd.

There were so many people, more people than she imagined possible. Her trips created gaps, and at the conclusion of each gap, she returned to find a burgeoning community. New Gleason consumed old Gleason, and each renovation dissolved another memory.

The Seventh Age

It appeared the entire town had come out to party. Christy brushed aside the annoyance and resumed the search for Rory. A mature, redheaded man with a full head of hair was a rare sight, so Christy spotted Rory at the bar. He sat next to Bill and nursed a martini.

Christy wore a skirt suit and sensible shoes, a poor combination for a romantic rendezvous, but she had time to change. Bill had a lengthy list of grievances, and he was just getting started. There was no danger of Rory escaping from Bill's diatribe anytime soon. She slung the garment bag over her shoulder and dragged the rolling suitcase behind her. Taking a cue from Superman, she headed to the women's restroom for a quick change.

The hallway was as crowded as the foyer and difficult to traverse. Gleason had few entertainment options: bowling, drinking, dining, drinking, dancing, drinking, and more drinking. Most of those born in Gleason chose to drink and then bowl, a troubling combination. The recent influx of avant-garde residents attended symposiums on the environment, politics, and overpopulation. When they grew bored, after about 6 to 8 weeks, they flew back to whichever city they called home, but the itch for Gleason's simplicity always drew them back. Christy understood it. No matter how far or how long she traveled, her thoughts frequently returned to her hometown and those she loved.

She pushed through the restroom door and came to an abrupt halt. A throng of women and a few inebriated men filled the women's restroom, but most massed around the mirror, freshening their cosmetics. Short and shiny mini-dresses appeared to be in vogue, and sexy lingerie – push up bras, thongs, garter belts, sheer hose, and thigh-high nylons – complemented the romantic mood.

When she passed by a couple of women locked in a passionate embrace, she tried not to bump them with her suitcase by turning sideways. She squeezed past them, but only just so. She rose up to her tiptoes and kept moving.

27

"Excuse me," she said and wriggled through the crowd. *There are so many people. I hate it when it is this crowded.* "Excuse me, please." She pushed between groups of women and came to an abrupt halt again.

A flush came from the end stall. Christy tried to work her way through the mob with little success. "Can you let me through," she pled. The gray door swung open, and a petite brunette emerged. She had the look of a college freshman out on a lark: black satin accordion miniskirt, overdone cosmetics, a black diaphanous top, black back-seamed nylons, and a neon blue push-up bra displaying her breasts. *Women are so competitive,* she thought. If one woman wears a new fashion, they all have to wear it.

A mature woman clad in tight leather slacks and a steel blue silk blouse, blocked the girl's path, kissed her, and ushered her back into the stall. "Get a room. Shit!" Christy huffed. She folded her arms and brooded.

A gray door opened for the stall next to the end. A mature woman – hiding her age with layers of makeup, a girdle, and an inappropriately tight dress – exited the stall. The flower of her youth faded long ago, but she still hungered for companionship, if only to drive the loneliness away for the night: she hungered for love, even if the love was an improvised lie. Christy had hurried into the stall before someone else stepped in front of her, but the suitcase caught on the doorframe. After wrestling it into the stall, she closed the door and huffed. This was harder work than going to the gym.

She hung her garment bag on a hook and placed the suitcase on the toilet seat. She stripped off her jacket and unbuttoned her ecru, silk blouse. The jacket, silk blouse, skirt, half-slip, camisole, black satin bra, slacks, black satin panties, and shoes ended up in the yawning suitcase. She stood barefoot in the stall: naked as a newborn baby, feet chilled to a pair of ice blocks, nipples popped, and skin covered with gooseflesh.

A knock on the door interrupted her. "Occupied," she replied with a strained voice. When the knock returned, she opened the door a few inches and peered out into the restroom. A tall man with alcohol-fogged eyes gazed at her and wobbled.

"I'm sorry. I was looking for Julie. Have you seen her? I was supposed to meet her here."

"Over here," a girl chirped and waved her hand above the stall.

It's a restroom for god's sake!

Christy was filled with renewed urgency: this was not a good place to be a naked blonde. However, the day's events popped into her consciousness and immobilized her. She wondered, *was John an angel? Did he really save that baby?* The obvious answer was impossible, so she attributed to holographic projection and some secret plan. *That is ridiculous,* she chided herself, *but what else could explain it?*

Orgasmic moans in the next stall stirred Christy to action. She grabbed a fresh black satin thong, stabbed her feet into it, and drew it up her legs, which caused her to ponder the inequity of female clothing. Nothing in a man's wardrobe approached the complexity or discomfort of women's attire. The mental image of men dressed in high heels and miniskirts caused a smile that wrinkled her nose.

She shook her head and continued dressing. After donning a pair of thigh-high stockings, the "stay-up" variety, Christy smoothed out the wrinkles and adjusted the back-seams of the black nylons. She unzipped the gown, and lustrous scarlet satin gleamed in the dim light. The gown was strapless, had a sweetheart neckline, a dangerous slit up the right side, and a form-fitting contour. She held out the dress and giggled, feeling like a 16-year-old out to impress a boy.

She held it above her head and drew it down her arms. The luxurious duchess satin caressed her skin, but the narrow waistline gathered above her breasts. She pinched, pulled, and tugged it over her fleshy globes. After the struggle, the dress slipped over her body and settle around her hips. She exhaled, pulled up the zipper; the bodice squeezed her torso, allowing in only a halted breath.

After putting on a pair of stilettos and smoothing her dress, she picked out a pair of black satin gloves from the suitcase. As a girl, she had watched classic movies, the kind where fashionably clad women wore satin gloves that extended all the way to their shoulders. She inserted her right hand into the black satin glove, shivering at the cool silky sensation, and drew it up to her shoulder. When they sheathed both arms, she draped a faux diamond encrusted necklace with a large pendant around her neck and a pair of matching diamond bracelets around both wrists, diamond on black making an elegant contrast.

After putting on her matching diamond earrings, with little other choice, dreading the fray to follow, she exited the stall, struggled through the crowd, and set her bags next to the tiled wall. Christy fought her way to the mirror and opened her purse. All of the women around her took note: it was as though she stepped out of a movie, and her leading man, Gregory Peck, waited for her in the lobby.

Despite many bumps and nudges, some deliberate, she set to work. She freshened up her makeup with a hint of blush, dramatic eye shadow, and long, cat's eyelashes. Her lipstick reminded one of candy apple red paint on a Shelby Cobra — a deep red base, vivid highlights, and a glossy sealer — which set her apart.

She brushed and set her platinum locks in a smooth wave, flowing over her shoulder, cascading down her back. The women beside her looked upon her with pouting faces. They applied fresh lipstick, preened their hair, and adjusted their clothes, but it was no use: they felt like the ugly stepsisters in Grimm's Cinderella, and they resented Christy for it.

Christy fought her way through the bathroom, much to the consternation of the other women. She emerged into the hallway but still found herself in a crowd. A set of double doors were open to her left, and they allowed her to see into a private hall. "The Gleason Leather Festival" stretched across a large banner. Some were "tops" and others "bottoms" — dominants or submissives — but all were dressed in fetish garb: leather, PVC, and latex — skin-tight pants, miniskirts, corsets, tights, and mini-dresses.

A group of leather-clad dommes lingered near the door. When a college girl wearing a white dress, with a floral print, wandered past them, a domme stepped into the girl's path. "Why don't you join us for a while? We have an open bar and plenty of seating. Come on; it would be fun."

"I don't know. I'm supposed to meet some of my friends, but I can't find them," the girl replied.

"It's okay. Everyone winds up back here. We'll keep an eye out for them." A hand in the middle of the girl's back, she ushered the hesitant girl into the hall and disappeared from sight. Christy smirked. *I see restraints, a ball gag, and a strap-on dildo in her future.*

A nubile brunette girl, just old enough to enter a bar – a nymph clad in latex tights, stiletto boots, a black diaphanous blouse, and a PVC pushup bra – decided to join the game. She stepped into Christy's path and opened her mouth to speak, but Christy spoke first. Anger rose up from Christy's core, and she preempted the girl saying, "Hmm, let me see." Christy cupped the girl's breasts and gave them a squeeze. "You have nice tits, perhaps a C-cup." She then spun the girl around by the shoulders, nearly toppling the girl; she grabbed the girl's right hip and pushed between her shoulder blades. The girl bent over at the hip and placed her palms on her thighs, straight brown locks draped past her face as she stared at the floor. Christy grabbed the girl's crotch and squeezed. "Very nice, I could pound this for a while. You are a bottom. Aren't you?"

With a girlish tone, the girl said, "No. I'm a top."

Laughter broke out from the assembled crowd. Christy smirked and shook her head. "Sweetie, you are a bottom if I ever saw one, but I'm here to meet someone; so I can't play." After strolling around the girl, she continued toward the main bar, leaving behind the deflated girl.

A dominatrix stepped out from the crowd and strode up to the girl: a sheep in wolves clothing. The domme examined the girl and said, "You belong to me. Turn around." She retrieved a leather collar from her purse and moved aside the girl's brown hair.

"But I'm a top, not a bottom," the girl whimpered.

"Quiet," the domme said and slapped the girl's ass. The girl yelped and grabbed her bottom. "Hands behind your back and head bowed." When the girl complied, she locked the collar and bound the girl's wrists with a pair of handcuffs. She spun the girl around and examined her prize.

The girl looked up through her bangs, a pout on her face, and said, "I really am a top; you know, dominant." The domme clicked a leash to the girl's collar and strode into the club. The girl shuffle-stepped after her and whimpered saying, "But I'm dominant."

Christy smirked and shook her head. She deposited her luggage near the coat rack, not concerned that someone might steal her dirty laundry. She took a deep breath and primped her blonde tresses. She locked eyes on Rory and put on her best smile. Hips undulating, breasts swaying, hands stroking her thighs, a symphony of sexuality, Christy passed through the bar with the grace of a tigress, eyes fixed on her prey.

She slipped onto a bar stool next to Rory. Rory languished in an alcohol-induced trance, but she waited, striking a pose, ready for a close-up. Rory sipped his martini, his glassy eyes fixed on the wooden bar. "Scotch on the rocks," Christy ordered from the bartender. The man set the drink on a coaster. She took a sip and waited. Still, Rory lingered in an alcohol fog. "Do you come here often?"

"Hmm, what?" Rory turned toward her, and his eyes lit up. "Christy!" he shouted and threw his arms around her. He smothered her mouth with hungry kisses and refused to release her. When she finally pushed him away, she saw tears rolling down his cheeks and the pain behind them: she had been away too long. "You made it," he said, as overwhelmed as if she rose from the dead, and dried the tears with a handkerchief.

"I caught an early flight. I wanted to surprise you." She scanned the bar and shook her head. "This place is so crowded that I could barely get through the front door, and don't even get me started about the restrooms."

"Bill's idea," Rory replied.

"Hello Christy," Bill grunted. "You look hot."

"What's Bill up to?" asked Christy.

"Democrats," Rory replied.

Christy frowned. "You are so full of shit, Bill. I don't see how one man can get things so wrong …." A war of words raged, and Rory hid in "no man's land." Bill and Christy spared on everything from global warming to school lunches. Christy was as far to the left as Bill was to the right, a militant Republican battling a liberal Democrat. Theirs was a peculiar relationship. One might assume they hated one another – one would be wrong. When Bill had a severe auto accident, Christy visited him every day in the hospital, and she waited until after Bill recovered to resume their verbal sparring.

"I have to piss," Rory said and slipped off his bar stool. He wandered back to the restroom and fought his way through the crowd. He passed by the leather bar entrance and more than one man leered at him. He dodged a few couples and entered the restroom.

When he entered, he saw a couple having sex and wondered if he was in the wrong place; seeing the restroom stalls, he shook his head and walked past them. People filled the stalls, but he hated using the stand-up urinals. There was no choice; he had to pee or wet his pants. He wandered over to a urinal and unzipped his fly. But as the urine flowed from him, he saw something out of the corner of his eye. The blonde, Bill's hooker, stood in front of a urinal.

What? He rubbed his face and shook off the alcohol fog. *What is happening?*

She had her satin dress hiked up in front, and her black thong was askew. Why was she staring at her crotch? Rory leaned over and saw her hands grasping a penis, a monster of a log. Laughter exploded from his mouth, and the couple paused from their lovemaking to see what was happening.

Rory hurried back from the bathroom, barely able to contain his laughter. He sat down between Christy and Bill. Interrupting their debate on the International Monetary Fund, he had them lean close and whispered in Bill's ear.

"WHAT THE FUCK!" Bill shouted. "YOU'VE GOT TO BE FUCKING KIDDING ME?" Laughter burst from Christy; she shook so hard that she spilled her drink. "This is bullshit, bullshit! Son of a bitch, a guy can't get a simple blowjob anymore." When he stormed out of the bar, Rory and Christy chased after him.

They walked back with Bill to the office and listened to a continuous string of profanity and railing accusations. They left his car in the parking garage and drove him home. During the trip, Rory had to pull over to the curb; Bill leaned out the door and vomited. After he had finished, they dropped him off at his house and waited for him to enter. Bill unlocked his door and waved to them. He then stumbled into his home and closed the door.

"I called Mrs. Darby. She's going to watch Michael tonight," Christy said. "What was Bill celebrating?"

The Seventh Age

"We scored a field goal, according to Bill." Rory put right hand on Christy's satin wrapped thigh and caressed her. "I really missed you. Three months is too long."

"I know, but it was important," she replied.

It was always important. When was Christy's family going to be important? When would they be her top priority? Sharing his feelings would only spark another fight, and she had just got home. If they only had a short time together, he wanted it filled with love and harmony.

Christy's left hand moved over to Rory's lap. Her fingers rubbed his member. With each stroke, she felt it grow full and hard. When it was stiff enough, she bent over and unzipped his fly. Rory held his elbows wide and looked down at his lap. He saw a mop of blonde hair bobbing, and he felt wet sucking on his manhood. His right hand slid down to her bottom and glided over the red satin covered slopes. It was wonderful to have her home.

Chapter 5

The delicious aroma of cooking bacon wafted through the house and wooed Rory from his blissful slumber. He sniffed the air, his stomach rumbling for food, and defied Christy's manipulation. It was Saturday, his day to sleep-in, and her list of chores would have to wait. He turned on his right side and snuggled into the soft pillow.

A shaft of purest white reached down from the heavens, the finger of God, and caressed his face. The day was bright; the sky was clear, and the birds sang: life beckoned him to partake in the celebration. "Damn it," he muttered and pulled the pillow over his head. The aroma of freshly brewed coffee now mixed with the bacon. He called out, "I'm not getting up! It won't work."

A minute later the pillow burst across the bed, and he shot up to a seated position. The blankets slipped down and piled around his waist. His hair tousled and his face long, he grumbled in frustration.

He rubbed his face and yawned. When he stepped out of bed, he detected the caress of silk underneath his foot. The scarlet satin gown lay on the floor beside their bed. A black satin thong still lay draped across a lampshade where it was flung the previous night.

"It isn't fair. Can't Christy let me sleep late one day?" he grumbled and shuffled to the bathroom. After a quick shower and shave, he dressed for the day: briefs, blue jeans, gray sweatshirt, sweat socks, and athletic shoes. Early fall demanded preparations – winter was coming.

The bedroom door burst open, and Rory strode into the hallway. The delicious scent of cooking food lured him like a siren song, through the hallway, and down the stairs. He charged around the banister and hurried to the breakfast table. Christy set down a plate before Michael. "Mrs. Darby brought him by earlier."

The Seventh Age

The young boy inspected his breakfast and made a face. Christy may have been homecoming queen, and she was brilliant, but she was a terrible cook, and the eggs somehow managed to be both burnt and runny. The bacon lay limp on the plate, undercooked and covered with fat. The toast resembled charred sacrificial remains or something one might find in the hearth.

Rory scooped up the plate from the boy and circled around the table. "Sit down, troublemaker," he said to Christy. She gave him her best "who me" expression and sat at the head of the table. She batted her long lashes at him and watched him work with her sparkling blue eyes.

Rory was an excellent cook and had once considered becoming a chef. He worked with speed and skill, and ten minutes later, he emerged carrying two plates of food. Michael's eggs were scrambled; his bacon was crispy, and his toast was golden brown. With it, he received a glass of orange juice and a glass of milk, both in sippy cups. Christy received two poached eggs and the same garnishes. By the time Rory returned with his breakfast, his wife and child were already finished.

"You inhaled breakfast."

"Three months of takeout does that to a girl," she replied.

"You lost weight," he replied. "You always do that when you're traveling."

"At least something good came of all that reheated restaurant food." She crossed her legs and watched him eat. When she saw a slight belly roll around his middle, she commented, "It looks like somebody found it."

"Huh?"

She patted Rory's belly: "Somebody needs to hit the gym."

"They closed the daycare." Rory shook his head and frowned. "They said it was, '… way too expensive …' for just a handful of children. Pete

37

Southern is a cheapskate if you ask me, and he keeps sleeping with the daycare staff. Sheila Daniels has a paternity suit against him."

Michael slid off his chair and scrambled out of the room. Adventure awaited him. His dad showed him how to construct a fort made out sofa cushions and a blanket. There was a horde of mythical creatures to vanquish. Christy cradled her coffee between her hands and took a dainty sip. She sat with arms tight to her sides and thighs pressed together. A sudden chill overtook her and stole away her warmth as if someone walked on her grave. Rory munched on a piece of bacon and followed it with a bit of egg.

"We have a lot to get done today," Christy gazed at him with a catlike stare. "You promised to help me."

"I know. It's just that there are endless jobs in that jar, and you just got home. I could work every Saturday for the next two years and never reach the bottom."

"If you don't want to help, we could always have my mother come for a visit. She loves to clean. It makes her feel young."

"Oh I see, you're going to play the mother-in-law card." He took a gulp of coffee and scalded his throat. "Go get the job jar." She leaped up from the table and scurried into the kitchen with a prance in her step. When she searched for the job jar in the lower cabinet, she made the mistake of bending over: her blue jeans stretched tight over her ass, and it wiggled like a sexual target.

Christy stood up holding the jar and felt someone standing behind her. Hands encircled her waist and Rory pressed against her back. When he kissed her neck, she said, "No. We have to get to work."

He ignored her protest and drew down the brass zipper of her jeans. When the material parted, his fingers pushed through it and glided along white nylon fabric. She clucked her tongue and said, "I'm serious. We have to get to work." However, her laughter only encouraged him, and he kissed the back of her neck. When his fingers traced down between her thighs, she gasped and reached back to run her fingers through his hair. Moving in smooth strokes on the white nylon, his fingers caressed her sex. His other hand moved underneath her forest green sweater, and she sensed fingers touching her breast through the bra cup.

She closed her eyes and absorbed his touch, her mind lost in bliss and her body reveling in his touch. He unbuttoned her blue jeans, and a few seconds later, her panties joined her jeans around her thighs. His hand moved to the middle of her back, right between the shoulder blades, and pressed in the middle of her back. She submitted to his desire and bent over at the hips. Waiting for him to take control of her body, she rested her elbows upon the countertop, her blue eyes looking back at him through golden tresses.

It had been a long three months, and her body yearned for his touch. When he entered her, she gasped and tossed back her head, accepting him in her secret place. His hips met her bottom; his manhood plunged deep inside her pelvis, and her sex throbbed. She tried to swallow, her throat was dry, and her heart rate quickened. She wanted to cry; they were one both body and soul.

They moved as a single entity; lovers entwined and hearts united. Her body tingled; his touched caused a symphony of pleasure. Her breasts swung like a metronome to the beat of his thrusts. A golden aura flooded her mind and enveloped her. The tempo reached a fever pitch, and the sexual ache reached a crescendo.

"Oh god," she whispered like a prayer. She tried to hold back, to linger in the moment, but her need was too great. Her body tensed, and she floated in the heavens – soaring in an ethereal world. She melted into him and lost herself.

His essence flowed into her, making her feel wet on the inside of her pelvis. All too quickly, the golden glow faded, and the clouds of the mundane overshadowed her. Her dress was ready at the dry cleaner; Michael's medical records had to be recorded in the computer; the yard was a mess; painting, cleaning, and weeding – there was just so much to do. She laid her head on her crossed arms and longed for a return to paradise.

"You are so fucking sexy," he panted. "You have such a great ass. It drives me wild when I see you walk away."

He brushed aside her blonde locks and kissed up her neck. She resisted a giggle, and her eyes welled up with tears. "I wanted to bend you over and fuck you right then and there. Of course, they would never let us back in the restaurant."

A laugh burst from her lips; "That's an old Joke."

Little feet thumped on wooden stairs and then charged through the living room. Rory jerked his cock out of Christy. She snatched up her panties and danced about as she drew up her blue jeans. She pulled up her zipper tab as Michael rounded the corner.

"Mommy, my toy broke." Michael looked with consternation at the action figure in his hands, a detached arm lying next to its body. "Can you fix him?"

She took the toy from him and snapped the ball shoulder joint back into the socket. "Here you go, sweetie. Now play nice with your toys." He nodded and skipped back into the living room.

A flush came from the lower restroom, and Rory exited. "That was an abrupt conclusion."

"Good, maybe now we'll get some work done." She crossed her arms and stared at him with a poker face. "I could still call my mom for help."

The Seventh Age

"You know one day that's not going to work you know." He reached into the jar and pulled out a slip of paper. A sigh escaped his lips as he read it.

"Pick out two jobs," she said with joy.

Rory snorted and rubbed his face. He fished around inside the bowl and plucked another slip. "Rake of the leaves and trim the hedges," he read them aloud. "At least they go together." When she moved aside the jar, he said, "You have to pick out two."

"I know what needs to be done."

"So do I," he replied. "Come on. Pick out two."

"Fine," she hissed. She picked out two slips, and her face grew long. "Till the flower bed, and wash the windows. Crap!"

"We could always go back to bed," he said and pawed at her again.

She wore her best serious face and slipped away. "We don't have time." He remained unconvinced and chased after her as she passed through French doors, pursuing her onto the rear deck. She danced, twisted away, and dodged him. She lifted her knees high and twirled, trying to avoid the ravenous man in pursuit of her. He chased her across the redwood deck and trapped her in the corner. Holding her wriggling body, he covered her with kisses and held her tight.

"I missed you so much," he said.

"I can tell." When his right arm embraced her, she swallowed and melted into him again. "We can't. There's too much to do."

"Fine," he sighed. "I don't care what we do as long as you're with me."

She brushed a blonde lock behind her right ear and felt the heat as her cheeks flushed. When he nibbled her earlobe, heat rose up from within her core. She chewed her lower lip and ran her fingers through his red locks. "I love you, too." She squirmed free and hurried off the porch, baffled but enthralled by the male mind.

She grabbed a garden spade and kneepads. As she dug up the decaying remains of last year's flower garden, she heard Rory raking the ground behind her. She glanced over her shoulder and caught him staring at her. His amorous overtures resurfaced in her thoughts, and her stomach fluttered. She sat up on her knees and chewed the tan leather tip of her glove. When she caught Rory leering at her bottom, she hurried back to work.

Rory smirked and continued piling leaves. He happened to look at the surface of their wood deck. The lacquer coating applied last spring was already cracking. He shook his head and frowned. "Nothing lasts," he grumbled. It would have wait for spring because it was too cold to apply a fresh coat.

When he bagged the last pile of leaves, he scrounged underneath the deck and found the fertilizer spreader. He wheeled it around the back of the garage and entered through the rear door. The smell of dust, oil, and raw gas vapors propelled him back to a fond memory; when he turned 20, he had restored a pickup truck and got lucky with Christy a week later. It was the best day of his life; she was his first, his only love. Christy's call snapped him back to the moment. In the back corner, near the workbench, lay a bag of fertilizer. He slung the bag over his shoulder and carried it back to the lawn spreader.

A chilly gust of wind swept over him, stealing the warmth from his body. Ready for an angry outburst, thick and gray like a wool blanket, a brooding cloud moved across the face of the sky, roiling as though offended by the land. Their time was short; a storm loomed. By the looks of it, it would be a bad one: the kind where you are sure God is angry.

Chapter 6

Howling winds slashed at the land like an icy knife. Drops of freezing rain stabbed at them and threatened a downpour at any moment. This drove Christy and Rory back into the house and, just as they went to close the French doors, a powerful gust shoved them backward and slammed them shut. If they were at sea, Rory would have said, "Batten down the hatches." The wind howled like some great beasts, moaning and clawing at the house, trying to break in, but they were safe and warm, protected from the rigors of winter.

Christy surveyed the house's interior and searched for more work, but the house interior was spotless. Rory always kept their home clean. With great reluctance, she said, "I guess we're done for the day."

Rory flopped into his chair. "Thank God for bad weather." He turned on the television and searched the channel guide. Although he seldom followed sports, it seemed the manly thing to do and said, "I'm going to watch some college football." When news played a video of an angel flying across the Miami sky played, he scowled and said, "That's stupid. It has to be a publicity stunt."

"Is college football on TV this time of year?" asked Christy. She was both high school and college cheerleader, and many urged her to become a professional football cheerleader. She knew more about football than Rory, and she ran the fantasy football league at work, but it made Rory feel manly when she acted naive. "I didn't know they started this early. Why is that?"

"The college football owners have to," Rory replied, "if they want to play enough games to qualify for the Superbowl."

Christy arched an eyebrow: most of what Rory said was wrong. There are no "college football owners," only colleges participating in various divisions. Although the fans and media would love it, there was no college equivalent of the NFL Superbowl, only different bowl games, but she let his many blunders pass, not wishing to correct him and sour his mood. "Oh I see," she replied and twirled a golden lock around her index finger. "It sounds sssooo complicated."

"It is," Rory replied, not perceiving her teasing. "There's an awful lot of statistics and stuff that goes into it. I don't really understand all of it, but I get the basics. I can't believe it. The receiver just fumbled!"

"No. That was a pass interference call. You're not allowed to grab the receiver's arms." When he looked up at her, she shrugged and said, "Lucky guess."

"Oh … well, it turns out you're right." He then baited her saying, "I guess they get an automatic touchdown."

"No, it's not. It's an automatic first down and a maximum of a 15-yard penalty." Then she saw him grinning at her: he knew all about her expertise. "You're a trouble maker."

She sat down on the sofa next to him and pulled a blanket over them. Rory's attention shifted from the game on TV to his wife. She kissed him and said, "You're adorable." When the news broadcast about the Miami Angel played again, he groaned and rolled his eyes. Christy remained silent about her eyewitness view of the event and made a mental note to contact her superiors about it. Even if it was a hoax, they would want a report in triplicate.

"MOMMY!" Michael called out in a shrill voice. The little boy was down for a nap and had a nightmare, something that had been happening for a month. Christy jumped off of the sofa and rushed upstairs. Rory groaned and rubbed his face. A cold shower was the only recourse.

Christy hurried into her son's bedroom. She woke him and held him in her arms. The confused boy awoke and rubbed his eyes. "Did you have a bad dream?" asked Christy. The boy nodded and yawned, and then he laid his head on her shoulder and closed his eyes.

"Let's have lunch," Rory called out.

Christy carried the sleeping boy down the stairs and into the kitchen. She shivered, picked up a blanket to keep Michael warm, and then set the yawning boy at the table. "Why is it so cold? It's still September. Shouldn't it be warmer than this?"

"I guess," Rory replied. "Maybe a cold front came down from the north. I'll get the paper, and you check the internet." He unlocked the front door and charged down the steps. Heading toward the driveway, he saw the Sunday paper lying in a small puddle. "I wish just once he could miss the water." He hurried down the driveway, the pavement turning his feet to ice cubes. He picked up the soaking wet paper and let the water drain out of it.

The front door opened and shut. Michael worked his way down the steps and plopped down on the front yard. He pretended to fly an orange and white toy airplane, accompanying its flight with buzzing sounds. "It's too cold. Daddy needs you to go back in the house. Christy … can you come get Michael?"

The throaty roar of an engine echoed through the streets. Rory searched for a low-flying airplane, but he saw a Harley Davidson Motorcycle. He walked a few steps and looked through a row of spreading elms that lined the street. 2523 Maple Avenue was hardly the place one would choose to ride – Morrison County included quiet streets and numerous stop signs – but every trip begins somewhere. He carried the paper and walked to the edge of the driveway. The engine roar grew louder until it transformed into thunderous booms. He took a few steps, stood on the sidewalk, and searched for lightning.

The motorcycle engine mixed with thunder and echoed like cannon volley, the distant sound of war. Using his hand as a visor, he gazed up at the sky and saw ferocious lightning emerge from black clouds and stab

45

the earth with relentless cruelty. It was an amazing display of raw power, more than he imagined possible, more than should be possible. Lightning bolts tangled together across the sky like a shattered windshield, fracturing it in a crazed pattern. He walked between the elms and stood on the grass that lay between the sidewalk and curb. Something emerged from emptiness – boiling air gave way to a specter – a long blur that ended with a motorcycle. Reality stretched as if it was made of plastic wrap – then it burst.

A stunning redhead – too beautiful to be real – rode a black Harley-Davidson Motorcycle. Sunlight glinted off her silver armor and helmet; a pair of swords handles emerged on either side of her neck, daggers strapped to her back, and glossy black material covered her like a second skin. Her silver boots rested on a pair of foot pegs, and her metallic gloved hands gripped the handlebar.

"Can I help you?" he asked. "Excuse me. What do you want?"

Rory grimaced in agony, and the newspaper slipped from his hand. He tumbled and collapsed onto the pavement, as though a marionette cut her strings. He struggled to draw in shallow breaths, and he slipped away as the world faded to dull gray and then went black.

"What happened?" He rubbed his temple and squeezed his eyes shut. Still seated upon the driveway, he searched for the girl and the motorcycle, but she was gone. He scrambled to his feet and sprinted to the house. Christy stared at the wall – mouth agape and face frozen. He grabbed her arm and shook her. "Christy, what's the matter?" She turned toward him, ashen, eyes hollow.

"What was that?" asked Christy.

Rory cocked his head. "You saw her, the girl on the motorcycle? She just vanished."

"What? No. I saw …" her words trailed into silence.

The Seventh Age

He grabbed her by the arms and led her over to the sofa. She moved her mouth as if to speak but no words came out. "What is it?" he asked with apparent alarm.

"I was up high in the air like I was flying. I looked down, and I saw smoke and fire. Flames poured out the windows of buildings and smoke turned the sun blood red. I heard screaming and then realized that it came from me. Everywhere I looked, dead bodies littered the streets."

He held her tight and pressed her head to his shoulder. "It's okay. It had to be some sort of hallucination."

"A hallucination?"

"Yes. We should check the news." He grabbed the remote control from off the coffee table. Julie, the weather girl, stood before a map and described a peculiar high-pressure area combined with icy wind. He changed channels, but everything was normal. He expected to hear of earthquakes, collapsed buildings, and crashed airplanes. There was nothing but a typical Kansas morning.

Both Rory's and Christy's cell phone began to ring. Rory worked for the FBI, and Christy worked for the State Department; this meant that they were both on call during times of crisis. Sure enough, their offices placed both them on alert. They rushed upstairs and threw on dress clothes. As Christy tucked her blouse into her skirt, she said, "I'll have Mrs. Darby babysit Michael."

"Good. We can drop Michael off on the way." Rory knotted his necktie, but it was too short; so he tried again. His phone chirped; another message came through. "We need to get going."

"MICHAEL," Christy screamed with a panicked voice. Rory charged down the hallway and rushed into the boy's room. A desk, chair, and books now replaced Michael's bedroom. "Where is he?" Her hands trembled as she rushed to the closet. Jackets and hats replaced his

47

clothes. "Where is he? WHERE IS MY BABY?" Rory took her in his arms, but she pushed away. "No. I want my baby."

He held his breath and scanned the room. There was no trace of Michael; not a single picture or toy remained, not a shred of proof that the boy ever existed. Christy ran from the room screaming Michael's name. Rory charged after her and ran downstairs to the living room. Her face was bright red, and she searched with hysterical eyes. "I want my baby?" When he tried to hold her again, she batted at him with her fists. "NO. Get away from me! I want my baby."

"I'll find him. I swear it. He can't just disappear. He has to be around here somewhere. You go to work. I'll find him." He held the side of her head and leaned his forehead against hers. "Don't worry. Trust me. I'll keep him safe."

"You will?" She expelled the fear and shifted consciousness, entering a trancelike state. Rory would find him. People just don't disappear. He was hiding, or perhaps he'd wandered off. Rory was a good father, the best according to many of her girlfriends. There was no reason to worry: Rory would keep searching until he found Michael. "Of course," she said, recovering her composure. "He's probably gone over to Bethany's house. You know how much he loves playing with her French poodle."

Rory perceived the expanding void in Christy's mind and brushed a golden tress from her face. She appeared to be sleepwalking, her sanity balancing on a razor's edge, and the slightest movement would send her toppling to destruction. He remained motionless, fearing that the earth would give way underneath him at any moment. He searched her eyes and saw a comfortable haze settle over her mind.

Rory said, "Right now you need to get to work. The State Department might know something about what is happening. You have to go."

She drew comfort and strength from his words. "You're right. He's just wandered off. The State Department will know something." She dried

48

her tears and grabbed her purse. Rory rushed into the garage after Christy and opened the garage doors. After unlocking the car door, Christy started the engine, held her phone away from her ear, and then lowered the window. "Tom Granger, my boss, has a helicopter flying into the county airport. He's going to give me ride."

"Okay," Rory said. "I'll find Michael and then get off to work." He touched his right side. The space reserved for his gun was vacant, and he rushed back into the house to retrieve it.

Rory returned to the garage just as Christy departed. The tires screeched, and the engine roared as she raced down the driveway. He stood in the open garage and watched her drive away; gnawing fear and a sense of doom ate away at him – where was Michael? What happened to his room? None of it made sense, and he was in the business of making sense of the world.

He stared at the driveway, trying and failing to comprehend his circumstances. Then he noticed tan pavers, interlinking blocks placed in an attractive pattern. He squatted and ran his hand across the rough stone. When did that happen? They opted to use asphalt instead of pavers when building the house. Who had changed it and why?

When he stood to his feet, he saw two rectangular flowerbeds where none had ever been. Even the front of the house changed, white siding replacing red brick, and black shutters, the functional kind that swung on hinges, stood ready to guard the windows. The yard, the garage, the house, and even the photos in his wallet had to belong to another family. Michael's existence, their existence, ceased to exist. How?

Sickly amber light washed over him like the coming in of the tide and stung his eyes. Rory wandered out the door and stood in the driveway. He gaped in awe at the strange display all around him. The sky was amber, but the yard, the trees, and even the driveway had turned sickly shades of brown. It was as if the entire world turned sepia, an antique photo hanging in some forgotten corner of the universe.

Scott Marcy

The glare hurt his eyes, but he managed to look up at the sky. The sun smeared across the sky, a long yellow stain, stretching from the horizon to the horizon like a yellow stripe. The very air rushed out of his lungs and fled the Earth in a great gust. Rory threw back his head as every cell in his body cried out in pain.

Rory screamed in agony and dropped to his knees. Slicing pain between his thighs doubled over. Both hands shot to his crotch and covered his manhood from some unseen attacker, and each breath released a cry of agony. A crack of bone came from deep within his pelvis, and more cracks came from his ribs. He doubled over into a ball and then rolled onto his side.

The world twisted into the distorted shapes of a funhouse mirror. The sun morphed, shrinking down to a dot while blades of grass stretched into a forest. He thrashed and twisted in agony; his flesh reshaped like clay, pinched and pulled; his hand began to wither, and his body assumed an unnatural contortion as if made of wet noodles. When he held it out his hand, it seemed a million miles away and traveling through space, stars racing past his fingertips and suns the size of coins. He sucked in a gasp and jerked his hand back to his body. His chest bloated while his manhood withered. Somewhere in the process, Rory passed out.

Chapter 7

Christy exited Maple Avenue and slid sideways onto Yarmouth Road.
She crushed the gas pedal, and the SUV rocketed, cutting a path down
the center of the 2-lane road. She passed a utility van and dodged into the
path of an oncoming GMC pickup truck. The oncoming car sounded its
horn and swerved off the road. She snapped back into her lane and raced
up the road at 80 miles per hour. She made a sharp right onto Simpson
Lane and flew over the Simpson Truss Bridge. Jennings Creek splashed
about like a tempest-tossed sea, angry and vengeful against all who
crossed it. Her SUV swerved onto Frontage Boulevard, nearly rolling,
and a brilliant brown flash of light blinded her for a moment. When her
eyes cleared a second later, she saw a delivery truck charging at her, and
she jerked the steering wheel, barely missing it.

Cars swerved and slid as if on the ice. They turned sideways and slammed
into guardrails. She heard the sickening sound of crushing metal and saw
bodies slapping about in the vehicles' interiors. To her right and left, the
rows of trees waved as if in a hurricane, and the road trembled as if
terrified. When her SUV skittered, she slammed on the brakes and slid
sideways on the road.

It only took her a few seconds to recover, but then she spun the wheel to
the right and hit the gas. The tires smoked, and the rear end of the SUV
swung around. Once again, she shot down the road. The traffic lights
danced as if doing a jig, and sparks erupted from an overhead
transformer, showering the traffic. She passed through the intersection,
nearly colliding with a white F150 pickup truck, and made a quick left
onto the Ruben Goddard Truss Bridge, charging onto Boardwalk
Boulevard.

The vehicle groaned and shuddered but regained control a moment later,
launching in the new direction. Far up ahead, cars danced on the road,
performing wild spins, brushing past other vehicles; some flew into the
Jennings Marsh, and others slammed sideways into a grove of trees.

Explosions blasted and rained down metal shards from the skies. A shockwave rushed over the land, and she slammed on the brakes. The truck jumped about like a bucking bronco. When it came to rest, she stomped the gas, and the SUV responded, rushing pell-mell into the fray.

She sped between cars and raced along Boardwalk Boulevard. Passing the school, she heard terrified screams and saw children fleeing from wobbling buildings. When she neared the underpass of U.S. 24, a pickup truck launched off the overpass, hurtled through the air, hit the ground nose first, somersaulted, and tumbled end over end, crumpling like an accordion. The airbag inflated, but the un-tethered driver slammed around inside the vehicle, showering the interior with blood and gore, the lifeless body tumbling like a rag doll.

She squeezed her eyes shut and charged under the bridge. Crashes and explosions surrounded her. When she burst through the opposite side, she sucked in a desperate gasp. An explosion rocked the power plant, bursting a metal building at the seams, and metal fragments, the size of an automobile, rocketed into the air. An ambulance to her right crashed through the lobby window of the Johnston Medical Complex, and a man burst through a third story window. Arms and legs flailing, he plummeted to the ground and hit with a bone-crushing thud, tumbled, and came to rest, a lifeless ragdoll.

Christy made a right turn on Airport Road. Several small airplanes jumped about Avery Airfield, and a helicopter sat on a pad. Cars and trucks littered the road, blocking it, so Christy swerved off the road and, plowing through the undergrowth, she drove to the north end of the airport, rocketing off mounds and slamming down again. She streaked past the terminal and recognized Tom's SUV.

She sprinted toward the helicopter, groans coming from the buildings around her, moaning as if giving birth. A hanger roof cracked and then toppled into the building, crushing the men and machines inside it, dust and debris launching into the air. A severed hand slapped the windshield, slid across it as if trying to hold on, and then fell away, leaving behind a bloody trail.

Tom stood by the helicopter and waved at her. She slid to a stop and jumped out of her car. The rotor blades sliced through the air and a whine came from the engines. She ran up to him, and he held the door for her. Christy scooted across the seat and secured her lap restraint. When the door slammed shut to her left, the helicopter lifted off the pad. She put on a pair of headphones and lowered the microphone.

"I almost didn't make it," she said.

"Me too," Tom replied. "The roof of my house collapsed. It's lucky that Joyce and the kids are in Atlanta visiting their grandmother."

Christy's thoughts turned toward Rory. She wanted to call him and see if he found Michael, but there was too much noise. It would have to wait until she landed. "He's okay, he's okay," she chanted in a whispering prayer. They lifted off the pad and flew into the sky.

The helicopter rose up ever higher into the air. Soon the streets were thin ribbons and the cars tiny dots, dots that slid about, slamming into one another. Christy sat up straight and looked through the cockpit window. The new shopping district, the office towers, and the West Glenn Shopping Mall waved like trees in the wind. Explosions erupted from gas stations, shooting fireballs into the air; burning debris rained down on the town, setting more buildings ablaze – thick, black smoke billowed into the sky, turning the sun blood red.

She looked to the earth beneath the helicopter. Brick buildings wobbled as though drunk, staggered about, and then collapsed. Clouds of dust erupted and billowed across the blackening sky. People, reduced to terrified animals, desperate to live, fled through the streets in every direction. Debris rained from the sky, severing limbs, causing deep gashes, and killing many. She covered her mouth and tears rolled down her cheeks.

53

Scott Marcy

The endless horizon fled away from them as if viewed through the wrong end of a telescope. The vista of fertile plains grew dark, mere blurs on a distant horizon. Like the snap of a light switch, the sunlight extinguished, and not even the distant stars lost their light, absolute darkness engulfing them, leaving the mind crazed and the eye hungry for light. A moment later, brilliant sunlight turned the Earth to bleached bones – the world held its breath. Strange Mountains rushed at them with the ferocity of invading Titans. Christy recoiled in horror, and a scream ripped from her lips. The mountains came to a sudden stop and surrounded the entire valley.

Alarms sounded, and lights flashed on the instrument panel. "We've lost the engines. We're going down," Tom shouted. He thrust the stick forward and auto-rotated toward the ground. Christy screamed as the ground rushed toward them in a freewheeling blur. At the last second, Tom wrenched back the stick, and the helicopter groaned and shuddered. The craft came to a rapid stop and then slammed into the soggy ground of Jennings Marsh.

Chapter 8

The distant drone of sirens roused Rory and awakened him to a severe headache, waves of nausea, disorientation, and agony. The discomfort subsiding, he drew in a shuddering breath and then exhaled. This was progress, and the pain evaporated with his next breath. He stretched out on the cool paving blocks and let it draw the heat out of his body, comforted by the firm support of the driveway. His relief, however, was short-lived. Upon inhaling, he sensed something wrong, not painful but out of place. His chest felt heavy and swollen, engorged as if filled with fluid. Elastic straps encircled his ribcage and traversed his shoulders.

He summoned his remaining strength and moved his right hand to his chest. His fingers touched silk, not cotton. His ribcage felt smaller, somehow, as if he was a teenage boy. Suddenly, he detected the peculiar layering of fabric, satin underneath silk. His fingers traced a semicircular arc across half of his chest. He stopped halfway across this arc and brushed something soft, like a pillow. His hand explored fleshy globes, and the globes felt fingers touching them.

A terrible aching void barged into his deliberations, a chasm focused at the junction of his thighs. Both of his hands converged on this point, reaching it simultaneously. His jeans felt unusually tight, his thighs strangely supple, and his sex wrong.

His eyes popped open, and he shot up to a seated position. Framing his astonished face, long russet tresses cascaded over his shoulders and flowed down his back. He gaped at the shapely thighs that merged into the smooth arc of a female crotch, and his female sex detected fingers grazing it.

"What the hell?" he gasped. The voice that came from his mouth was lyrical and most definitely feminine. "What's going on?" The strange voice came from his mouth again.

He scrambled to his feet and tried to comprehend the cacophony of confusing sensations. Dizziness made him stagger for a moment, but it soon passed. His right hand shot to his breasts, and his left hand grabbed his backside. He could not breathe. His fingers confirmed with certainty what his mind detected: a pair of fleshy globes, breasts, teardrop shaped and heavy, hung from his chest. His other hand glided over a heart-shaped bottom that melded into a pair of thick thighs.

A violent epiphany erupted in his consciousness. *I'm a girl.* The male pronoun no long applied, "she" examined herself and "her" environment in confusion. The maple trees were bare skeletons as though far into fall. A carpet of brown leaves covered the yard, sidewalk, and parts of the street. Rory saw an overcast sky and the glowing yellow sun, a mere dot, on the western horizon. It was still morning, but it appeared to be sunset.

How?

Rory turned and saw the closed garage door. Who closed it? No, it was more than closed; someone secured it with padlocks, and boards covered the first-floor windows. Nausea hit her stomach like a punch to the gut, and she doubled over, vomit spewing from her mouth. The contents of her stomach splattered onto the pavement at her feet. She dropped down to her hands and knees. After sucking in desperate gasps, more dry heaves tormented her. "Oh god," she gasped, and yellow bile then spewed from her mouth.

Nausea turned off like a switch, and she sucked in desperate gasps. "What is happening?" she moaned and sat back on her feet. Her eyes closed, her face raised toward the sky, a cool breeze caressed her cheeks and soothed her troubled mind.

When she opened her eyes, she saw clear blue skies. Caressing her cheeks with its loving warmth, the sun jumped again and stood directly overhead. She struggled to her feet, wiped her mouth, and noticed something peculiar: long dried vomit lay on the ground at her feet, and it appeared to have been there for days, perhaps weeks.

The Seventh Age

She hurried up the walkway to the front door. In the dim reflection of a glass pane, she noticed her reflection. A redheaded beauty – the kind starring in movies or gracing magazine covers – stared back at her. She took a step forward and touched her face. Her fingers glided over baby soft cheeks and crimson lips. She looked deep into the girl's amazing blue eyes, a pair of perfect sapphires with flecks of black. Her brows formed a thin scroll above her eyes. She licked her lips and then touched them. They formed a pair of perfect Hollywood, crimson lips. Her angular chin and graceful neck added up to a stunning beauty.

The wind caused her red bangs to dance on her forehead, and she shivered, but not from the cold. When she drew in a breath, the sunlight danced on her copper silk blouse. The silk fabric sculpted around her breasts and slim torso. It had to be a dream, yet she was awake.

The girl in the reflection was no more than 18, still in the flower of youth, an innocent beauty. A drop of rain on her cheek broke the trance and demanded action. She tried the doorknob, but it was locked. She charged down the steps and found their hide-a-key rock planted in the shrubs. After retrieving the key, she unlocked the door and hurried into the house.

When the door opened, the very first thing she saw was a wedding photo. Rory wore a pristine, white silk gown with a long train wrapped around her legs and laid in a fan before her. She clutched a bouquet of flowers and had an arm around her side, Christy's arm. Christy's golden locks draped over a black waist jacket that she combined with a matching satin pencil skirt. This was not one friend congratulating another, but a wedding photo.

Rory became light headed. She staggered over to the sofa and slipped down onto the seat. When she began to feel faint, she doubled over, mashing her breasts against her thighs. After several minutes, she recuperated and stood to her feet.

All of the photos were of Christy and the red-haired girl, Rory. Other peculiar items lay strewed about the living room. Candles, lots of them, were burned down to the base, and icicles of wax hung from the sides. Folded blankets lay next to the wall, and others lay on the coffee table. She picked up a lantern, turning it this way and that, and she remembered that they bought it on their last camping trip.

She rose to her feet and strolled to the kitchen. Cardboard boxes filled with food sat on the dining room table. Five-gallon containers of water sat on the pass-through countertop. Two gray tubs sat next to the sink, filled with dishes and provisions.

A single thought flashed in her consciousness, "Michael." She charged up the stairs and hurried to his room. All signs of their son vanished from the spare bedroom. She slipped down into a chair and wept, great heaving sobs shaking her; her missing baby, her body, and the trauma proved to be too much for her. The emotional storm thundered within her soul and showered tears from her eyes.

The emotional storm slowed and then subsided. Rory sniffled and wiped away the tears, feeling refreshed and cleansed, like the forest after a spring rain. There was nothing left of her previous life. It was gone, vanished like dew upon spring flowers. Suicide flashed in her mind and departed just as quickly. Whatever happened, she was going to get her life back.

She wandered through the hallway to her bedroom, and it too was different. The white comforter was gone, and a forest green comforter replaced it. Two makeup tables confused her, but then realized one was hers. When she opened her top dresser drawer, she saw an assortment of panties – silk, satin, and nylon. She pulled out a pair of panties, pink satin and trimmed with white lace, and held them to her hips. The female undergarment was a perfect fit.

The Seventh Age

Even the walk-in closet reflected her new life. Most of the skirts, dresses, and scores of shoes belonged to her. Most of the pantsuits and blouses with big floppy bows belonged to Christy. This provoked a question.

Do I still work for the FBI?

She exited the closet and spotted a brown leather purse lying on her dresser. After she had rifled through it, she found her driver's license. Her name was still the same, but her age was just 21; and then she found a photo ID; "The Barrymore Lounge" was printed in bold letters on the badge. She knew the restaurant well. It was a high-end establishment frequented by stockbrokers, lawyers, and doctors. Most of the waitresses, all beautiful, supplemented their income as exotic dancers and escorts, some providing their services on premises. She hurried back into the closet and circled around the rack of dresses. A row of black satin cocktail dresses and costumes, useful only when swinging around a brass pole, hung in the closet. She pulled out a dress and held it up to her torso. The dress's loose pleats stopped at her upper thighs and had a fitted bodice with a push-up halter top. A mini-crinoline gave the skirt a slightly fluffy appearance, exposing a hint of lace.

"I'm a Special Agent for the FBI," she huffed. "I'm not a stripper."

She hung up the dress and marched back into the bedroom. She slapped down the ID badge, and another revelation emerged into her consciousness. If she was 21-years-old and a cocktail waitress, then she had attended neither college nor graduate school. All those years of study vanished in the blink of an eye.

The house began to shudder, items dancing about on the dresser top, and the earth groaned, splits ripping across the face of the land. Rory ducked underneath a makeup table and covered her head. Screaming, she held onto tightly to the legs. Knickknacks leaped off their perches, smashing on the hardwood floor, and picture frames fell off the wall. Splintered glass was all about Rory. She shouted, "What is going on?" The aftershock faded, and the land once again slept.

She hurried to the living room and turned on the TV, but there was no power. She turned on radio, but she heard only static. When she stood at the bay window and looked through the boards, she noticed that the sun was missing from the sky, but a moment later it returned with a brilliant flash. Green and red streamers of the aurora borealis danced across the sky like flags in the wind.

Rory grabbed her keys from off the wall and sprinted into the garage door. When she flipped the light switch, nothing happened. She tried it several more times, but the power was out, and the garage doors were shut. A few shafts of sunlight passed through windows, illuminating the garage interior. Her sensible SUV had been replaced by a four-wheel drive, lift kit, knobby tire, roll bar, chrome pipe, brush breaker, Baja kit pickup truck. The blue behemoth loomed like some extinct species of a dinosaur resurrected. The one accommodation to prudence was the topper or cap on the back bed of the truck. Otherwise, it was a 4X4 monster.

She tried the garage door control, but it too was dead too. So she grabbed the manual garage doorknob and pulled. She heaved with all her might, but given her feminine body, which was weaker, it failed to move. The earthquake shifted the house and skewed the house's frame, wedging the door. Lying on her back, she pushed with her legs, and still, nothing happened. After exiting the side door, she examined the garage doors from the outside. Hasps, secured by padlocks, sealed the doors. Rory returned to the garage and found a set of keys.

After unlocking and opening the garage doors, she climbed into the driver's seat, stabbed in the key, and twisted the ignition. Nothing happened. She tried it several more times, but the ignition was dead. A fuse, perhaps, or something more serious, she had no way of knowing.

With little another choice, she re-entered the house and searched for a flashlight in the stand drawer near the front door. She pressed the button, but it emitted no light. The bulb was burned out, and the glass was opaque.

The Seventh Age

Finally, Rory found a strawberry scented candle and an old pack of matches in the miscellaneous drawer near the kitchen stove. She struck a match and lit the candle. At least fire still worked.

She carried the candle down into the basement, using her hand as a shade to keep the flame lit. The basement was unfinished, much to Christy's annoyance, or at least it had been. Now it was completed and fully furnished.

An area rug lay over brown tile, and comfortable furnishings sat in the center of the room. They even had a large screen TV. She crossed the room and entered the laundry room. When she stepped on some clothing, she saw a pair of fuchsia silk panties. They spilled over from a load of soiled laundry lay on the floor. At first, she assumed they belonged to Christy, but then she noticed that they were her size.

With a pout and a slouch, she crossed the room. She opened the fuse panel, but none of the breakers were tripped. This fact did not stop her from trying them. After the last breaker had snapped shut, she huffed and put her hands on her hips.

"The power is out," she groused with girlish annoyance. Even her curses were cute, which further annoyed her. They were supposed to be angry and thunderous, not cutesy like a miffed girl.

Rory carried her candle back through the basement and returned to the main floor. The transistor radio crackled and hissed. A woman's voice came from the speakers: "Ladies and gentlemen, let's settle down so that we can get started. Please, if I could have your attention, we can begin. This calls together an emergency meeting of the city council …."

The auditorium grew quiet, and Mayor Orville's voice rumbled. "… Events over the past two months took our community by surprise. Most of our infrastructure was destroyed or near failing. Just when you thought it couldn't get any worse, it did. Another wave of quakes destroyed what remained. Only a fragment of Gleason has electricity."

"Thanks to our local FEMA director, David B. Jones, relief efforts are progressing at a reasonable rate." He rubbed his heavy jowls and snorted. "All of our water conduits were cut off, and every road out of the valley is blocked or simply erased. It's hard to fathom …."

"… Fuel capabilities are limited. Only official vehicles are allowed on the road. Fuel conservation is paramount. Even with these efforts, it will be exhausted in three months. All grocery stores are closed in an attempt to provide an equitable distribution of food. Mid-winter will find us with critical shortages. Water management is the only bright spot. We should have the city water back within a day or two, once crews repair the mains. As for your waste elimination, please use your best judgment, and if necessary, bury your waste in your backyard: untreated waste can cause many fatal diseases. All of the bridges appear to be intact, but they have not been inspected by engineers. At this time, only foot traffic may cross them. They may not support your vehicle."

"We have repeatedly tried to contact the outside world via shortwave radio. None of our efforts have met with success. Also, we made several attempts to fly airplanes out of the valley. They all suffered engine failure and were forced to make an emergency landing. In short, we are cut off from the outside world."

A noisy din broke out from the audience. "Please settle down. Martial law is still in effect, and the local civil defense forces have been activated. They are supplementing our local law enforcement. If you see a soldier, please follow his instructions. They carry the weight of law. Looters will be shot on sight."

"Ladies and gentlemen, we must provide for ourselves. No one is coming to our rescue. We have crops that require harvesting and processing. Bottom line, if you're a farmer, you've just been drafted. We want every backyard turned into a greenhouse. You cannot rely on someone else to grow your food. We have plenty of seeds; please see Thomas Benjamin."

The Seventh Age

"We also need volunteers to repair the old mills on Jennings and Cougar Creek, which leads into the next topic: all of our rivers are swollen beyond their normal capacity. They are unsafe, so stay out! Any attempt to cross them may result in injury or death. And there will be no one to rescue you. Furthermore, the mountains present an implacable barrier …."

Mountains, what mountains? This is Kansas. We don't have any mountains, Rory wondered.

The sound of children at play distracted her. She turned off the radio, walked to the window, and pushed back the curtain. Through a gap in the boards and beyond the overgrown front yard, she saw children at play on the street. Her neighbors wandered about and formed small conversational groups.

I wonder what's happening. Rory walked to the door and grabbed the knob. A sudden epiphany occurred to her. *I'm wearing a bra and panties.* Her mind traced the peculiar sensation of smooth satin cups cradling her breasts, elastic straps digging into her flesh, and satin panties smothering her bottom. Pressing her chin to her chest, she saw rust color satin tented over a pair of impressive peaks. They gleamed like a pair of glossy mountains, and looking past them, she saw wide hips – all out of place to her male mind. She plucked open the neckline of her blouse and gazed at the pair of swells rising from her chest. How peculiar: she could feel them.

Perhaps it was ridiculous, but she worried that they might find out her true identity. Boys turn into men, and one of the worst insults in the male world was to be compared to a girl. It was an insult like none other. To throw like a girl, to run like a girl, and to fight like a girl was shame personified. Both men and boys freely ridiculed such people. Wimps were socially ostracized, rejected by girls, and received vague expressions of revulsion. In fact, even a subtle feminine gesture resulted in abuse and rejection. It could even threaten a man's survival – beatings and murder often resulted.

63

Rory's fears were rational, and yet she was without escape. She was a woman, and nothing could change that. In the end, she summoned her courage. *No one will recognize me. I'll just say I'm visiting from out of town.* The tension left her body, and she drew in a cleansing breath. *Okay, that will work. Let's do this.*

She grabbed a silver polyester sweatshirt from the coat closed and pulled it over her head and arms, but it stretched taut over her ample cleavage, designed to amplify rather than hide the feminine form. She then opened the front door and jogged down the steps, her breasts heaving with each impact, a disconcerting sensation. As she crossed the lawn, she came to a slow stop and searched the skies. White capped mountain peaks loomed over the trees like brooding gods. She gaped at them in astonishment, unable to fathom what her eyes beheld. The mountains spread out to the right and left until the trees blocked her gaze. Who were these strange mountains, and where did they come from?

After crossing the lawn, she cautiously approached a group of gathered men, unshaven, dressed in a mishmash of warm clothing, and their faces showed their fatigue. She searched for a hint of revulsion and danger. The men congregated before a deep gash in the street and stared at their feet. It was wider than a man could jump and extended across the street and into several yards. Rainwater filled the gash and hid its depths.

Tom Reynolds primped a comb-over back over his balding head and patted his round, beer belly. "When do you think they're going to get the electricity going? I'm sick of cold food and no heat."

"I'm visiting from out of town," Rory blurted.

They all looked at her in unison, furrowed their brows, and dismissed her as peculiar, yet another stranded tourist. Who knew what motivated teenage girls? However, when in the presence of a beautiful female, men conformed to social custom and introduced themselves. After their introductions, she said, "I heard the mayor on the radio. The power is out all over the county, and the water mains are broken. I don't think the power is going to come back anytime soon."

"I suppose not," Tom replied.

As Rory stared at the water-filled crevasse, a peculiar sensation pricked her thoughts – *someone is watching me.* She looked to her right and left; several men lingering behind her, their gaze fixed upon her. She blushed and turned away from them, but this only caused further stares.

Tom asked, "Are you okay? You could come over to my place and lie down." Not once in five years had Tom ever offered to have Rory over as a guest. On the other hand, he did have a history of sexually harassing every woman he met, which included Christy.

"That's okay. I'm all right," Rory replied. "Where did the mountains come from?"

"Where have you been? No one knows." Tom took a step back and rubbed his belly. She met his lustful eyes with an angry glare, but Tom never looked up to acknowledge it, and Rory grew more upset by the second. Rather than getting into an argument, she said, "I need to get back to my house and get a jacket."

"You can use mine." Without waiting for a reply, Rick Barns removed his worn, brown leather coat, revealing a flannel shirt beneath it. He thrust his jacket onto her shoulders and wrapped it around her. "Here you go," he said. "This jacket has kept me warm through 10 winters."

The men appeared feral, reverted to a wild state, and their eyes had the gleam of a predator. They ran out of disposable razor blades over a month ago, and electric shavers required electricity. He and all the other men had to grow beards, to grow long hair, to lose body fat, becoming sinewy, and to become hard: exemplifying their dire circumstances, primitive, hungry, on the edge of survival, the shadowy past of human ancestry.

Rory looked at the brown leather jacket wrapped around her shoulders and then up at Rick. It was a transformational moment. To refuse the gesture would deeply wound the young man. To accept it meant to accept her new role as a woman. In the battle of the sexes, women were "us," and men were "them." Beyond those reasons, she was cold, and the jacket was warm; and it made her feel safe.

She slipped her arms into the sleeves and wrapped the jacket around her torso. "Thanks," she mumbled and lowered her gaze. Seeking to shore up her damaged masculinity, she said, "I once went camping in Alaska with my friend Bill. We had to bathe in ice-cold water."

Tom let out a lustful laugh and made a crude joke. Rory gaped, unable to believe what she heard. "I bet you two kept warm in the tent that night."

Brent McClain, a retired NYC cop, and church elder said, "Keep it clean Tom. She's no hooker. I have a granddaughter her age. She's going to college at the University of Chicago."

"She's going to UC," Tom laughed. "She lives in New York City, the greatest city in the world, and she goes to Chicago. That's hysterical." Brent failed to see the humor. Rory's mind was a blank: other men were fighting over her. She corrected that thought; they were not "other men" since she was now a woman.

Tom fumbled and dropped a silver pen on the ground. "Could you get that for me? I have a bad back."

"Sure," Rory said. When she bet over to pick up the pen, she sensed eyes staring at her. She picked up the pen and hurried back to her feet. She handed the pen to him.

"Thanks, I've got some arthritis in my hands," Tom said. "You've got a beautiful body. I bet you do a lot of bicycling."

Before she could reply, there was activity in the home across the street, and the front door flew open. A young man scrambled down the steps

66

and spun around to face the door. Pierce Ripley charged out of the house holding a shotgun. He pointed it at the young man shouting, "Get out of my house. I should shoot you as a looter."

"I'm not a looter. I'm you son, Jeff! I live here." Fear and desperation mixed in the young man's voice. Brent hurried over to them.

"Lower the gun, Pierce. Let's talk this out," Brent said.

"This thief was inside my home. He just walked past Jeanie and me. Then he sat down on the sofa like it was nothing. Can you believe him?" Pierce said.

"What are you talking about? You're my father," Jeff pleaded. "I just woke up. I was out late last night."

"I don't have any children, not living ones anyway. Kurt died in a bank robbery gone wrong. He was 'on the job' with the sheriff's office. My girl, well, I have no children left. They're all gone."

Rory hurried to the disturbance and stood by Brent. Jeff wore only a T-shirt and pajama bottoms. He shivered from the cold, and his bare feet were numb on the wet concrete sidewalk. Brent approached Jeff. "Son, are you having an episode? I've known Pierce and Jeanie for years. They only had one son."

"This is insane," Jeff said. "You taught me how to pitch baseball. You coached my little league team. He's my father, and she's my mother."

Rory charged past all of them and spoke to Jeanie, "He claims he lives here. Show me his room."

Jeanie hesitated for a moment and then nodded. "Okay, fine. Let me show you." Rory followed Jeanie into the house despite Pierce's objections. They passed through a small living room and turned left when they reached the kitchen. The hallway was narrow and covered with family photos. She threw open the door and said, "See. It's just a —

" Her words trailed off into silence. An unmade twin bed, sheets and blanket lying askew, clothes spilling out of a laundry basket, and a pile of dirty athletic shoes lay before her. Three little league championships trophies were displayed on the mantle case, a layer of dust covering them. "Pierce, get in here," Jeanie shouted.

The burly man pushed past Rory and entered the room. He combed his fingers through his gray locks and examined the room. "What is all this? This was my den."

Rory glanced at the dresser and saw a framed photo. In the picture, Pierce stood with his arm around Jeff. Jeff looked to be 10-years-old. He wore a yellow and white baseball uniform with "Ripley's Mufflers" stitched on it. "Take a look," she handed them the photo. There were others scattered about the room and hallway. Brent entered with Jeff following behind him.

"When did you put all this in here?" demanded Pierce.

"Put what where?" pled Jeff.

"All this stuff," replied Pierce.

"This is my room. It's always been here. Where's Jessica?" asked Jeff. "At least she will remember me." He walked down to the hallway and threw open the second door. "Jessica, will you tell mom and dad who I am."

A little blonde girl rubbed her eyes and yawned. She shuffled out of her room wearing a white cotton nightgown and pink bunny slippers. "I was still sleeping." She crossed her arms and shivered. "What's wrong?"

"Mom and dad don't remember me," he replied.

The little girl cocked her head and furrowed her brow. "What? Are they sick?" Jeanie pushed past everyone and threw her arms around the little girl. She held her tight and began to sob. "Mommy, are you okay?"

"Mommy is okay. I'm just so happy to see you. That's all," Jeanie replied. Rory knew the story; it was in the local newspapers last winter. Jessica and her friends took a short cut across an ice-covered pond. All three of them fell into it and drowned.

"Hey, mom, dad, where are you?" A uniformed officer hurried into the house. "I have to get back to work soon. Looters are on a rampage all over the city. We need to this place boarded up."

Pierce's face went ashen, and the gun slipped from his hands. His son Kurt stood before him, whole and healthy. He charged toward the Kurt and threw his arms around him, tears flowing from the big man's eyes.

"What's up pop?" asked Kurt.

"You died two years ago in a bank robbery. I buried you," Pierce said. "How?"

"No, I didn't. I had to take the day off to take Jeff to the doctor. You two were busy, and Mary asked her mother to babysit the kids. Jeff threw up all over my car, and my mother-in-law moved in. What a day that was." He looked at the stunned faces. "I don't know what your problem is, but we need to get working. I want you guys safe. Mary is using my Jeep to pick up the girls, and she's meeting us here."

Jeanie hugged her son and kissed him. She wiped away the tears and asked, "What about Jessica? Did you save her?"

"Save her from what?" asked Kurt.

"She fell through the ice on her way home from school," Jeanie said.

"Jeff, you're supposed to pick the girls up from school. That was the deal. If I gave you my old car, you promised to give them a ride home. Are you trying to get her killed?" Kurt shouted.

Jeff searched his mind. "I did. I do every day. Jessica never fell through the ice." The little girl held onto Jeff's hand, and her eyes welled up with tears. "Mom and dad think you're dead, and they don't remember me. It must be a gas leak from the earthquake."

When an argument broke out, Rory left the house and wandered back into the street. Tom asked her, "What's going on. Are the Ripley's smoking dope?"

Rory was about to reply when Greta trudged up the street. The heavy set woman lugged four shopping bags and wore a fierce expression. "Tom, what's the matter with you? Why didn't you pick me up from the supermarket? I managed to buy a few cans of tuna fish that were still on the shelves." She stuffed the grocery bags into his hands. "Carry these. I cannot believe you. You are the most unreliable man I've ever met. My mother was right – I should have told you no."

"You're dead," Tom said. "You died three years ago from colon cancer."

"Are you drunk again? I had a colonoscopy and had my polyps removed. You know that not that you care." The pear shaped women rubbed her back and grimaced. "I need a back rub."

"But you're dead," Tom insisted and chased after her.

A disturbance broke out down the block. Several women were crying, and men were calling children's names. There was no need for Rory to investigate. She understood what was happening. The entire street was alive and abuzz with conversations. Rory strolled through the midst of the chaos, but her thoughts remained on her baby son, Michael.

Chapter 9

The fire department lacked water; the police department lacked bullets, and both lacked fuel to power their vehicles. Exhausted, outmatched, and disheartened, they abandoned the commercial districts, only rubble and dead bodies remaining, and shifted their efforts to the populated suburbs. Christy worked with the sheriff: she trained and organized neighborhood watch teams, authorizing ordinary citizens to use deadly force.

After a long, dangerous day, they traveled a long and uncomfortable journey home. Christy drove her black SUV, packed with ten relief workers, through the winding streets of the East Commercial District. The only traversable route home took them straight through and then into the old downtown district – both were disaster zones: debris blocked streets, vehicles burning, collapsed buildings, girders jutting like broken bones, and bodies strewed on the ground, uncollected and rotting. The city of Gleason was under siege and in chaos, looters smashing windows, fires reaching into the heavens, bands of roving men – stealing and raping – and shots, sounding like the snap of firecrackers, occurring day and night.

Despite the bitter cold, the passengers kept the windows lowered, and their weapons ready. Like the flash of a camera, gunfire erupted in the night. They returned fire but hit nothing. It was too dark, and the shooters too well hid, but it let looters know that they were serious. It was too dangerous to stop; the dead and dying would have to wait for morning. Watch groups collected the bodies and left them on the curb, along with the trash, waiting for the horse drawn cart to collect them, depositing both in makeshift bonfires.

After they had passed over the Simpson Truss Bridge, Christy marveled at the transformation. The residential streets were so peaceful, a stark contrast to the chaos of the commercial districts. A candle lit every window with a gentle glow, making her feel as if she had stepped back in time. Runny-nosed children squealed as they played a game of "hide and seek," the dark providing perfect cover. A pair of young lovers walked hand in hand, enjoying a private stroll. Adults lounged in their living rooms, reading books, talking, and listening to the radio. Overhead, the aurora borealis danced across the night sky like a great satin ribbon. It cast an eerie, otherworldly glow upon the suburban street. How long would it last? How long would it be until the chaos spread like cancer to the populated suburbs?

Her coworkers pressed her for news: "Had she heard from Rory? Did he find her baby?" she answered every question with a diversion or numb indifference; she shrugged and assured them that Rory would find Michael, dismissing the topic. When Tom Granger pressed, she launched into hysterics and screamed at him to mind his own business. Only then did they realize the depths of her pain and the severity of her mental illness.

She hated going home. It would be yet another lonely night while Rory was searching for Michael. In her heart, she began to fear the worst, but she pushed away the gloomy thoughts, choosing to believe that Rory had found Michael and was keeping him safe. They would return to her, she was sure. Rory would have a great tale to tell. It provided her with a safe place to hide, a shelter from the harsh truth of reality. She even imagined the reunion; joyous celebration would erupt, and the terrible ache in her soul would finally go away. It made little sense, but such is the nature of a troubled mind.

When she turned onto her street, Maple Avenue, she slowed to a crawl and drove around the crevasse, circling across a neighbor's yard. She put the SUV in park and stepped out of the warm vehicle. The sudden sting of crisp air pinched her nose and cheeks, turning them red. Wearing a skirt in the middle of a disaster was a huge mistake, but all of her other clothes were dirty, and she ran out of laundry soap a month ago, and she hated dragging her dirty laundry down to the river.

Christy slung her purse over her shoulder, closed the garage door, and secured the padlock. A recent rain left their front yard cold and wet. A group of young men rounded a large oak tree and emerged from the night. When they saw her, they shared quiet whispers. No one would blame them for mistaking her for a 20-year-old woman; she appeared to grow younger, instead of older. "Hey baby, want to party?" called out a teenager, his buddies lingering behind him, hoping for a "yes."

"No, but if you have a generator, I'll take it," she said.

The teen laughed. "I haven't got one of those, but I have a bottle of gin. That'll warm you up."

"No thanks," she said and continued on her way. When the young men departed, she released her grip on her service weapon and closed her purse. Many thought it was the end of the world and gave into despair. Sexual assaults and theft were so common that they no longer collected the reports; watch groups had to settle disputes within their neighborhood.

She cut across the lawn to her front door. The flicker of candles illuminated the bay window with a soft glow. She scurried up the steps and inserted her key in the lock. Her joyous reunion had finally arrived – they were home! She entered the front door: her thoughts consumed and heart aching. "Rory, Michael, I'm so glad that you're finally home. Mommy loves you, baby."

She set down her keys in the dish by the door with a clatter and put down her purse. After closing and setting the dead bolt, she circled around the sofa, entering the living room. Dying embers burned in the hearth and cast a warm glow over the room. Their house was the only one on the block to have multiple fireplaces, a fact that she once cursed but now relished.

Where were they?

She stripped off her coat and warmed her hands by the fire. Rory and Michael were asleep upstairs; she was sure of it. When turned around, she saw a redheaded woman lying on their sofa. The young woman clutched a blanket up around her neck and lay fast asleep. Who was she? Where was Rory?

Christy raced around the sofa and returned to her purse. Weapon drawn, she returned and circled around the couch. She demanded, "Who are you?"

Rory awoke and saw Christy pointing a gun at her. She sat up and yawned. "It's me ... Rory, your husband." She palmed her breasts and bounced them. "I guess 'wife' is more appropriate now. You never told me you were really a lesbian. Of course, I am too since I married you." She took note of the disbelief in Christy's eyes. "Don't believe me? I understand since I don't really believe it. I keep thinking this is all going to end. I'll wake up and find that this was all a nightmare."

"What are you talking about? Are you on something? Is anyone else here with you?"

Rory snorted and tossed aside the blanket. She stood to her feet. "It is just me, and I am not high, although I wish I were." She held out her hands and said, "It's me, Rory." Although female and beauty incarnate, Christy detected hints of her missing husband in the girl's face. "A funny thing happened to me after you left: I changed into a woman. Of course, that explains why Michael disappeared."

Christy held the gun on Rory as she walked past her. Rory picked up a wine bottle and filled it to the brim. She held it out for Christy to take. "You might as well have it. I can't get drunk. Lord knows I tried. I drank an entire bottle of scotch, and all I did was pee." When Christy failed to take the glass, Rory set it down on a small table next to the wall.

"Look Christy, either shoot me or put the weapon away." Rory returned to the sofa and drew the blankets over her. As she recounted her day, Christy lowered her weapon and tentatively took a seat across from Rory.

Rory recounted her strange tale, about her transformation, about the people who were alive again, and about the missing children. As she told the story, a single word "nevermore" from Edgar Allen Poe's work "The Raven" kept popping into Christy's mind. It was all so unbelievable, but she had seen so much over the past two months. It made sense.

Christy put her gun on a lamp stand next to a candle, and the torrent of tears flowed at last. She covered her face and wailed like a woman by the side of a grave. Her tears suddenly stopped, and she growled, "I don't believe this. People just don't disappear. We will find him. Even if you are a girl, you came back – he can too! I know he exists. I gave birth to him." Her words trailed into silence, and more tears streamed down her cheeks. When Rory tried to comfort her, Christy pulled away.

Her entire body sagged, and her eyes fixed on the floor. "It all makes sense. I've been looking for you and Michael for the past two months. There was no sign of either of you. Every day at the Federal Center, new employees showed up that no one had ever met, and other people vanished, as though they never existed. Albert Benson was by my side, telling me about how his wife made it home. We were walking to a meeting, and then he stopped speaking in mid-sentence – he vanished."

Rory wrapped the blankets around her. "It's late, and I'm going to bed. We can talk about all this in the morning." She shuffled away and climbed the stairs to the second floor.

After blowing out the candles, Christy followed Rory, still carrying her gun. Part of her still refused to believe the story. She would find her baby.

When she entered the bedroom, she saw a fire in a small hearth. They used it for romantic evenings. Technically, it was illegal – air quality control precluded wood burning fireplaces – but they risked it occasionally. Now that society had collapsed, many homeowners had a bad case of chimney envy.

Rory stood with her back to Christy. She stripped off her blouse and tossed it onto her dresser. When Rory turned, the warm firelight reflected off her black satin bra cups. Their size surprised Christy. They had to be at least a D-cup, a pair of ideal globes. Rory unbuckled her blue jeans and stripped them off. A matching pair of black satin panties cleaved to her wide hips, and more importantly, to the smooth arc at the junction of her thighs.

Rory combed her fingers through her hair. "I'm sorry I was such a jerk to you. But I spent the entire day worrying about you, and then, when you did show up, you point a gun at me. It's about as bad as I imagined." She reached around her back and struggled to find the clasp.

"Here, let me," Christy said. She unhooked Rory's bra and admired the smooth tanned skin. Rory squatted down and opened her pajama drawer. She moaned and rolled her eyes. Not a single pair of flannel pajamas lay in the drawer. It was filled with silky, satiny, or gauzy nightgowns. She was too tired to care. "Whatever," she sighed. Fatigue and regret robbed her of pride. She picked out a gold silk chemise and matching panties.

Christy's mind was a blank: her strength of will was gone, and her sanity rested upon the edge of a knife. She acted out of mechanical repetition, walking a familiar path without thought or introspection. It was late, time for bed. Christy stripped off her suit jacket and unbuttoned her blouse. She watched in fascination as Rory stepped into the panties and whisked them up her legs. A second later gold silk smothered her. She held the nightgown above her head and drew it down her body.

Rory hurried underneath the blankets and curled up into a ball. She shivered as the cold sheets stole her body warmth. From underneath the covers, she watched Christy undress as she had a million times. Somehow, it seemed different now. When Christy was down to her lingerie, Rory was contemplative rather than enticed.

After Christy had slipped into bed, Rory began to shiver from the cold. In desperate need of body warmth, she rolled over and scooted up next to Christy. Christy felt a feminine body clad in silk pressed up against her back, and a woman's arm draped around her hip. Rory's hot breath burned the side of her neck, and her long hair tickled it.

Rory whispered, "I was terrified I would never see you again." Her right hand glided over the silk covering Christy's stomach. Christy lay wide-awake as a delicate female hand caressed her. She pulled away and sat up in bed.

"I just can't do this. Look at you. I'm not even really sure you are Rory. You're some girl that I just met. This is impossible."

Rory sat up and let the covers fall down into her lap. "How do think I feel? I am the one on the inside of this body. Besides, you had a fling with a girl in college once," Rory said. "You told me all about it."

"Well yes, but it was with my English Literature professor, Claire Dewitt. She invited me to her house and ... um ... we did some shots, and we smoked a joint – the next thing I knew we were sleeping together. We lived together for a while, but it was all wrong." Christy crossed her arm, tightened her face, and shifted to one hip. "She kept on pushing me for riskier sex like it was a drug or something. We almost got caught in the Stern Library. I told her no more. Then I came home from class and caught her in bed with a freshman, Leeann Lawson. She had the nerve to ask me if I wanted to join them. I knew it was over, so I moved out that day. The next weekend, we went on our first date, and I knew that I was straight."

"Actually, you're not," Rory quipped. "You and I are married. You're a lesbian."

"Lesbian" was a word Christy never used to describe herself. It was a college fling, and it was a memory, not a lifestyle she chose to pursue. She was married to a man and had a baby. College and sexual experimentation were faded memories. "We are not married! I don't want you. I want my husband. I want my baby! I want my life back," Christy screamed, her fists clenched in rage.

Rory scrambled to her feet. "Do you think I want to be a girl? I don't. I want my body back. I want my life back. You have no idea how much I'm going through."

"No idea? You're the one without a clue. You have no idea what it means to be a woman and suffer from PMS. Every month you suffer from it. Then one wonderful day I got pregnant, and I had a baby, a beautiful little baby boy. I loved him with all my heart, and my life was everything I dreamed, and then God shitted on me. My husband turned into a teenage girl, and my baby disappeared. My baby is gone, not dead, just gone. There isn't even a body. He just vanished." Tears streamed down her cheeks. "Then that girl says, 'You have no idea how much I'm going through.'"

Christy grabbed a pillow and stormed out of the room. She slammed the door behind her and marched down the hall. Rory heard the door to Michael's room open and slam shut. As quiet returned to the house, Rory wept.

Chapter 10

The next morning, Rory opened the valve to the propane tank and started the barbecue. During moments like these, she was grateful that they kept the cast iron pans; Christy had wanted to give them away to the First Baptist Thrift Shop. She opened a can of spam, dumped it into the pan, and then mixed some sausage with it in an attempt to make it a little more palatable. She was not alone in this task. The pungent aroma of cooking meat came from all around the neighborhood.

Despite wearing a blouse and fleece top, the frigid wind stole her warmth, and she soon found it necessary to return indoors. Although Rory was tempted to start a fire in the hearth, she reserved the firewood for nighttime. She rubbed her arms and decided to have a cup of tea. When she held the kettle to the faucet, no water came out and sighed.

Shuffling and thumps came from the foyer. Rory set down the kettle and exited the kitchen. Christy stood in the foyer, five suitcases lying at her feet. Christy searched her purse for an ID badge. When she looked up at Rory, her expression turned to ice on a winter's day. "I'm going to stay with Tom."

A horn blasted from the driveway. Christy opened the front door and waved to Tom Granger. He put the car in park and stepped out of it. After opening the trunk, he hurried up to the front door. "I was a little surprised when I received your message this morning. After the roof had collapsed, I had to move into my rental property on the other side of the city. I had no idea you knew where it was. You must have paid a fortune for that kid to ride his bike all the way to it. Is everything okay?"

Christy turned to Rory. "This is what's left of my husband – correction, my ex-husband."

Rory took a step forward; "You're leaving me?"

79

"Leave you? I am not even sure who you really are. I married a man, not you. You can keep the supplies and the gas. The house is yours. We only had a few thousand in equity anyway. As far as I'm concerned, the bank can have it." When Christy turned to leave, Rory grabbed her arm. Rage burned in Christy's eyes, and she jerked her arm free. "I never want to see you again."

Rory lingered in the doorway, her soul instantly numb, and she watched Christy stride down the walkway to the parked car. It had to be a dream. Christy took a seat on the front passenger side and fixed her gaze straight ahead. Tom's face grew long, all thoughts fled his mind, and when he met Rory's distraught eyes, pain filled his heart. There was nothing to say, so he picked up the bags. He hurried to the trunk and placed the bags in it. Rory walked down the step, tears streaming down her cheeks. The car backed out of the driveway and cruised away.

Christy never looked back.

Rory dropped down and sat on the steps. She had cried more that day than she had in the past 10 years. Her entire world was shattered. The only person she had ever loved abandoned her in the hour of her greatest need.

The smell of sizzling meat urged her to action. Rory circled around the outside of the house to the grill. She flipped the meat and wondered what she would do. She was without a car, a phone, running water, and electricity. The canned goods would last about three weeks to a month if she rationed them.

She considered going to her parents home, which in this case was 'The Ridgeview Resort' north of town, but how would she face her parents? How would she tell them that their son was now a daughter? Rory was more alone now than she had ever been in her life.

The brooding skies left them in perpetual twilight. Winter came with sudden ferocity. A snow flurry landed on the tip of her nose. She warmed herself by the grill and pondered what to do. While their vehicles were out of gas, the bicycles still worked.

After packing the cooked meat away in an insulated cooler, Rory forced herself to eat a hearty breakfast. There was no telling when she would have a hot meal again. She left the dirty dishes in a tub and put on a warm coat with a scarf. Five hundred dollars would buy some food, or she hoped it would. She hid the money and five silver coins away in her right sock and strapped a fanny pack around her waist as a decoy.

When she entered the garage, she saw the black SUV. Did it work? Would Christy come back for it? Then again, who cared? Christy had abandoned her. She considered taking the SUV down to the market, but there were no keys on the hook, and she had no idea where Christy had left them. Besides, the bicycle would attract less attention, so she opted to take it. After wheeling the bike through the side door, she locked up the house, strapped on an empty backpack, and pedaled down the driveway.

She cruised through the shattered street. A few of the neighbors were just starting to wander out of their homes. The children, however, were already out in force. They chased one another and screamed. A few boys played football while other shot hoops. Rory waved at them and continued on her way. It might have been idyllic if not for the distant gunfire, growing closer every day.

The nearest supermarket lay 23 miles away, requiring her to go north to Route 223 and then traveling south on East Grove Blvd. By car, it was a 20-minute trip, but on foot, it would take most of the day. The bike added some mobility but was still a long journey.

Debris obstructed many of the roads, and long fissures scared the earth. When necessary, she carried her bike and navigated around these obstacles. After 20 minutes, she actually began to enjoy the trip, the cool wind on her face, and the brooding gray skies. The trees were bare skeletons, and brown leaves contrasted the rich black road. She saw movement at the edge of the woods. Armed men clad in camouflage emerged and four more emerged from the woods on the other side, everyone armed but her. She cringed and sped past them, not waiting to speak with them. The men rested the butts of their rifles and shotguns in the crook of their arms, and they eyed Rory with hungry, lustful glares as she raced past them. On an adjoining dirt road, she saw two cars with drivers behind the steering wheels, ready to block the road – self-defense or a trap?

As she neared the Eastern Road, the crowds grew dense. A slow procession of men and women, many of them weary to the point of collapse, trudged down the middle of the road, blocking the path of vehicles, the drivers blaring their car horns. The side streets became tributaries, and the main streets became rivers. They took the long way and walked up toward Rt. 223.

Rory wondered if there was some sort of rally or public meeting. She pedaled through the crowd as best she could, but progress was slow. Hunger a constant companion, children clutched their parent's hands and whined. The sea of humanity soon avoided the forest and stayed to the road.

She opted to take a shortcut, traveling up Eastern Road and then turning right onto a dirt trail. This led her to the Power Line Service Road. It was little more than a dirt road laid down the center of a bald strip of earth that cut its way through the forest of scrub oaks and pine trees. Towers, appearing like metal giants with outstretched arms, clutching power lines, lay in the middle of this strip. Before the crisis, they supplied power to the exclusive communities north of town. Now they were bare-boned skeletons, artifacts of a bygone era.

She dismounted her bike and climbed the gravel road traversing the top of a hill. Once at the top, she saw rolling land and leafless trees. She walked alongside her bike, the tires too thin for off-road cycling.

The Seventh Age

A shot rang out and then another, so close — Hunters? Perhaps it was but perhaps not. Rory worried what else they might be doing. Only a short way further on the road, she spotted shredded rags that had once been clothing. Pink floral, nylon panties lay underneath the brown scrub brush, and the matching bra was only a short pace away. She tried to imagine a benign scenario where a woman might remove her undergarments and then discard them. None of them seemed plausible.

Two more shots startled her. Her hand touched her right side, seeking the comfort of a handgun, but she left the house without a firearm, and it was too late to turn back. The shots grew near. She continued at a brisk pace, curious but fearful of what else she might find in the bushes — a body perhaps?

Upon hearing voices, Rory ducked down and hurried into the dense undergrowth. Her heart hammered within her chest, and every footfall sounded like thunder. From her hiding place, she saw a pair of dirty basketball shoes and soiled blue jeans, the barrel of a shotgun pointed down at the earth beside them. The man trudged past her on his way south and then by two more men.

Rory pushed a branch aside and saw three young women. Rope bound their hands behind their backs, and cloth filled their mouths, their whimpers stifled. Ropes circled the last girl's neck and led to the girl before her. This line eventually led to the man leading the procession. He had a face that appeared weathered, like old leather, and he had a rough beard and tangled graying hair. He fixed his dead eyes on the trail before him, his ripped bib-overalls, and soiled athletic shoes, a testament to the harsh conditions that overtook him. He clutched a rifle in his right hand and the rope in his left. The terrified girls followed him along the trails, every footfall carrying them farther away from home and rescue.

Two men stamped the ground and pushed. The rubber wheels of a trolley rolled past Rory, the type one might use the kind at a construction site. Canned goods, filled red plastic gasoline containers, and other goods were stacked high and lashed in place with rope. A second wagon followed the first, and then a third.

After the procession had passed her by, she drew in a traumatized breath. She kept hidden not wishing to abandon her cover. It was then that she spotted a pair of teenage girls exiting the woods farther down the road. When the girls saw the men, they froze for a second and then fled, terrified cries coming from them. The men gave chase and charged into the woods. Screams ripped through the woods and then suddenly turned silent, turning Rory's blood cold.

Clutching the ground, she buried her face against the moist loam, not daring to look up at them. She wanted desperately to flee, to run as fast as her feet could carry her, yet she remained hidden, her gaze fixed upon the ground. She heard footsteps a pace away from her and dreaded discovery.

The men returned with a pair of girls in tow. The girl's clothes were disheveled, their hair tousled, and their hands bound; they sobbed and cringed, looking for mercy in their captor's eyes but finding none. After tethering the girl to the rear of the line of captives, the crew resumed their slow march south toward their dark destination.

Rory watched the men trudge out of sight. When they exited a side trail heading east around "The Loop Shopping Center," she arose from her cover and stole a quick glance around it. The trail was empty once again.

After grabbing her bicycle from the bushes, she ran beside it and passed through the forest. Keeping the water tower on her left, she fled for the main road and safety. Every so often, she dared gaze up at the majestic peaks stretching up into the sky. She tried to distract herself and explain their sudden appearance. Every attempt to explain them seemed more ridiculous than the previous theory.

The water tower marked her final destination. When she came upon a paved road, East Grove Boulevard, she mounted her bike and followed it. The road carried her down a gentle hill and toward the rear of Dawson Groceries.

At the crest of the hill, where the trees gave way to bare ground, she paused and scanned the surrounding terrain: dead grass, naked trees, and a dirt road. She was alone in the woods once again. Off in the distance, she heard a dog bark and the snap of gunfire. The rush of the wind flapped her clothes, stung her nose, and turned her cheeks red. Waves of emotional pain seized her soul and crushed her. Agonized by her cowardice, she leaned over the handlebars and closed her eyes. *I am a Special Agent for the FBI. I should have helped them. But how? I should have thought of something. But what could I have done?*

She walked in silence, her sense of self-worth still stinging. Her mind began to drift, and she looked to the horizon. The enormous mountains seized her imagination. Taller and broader than she imagined possible, they jutted into the sky and sliced through the passing clouds. Each mountain stood shoulder to shoulder with its cousin, an implacable barrier. Gleason, now a valley, sat in the middle of this mountain range, a great basin, a place where the rivers, both old and new, converged.

Across a parking lot, she saw a discount store, a local retailer rather than a national chain. She circled around behind it, locked her bike to a tree, and then covered it with sticks and leaves. After making sure no one saw her, she hurried down the hill and across the grassy strip that bordered the parking lot. When she rounded the corner, she came to an abrupt stop. A crowd of people filled the entire lot.

A woman with a megaphone spoke, "I am Debbie Gauge, the official information officer for The City of Gleason. Dawson's Groceries and Evan's Sundries will be emptied soon. Reliable reports indicate that produce, meats, and most packaged goods are exhausted. Other stores may have a few supplies, and we have done our level best to allocate them fairly; but those too will be expended in a few minutes. If you need food, please go to the armory on the west side of the center circle. They still have some supplies of fresh drinking water. The sheriff reports that most of the transformers — required to provide electricity — were destroyed by an electromagnetic pulse or EMP. There are no estimates as to when power will be restored."

"What about us? We need food!" shouted a man. "Downtown is a killing zone. We can't go there."

"The mayor is working with law enforcement to quell the violence, and local farms are bringing in their crops. We will have flour available in a few weeks. Please conserve your food until then."

"Conserve our food?" the man shouted. "I'm already out of food. We're hungry. We need food now!"

"People, we have lost touch with the outside world. We are on our own. No one is coming to save us. Take care of your family and friends. They are your best hope now. God be with you," she concluded.

"This is ridiculous," a man said. "Do something!"

Rory passed through the crowd that formed behind her and searched for an officer. She spotted a man wearing green fatigues and carrying an assault rifle. "Excuse me," she said. The young man, a private on leave from the army, turned toward her. She then told him what she witnessed on Power Line Road. "... They are south of the shopping complex. You still might be able to catch them."

"Thanks," the young man said and ran to speak with his sergeant. After relaying her story to the sergeant, a squad of men loaded into a pair of jeeps and raced south, leaving Rory to watch them drive away. She waited for a minute and then decided to leave.

She circled around the back of the store and retrieved her bicycle. The shortcut was out of the question, so she stuck to the road. After she was a half mile away, the store tried to close, and angry protests ensued. The mob smashed in the store windows and rushed into the facility. Several shots rang out, and screams erupted.

The Seventh Age

Against the flow of pedestrian traffic, desperate for safety, she pedaled as fast as she could. Rory felt sick to her stomach. Where would she go? What would she do?

The road passed in a blur beneath her tires. It weaved its way through the woods and up to Rt. 223. No sooner had she passed over the north bridge spanning Jennings Creek when armed men arrived and blocked traffic. When angry shouts and defiance erupted, the volunteers fired shots into the air and drove back the unruly mob.

A man clad in blue jeans, western boots, a brown suede jacket, and a cowboy hat climbed onto the hood of a Jeep. "There is no food in the shopping district. None! The shelves are bare. They don't even have clean water. Go home, or better yet, go fishing. You are going to have to forage for your supper. I run a fish-camp two miles north of here. We are showing people how to process acorns and make bread. If you come up, I will be glad to show you how, but going grocery shopping is not an option …."

Rory turned, her heart filled with dread. She looked toward home and saw great plumes of smoke rising up into the sky, thick and black, as though the world burned. Scattered gunfire erupted, and then a thunderous boom shook the ground: a mushroom cloud of fire and smoke rolled into the sky. She rode south on Eastern Road, standing on the pedals and pumping as fast as her legs allowed. An army convoy raced past her. Soldiers armed with automatic weapons looked back at her with weary eyes.

It was late morning when she reached her neighborhood. A gathering of her friends and neighbors formed in the middle of the street. Brent tried to settle them down, but raw fear seized them, growing stronger with each bit of bad news.

Ellen Garby objected saying, "… You have no idea if everything is going to be okay. We need to know what's happening." Rory stepped off her bicycle and walked toward them

"I know fear isn't going to help," Brent said. "We need to stick together."

"I just came from a trip to Dawson's Groceries ...." Rory relayed to them all that she saw and heard. "... I left when the rioting broke out. Stores were looted and burned. I rode by a column of soldiers on their way to stop the violence."

"You're sure of this?" Brent asked.

"Very," Rory replied. "No one is coming to save us. There is no food, no water, and no gas. And the woods are filled with looters. They could be here at any time." Even Brent showed signs of panic, combing his fingers through his gray locks. The assembled crowd dissolved and families rushed back to their homes.

Honking sounded in the street. Rory walked over to a window and brushed aside the curtains. Several cars waited in the streets, fueled by hidden stores of gasoline. People rushed out of their homes and piled into the car, and more cars joined them. A knock came from her front door and startled her. When she opened the front door, she saw Rick Barnes on her stoop.

"We have a little room in our van. It's going to be tight, but you can come with us," he had a hopeful look in his eyes. The driver of the van honked the horn. "Wait a second," he shouted. "What do you say?"

"Where are you going? All of the roads are blocked. There's no way out of the valley," she replied.

"We're going to drive as far as we can, and hike out the rest of the way. We figure we can hike over the mountains in a week or two. We have poles to catch fish and plenty of ammunition to hunt. It may take us a month, but we figure that we can make it to civilization by then. I camp out in the backcountry all the time. It will be an adventure. What do you say?"

"No thanks. I'm staying here. If you make it, send help back for the rest of us," Rory replied.

"Oh … ah … okay," Rick said. "No promises but I will do what I can. I'm not sure if I will be able to find you after all this is over, but I would love to go out for a beer."

"Sure, I would like that." Rory closed the door and locked it. When she returned to the living room window, she saw the van drive away. It was then that she spotted the official government plates on the back. They stole the van. Who knew what happened to the driver.

After the last car had departed, a sense of doom and loneliness filled her. She leaned her forehead against the glass, her breath creating an oval patch of condensation. Her eyes closed, she considered her situation and realized that she might have made a mistake. She ran to the front door and flung it open. After leaping off the stoop, she sprinted to the street, but it was empty: Rick was gone. She waited in the middle of the street, hoping someone would return, but as the minutes passed, a growing sense of futility took hold of her. She trudged back to her house and closed the door behind her. Now she truly was alone.

Rory took two steps away from the door, and then she heard a scratch. She turned around and opened the door. A medium size Australian Sheppard with a black and white coat, long hair, and pointed ears waited on her stoop. The dog cocked its head, perked its ears, and gazed up at her with its dark brown eyes.

"Well, what do you want?" The dog walked past her and entered the house. It circled around the sofa and curled up on it. "Oh, I see, you're looking for a warm bed for the night."

She knew the dog. His name was Jake, and he belonged to the Straus family. She walked down the steps and shivered in the cold. The Straus home lay three doors down on the opposite side of the street. She was sure that they left earlier in the day, abandoning the dog. The afternoon sun cast long shadows across the Straus yard. The windows were dark, and the house reminded her of a lifeless tomb. Like all the other residents of Gleason, they were trying to hike out of the valley.

In many people's eyes, Jake was a liability, another mouth to feed, but Rory knew the truth: dogs give far more than they take. They warn people of danger, protect people when they slept, and loved them when no one else would.

Jake looked up at her, wondering if she would expel him. Rory's heart melted at the sight of his big brown eyes. "If we are going to do this, then we have to get some things straight. I'm the human; therefore, I'm in charge. You do what I say. Clear?"

Jake let out a bark, which Rory took as "yes." She rummaged around in the kitchen and found a can of hash. After opening it, she set it down on the floor and called him. The dog's nails clicked on the tile floor. He sniffed the food and then gobbled it down. Panting, he looked up at her and then passed under her hand by way of thanks.

"Okay," she said. "You're welcome."

When she returned to the sofa, Jake hopped up and lay down next to her. He curled up and laid his head on her left thigh. "It's a good thing Christy left me. She would never have let you stay." Jake looked up at her with big, dewy brown eyes. In a world gone insane, it was nice to have a friend.

Sunset came early thanks to encroaching clouds, and the suburban street had never been so dark. Even the stars hid from her. After checking the doors twice, she retrieved a Sig Saur, 9mm handgun. She and Jake headed up to her bedroom. After which, she locked the door and started a fire in the hearth.

Chapter 11

Rory cycled to other neighborhoods and abandoned shopping malls, craving human contact, and yet another family fled Gleason. When she questioned them about their destination, vague descriptions of unsure destinations ensued. They decided to leave, and hiking out of the valley was popular. Most felt that the rest of America, and rescue, lay on the other side of the mountains. The assumption might have seemed reasonable if Rory understood how the mountains appeared in the first place. Absent from that explanation, she worried about what they would find. Would New York City be flooded by the sea, or would Florida be an island; or would California be missing, sunk into the ocean?

The second week of the exodus left the neighborhood a ghost town. Gleason was an ominous void, and even the gunfire fell silent. At night she dreamt of the destruction and looters that chased her. When she awoke, she would grab her handgun from off the nightstand and creep to the window, worried that looters moved through the darkness, murdering those that remained, and peering out through the blinds, her every sense focused on the emptiness, straining to penetrate the veil of darkness.

Rory crept back to her bed and caressed the handgun. Jake followed and lay down next to her. The dog pressed up tight against her and shared in her anxiety. She ran her fingers through his silky coat, and Jake nuzzled her with his wet nose. While she loved Jake, their food was low and would be gone in another week. Then what would she do when he whimpered for food? For an instant, she envisioned pressing the gun to Jake's head and pulling the trigger. She extinguished the disgusting thought and assured herself that it would never come to that. Help would come. It just had to.

When morning arrived, she brooded over her dwindling supplies. The dry dog food, scavenged from several houses, was half-gone. She watched Jake wolf down the gravy mix and then thank her with a little

91

dance. As she combed her fingers through his hair, she recalled the previous night's imagining. Would she have the courage to do it, to end Jakes life, when the time came? What would she do? Would she commit suicide? With the world gone insane, it seemed the only rational choice.

Whether an internal voice or an external presence, something urged her to do it now, to take action, to end her angst, to end the constant drone in the back of her mind. They were safe, comfortable, and well fed. Perhaps that was the time to end her life before things got bad. Then Pastor Prescott's words resurfaced in her consciousness: "Death comes for all of us. It needs no help from you."

If suicide was out of the question, what would she do? The answer terrified her. She had to hike out of the valley, leaving safety and home behind. Rick was right, she was a fool. Whatever lay on the other side of the mountains, whatever hardships she encountered had to be better than this. She chided herself for not joining Rick. She passed up a well-supplied and armed group, and now she had to go it alone.

"I'm such an idiot," she lamented.

The decision made itself. They would hike out tomorrow at sunrise. She searched the attic and found a sleeping bag, backpack, and camping gear. But what could she do about Jake? The Straus family owned several dogs, and they ushered them out the back door and abandoned them when they departed. Most wandered away, dying or becoming feral; only Jake remained. She searched the Straus's house and found a canine backpack, once used for camping. After they were packed, she spent the day planning their escape from Gleason.

Rory woke early the next morning, eager to begin their adventure, eager to leave Gleason and sorrow behind her. Although she was loath to wear women's undergarments, she yielded and donned comfortable lingerie, a black Lycra polyester pair of panties, shiny and hugging her feminine curves. She opted to wear an athletic bra and donned a long sleeve cycling jersey, which gleamed like polished chrome, emphasizing her chest. With them, she wore a pair of ankle length, Lycra spandex jogging tights. They felt a bit too body conforming, but she appreciated their elasticity and their warmth. And although she found a ski jacket, snow pants, and heavy boots packed away in the guest room closet, the weather had turned warm, making it far too warm to wear them, but she brought them for when the weather turned – and everyone knew that mountain weather could kill.

The sum effect of the garments enhanced her beauty and sex appeal, much to her chagrin. Of course, fashion designers created female attire with this goal in mind, but she was not the average woman; and the notion of ogling repulsed her. She exited the bedroom and scrambled down the stairs, excited to begin the adventure.

She strapped her backpack and winter gear to the cycle, but she paused to eat a last hot meal. After kneeling and offering a simple prayer, awkward but sincere, the first earnest prayer in years, she strapped a knife to her hip and took a last look around the living room. She debated whether to bring her handgun. Her FBI training made it clear that guns usually made things worse, not better, and the public seldom hit what they shot at, often resulting in tragedy – yet she could not resist the power of the gun, and she decided to bring it.

A flood of memories cascaded through her consciousness. She recalled Christy's laughter as she played with Michael: a perfect spring day filled with barbecuing and cold beer. Although her heart begged to linger in the memory a minute longer, she pushed it aside and exited the house.

"Come on Jake," she said, stuffing the gun in her already filled pack and mounting her bicycle. There was no need to keep him on a leash. Such laws disappeared with society. Jake hurried up to her side and matched her pace. As she pedaled through the street, she heard the lone pop of gunfire and smelled smoke in the wind. It had a plastic, synthetic aroma, the kind of smell that made your lungs seize, unlike the smell of a campfire. She searched the treetops and saw a black column rising into the clear morning sky, yet another house burned. She hoped that it was unoccupied, but a flock of crows that circled about the treetops hinted that someone else died.

They weaved through the connecting roads and traveled to East Grove Shopping District. Litter and clothes lay strewn about the ground, and looking down the gradual slope of Grove Boulevard, she saw miles of abandoned cars and trucks. A gray tabby, a mouse in its mouth, snuck across their path and darted underneath a sedan. When Jake sniffed at the cat, it hissed and moved deeper underneath the vehicle.

She rode between the cars, mindful to avoid the broken glass on the pavement. Felled to provide firewood, stumps, like razor stubble, marked what had ones been decorative groves. Smashed windows, sooty stains, fire scorched wood, collapsed roofs, and looted shelves replaced what had once been an upscale shopping district. A dead man lay on the sidewalk; his jacket and shoes missing. He lay face down and halfway through a shattered store window; a round bloody stain marred his once white sweater, and a fist size hole lay in the center of his back, exposing his internal organs, blood congealing upon the concrete sidewalk.

Only the cinderblock walls of Dawson Groceries remained. A vague stench of death wafted on the breeze, fading in and out, a promise of what lay in store if she lingered. When she rode past three abandoned army transports, she drew in a frightened gasp. Three soldiers, clad in fatigues, dead fingers clutching spent weapons, lay between the trucks, their killers nowhere in sight. She retrieved her sidearm from the backpack, but she forgot the holster; it lay miles behind her back at the house. Turn around? Not an option. She would have to do without it and anything else she forgot. She returned the gun to her pack, hoping she would not need it in a hurry.

She sped down the hill and arrived at the end of the loop. It was time to leave the convenience of the road and civilization. It was not until she trekked through a mushy field, dampening her feet, that she had an epiphany. A road, like bread or gasoline, was the product of civilization, a commodity that she would come to miss.

The Seventh Age

"The Simms Memorial Trail" began. She turned left, and the gravel path flowed underneath her. It cut a trail through the forest and headed straight toward the river. It was much faster and safer than taking a car. That would have required passing through town, and she was afraid of looting and what remained after the looting ceased. Also, these strange mountains were probably devoid of roads, and the truck would not start. She was unsure if she could repair it.

Jake trotted alongside her, glad for the adventure. Every so often, he stopped to sniff the ground. Falling behind, he raced to catch up with Rory. When they arrived at the Westerly River that flowed into Prospect Lake, she noticed that it was swollen and turbulent, an oddity in the fall. That only typically happened in the spring with the winter melt off. Although the red steel trestle bridge was wide enough to ride, she opted to walk her bike across it. As she passed over its length, the wooden boards thumped underneath her feet. She peered over the side and stared down into the swirling water and started in shock – red algae made it appear like a river of blood – and then a body floated past, making her wonder if it was red algae, or something more sinister.

They passed over the bridge and saw the waters lapping on the opposite shore. She began to jog and heard a disconcerting rattle beneath her feet. *It will hold*, she told herself. When she reached the concrete footing, a sigh of relief escaped her lips. Jake rushed passed her and continued up the trail.

Rory mounted her bike and began to peddle. She came to a strange and frustrating conclusion. Bicycle seats hate the human body, and all of her weight balanced on her the most sensitive areas. Shifting her weight, she scooted back to the saddle, but it was too narrow to support her.

The trail circled through a bare thicket. Brown leaves covered the ground, and a recent rain turned them into a thick matt that partially obscured the trail. A brisk wind swept down the mountain and shoved her left side. She slowed to a crawl and shifted gears. The icy wind stung her nose and ears, a taste of misery to come? She leaned forward, putting more pressure on her crotch, and pushed hard. When the trail made a sharp right turn, the wind nearly toppled her. She fought to keep her balance and keep moving.

Apprehension panged her when she left the trail for a dirt road, the vivid recollection of the captured women still dominating her thoughts. The road skirted along the base of the mountain as if laid that way on purpose. When she rounded a grove of leafless trees, she stopped. Something cut the house in half, sliced right down the middle, the back half gone. The front half butted up against a rough boulder. It reiterated the point that something very strange happened and was still happening. She resumed riding and saw more oddities. Half a car lay next to a half a fire hydrant. The road made a left turn and came to an abrupt halt at the foot of the mountain. She squeezed the brake and then straddled the bike. Gazing skyward, she saw the mountain looming over her like a disapproving giant. It rose up so high that it passed through the clouds, disappearing from sight and shattering her confidence.

She tried riding through the woods, but her bicycle tires were too narrow. The tires sank into the mushy earth, and muck soon mired them. Rory dismounted her bike and walked it through the woods for a mile. After that, she happened upon a dirt road and continued despite the effort. The ground became rough, covered with jagged stones. Predictably, a minute later a pop and a hiss came from her rear tire. A flat. Albeit reluctantly, she leaned her bike up against a tree, removed her backpack, and left it behind. Whatever path led through the mountains, she doubted a street bike with a flat tire would be useful.

Stripped of her last technological comfort, she set out on foot. The lifeless forest skirted along the base of the mountain and started to appear scorched. The charring grew worse with every step she took until the trees looked like burnt matchsticks. It was then she happened upon a deep trench, a long, straight gash cut into the earth, pointing away from the mountain. She scrambled down the bank and stumbled into it. At the end of the trench, she spotted the nose section of a passenger airliner, the body snipped off in the middle, lodged in the earth like a silver bullet. She walked slowly toward it and saw debris scattered about the ground, an all too familiar sight these days.

A business suit and patent leather shoes lay at her feet as if laid out for someone to wear. When she kicked it, a bony hand emerged from the leaves and fell over like a stick. She scrambled backward and fell to the ground, a yelp ripped from her lips. She sucked in gasps of air, and her heart pounded. She retrieved her handgun and pointed it at the corpse as if to fend off the nightmarish image. Every horror movie she'd ever watched flashed in her mind, and she halfway expected eerie music to play and a zombie to arise. For a moment, she waited, gun ready. Jake trotted over and sniffed the corpse. "Jake," she hissed, "get away from it." Jake ignored her and continued his examination. But the dead didn't rise, and she felt foolish.

Rory struggled to her feet, wiped the sod from her bottom, and shifted the load on her back. The dead bodies of the airline passengers lay scattered on the forest floor. Some were still strapped into their seats, arms and legs broken, but all were badly decomposed. As she passed through the carnage, she happened upon an orange suitcase. She opened it, searching for something useful. The lid opened revealing a little girl's teddy bear. The stuffed bear looked up at her with one black eye, hoping for a child to hold it. Overwhelming loss flooded her soul as she gazed upon the abandoned toy. She wrapped her arms around Jake and pressed her face into his neck, finding comfort in his presence.

She closed the lid and secured the latches. Rising to her feet, she left the remaining luggage unexplored. She thought she was beyond the carnage when she came upon a headless skeleton. It hung upside down in a tree, its arms waving in the breeze as if calling for help, its trousers caught on a branch. She hurried passed the macabre scene and began to jog. The heavy pack heaved, as did her breasts, and both soon forced a slow, deliberate pace.

As she continued her trek, she pondered the weather. Why was it so comfortable? Except during the months of July and August, most women were perpetually cold. "Turn up the heat," was Christy's recurring demand. But Rory felt more than warm, she felt snug, toasty as if seated beside a warm fire. She attributed it to physical exertion, but part of her doubted this conclusion. There was more to her new body than just a change in gender, but what it was defied her comprehension.

The pair followed around the base of the mountain, searching for some means of passage. Its hard, gray face remained implacable and impassable. Rory began to fret and regret her decision. Without a valley or ravine of some sort, she would never be able to pass through the mountains.

They searched without success, but after passing through some dense undergrowth, she scampered down a slight embankment and found herself on the outskirts of U.S. Highway 24. Abandoned cars littered the four-lane highway, some rolled off into the ditches but most scattered about the road like discarded toys. A slow procession of humanity, beleaguered survivors, stretched off and disappeared into the horizon, all seeking safe passage through the mountains.

She scrambled down the embankment and then climbed the shoulder to the highway. Rory hurried up to a family of four, all of which gazed at the ground with weary eyes. "Hello, where are you going? Have you heard anything about a rescue coming?"

"No. Sorry," the man replied. "My name is Steve Martin, like the actor. This is my wife Stacy, my daughter Emily, and my son Brandon."

"Rory Vakhal," she replied.

"Someone told me that it connects to a road that passes through the mountains," Steve said.

The Seventh Age

Rory looked back at the forest. "I left my bike a mile back in the woods. Damn it, I knew I should have kept it. But I don't suppose I'll find a spare inner tube anywhere along this road."

"I left my car along the side of the road 20 miles back, ran out of gas. It was a Mercedes. I had two payments left on it." Steve clasped his wife's hand. Stacy appeared too weary to speak and carry on a casual conversation. The boy and girl trudged behind them as if half dead.

Wanting a bit of distraction, Rory asked, "Do you live in Gleason?"

"We decided to get off the highway and see rural America, Gleason was supposed to be some sort of art Mecca. We had to go." He shook his head and rubbed his eyes. "We stayed at the Spring View Motel. It was okay as far as motels go. Then the world turned to shit."

Rory grunted, "Yes, I know."

"We paid for a full week, and we had food in the car. Why worry? The military or FEMA would come to save us. Two weeks later, we were out of food and money. Hell, we used debit cards to pay for everything. Who carries cash? Luckily, the manager accepted a check, and he let us stay another week. It was encouraging. Everyone was pulling together. The sheriff's office handed out food and water. Then, one day, when we went to get our food ration we were told it was all gone."

"I still remember the night when the motel manager came to our door. He had a huge man standing behind him. I mean he was enormous, arms the size of trees, tattoos all over them. I offered to write him another check, but he wanted us out. I gave him my gold Rolex. It was worth $10,000. It only bought us another three weeks. The next time he showed up with a shotgun and threw us out at gunpoint. Can you believe that? He just threw us out. He pointed his gun at my children!"

"Well, I know where there are plenty of empty homes." Rory sighed and moved the shoulder straps of her pack. "There's no food, no power, and no water, but they are available."

Steve grunted and shook his head. "No thanks. I figure we have just enough food to make it through the mountains."

"I thought you said the town ran out of food," asked Rory.

"They did. A group of us broke into the motel manager's home and raided his pantry. I could not believe how much food was in it. He was supposed to distribute it to us. We cleaned him out. Oh, and I got my watch back. Then Charlie set the man's house on fire. I thought that was wrong, but there was no way I was going to fight him." Steve smiled and slid up his left sleeve, exposing a gold watch. "I wish I could have seen the manager's face when he got home."

"I know the man who manages that motel. Elton always has been a bit of a miser. He cannot keep an employee. He pays too little," Rory replied.

"So you're a resident?" asked Steve.

"All my life," Rory replied.

"I'm sorry about your town." Steve stripped off his ball cap and ran his fingers through his thinning hair. "It's pretty much finished. I only hope we find civilization on the other side of the mountains."

They walked in silence for an hour. Even Jake began to grow weary. They stopped as a group and rested on a soft patch of ground for a half hour, all the while watching half-dead people trudge past them. After eating a meager meal, they resumed their trek.

The road ended in a sharp V-shaped ravine. Twenty yards to the right was a dirt road that passed through the valley. Patches of snow marked the corners where the road met the mountain. Rory scooped up handfuls of snow and stuffed them into her canteen. The others copied her and refilled their water bottles.

They traveled into a shaded valley, and the sun sank behind the mountains, freezing them and the ground. They found a small flat spot on the trail and stopped for the night. Other travelers kept walking, confident that they could navigate by starlight. Rory watched the refugees and ate an energy bar, sharing it with Jake. When the last person schlepped past them, she unrolled her sleeping bag and settled down for the night. Sleep came swiftly and deeply.

A shrill scream ripped through the night, and Rory awakened. She searched the darkness and drew her weapon. The gun burned her hand as though on fire. She hissed and let it tumble to the ground. She tried to turn on her flashlight, but the batteries were dead. She slapped it a couple of times and unscrewed the end cap. Leaked battery acid coated her fingertips. She tossed it aside and wiped her fingers in the brown dirt.

Another scream pierced the night. Rory jumped to her feet and drew her knife. A few stars twinkle through broken clouds and cast dull light upon the road. Steve moved to her side. "That sounded like a woman screaming," he said.

Stacy clutched her terrified children and asked, "What's happening?"

Primal instincts awoke within Rory. They made the hair on the back of Rory's neck stand on end. A man shouted, "No. Please."

"I'm getting out of here," Rory said.

"Where are you going to go?" Stacy whined.

"I'm going back. Those screams are getting close." She turned toward Steve and asked, "Are you coming with me?"

"We can't go back," he replied. "There's nothing back there for –" another scream interrupted him. He rubbed the back of his neck. "We have to keep going."

Rory put on her pack and then strapped a pack on Jake. "We need to get out of here." The sound of dying was unmistakable. "We have to go." When Steve hesitated, she strode away without them.

Four hours passed, and her eyes adjusted to the starlight. It was sufficient to illuminate the road and keep her from wandering off the edge. The nearing screams, however, caused her to quicken her pace. "Get away from me," a woman screamed. "Let me go!" Rory stripped off her backpack and Jake's pack. After tossing them aside, she began to jog.

Her feet flew over the dirt road. The screams grew nearer still. Horrible roars and shrill screeches echoed throughout the canyon. The sound awakened some deep instinct within her and launched her into a primal frenzy. Her feet ate up the ground. Although both her legs and lungs burned, she kept up the pace. Jake ran by her side, no explanation required. They both sensed the unseen danger pursuing them.

She lost track of time and distance. The road became level and then stopped. Finally, she was back in the valley. She crept through the woods and drew in gasps of air. They navigated a small embankment, and she felt the smooth asphalt surface. The race resumed. They followed the vague outline of the road as it passed through what had once been a small grove of trees. Something was chasing them: she could feel it.

Her body yearned for rest, but she kept running. Primal responses flooded her body with adrenaline and other hormones to dull the pain. She was no longer human, but a fleeing animal.

A red sun rose over the mountains to the east. It set the clouds and white capped mountains ablaze. She ran up to the crest of a hill and dared to pause. When she turned back, she saw the mountains far behind her. There was no sign of Steve or his family on the road.

Men on horseback, dressed as knights in metal armor and helmets, thundered past her. Their hands gripped weapons, ready for action. She watched them race toward the mountain road.

Rory turned away from the mountains and continued toward town. She tried to jog, but her legs failed to respond. As fear faded, fatigue made her limbs and eyelids heavy. There was still enough fear to drive her to keep moving.

More soldiers rode past her at pell-mell speeds. Eventually, the sun rose and burned away the night chill. It rose up into the sky, 10:00 A.M. by her estimates. The endless array of abandoned cars continued, littering the highway. She found an unlocked sedan and crawled inside it. After locking the door, she and Jake fell fast asleep.

Chapter 12

The afternoon heat turned the car into an oven, and Rory roused with strands of hair matted to her glistening cheeks. The car smelled of sweat, urine, and unwashed socks: someone had lived in the car for quite a while. Her throat parched, she reached behind her for her water bottle, but then she remembered the trail, discarding her belongings while running for her life. Recrimination stung her spirit. Why did she run? What was she afraid of? *I'm a coward. It was probably a mountain lion or some coyotes.* But she continued to ponder the situation, and she decided that the sounds came from something else, something dangerous.

Jake scratched at the car door; he wanted out of the oven. When Rory opened the door, a blast of cold air washed over them, swirled about the car interior, and escaped, carrying away the warmth. She rose to her feet, her legs aching, and stretched her arms. "Oh god, my back aches," she groaned. Jake was otherwise occupied: he sniffed a bush and lifted his leg. The road was familiar. She looked about and surveyed her surroundings. The outskirts of downtown lay only three miles away.

Stripped of gear and without breakfast, the pair resumed their hike. Rory saw piles of brick, and broken lumber, much of it scorched, that had once supported businesses. Bare ribbed buildings rose into the sky, their façades and walls fallen away. Men, like scavengers, picked through these corpses, searching for something useful. With a sharp clip-clop of hooves, a horse drawn cart trotted by her. Men clad in brown and tan cotton clothing stared with naked lust. They appeared like peasants escaped from some medieval movie, and after they were a short distance away, they laughed and joked; she tugged on the hem of her jacket and crossed her arms. She wanted to shout some witty rebuke, but she was far too tired, and they were too far away.

The Seventh Age

Two hours of walking through ruins left her exhausted and depressed. Where were the reporters, the FEMA advisors, and the military relief? Where was everyone?

Piles of rubble lay all about her, and the stench of burning flesh arose from many fires that burned the dead. A group of men and woman congregated in the streets. She recognized Ned Travis and walked over to him. "Hey, Ned, what's happening?"

Ned cocked his head and puzzled for a moment. He shrugged and said, "Soldiers from up north arrived in town late yesterday. They are from the Kingdom of Salvia in the Wolf's Maw Mountains, and this planet is not Earth. It's Eden. Is that messed up or what?"

"Has the world lost its mind?" she exclaimed. She told them of her hike up the mountain. They listened carefully as she described the screams in the night. "... What was all that?"

Judy Cosgrave spoke up. "The soldiers said that monsters, called daemia and haugr, live in the caves. They come out at night to feed. You have to be in one of the traveler's compounds at night, or they eat you."

Rory wanted to ridicule the idea, but the screams still reverberated in her imagination. "I was terrified. I just ran as fast as I could. Did anyone survive?"

"Not unless they made it to a Waypoint Town." Ned rubbed his face. "A soldier told me that the towns are 40 miles apart. He said that most of them have only a single inn, a tavern, and high curtain walls. The inns are so expensive that almost everyone sleeps in the courtyard. You really do not have a choice though. You have to make it there by nightfall or get eaten." He paused and shook his head. "What the hell is going on? The world has gone insane. What do they mean this planet is Eden? It doesn't make any sense."

Rory gazed at her chest and spandex material tented over a woman's breasts and then at her feminine hips. "No. Actually, it does make sense."

They looked at her in surprise. "Those mountains had to come from somewhere. They don't just spring up. Our valley had to jump to another planet. Maybe this is in our dimension, or maybe it is another. I don't know. But it's the only conclusion that approaches an explanation."

Ned shrugged. "Yeah, I guess, but it means we're stuck here. There is no United States and no one is coming to help us." This observation caused a corresponding period of silence: everyone pondered their fate. Ned finally broke the silence. "I need to get home. Phyllis and the kids are waiting for me."

"I have to get home too," Rory said.

"Do you mind if I walk with you?" asked Judy.

"No. I could use the company." The midday sun blazed with unexpected heat. Rory stripped off her sweatshirt and jacket, tying both around her waist, the light gleaming off her silver top. Men dressed in rusty armor and dreary garb leered at her, their desires unspoken but evident in their eyes.

"I don't like these people," Judy whispered. "They keep looking at me like I'm some sort of prostitute."

"I know what you mean."

Rory took note of the horse-drawn carts and the medieval garb. There were a few women she saw among the newcomers. Although it was a warm day, they wore skirts over crinolines and both extended all the way to their ankles. Likewise, they wore long sleeved peasant blouses with restrictive corsets overtop of them. Some of the women wore straw hats, held in place with a colorful scarf.

"I guess I can understand why. Look at the way we are dressed. You're wearing shorts and a tank top, and I'm wearing athletic gear. They wear more underwear than this. It must seem like we are naked," Rory replied and crossed her arms.

The Seventh Age

A peasant woman stood atop a wagon with her hands on her hips. The deep crevices in her face testified to long winters and many hardships. "His Excellency King Leopold Justinian the IV of Salvia has graciously provided these supplies to the people of Gleason. Come and partake in his bounty." Rory and Judy joined the crowd gathered around the wagon. When the woman saw them, she scowled and handed them both a heavy burlap sack. "Take your food and move along, whores."

Judy's mouth hung agape, astonished at the grim woman's gruffness. She was about to say something when Rory dragged her away by the arm. She whispered. "Go home and change. We don't want these people getting the wrong idea about us."

"But she called us whores," Judy protested.

Rory scanned the guards gathered around the perimeter of the food distribution. "They are feeding us, and the guards have swords. Don't give them an excuse to use them."

"Use them?" echoed Judy.

"Yes. This King Leopold is trying to act like a big shot. He doesn't want a couple of women embarrassing him, especially women he thinks are prostitutes."

Judy nodded: "I guess."

Rory opened her sack and examined the contents. "I have a loaf of bread, ten potatoes, an onion, and lots of dried beans. I need to get this home before someone tries to steal it." The last observation struck a chord of fear within Judy. She bit her lower lip and nodded. They separated, and Rory headed for home.

Rory walked along Frontage Boulevard. The broad, 4-lane road was free of abandoned cars and trucks, cleared by the sheriff's department. It felt strange to walk down the middle of the street without concern. She kept expecting traffic to top the hill and rush at her; a crowd, growing denser by the minute, passed her by, heading toward the food giveaway. She left the main road and turned onto Simpson Lane, spanning the Simpson Truss Bridge. Jake paused at the edge of breakwater and peered underneath the guardrail. The swollen waters of Jennings Creek rose up perilously high, almost reaching the bottom of the Simpson Truss Bridge. She walked across the bridge in the middle of the road, staying well away from the raging river.

Rory trekked back through the Heritage Woods Estates feeling a little less desperate. She had food, and more would follow. It was simple fare, but it would sustain her. She also knew what had happened to her town, which was more than she knew the previous day. Many questions remained. What was this Kingdom of Salvia, and what did they want? No one gave away food without wanting something in return. She tried to accept it as a generous gift, but dark suspicions gnawed at her.

The golden sun beamed upon her and soothed her troubled mind. While things always seemed worse at night, they seemed better during the day. She resolved to go home and cook dinner. Tomorrow she would find her bicycle and perhaps her discarded backpack, although the latter seemed unlikely. She still felt compelled to try, though.

Jake ran ahead and chased after a squirrel. Part of Rory wished he would catch it. Every animal he caught and ate was less food she had to supply. This shifted her thoughts to her melted gun. What had caused that? She had more guns in the safe at home. She could use them to hunt for meat, and she could always go fishing. She enjoyed it, and there was plenty of time for it now.

Yes. Things were much better. Reality had righted itself, and the world seemed a little less topsy-turvy.

She passed by the large wooden sign that marked her neighborhood. The streets were still empty, and scattered debris still lay untouched in overgrown yards. Everyone would return soon. Where else could they go?

Chapter 13

Rory prepared and consumed a measured portion of her supplies. She had no idea when or if more would follow. The pumpernickel bread was terrible and filled with fibrous fragments of seedpods. Just a few bites of the heavy bread filled her stomach, and because of the cardboard taste, she was glad for it. But it was good to have food, and more importantly, it was good to hope.

She shared the bread and some bland beans with Jake. The dog was far less picky than she, and Jake wolfed it down in seconds. She learned a lesson from Jake. When an animal is hungry and someone presents it with food, it eats. She returned to the beans and consumed them all.

They hiked back to the bicycle, but the supplies abandoned on the trail were too far and probably scavenged. After Rory had returned home, walking her bike, end of day found her back where she started. Rory opened one of her last bottles of red wine, and a glass of wine in her hand, she watched the dancing flames in the hearth. She pulled up the blanket and settle back into the plush reclining chair. "Well Jake, just between you and me, it's weird to be a girl." The dog raised its head, and his ears peaked as if what she had to say was the most interesting thing he had ever heard. "But I guess I'll have to get used to it, not that I have a choice. I wish I knew how that happened." She swallowed the last gulp of wine and sighed. "I wish Christy was here."

Jake laid his head on her and closed his eyes. Rory joined him and drew up the blanket. The warm fire and fatigue finally wooed Rory into a deep sleep. Jake stretched out, and with a groan, he fell fast asleep as well. His belly was full, and all was right with the world.

A rainbow of blue, yellow, green, and red sparkles danced in the air, like a shimmering mist. They burst into existence, gave birth to others, and then disappeared a moment later. These tiny flashes spread through the air like a growing swarm of insects, exponentially multiplying, engulfing, and absorbing. The air became thick like molasses and wrapped around everything like a heavy blanket. The flames dancing upon the logs slowed as if fatigued and then came to an abrupt halt. As if caught in a video freeze frame, everything froze. The constant that defined human existence – the passage of time – stopped.

Chapter 14

Rory dreamed of stars – dancing as ballerinas before a black curtain – and galaxies shimmered like diamonds as she passed through endless night. She drifted without form or care; her soul rested in the arms of the heavens, cradled like an infant in her mother's arms. Such dreams were sweet and not easily surrendered.

The rising sun took her by surprise, the yellow ball of fire a stranger to her eyes. The first rays of dawn stretched across the room and caressed her cheek, gently pulling her back to the world of the living. Her eyelids fluttered, and she beheld her bedroom, bathed in light and as fresh as the first dawn upon a new world. She yawned and sat up to greet the new day. The ease of night and slumber were cast aside like a warm blanket, their comfort lingering in her memory.

She rubbed her neck. A peculiar angle created a slight cramp on the right side. For a moment, she opened her mouth to call out for Christy. Then the memory of Christy's departure resurfaced, and the lament of her soul returned with crushing intensity. She lay back and tried to fall asleep. Why get up? Why dress? Why eat? Why exist?

Jake sprang to his feet and jumped on the bed. When he licked Rory's face, she blocked him with her hands and pushed him away. He paused for a moment, sniffed the air as if searching for a cat, and then he rushed out of the room. Rory sighed and pushed aside the blankets. The day and new challenges awaited her. She rose to her feet to meet them but did so with a heavy heart.

She pushed aside the curtains, surveying her world; she shielded her eyes from the painful white light; it was just as she left it. "I must have been tired. It's mid-morning." She yawned again and shuffled into the

111

bathroom. After stripping off her clothes, she poured some water into the sink and partook of a cold sponge bath. She then transferred the wastewater to the toilet tank located behind the seat. When it was full, she sat down and relieved herself. The gray water then flushed away the waste.

She dumped her clothes into the hamper and opened her underwear drawer. Women had many options when it came to undergarments, but none of them suited her masculine sensibilities. She rubbed her face and tried to decide between the various options. Her plan was simple. She was going to go to the Federal Center and check in with the FBI. She still had a job to do, and she was sure that they needed her help.

Two wardrobes hung in the closet, her clothes and the remained of Christy's clothes. Rory's wardrobe included few conservative outfits, which is to say that most were rather revealing, but Christy took most of her clothes. One by one, she perused and rejected each outfit. Women's fashions and the current trends were a mystery to her. When she came upon a pantsuit, a clear safe choice presented itself. The material was black, elastic, and satin – a bit shiny, but the best she could find. Now, Rory was new to dressing as a woman, but she understood the embarrassment of panty lines. She did not want to admit to wearing panties, let alone have someone see their outline.

A thong seemed to be the right choice. A black color satin thong and matching bra appeared to be the best combination. Rory held out the thong and twitched her nose. The remains of her masculine orientation chaffed at the notion of wearing a thong. Should she go without wearing underwear? That was worse. She meditated on the matter – yes – it was worse.

She stepped into the thong and whisked it up her legs. The narrow ribbon cleaved deep between her cheeks, making her very aware of her bottom. She stabbed her arms through the shoulder straps of a bra and secured the chest strap with one deft move. The satin underwire cups lifted and shaped her breasts, creating a pair of grapefruit size, bulging globes that swelled out from her chest. Yet as she made a few final adjustments to the shoulder straps, an oddly comforted and controlled feeling settled over her. It was only after she picked up her slacks that it occurred to her how easily she had hooked her bra – a lucky try?

She stabbed her legs into slacks and did a little dance as they sheathed her legs in black satin; it caressed her legs and then hips, sculpting to her feminine curves. Her fingers slid on the smooth arc of her satin wrapped between her legs but found no zipper; then she saw the strange side zipper on her right hip; the garment had all the same parts but was so different from men's attire. A white silk blouse with a Peter Pan collar came with the outfit; it had a black ribbon tie and was so cute that it screamed I'm a girl, but it created forward momentum, and that eased her troubled mind.

After putting on a pair of ankle boots, she stood before the dressing mirror, and a teenage girl stared back at her – the face of a stranger. "Oh my god, this is so weird."

She tugged on the lapels of her bolero style jacket, a fact she failed to observe, and found that it emphasized her womanly assets, white satin fabric tenting and sculpting around her chest. Meanwhile, the slacks sculpted to her heart shaped bottom in a very disconcerting fashion. Still, it was better than jeans and a sweatshirt – she guessed.

She brushed her hair, but something was still missing. She studied her appearance for a moment or two, not certain of what it could be. Then it occurred to her: women wear makeup. The masculine half of her exclaimed, "Hell no! I can go without." She exited the room only to return a minute later. She muttered curses and sat down at the makeup table. She needed a job, and women without makeup appeared half-dressed and unprofessional, or so Christy used to say.

The array of cosmetics was daunting. Rory took a seat and set about to perform this unwelcome task. She watched Christy apply her makeup on many occasions and knew the basics. Foundation came first, as implied

113

by the name. She then applied a touch of rouge to the apple of her cheeks, luscious red gloss to her lips, and a hint of taupe to her eyelids. Even her lashes got a quick coat of black.

She pouted at her reflection; the girl in the mirror was a rare beauty, dressed like a teenage girl seeking her first job. "I hope this works." She arose and exited the room.

Jake followed her from the bedroom, eager for a morning meal. Rory opened a can of ravioli and dumped it into a dish. A gassy hiss emanated from Jake, and Rory screwed up her face; waving her hand, she said, "You really can raise a stink." Dogs, however, went out of their way to smell urine and feces. It made no difference to him.

Rory grabbed a set of car keys and tried to slip them into her front pocket. Of course, neither her slacks nor her jacket had pockets. Her male ego burned hot and railed at the poor functionality of female attire. Appearance rather than function defined women's clothing. The thong assured of this conclusion. Rory sighed and slouched. With little other choice, she marched back to her room and fetched a purse. She placed a handgun, a few makeup items, some tissues, and a set of keys in her purse.

"You stay here, Jake, and guard the house." The dog seemed to understand and settled down onto the sofa. Rory tried to open the garage door, but it was stuck. It was then she remembered the padlocks. She could not help but wonder why Christy placed them there. Rioting and looting were provocation enough, but she worried that there might be a specific reason.

When she exited the back door, their world was mute and lifeless. The brown of the tree trunks, the white house trim, and the blue of the sky was swallowed in murky shades of gray; even a set of burnt red lawn chairs appeared dull and lifeless. The sun burned bright overhead, but its efforts were unappreciated by the land.

The Seventh Age

The world popped, and sudden colors and sharp sounds assaulted her senses. She sucked in a gasp and arched her back as if bursting out from frigid waters. A moment later, she opened her mouth wide and rubbed her ears. The world exploded with life and hot air gusted with sudden power, and it carried with it the scent of mature crops, ready for harvest. But it was fall. How could it be so hot? She used her hand as a visor and gazed up at the sky. The sun stood straight overhead and not off on the northern horizon, as though it was midsummer.

There was no time to ponder the inconsistencies of the weather. Rory circled around the garage and removed the padlocks, then pushed open the door. Christy's black SUV was a bit roomier and more comfortable, and unlike her truck, it worked. It was the only choice. After closing the door and replacing the padlocks, she was on her way.

She drove along Maple Avenue at a crawl. Homes with padlocked doors, shutters swinging idly, and boarded windows reminded her of a corpse. Children's toys still littered yards, and bicycles leaned up against trees. Laundry still hung on the line behind one home, never to be collected. Heaviness hung upon her as she witnessed the void left behind by the exodus. Perhaps the others would return, but she doubted it. Maple Avenue was a graveyard, and the homes were mausoleums.

When she arrived at the stop sign for Yarmouth Avenue, the SUV rolled to a stop. A vast circle, having a crisp edge, stretched 2 miles in diameter; the circle appeared sharp as if drawn with a compass. Fallen leaves and skeleton trees were behind her, a testament of fall. However, the trees ahead of her were laden with green foliage, and thick grass filled the empty spaces.

She pressed on the gas and entered the green world. The SUV's tires began to bounce on rubble; grass sprouted around broken chunks of pavement, and dense vegetation pressed in from both sides. Great roots stretched across her path like barricades, and the SUV rocked as it scrambled over the undergrowth.

115

She scanned for some sign of the familiar. This was Yarmouth Road; she was sure; she had driven it every day for seven years. Between the heavily laden branches, the dense undergrowth, and the dark shadows she caught glimpses of houses. Broken windows, collapsed roofs, devouring black mold, and scattered detritus replaced what had once been homes. A few homes were nothing more than foundations filled with debris and stagnant water. Eaten by rust, tires flat and decayed, dirt covered the abandoned cars. Bullet holes pockmarked the sheet metal and shattered filthy windshields.

In the rearview mirror, she saw the fall scenery. Yet an abundant forest lay ahead of her. The trees closed in on the road as if engulfing it, their leafy branches swaying in the breeze and stretching high toward the sky. They were larger than she imagined possible.

She made a right on Simpson Road and drove downtown, finding it in terrible condition. Only snatches of the pavement remained as the earth digested the work of man. The encompassing foliage left behind only a vague hint of the road. She cruised to the Simpson Truss Bridge, spanning Jennings Creek, and stopped. The bridge appeared weathered beyond its years, and the swollen river spilled over the banks.

The dense forest lay behind her, and the only sign of civilization lay on the other side of the river. She decided to risk it, but she lowered her window, in case the bridge collapsed, forcing her to swim free of the SUV. Wide planks rattled when her tires rolled onto the bridge. The bridge groaned with noisy complaint, and it appeared to be more rust than metal. When the SUV reached the halfway point, fear stabbed her. Swirling waters, a swift current, brown with mud threatened her with death. She risked a little more speed and hurried across the second span. When her tires reached the other side, she rushed up the hill, expecting to see the bridge collapse behind her, splashing into the river. However, it remained intact and resolute.

A small hill carried her onto Frontage Boulevard. It was in better shape, but not by much. Grass grew in the crazed fracture lines that marred the once smooth surface. Rory turned on the radio and heard a static hiss. Snaps, whirs, and hisses replaced what had once been "Easy Rock 950 AM." As she cruised toward the city, she passed by an old flatbed truck. To her amazement, a team of horses pulled it. Ears of corn filled the bed and were piled up high on the wooden sides. The reins passed through the opening that had once been a windshield, and the driver clutched the leather straps in his calloused hands. The old man removed his hat and scratched his balding head as if she was the peculiar one.

She cruised around the vehicle at a slow speed, but it seemed so fast. There were dozens of rusted, abandoned cars. Like those she observed earlier, they were little more than rusted hulks, buried in dense undergrowth between towering trees, time capsules awaiting some future archeologist. One tree actually grew up through the middle of a sedan, impaling it. Layers of leaves now covered the automobile roofs, and packed dirt turned the windows opaque. The tires were flat, cracked, and rotted.

When she entered the town, new structures replaced toppled buildings, as if this had all happened just days ago. How could anyone rebuilt so soon? It was just another impossibility in a day full of them.

She recognized the red brick, concrete trusses, and gray slate roof architecture, yet the buildings and the town were strangers to her. The builders used debris from the ruins, and constructed buildings with a maze of tight alleys, stairways, and walkways. Most of the buildings had balconies covered with green awnings, heavy plank doors, and shuttered windows. Men and women reclined on handcrafted furniture and looked down at her vehicle as she passed.

Girls paused from playing jump rope to stare at her. They wore homemade dresses of simple tan cotton fabric. The dresses hung down to their ankles and hung loosely on their bodies. Their hair was captured behind their heads, some worn in ponytails, and others pigtails. A boy rushed out of the house, leaned against a round log railing, and watched her with fascination.

Women with their hair gathered behind their head in brightly colored handkerchiefs – wearing peasant blouses, knee-length skirts, and leather shoes – carried baskets filled with goods. They sold fish, bread, fabric, fruit, produce, and other consumable products. Other women worked down by the river washing clothes; they rubbed soiled laundry against scrub boards. Yet some of the women wore fine dresses made of silk, satin, and velour, hand embroidered and striking. These wealthy women gathered in small clutches in front of shops as eager merchants vied for their business. Both groups paused to gawk at her as she passed them by.

The shops grew more numerous as she neared Main Street and the downtown shopping district. The polished and abundant goods of an industrial society were gone. What replaced them was a handcrafted and homespun economy. The dresses, furniture, brass oil lamps, and pottery goods all indicated local production. Smoke arose from many chimneys as restaurants prepared meals. They tantalizing aroma of cooking meat and vegetables caused her stomach to grumble in complaint. A pair of old men paused from a game of checkers and stared at her. Rory was beginning to feel conspicuous and more than a little worried.

A man holding a stop sign ordered her to halt. He moved aside as a convoy, a ragtag assembly of patchwork vehicles, approached the intersection. The pickup trucks, cars, and a flatbed truck was so much automotive scrap, slapped together in random fashion. Clouds of choking dust billowed in the air as they passed her by. She noticed a blue triangle on the side of the road but failed to comprehend its significance. It marked a rhunite free road, safe for automobile travel. The officer waved at her, and she cruised past him, feeling afraid, like a small child lost in a strange land.

———

Miles away, Bill Kendal released the lever and opened the gate to the lift. Jackhammers, drilling, and heavy machinery created a deafening din all around him. He crossed the metal ramp and dodged several work parties. When he entered administrative building number 3, he removed his hard hat. A thick layer of dirt covered his work boots, jeans, and a navy tee shirt. Even his orange vest was reduced to a dirty brown. It appeared as though he was a mud creature risen from the earth. It was best to avoid the offices.

He made a quick right and pushed open the locker room door; separate male and female facilities were no longer possible. A locker lay open to his right; two bras and pairs panties lay inside it. Trina and Jessica were showering. It was best to avoid them. They did not want men to join them. In fact, it would probably result in an assault.

Bill wandered over to a sink. Decades of grime and paint covered the sink's dingy enamel surface. He turned on the tap, and cold water flowed through his fingers. He splashed his face and washed away a layer of filth, and then his hands glided over his balding head. The water ran muddy brown for a moment, and a man appeared from the pile of mud.

Tom Riften, the operations foreman, was a grizzly bear of a man with a gravelly voice and a manner to match. He exited his office, stood in the doorway, and shouted: "Bill, I need to see you."

"What?" he snapped back.

"Come in and shut the door," Tom replied. Stacks of papers, drawings, and broken parts lay scattered about his desk. Tom put on a pair of reading glasses and held up a piece of paper. Bill stood in front of his desk and scratched his neck through layers of dirt. "The mayor's office is sending another inspector."

"Why? What's up?"

"According to him, we are behind schedule. They want to see what the holdup is," replied Tom.

"Schedule, what schedule? We're just making this up as we go. Geothermal power is new to all of us," Bill said. "If they wanted a professional job, they should have hired that Solva contracting firm."

"Good point," Tom replied. He smelled as if he had been too near a brush fire and his teeth were stained yellow. "But we were the lowest bidder, so we have to deliver. The King's Development Panel is unhappy with our progress. According to them, we should have turbine number three up and running. They want the reserve power available before winter arrives."

"Yeah, and I want to leave this goddamn valley, get back to Earth, and retire to Florida. We are working as hard as we can." Bill rubbed the back of his neck. "Have you noticed how our leadership caves in all the time and they never get their hands dirty? They sit up in their offices and live in homes like the aristocracy. They get fat, and we work to death."

"With a speech like that you should run for office. Oh wait a minute, this isn't a democracy. That went away with Earth and the USA. They have all the power, and we have none. No more talking about the King, the Royals, or the aristocracy: you'll get us executed."

Bill just grunted at Tom in reply. He knew Tom was right; spies lurked within earshot of every conversation. Tom added, "Anyway, meet with the rep and get him off my back." Tom handed Bill a whiskey bottle. "Give him this. It's the good stuff from before the Cataclysm. That is a single malt scotch, so don't break it or drink it. It should buy us some good will for a while."

Bill held up the bottle and gazed at the amber liquid. "I used to love scotch. It seems like a lifetime ago." He sighed and shook his head. "I'm tired. That bedrock is some tough stuff. I mean we risked our lives and worked all night long. If we had hit one patch of low-grade rhunite, we would all be dead. As it is, we only cleared away a couple of meters of granite. I need a cold beer and a hot woman."

"Stay away from those shanty brothels. They'll cut your throat and eat you for dinner. Besides, you own half the docks and all of the girls. Sleep with one of them," Tom said with a raspy cough.

The Seventh Age

"I may own the building, but I still have to pay for sex. Those girls don't work for free. If a guy tries to rip them off, they cut him, or worse yet — they give him the serum. After the gender transition is complete, they sell him as a slave girl. That's worse if you ask me," Bill said.

"You have a point," Tom said. "Just don't screw this up, or I'll toss you down a shaft." Tom scratched his graying beard and brooded oversupply invoices.

Bill slapped off some of the dust. "You should come down and enjoy yourself. I have several girls just off the farm. You just can't beat it."

Now it was Tom who grunted. Prostitutes and liquor cost way too much. Fondness for either of them bled a man dry. Tom said to Bill, "Get a shower. You stink."

Bill exited the office but opted not to take a shower. Trina and Jessica might still be using the facilities. He exited the locker room and grabbed his hard hat. When he entered the administrative offices, the women paused from their labor to watch him pass. "Good afternoon ladies," he said with a smile. However, he sensed their anger at his intrusion into their world, a "dust bunny" on its way to some hidden crevice. Gladys, the receptionist, eyed him as he approached her desk.

"I need a visitor's badge. I have to show some big shot around," Bill said. Gladys sifted through her upper right desk drawer and fished out a badge. She noted it in her log and slapped it down on the counter.

"If that goes missing, it's your neck, not mine," she said.

"It's not like I'm gonna sell it on the black market." Bill felt a chill coming from the woman and picked up the badge. He failed to comprehend why the office workers were so miserable. They worked in air-conditioned offices.

Cars, trucks, and heavy equipment scurried about the construction site. Bill waited under the covered carport, hat in hands. A black SUV swept around a dump truck and raised a cloud of dust behind it. *If I was a corrupt official, that's what I would drive,* he reasoned. *It looks new. It must be worth a fortune.* The SUV rushed up to him and stopped.

The driver's side window lowered. Rory removed her sunglasses and parted her lips in astonishment. Through the soiled clothes, filthy mud, and rags, she spotted a vestige of her former boss and best friend. "Bill, is that you?"

Bill rubbed his chin and strolled up to the car. He glanced at the gleaming slopes of her chest, and he wondered if she was the driver. She appeared too young to be the royal inspector.

"Bill, it's me, Rory."

"Rory who?" asked Bill.

"Rory Vakhal," she replied. "We worked together for the FBI. What are you doing out here? What happened to you? What is going on here?"

"Rory Vakhal was a man, and he's been dead for over 50 years," Bill replied. "Is this some sort of bureaucratic test? I don't need this. I am tired. Take the bottle of booze and get out of here."

The door swung open, and Rory stepped out. She removed her sunglasses and scanned the construction site. Bill furrowed his brow and cocked his head. Russet tresses framed the most beautiful face he had ever seen. Her jaw was delicate; her button nose was perfect for Hollywood, her skin had a slight glow, her cheeks were rosy, and her eyes sparkled like emeralds.

"What the hell is going on?" she asked, and then she told him a condensed version of her story.

When he heard about the circle of leafless trees, his face lit up. "Get in the truck. We need to go somewhere private to speak." He darted into the office and handed the bottle to Gladys. "Give this to some stiff inspector when he comes." He raced out of the office and circled around the truck. "Get in the vehicle before someone sees you."

"Okay," Rory said and got back in the SUV. The passenger side door opened, and Bill jumped into the seat. His body odor stung her nostrils and made her eyes water.

"Go straight ahead. I know of a private place where we can talk." He pointed toward the quay along the harbor. "I have an apartment where we can speak in private."

She gazed off to the west and saw vast, calm waters of Hope Lake; the gleaming waters reflected the sunlight like a huge mirror. Sailboats skimmed along it, dragging fishing nets. Towering mountains bordered the lake like giant walls of sheer rock. The lake extended far off into the distance, and she could not make out the opposite shore. "Where the hell did that come from? It's as big as Lake Michigan. There aren't any lakes that big in Kansas."

"We sure aren't in Kansas anymore," Bill proclaimed with a raspy laugh. "Drive on Boardwalk Boulevard toward the docks;" he pointed toward the lake and quay trimming the shore. She pressed on the accelerator and cruised toward the coasts. "After the Cataclysm, we were all wandering around in the rubble. Most of us wound up by the lake and wondered if we had gone insane. Hope Lake empties into the Corsair River and then empties into the Arner Sea. Like the whole valley, it is geothermally active. It never freezes, and fish thrive in it. It kept us from starving that first winter."

"What happened?" asked Rory.

Bill glanced at her, "No one knows. There are all kinds of crackpot theories, but no one really has a clue. At first, we thought the entire planet changed around Gleason. Then we realized that Gleason had jumped to a new planet. Later we learned it was Eden. Eden – HA – this isn't paradise — you can be sure of that."

"Just a few days ago everything was so normal." Rory shook her head and gazed in astonishment. "The city and the county were fine. We celebrated our department's 'field goal.' We went to the bar, and you had sex with that … um … woman. Christy was with us. This is unbelievable."

"Christy manages all of the docks and the brothels; I suppose you would call her a madam. This must be unbelievable from your perspective." Bill surveyed the redhead seated beside him. She had the body of a swimsuit model and the face of a movie star. "Think about what it's like for me. The guy I knew 50 years ago, my best friend, is not dead but a sexy redhead. We live in strange days. I thought I was going to die 100 times over the past 50 years. Instead, I keep hanging on in this purgatory."

"You still haven't answered my question," Rory said. "What happened?"

"There's not much to tell. It was rough the first year. We all worked together to survive, and we were making it. The King of Salvia sent emissaries to us and gave us food. Then more strangers began to arrive in the valley. They claimed to be merchants from villages deep in the mountains. We were more than glad to trade with them."

Bill pinched the bridge of his nose between his eyes and rubbed. "We were such idiots. We traded anything that we could find. They had food, medicine, and, more importantly, native plant stock. Everything we put in the ground shot up. Orville, the mayor, declared a harvest celebration."

"I remember it like yesterday. It was the middle of September, but it was still warm. Some dark gray clouds were moving in from the west, but we had no worries: we harvested all of the crops and stored them in silos or in jars. We were set for the winter. The whole town was alive, and since there was no gas for cars, we set up tables in the streets. The entire town smelled like a kitchen with cooking food. Anyway, we were smiling and laughing. Our bellies were full, and food still filled the tables. It was great."

The Seventh Age

The smile disappeared from Bill's face. "Then the sun was setting behind the Wolf's Maw Mountains, and we lit the bonfires. I had a real mug of cold beer. That tasted so good. People started running from the north side of town. We heard screams and gunshots. A tsunami of people rushed down Main Street, and someone shouted that we were being invaded."

"The king of Salvia had sent an army, all dressed in armor and carrying swords. At first, I thought it was a joke. Then the archers lobbed a volley of arrows into the crowd. Bodies hit the street, and screams erupted. I joined the crowd and ran for my life. More soldiers showed up at the south end of town. We were trapped."

"Our friend, the King of Salvia used the merchants as spies. We were so naive. We gave them the grand tour, and we even supplied them with maps. Can you believe that? We gave them maps of the entire valley, and we even pointed out our few meager defenses."

"You have to picture this. We were terrified. They gathered us all into the center of town, and they dragged Mayor Gruber, the City Council, and other dignitaries onto a platform – the one we built for a music festival near Circle Park. We didn't understand what was happening. Orville was still trying to reason with them as they chopped off his head. Blood squirted out his neck and sprayed the crowd. One by one, the others were forced to kneel and were executed. I pissed myself."

"They informed us that we and the entire valley were now the property of Salvia. They knew who owned weapons, thanks to the merchants, and they seized their guns; and they killed anyone who resisted. A month later, the soldiers returned in the middle of the night, and they threw us out of our homes. We huddled together in the freezing cold, staying warm as best we could. The next day, those who pledged loyalty to the crown could go home. Your dad was the first. He burrowed in deep with them like a tick in a hound dog."

"What about those who refused?" asked Rory.

"They were put in chains and sold as slaves. Most of them died of exposure. We saw their bodies half exposed in the snow." He looked straight at her. "In case you are wondering, I held out for the entire winter. By spring, I was a walking skeleton. Rather than die, I pledged loyalty."

He settled back and sighed. "I've had a few years to think it over. Your dad was smart. He accepted reality and got himself a honey of a deal. King Leopold assigned him as 'Viceroy of the Realm.' He's in charge of the entire valley."

"What happened to me?" asked Rory.

Bill could tell Rory was near mental collapse. "You were caught in a gray zone. There are four types of zones: gray, red, yellow, and green. Green speaks for itself. Plants grow like you would not believe; most of the valley is like that. Yellow zones are tricky: time moves twice as fast. No sooner do you step to one side then you shoot out the other side. It's kind of funny to watch people land. Red zones are thermally active zones. The geothermal power plant is on a red zone. Gray, I told you about: time slows."

"Everyone took off out of the east side neighborhoods after the Cataclysm. Then, BAM, a temporal vortex settled over the whole area. If you ask me, you got off lucky," Bill said.

"I used to go up there from time to time. I got as close to the border as you are to me. The whole thing was a dull gray. The further in I looked the grayer it got. I saw this guy running to the border. He was sprinting toward me, frozen in mid-stride. I thought he was dead at first, like one of those bugs caught in amber, but he was moving. I stood there for two hours, and he only moved a few millimeters. It was unbelievable. As the years passed, people forgot about it and accepted it as part of life."

"What happened to the people who were stuck; I mean, when they emerged like me?" asked Rory.

The Seventh Age

"Well," Bill said, "I remember this one guy. He escaped the gray zone about 10 years ago. He marched right into the center of town and started spouting off about the Constitution and liberty. He was executed at sundown."

When they came to a trench, the weight of the truck made the steel plate covering the trench rattle beneath them. A chorus of jackhammers came from their left, and a bulldozer dumped a load of rock into a truck to their right. The smell of biodiesel and smoke hung in the air.

They raced toward the harbor. The masts of sailing ships rose above the port warehouses. Many were small by modern standards, but a crew of six could easily handle it. Without the benefit of refrigeration, the catches had to be small. The other ships were heavy haulers, with tall masts and white sails. When they passed over the bumpy dirt road, Bill stole furtive glances at Rory. They swept around a wide curve and headed toward the quay. They passed through a growing crowd of people; sailors milled about the docks. Some compared fishing techniques, others drank, and others visited second story brothels; bawdy women strolled about the second floor; they wore only lingerie and lounged on second-floor patios, and they called out to passing patrons. "We gave up on policing drugs, prostitution, and gambling a long time ago. As long as no one dies or steals, the law ignores it."

Reading her expression, Bill said, "We don't have the resources or the prisons to regulate human vices. Besides, the kinds of vices you find down here are legal in Salvia. All of the others crimes — there are damn few — result in execution or involuntary servitude. It's slavery by another name if you ask me, but the king doesn't see it that way. He proclaimed, '… These people need to be punished, and we need someone to do the work ….'"

A blonde, clad only in black satin lingerie, bent over a railing and waved. Bill returned her wave and said, "That's Trixie. She's my favorite." He lowered the window and shouted, "I'll be up to see you later — after I take a bath."

Rory saw a pair of young women speaking with a man outside the brothel. When Bill saw what Rory was looking at, he commented, "More of them show up here every day. Harvest time is twice a year and lasts over a month. The farmers and laborers work 16 hours a day, and it is hard work. It beats the pride out of them, and back breaking labor is a great motivator for change. Besides, being a whore isn't so bad. It's a good life for the girls. They get to drink, to dance, and to have sex. What's not to like?"

Rory was not convinced. Trite male mottos rang hollow to her female ears. Would Bill want his mother or sister to work in such a place?

They pulled into a parking lot, gravel snapping and crunching underneath the tires. Most other vehicles were horse-drawn buggies or modified compact cars, reminding her of a bizarre antique carriage. The others appeared to be road warrior cars. Bill paid the attendant and procured a safe parking spot. When they exited the SUV, a humid breeze carried the pungent aroma of fish, cooking food, and perfume.

They stepped onto a boardwalk, their steps causing a rhythmic tap on the wooden planks. The boardwalk and most of the building around them were constructed from scavenged wooden logs. Most of the rental log cabins nestled in the foothills collapsed during the Cataclysm. Entrepreneurs used the debris to build the wharf.

When they emerged from the alley, Rory found herself in a fishhook-shaped lagoon. With their boats safely moored at the docks, crews had time to relax or get rowdy before returning to the sea. Casinos abounded on the first level, filling every other building; stairs led up to the second-floor brothels, and guest accommodations lay on the third floor. Sail material had been adapted for use as awnings, so those alfresco dining could avoid the hard midday sun. Bill led her to the left and past several shops. Buoys, lobster traps, and nets filled the display windows.

"Is this lake salt or fresh water?" asked Rory.

"Huh, what? Oh, the lake is fresh water, and the ocean is salt; the mouth of the river, where they meet, is brackish. The lobster is great if you can afford it. Most of the time I just eat bass, mackerel, or whatever the catch of the day is." When they passed by a girl wearing nothing but sky blue silk panties and a diaphanous top, Bill gave her a playful smack on the bottom. "Don't let the dock master catch you on the quay. He'll throw you in the harbor."

The girl screwed up her face and nodded. "Okay," she said and hurried up a set of stairs. Rory heard music and laughter spill out of the second floor of the building.

"The dock master makes sure everything runs smooth," Bill replied. "It's an informal rule that working girls stay off the streets. It's safer for them and keeps the partiers indoors." Bill pointed at a third-floor loft. It had an encompassing balcony, French doors, and a private walk up. "I invested all my credits here on the docks. This is prime real estate."

They walked around to the fishhook-shaped dock where Bill had a private residence. He charged up a private set of stairs and retrieved a set of keys from his pocket. They jangled as he unlocked a door on the side of the building. After Rory had followed him into the building, Bill threw a deadbolt across the door. "You can never be too safe around here. Things can get wild at night. You don't want a drunk staggering in and passing out on the floor. It's happened."

Bill strode through a narrow corridor. Bedrooms and baths lay to the right and left. They emerged into a large living room. A pair of barrels with a wooden plank on top of them served as a wet bar. A curious conglomeration of scavenged furniture from the salvaged cabins furnished the room. Against the far wall, she saw a rhunite-modified oven, cooking without smoke or gas, and a round dining table. An empty whiskey bottle and shot glasses lay scattered about on it.

"I know, it's a mess," Bill said. "I had a poker game last night." Rory picked a dirty sweat sock off a cappuccino leather chair and tossed it onto the floor. She took a tentative seat, ready to rise up at a moment's notice. Bill handed her a glass of whiskey. "It's rotgut, but it hits the spot."

Rory took a sip and grimaced saying: "You weren't kidding." She set the glass down on a small table. "It looks like you've done well for yourself. Why —"

"Why do I work at the power plant?" Bill finished her question. He finished his drink and refilled it. "When the Cataclysm happened, money became worthless. I had $10,000 locked away in my home safe. Suddenly, it was just kindling. Only gold, silver, or trade paid the bills. Fortunately, I put aside some gold for emergencies. I am glad that I did. Anyway, that was when we set up the barter exchange." He shrugged and gazed up at wagon wheel lamp overhead. "Different jobs pay different wages. Management calculates p ay by the hour and by the type of work. Field labor pays four credits a day while nursing pays 20 credits an hour; doctors get 80 credits an hour. It all depends. When the power plant ran out of fuel, a bunch of us got together and contracted to complete the upgrade. We built 'Thermal Power Plant One' forty-five years ago. Every ten years we added another power plant. All of the lines have to be grounded, so we have to shield the hell out of them; then we lay them down all zigzagged. It's because of the rhunite that permeates the granite. It can turn the electrical power dirty, creating all kinds of spurious frequencies and current spikes. It's so frustrating. Anyway, we get most of the high tech gear from Midway or Solva."

He stripped off his soiled coat and tossed it aside. "You can forget about working for someone else. Those jobs pay crappy wages for hard work. I mean, they grind you down to a nub." Bill took another swig. "Where was I? Oh yes, you have to be self-employed."

"I'm going to be honest with you. You're beautiful. I mean it. I know what you must be thinking, but just hear me out. In one day, you could earn a year's field worker's wages." He took another swig and paused. "I have a sweetheart of a club on the other end of the dock. It's private and very high end —invitation only. I have guys who would pay huge money to sleep with you. You used to be a guy, but now you're a hot girl. That turns a lot of guys on."

He refilled his glass and took another swig. "I've seen plenty of guys who transition from male to female. Some are good looking, and some are not, it all depends – but they all earn decent wages. Some guys look like a mannish woman. I don't get it," he shrugged, "but it's not me."

"You want me to be a prostitute?" asked Rory in disbelief.

"Not a hooker, an entertainer who happens to have sex. You would get to wear fancy clothes and eat lobster dinners, every night if you want. That outfit you are wearing now is kind of sexy. I bet you could earn 3 silver coins per man. Do you have a vagina? The reason I ask is not all the transition girls do."

"What?" She spread her thighs wide and gazed down at the smooth junction between them. "Yes. I have …" she faltered, "well, I have a vagina. But I'm not …."

"Don't say no. Say maybe." Bill rose to his feet. "If entertaining isn't for you, I have other jobs. I am part owner of a shipping fleet; they are always looking for female crew. If you get too many men in one place for too long, some men transform to female. The locals call it 'nature's calling.' It's an evolved response to perpetuate the species. If you think about it, it makes a lot of sense. Fish, turtles, and trees do it back on Earth. From nature's point of view, it's just a different set of sex organs."

"I suppose," Rory said, "but I get seasick. Besides, I want to find my mom and dad. Are they still around?"

"Walter and Meredith," asked Bill. "Sure, but they spend most of their time up at the castle with the king. I'll tell you what. I will send out a courier and get word to them. They can come here to meet you. In the meantime, you and I can hang out and have some fun." He turned toward the hall. "I'm going to wash up and change. We'll go out to eat and talk. Think about my proposition. You can stay with me for a week or two."

A brunette, Sienna, slept in his bed. Rory assumed she was a conquest from the previous night. Bill nudged her: "This isn't a flophouse." She yawned and sat upright. He fished around in a box full of lingerie. He then tossed her a pair of gold metallic panties and a matching Basque corset. "Go to the 'Mermaid House' and tell them that I sent you. Christy breaks in all the new girls. She'll teach you how to please a man in bed."

"Okay," she said and rose up from the bed. She stepped into the panties and whisked them up her legs. "How much do you think I can earn?"

Bill set his drink on his dresser and stripped of his shirt. "I don't know. You have a beautiful face. I bet you could earn three silver coins a night."

"That's great," she said with a grin. "It's better than being a slave."

He left out a few details. Most girls imagined handsome men and romantic encounters. Reality was ugly sailors that smelled like fish. Even so, she was right; it was better than being a slave.

Bill purchased slave girls and set them free. A few decided to leave, but the majority stayed. There were few opportunities for improvement, and it was far easier than harvesting. Marriage was a possibility of course, but such a woman would never be a first wife. As such, she would be bound to the will of her husband and the other dominant wives. This created a situation where they were little more than slaves, a fate which they had just escaped.

Bill called out from the bedroom. "I keep telling your old man that he needs to diversify. That resort is a gold mine. All he needs to do is add a few gambling tables and some girls. He would make a fortune."

After Sienna had secured the corset's hooks, Bill grabbed the laces and put his knee on her back; each tug of the laces compressed her body into the ideal female form. After tying and tucking in the laces, he said, "I almost forgot one thing." He handed her a silver medallion, suspended from a silver chain. After securing the clasp around her neck, he gave her bottom a smack. "That medallion is your passport to all the clubs on the docks, free of charge of course. Don't lose it."

The girl's hand explored the pendant, and she studied its features. "Okay," she replied with a meek tone. "I really appreciate your setting me free."

"Good. Then while you're here, you can give me a scrub down." Sienna poured a basin full of water. After washing him down, she began to scrub him with soap. From out in the hallway, Rory called out, "I need to get going, Bill."

Still naked and wet, Bill hurried out into the hallway. "Are you sure you can't stay? There are some great places to eat around here."

"I need to get going. I want to find my family and explain things in person," Rory replied.

"I get it. You haven't seen them since you switched teams," Bill said. "But ...."

Rory opened the exterior door and stopped. Drawing in a sharp gasp, her heart in her throat, and her mind frozen, she gaped at Christy. She was more beautiful than the day they married. Rory's conscious mind was blank, but her subconscious screamed, "RUN!"

Chapter 15

Rory raced the SUV over the gravel road as if being chased, feeling better with each mile passed. Bill, the docks, and Christy assaulted her reality. When she passed by the power plant, feelings of panic began to subside. Men paused from their labors to watch the SUV rush past them. She left them gaping and choking on her dust.

Dirt soon gave way to broken pavement and smooth road. The vestiges of her former life and civilization returned. "The Johnston Medical Complex" where she had her tonsils removed as a child and Christy had given birth to Michael was on her left. She recalled how blissful Christy had appeared that day. Disheveled, as though she just passed through a great storm, but peace and joy overshadowed her. The nurse wheeled in a baby carriage, and she picked up the newborn saying, "I would like to present your new baby boy." Rory held the infant, a fragile life, marveling at the wonder of it.

Christy's sudden departure and just as sudden reappearance barged into the comforting memory. From Rory's point of view, it was yesterday that Christy's love turned to hate. For Christy, 50 years passed since that fateful day, the memory becoming sepia, a distant memory in some forgotten scrapbook.

Rory glanced at her lap. Black satin wrapped around feminine thighs and merged together forming a sharp "V." Beneath the layers of clothing, her mind sensed the subtle presence of a vagina and the lingering, phantom ache of her missing male genitalia. A vague sense of vulnerability replaced the full sensation between her legs.

The road weaved through the familiar landscape. Rory spotted the county school, Nesbit K-12, and she recalled endless summers of baseball. She and her friends hung out in the student union, ate pizza, and fell in love. She first danced with Christy in the Gray Auditorium and kissed her underneath the bleachers.

The Seventh Age

Field grass, grimy windows, faded trim, and chained doors turned the building into a lifeless shell; cattle grazed on the athletic field, a place where children once played; it was all so sad as if she saw ghosts. Most educational centers required school buses, automotive travel, utilities, and teachers. Education, it seemed, had ended when freedom died. Children studied at home, if at all. She wondered if parents, weary from 16 hours of labor, even took time to teach their children to read and write.

She passed by a bodega set in a strip mall and a small grove of trees with horses and buggies lingering out front. A winding road carried her past trees and the marsh. She left Boardwalk Boulevard, passed over the Ruben Goddard Truss Bridge, which spanned Cougar Creek, smelling like an open sewer, and emerged onto Main Street on the south end of town.

Earthquakes had fractured many of the sewer lines, and repair crews no longer had the gasoline-powered equipment to repair them; thus, chamber pots came into fashion once again. Human waste floated in the rivers and then out to sea. This made the waterways non-potable and contaminated with deadly bacteria.

She breathed a sigh of relief when she entered the sheltering arms of the town. Red brick buildings greeted her, and she saw Kent's Barber Shop, filled with men awaiting their turn in the chair. Gail's Gowns was likewise filled with ladies searching out a bargain. The ice cream shop was gone; milk was stored as cheese or not at all. She never realized how much cold was fundamental to society. Sorrow pressed down on her – she would never again taste ice cream's cool sensation.

As she drew near the center of town, pedestrian traffic choked the road. Men and women appeared surprised by the fact that a car was trying to drive on the road. She slowed to a crawl and honked her horn. Shoppers turned and gaped at her; but they gave way, letting her pass.

What had once been a park, located in the center of town, was now a market, filled with mercantile booths. Most were made of wood and cloth, once improvised but now permanent. In her mind, the crisis was still fresh; they were isolated, hungry, and afraid. But that was long ago, a matter of history to the residents. Cheese, fruit, bread, and vegetables filled the stands to overflowing. There were pens filled with goats, pigs, sheep, and cattle. A dozen men wearing bloody aprons hung chunks of meat from hooks, and eager customers purchased the bloody flesh – her lip curled in disgust. She preferred her meat wrapped in Styrofoam and plastic, without an introduction to the creature she would consume.

A wagon filled with ears of corn passed in front of her and forced her to stop. She looked to her left and scarcely believed her eyes. A nearly naked woman with golden skin and a fit body stood upon a raised wooden platform. Her bare breasts heaved as she drew in anxious breaths. Her sole covering was a meager leather thong: a triangular patch covering her sex. Her raven black locks cascaded over her bare shoulders and flowed down her back.

What was she doing, and what was in her mouth? Rory put her SUV in park and exited it. She joined the crowd and moved toward the stage. The woman's lips strained around a ball gag; black straps stretched across her cheeks. The truth came to Rory all at once. This woman was a prisoner.

The woman stood in the center of the stage and tugged at something behind her. Rory moved to the right for a better view. It was then that she saw the woman's wrists. Leather cuffs bound them behind her, and a cable tethered her to the center of the platform.

A bald man strolled to the center of the stage. His purple robes and gold tunic struggled to cover his ponderous belly. He held up his hands, and the crowd became silent. It was then that Rory recognized him; Jerry Travis, he owned and operated a bait and tackle shop on Philo Creek. The last time she saw him, he was young, thin, and had a mop of red hair. He was engaged to marry Molly Russell.

The Seventh Age

Jerry appeared to be in charge. He held up his hands, and the crowd fell silent. "… by order of His Excellency King Leopold Justinian the IV of Salvia, Karen Champlain was arrested, tried, and convicted for failure to pay taxes. Her freedom is forfeit, and she is being sold to pay her debt to society. We will start the bidding at 100 silver coins."

Rory could not believe her ears. She knew Karen; they graduated high school together. Karen went on to graduate from the University of Chicago Law School. After passing the bench, she returned to Gleason and worked for The Kansas State District Attorney's Office.

Impossible, it couldn't be, but it was, and right before her eyes. She had to remind herself to breathe. The enraged woman shouted out stifled curses when the auction began. Her price quickly rose to 180 silver coins and then slowed. Men and women pressed in around Rory. Both genders called out bids and drove up the price. A woman to Rory's far right called out the winning bid of 205 silver coins.

The winner climbed up the stage stairs and examined her prize. Karen spewed out garbled threats and tried to move away. A pair of guards seized her by the shoulders, drove the woman to her knees, then shoving her head forward. Jerry signaled a female guard. The auctioneer picked up a long staff from off a table with a crystal mounted to the tip. It glowed with the brilliance of a naked spotlight, which pierced through daylight. The winning bidder removed a gold ring and handed it to the auctioneer. The auctioneer then mounted the ring to the tip of the crystal.

After wrapping a black choker necklace around her neck, he stabbed the signet ring into the front of the woman's neck and marked it. Karen screamed and struggled as they drove her head down to the wooden platform. Karen tried to plea for help, but her gag reduced her words to an unintelligible mew. "By edict of the king's court, you are hereby stripped of your memories and condemned to a life of servitude."

Jerry turned to dark sorcery long ago, and he studied the forbidden ways, the dark ways, how to reshape the mind. He touched the staff to the small of Karen's back – just above the buttocks, and centered on her spine – and chanted in a low, rumbling voice. Fine golden lines scrolled along the base of her spine, radiating a white glow. Rory saw another red glow in the core of Karen's body; it grew up her core toward her head. As it did so, the glowing silver scrollwork and flourishes flowed with it, marking her flesh. They crept up the woman's spine and moved to her neck. White-hot light exploded from her eyes, nostrils, and around the ball gag. Her face lost all expression and limbs went slack. She snorted in rapid but shallow gasps. The light flowed down her necklace and glowed deep in the core of her chest.

When the auctioneer removed the staff, he inspected the small of the woman's back. The glowing golden embers flashed across the scrolling lines that marked her back. The intricate detail of the crest, including its colors, now marked her flesh. As to the necklace, magic bound it to her body: she could remove it to bath, but if she moved more than a hundred paces from it, the choker would reappear on her neck. Her mistress' signet ring controlled the collar by powerful magic. This was true of all slave necklaces.

Satisfied with the branding, Jerry signaled the men. They released her, and they dragged Karen to her feet. They had to support her for a minute or two; her legs were too weak to bear her weight. She gazed at the faces of the assembled crowd with vacuous confusion. A void replaced a lifetime of memories.

As the owner led Karen from the stage, the woman waved to the crowd and smiled, as if she batted the winning run at a baseball game. She descended the steps and met her family. They examined the slave girl, complemented her on a fine purchase, and joked as they passed through the crowd.

They hauled next debtor onto center stage. Rory recoiled in horror: it was Rick Stannish. They had camped, fished, and played baseball as children.

The Seventh Age

Rory, Bill, and Rick were the three musketeers; they did everything together. They shared a limousine for the prom; both Rory and Bill were best men at Rick's wedding. Rick had took over the ranch after his father died of a heart attack. It was hard going the first few years, but Rick had a will of iron. They carved out a life together and settled into wedded bliss.

Rory's second best friend stood on a stage wearing only a thong, his wife and children cowering behind him. Rick struggled and uttered garbled protests as they were dragged onto the stage, his powerful limbs and ripped muscles fighting them. He spewed out impotent threats at the crowd. Lisa squatted and held two terrified children; she squeezed them to her and covered their eyes.

Rory felt sick. She pushed through the crowd in a dazed sense of panic. A few men leered at her, perhaps hoping she would be the next person auctioned. A handgun rested in the side pocket of her SUV. She ran to her car, reeling at what she just witnessed – her stomach twisted into a knot; her heart pounded, and her mouth went dry. She stood in the open door and gripped the weapon. She had to do something – but what?

Had the world had gone insane? What had happened to everyone? What had happened to the town?

She thought of opening fire, affording Rick a chance to escape. She could shoot Rick's captors, but there were too many of them. Most were armed with swords and spears, but a few carried assault rifles.

An explosion rocked the street and jerked Rory's feet out from underneath her. It threw dust and rocks high into the air, and the blast shoved Rory into the vehicle. When she looked into the rearview mirror, she saw screaming people running from the town square. A flatbed truck raced up to the stage. Armed men pointed rifles at the guards, and rifles cracked with sharp snaps of gunfire. Bullets ripped through the guards, causing a cloud pink mist. A man leaped onto the stage and cut the family's bonds, and they jumped into the truck bed.

The truck tires smoked, and it raced away from the auction platform. Rory watched in astonishment. Flames blasting from weapons, the guards groaning from mortal wounds, smoke jetting from squealing tires, men dressed in cowboy hats firing at the city defenders. The truck swept past Rory, made a sharp left turn, and raced back toward the harbor.

Rory stared out the windshield and looked to where the truck departed. Her mind was a void. She rose to her feet and gaped at the carnage. A truck filled with defenders raced around the corner and then surged past her. Men riding on the back of the truck wore armor and carried spears, swords, and assault rifles – a strange combination of weapons. They chased after the escaped fugitives.

"This can't be real. You need to wake up now." She pinched herself, but it was no use; she was awake. *This is insane. I don't want to be here. I want to go home.* She had but a single desire, to go home, hide in her bedroom, and never come out again. She cruised out of town and left the chaos behind her.

Chapter 16

Rory exited the northeast side of Gleason, glad to leave the chaos behind her – she hoped. The transition from East Main Street to Garrison Street and the Clinton Road (Highway 191) went without incident; for a few precious moments, she let herself believe that she'd left all the chaos behind; the road would carry her back to The United States, and she would have an interesting, if not unbelievable, story to tell. Further sustaining this delusion, she happened upon the Golden Nugget, an Italian restaurant. She'd spent most nights of her youth within its wall; dining patrons carved their initials into the wooden booths and barnboard siding. When she grew old enough to work, the owners hired her as a dishwasher; only girls waited on tables, and she was very much a boy at that time.

She passed the Elegant Vintner. Her father owned part interest in the business. Darby Street, Bare Rock Lane, and Broken Pine Road brought to mind fond childhood memories; the mapmakers forgot these dirt roads even though they led to adventure. She spent many summers camping out, swimming, fishing, and cycling off these roads. Then she passed through the woods and came to a reddish rock.

The Ridgeview Resort rose up from the pines and oaks like a welcoming friend, a safe port in a vast wilderness. The spires of the great building jutted into the sky; red and gold pennants flapped from them in the breeze. The ballroom rose through the tree line: a battlement of old, a great ship – gray stone slicing through a troubled green sea. It overlooked River Run Canyon. The stone edifice stood over the town and surrounding valley as a proud monument. It appeared to emerge from the face of Knob Hill.

The resort was a transplant from Scotland in 1892. Real estate speculators dismantled the mansion and reassembled it in Gleason. By 1933, it fell into disrepair and tourism faded. No one wanted to invest in a dilapidated building. Everything changed in 1983. Real estate speculators, Verde Vista Properties, rode the crest of the timeshare market; they wooed investors and took in millions. The multitudinous buildings, corner towers, and halls were now comfortable condominiums. A third of the facility provided lodging to short-term guests, resembling typical hotel rooms. However, real estate speculation trends were dangerous, and by 1987, Verde Vista Properties filed for Chapter 11 bankruptcy – one year later they filed for chapter 7. The property changed hands several times, and Walter Vakhal, Rory's father eventually bought it.

Tall, arched windows adorned the exterior sides of the ballroom, and through them, one could see the fresco ceiling, chandelier lights, and balconies. During the day, a million splintered prisms painted the interior. A large patio trimmed the hall, which provided a choice view of gardens, growing produce rather than flowers. Walter appreciated a bargain and thought vegetables were every bit as pretty. However, even Walter's penny-pinching ways could not diminish the grandeur of the resort. Many weddings – including Rory and Christy's wedding – took place in the private chapel, and the receptions took place in the ballroom.

The resort's interior conjured up images of European royalty. Great stairways, two in the foyer and four in the hall, provided access to the main facility. The resort was a vast labyrinth, a great collection of suites, libraries, halls, studies, gymnasiums, and even an observatory. Rory spent her childhood scurrying through the many hidden passages, like a rat in the walls, and she would pop up when least expected and disappear just as fast.

The Vakhal Family maintained a private residence located on the western bluff. Green-peaked metal roofs, dormers, balconies, walkways, round towers, and even a widow's walk marveled the eye. The great house stood upon the highest point, looked out from the side of a sheer cliff, and connected to the resort via an underground tunnel.

The Seventh Age

The private residence stood three stories tall, included all the amenities of a royal estate, and was the best architectural example of the Gilded Age. A wine cellar, storage facilities, and other structures lay deep in the rocky hill. A full gymnasium and pool lay at the bottom and rested on the edge of a canyon with a sheer rock wall. A zero point pool allowed one to look right off the edge of the canyon.

A winding road traveled around hairpin turns and thick forests. The resort grew larger by the second until Rory felt like a child approaching the house of a giant. The main road passed along an imposing curtain wall, capped by jutting black spikes and skirted the entire property.

A high black iron gate stood sentry at the entry road. The sum effect made it appear impregnable, like a fortress built to keep out rampaging hordes. As she neared the gate, she saw sentries; men stood watch, carrying weapons and wearing tarnished steel armor.

Rory made a quick right turn and entered the resort. One of the men held out a hand and motioned for her to stop. She slowed and lowered her window. "What business do you have here?" the man barked. "Speak quickly."

"I live here," she said.

He furrowed his eyebrows and scanned the SUV's interior. His eyes then fixed on the silk blouse molding around her breasts. Presuming her to be a courtesan, he said, "Let her pass."

She cruised past the men, and her sense of safety evaporated. Six armed men, riding on horseback, watched her pass with evaluative stares. They appeared to be on patrol and disappeared behind the riding stables. Parties of workers trained horses, tended to livestock, and harvested apples. Two things were peculiar about this: First, it was not the harvest season. Second, the trees were enormous, and the apples were the size of grapefruits.

The driveway, like a rich black carpet, carried her toward the breezeway. Three white flag posts jutted into the sky, and a flag, which she did not recognize, flew over the estate. It bore the symbol of a beautiful white flower set on an azure field.

She looped around the drive and stopped under the covered breezeway. More armed men stood sentry at the glass doors, and others walked patrol in squads of four, the men bearing swords rather than guns, a fact which she found peculiar. Rory unlatched her door and rose to her feet. She pressed her hands to her back and stretched, which drew the attention of every man around her.

Two of the glass doors swung open and Walter, her father, exited the resort. He stared at her a few seconds, unsure if the woman who stood before him was his daughter. He had never seen her since her abrupt transition from male to female. When he was sure it was her, he rushed up to her and threw his arms around her. "I thought you were gone. We talked to Christy just after you were lost in the gray zone. There was nothing we could do." He took a step back and inspected her. "You look just like the pictures in the family photo album. It's hard to believe. We were shocked for years; our entire lives changed in a split second."

Meredith, her mother, rushed out and shouted, "Rory, you're home," Rory was astonished at her mother's appearance; golden locks framed a youthful face, and she moved with the vigor of a woman in her prime. The family embraced in sweet relief. Her mother began to cry. "I missed you so much." Rory, too, began to tear up and clung to her mother.

Walter rubbed Rory's shoulder and moved to the open door. Gus Myer, the stable and vehicle manager, walked up the hill from the maintenance garage. He and his wife, Sophie, lived in a small house near the stables. Tommy, his nephew, lived in a studio apartment above the stables. Gus Myer strolled over to Walter and cleaned grease from his hands with a rag. "I can tell she is your daughter. She looks just like the painting in the foyer. She must have escaped the gray zone. Is she okay?"

The Seventh Age

"So it would appear," Walter said. He stroked his chin with his index finger and pondered for a moment. He closed the SUV door and told Gus, "Take the car down to the garage and store it out of sight."

"Shouldn't we contact the sheriff? He will want to know that she's back and the gray zone has lifted," said Gus.

"Not just yet," Walter replied. "I want her to settle in first." He followed his family into the resort and jogged up the flight of stairs. Walter was a head taller than most men, and he still wore the same size trousers that he did in the army, which testified to his iron will and fierce nature. Despite his advanced years, 128 by human reckoning, Walter appeared younger than Rory's memory of him, no older than his mid-thirties. Years of hardship and toil vanished, by what means Rory could only guess, but she suspected it had something to do with her transformation – whatever that might be.

Walter passed by the reservation desk and followed them up to the restaurant and bar. When he entered the restaurant, he saw Meredith seated next to Rory and holding her hands. Monica, a Hispanic woman, and another childhood friend hurried in from the kitchen; she gave Rory a hug and then sat down at the table. The ladies listened as Rory told her strange tale.

Walter drew up his trousers and crossed his legs. Walter still wore trousers with a sharp crease, a pristine white shirt, a silk tie, and a suit jacket with a handkerchief in the pocket. His generation wore a suit for every occasion. Rory had once found him chopping wood in a Brooks Brothers suit.

He studied Rory's face and paid careful attention to her every word. The day after the Cataclysm, Meredith noticed the changes to the family portrait. Home movies and legal records all reflected the same thing. She gave birth to a daughter. Her son and grandson vanished from existence.

Walter refused to accept Rory's transformation, and he spent a year building his case as if going to court. The harder he worked, the more the evidence weighed against him, and the prosecution, his own conscience, won – his son vanished and was replaced by a daughter. Of all the twists and turns, of all the hardships and sorrows life gave him, losing his son was the greatest burden to bear. Every father imagines his son's future, and Walter was the same, but his imagined future died. His son vanished. He would never father a child, and he would never feel the comradeship fathers have with sons. But his daughter lived.

Rory started at the beginning, as any good tale must, and she unfolded her story. Her mother gasped when she heard of the bombing and the rescue. Walter listened with stoic patience, a thermos bottle of hidden emotions. He leaned forward when Rory discussed the act of violence that took so many lives. A slight sigh of relief escaped him, and the tension left his body. "Then you were well away from the area when it happened?"

"Um, yes," Rory replied. "I ran back to get my gun. How could everyone let this happen?"

Walter paused and collected his thoughts. "Rory, the world changed around us. That much was evident from the first day of the Cataclysm. The others were so eager for relief that they accepted aid with few questions. The traders offered scant details about their dealings and conflicting testimony. I suspected them from the start."

He stroked his chin with his index finger and gazed at the table top. "Questions reveal much about a man. At first, they asked about our origins while providing us with only vague references. All of their questions were entirely reasonable, at least on the surface. They wanted to know our crop production, our distribution channels, and such the like. Of course, they had to know about our security arrangements: thieves were everywhere, according to them. Mayor Gruber accepted them with the innocence of a child, and he showed them our few defensive fortifications."

The Seventh Age

"I served as an intelligence officer in the Army. I warned Orville – not that he listened to me. He gave me vacuous assurances of their sincerity and a friendly pat on the back. 'You worry too much. Whoever they are, we need the trade,' he said to me. The very next day, he sold them an assortment of guns and ammunition. The stupidity of it all astounded me. So I withdrew from the city council and hid my thoughts."

"I probed the merchants and hinted at my cooperation." Walter stiffened and narrowed his eyes. "I made myself indispensable to the merchants and a trusted ally. When the invasion came, I was the first person they turned to …."

Rory settled back and let these revelations sink into her. Her father was not only a collaborator but a co-conspirator. Walter rode the political tides like few could. His contacts rose all the way to Washington D.C., and yet he was a loyal American, or so she thought. This man was a stranger, yet she knew better than to speak her mind – her footing was tenuous. She could sense it.

"… Courts sentence convicted criminals, murders, and rapists to execution or to servitude. The Royal Court dispenses justice on a whim and evidence is a nuisance. Some people, lawyers mostly, insisted that Salvia follows United States law and accept our constitution. They were among the first convicted of theft, trespassing, or other petty crimes. As such, the penal system dealt with them. Peripheral supporters were found guilty of debt and tax crimes."

"No one is safe. Political opponents face trumped up charges. The King and Prince Gregory have a long history of removing opposition. Five years ago an inspector by the name of Vladimir Sabitov traveled from the capital city of Kurio to Salvia. The High King of Asgard commissioned him to audit the Rhunite powder extraction and the reported tonnage transported out of the mountains. The Asgard Parliament is responsible for most of the territories outside of the Regal Mountains and levies taxes upon goods that cross their territories or seas."

"Anyway, a supposed group of bandits attacked him and his family on the way to Salvia. He and his wife had their throats cut. Their girl, Sienna, was kidnapped and smuggled out of the country. Rumor has it that she was sold as a slave."

Walter concluded by saying, "We woke up to a world and a way of life we hardly recognized."

Grace brought over cups and set them on the table. She took a seat and joined them. Walter took a sip of the steaming coffee and resumed. "They ordered all citizens to surrender their weapons to the police. The king's army then collected them and took them away. Only the official army is allowed to carry or use weapons."

Monica added, "That's right, and then came the taxes. Those who resisted or refused to pay found themselves arrested and convicted of insurrection. The king seized their lands and possessions. Tell her about the secret police."

Walter gave the young woman an icy stare. She gazed down at the table and bit her lower lip. He then resumed, "It is not wise to discuss such things. It suffices to say that sometimes those accused of crimes become criminal informants."

"This discussion is dangerous. We are all very close, and I think of everyone as family. However, people under stress do things they might not in other circumstances. Your best friend would betray you if faced with the gallows."

Rory detected a hint of pain and fear in her father. All she said was, "I see." They shared a knowing glance and understood that which they left unspoken.

"All those people outside, do they work for you?" asked Rory.

"Most," Walter replied. "They earn a small wage, and I provide them with room and board. Most of them live in the cabins down in the canyon."

Rory focused on the word "most." "Most" meant many but not all. Where there any indentured servants? She wondered but said nothing. "What did you mean by the castle?"

"Oh that," he said, "The King of Salvia lives in a castle 78 miles to the north of the valley. It's quite impressive. I have business there tomorrow. We can go together." Walter tapped his chin. "You came from your house over on the east side?"

"Yes," she replied.

"Hmm, I'll send some men over to collect your belongings. We should also guard the vacant homes. We don't want them to be looted," he said.

"I guess that would be okay. Tell them to bring my dog, Jake. I adopted him, or he adopted me; I'm not sure which."

Walter and Meredith left the table and exited the room. Rory leaned close to the ladies and asked, "This place is insane. It's like I stepped back into medieval Europe."

Monica wrung her hands. "It's not safe. I'm surprised your father said as much as he did. I've never seen him open up like that." She paused a moment, and the whispered, "We'll talk later. There are too many ears."

Chapter 17

Rory slipped out of her bedroom, as a thief fleeing justice, just as the sun broke over the horizon. The first rays of dawn cast somber shadows across the Wolf's Maw Mountains and bathed the valley in a soft glow, casting off the night's chill. Both men and beasts labored in the fields, tilling the green earth, sowing seeds for a spring crop, harvesting winter wheat. Smoke arose from many chimneys as peasant women prepared for another day's labor; every loaf of bread, every cooked potato, every shank of broiled meat, and every bit of greens had to be prepared by hand – 7 days a week, 365 days a year – they fed their families.

Rory lingered near her bedroom door, peering around the wide, paneled doorjamb. A flock of chambermaids passed through the hallway, chatting in quiet voices. Rather than the dowdy uniforms she remembered, these girls wore rather tight and revealing uniforms, standard Asgard fare but taking Rory by surprise, a compromise between the elegant style and sensuality; the satin uniforms, both bodice and sleeves, were fitted and had a low-cut neckline – exposing a tantalizing glimpse of their white satin corset cups, causing their breasts to bulge in wonton display – white lace trim, a loose pleat skirt dancing around mid thigh, and a white satin apron, draped across the front and a large bow tied in the back. Black nylons sheathed the girl's legs, and they walked on rather tall, impractical high heels. More peculiar than anything else was the girl's black choker necklaces. They had an oval setting in front with the Vakhal family crest upon it.

They're slaves!

Rory's lips parted, and she sucked in a gasp. Her mother and father were slave owners, the knowledge shattering her frail sense of well-being, giving rise to a feeling of dread. She lingered in the doorway for a moment, indecision stealing her resolve. What could she do? Where could she go? She had nowhere to run.

The Seventh Age

The maids selected different doors and knocked on them. One by one, they entered the chambers of the honored guests. The men and women, like spoiled children, insisted that the maids bath, groom, and dress them for the day. It was only a matter of time until they reached her bedroom.

Dreading pursuit, she hurried through the side hallway, the window light marking a dotted path down the long hallway. Off in the distance, through the window, she saw crews hard at work, laboring in the cool of the morning, wisps of mist-draped like a white blanket around their feet, hurrying before the heat of the day. The men dug trenches the old-fashioned way, with shovels and picks. They laid a new water main, and rather than use metal pipes, they used hollowed out trees. Each tree plugged into the one before it, forming a tight seal, and their ultimate destination was the orchards.

Are they slaves too?

The faster her steps became, the more her breast heaved, tugging at the elastic shoulder straps. It might have been her imagination, but she was sure that her breasts were larger, heavier, and rounder. Her blood rushed in her ears, and her heart beat in her throat. The hallway seemed eternal, and she broke out into a run.

What's wrong with everyone?

Several maids entered rooms and began stripping the beds, leaving the red carpeted hallway an opportune void. Seizing the opportunity, she sprinted through the hallway; her foot falls quieter than a cat. After she had rounded the banister, she scrambled down two flights of stairs, taking the steps two at a time. *I can use the service tunnel to get to the garage. Christy's SUV should be there.* It was a thin plan, but the best she could devise.

Upon arriving at the upper railing, her hands slid over the taut denim fabric, exploring her new curves. There were many other clothing choices. Elegant gowns, dresses, and skirts filled her closet— not a pair of slacks remained. Yet her persistence paid off, and she found blue jeans in the back of her closet, buried inside a box. They were a bit tight, but they made her feel normal, a point of normalcy in a world gone insane.

A large crystal chandelier hung over the foyer, sunshine beaming through a thousand crystals, showering the foyer with rainbow splinters. Rory wished she had left while it was still dark, and she stole her way across the expansive hallway. All she wanted to do was run, run until she left the insanity behind. To her left lay the grand parlor, the formal dining hall, the kitchen, and the storage rooms; these rooms then provided discreet access to the tunnels.

Most homes could have fit inside the expansive parlor, an ostentatious room by most people's estimation. French Pavilion furnishings, black marble coffee tables with silver scrollwork, matching end tables, ornate oriental area rugs with an intricate red and gold pattern, towering chandeliers, two massive hearths, long red curtains, towering windows, and fresco ceilings created the impression of a palace – Rory would have traded it all for a studio apartment in New York City.

She broke into a jog, feeling as though she needed to escape some unseen pursuer. "Where do you think you're going dressed like that?" asked Meredith. Rory cringed and froze in place, a moment later turning to face her mother. "Only warriors wear slacks, and you are no warrior. You go right back up to your room and change."

Rory shrank like a turtle into its shell. "What are you talking about? What I'm wearing is perfectly fine. Everyone wears blue jeans."

"No, they don't. Only vagrants and the lowest commoners wear slacks, and we are not commoners. We stay in power because of perception." Meredith noted the terror on her daughter's face, and she closed her eyes, taking a deep breath. "I'm sorry I lost my temper."

She moved to Rory and took her hands. "I know all this must be very strange for you. From your perspective, less than a week has passed since the Cataclysm, but for us, it has been fifty long years. We do what it takes to survive. The royal family and aristocrats must perceive you as being one of them. To appear any other way is to show weakness and invite political attack."

"So that means owning slaves?" Rory said.

"Yes, the mere idea of slavery offends your father and me … but we do what it takes to appear as one of them. Aristocrats own slaves; it's just that simple." Meredith looped her arm through her daughter's arm and led her back to the foyer. "Your father is Viceroy of Gleason. Except for the king, he is the most powerful man in Salvia. We are expected to maintain a certain lifestyle. I know this must sound outrageously hypocritical to you, but you need to adapt. You're our daughter: everything you do reflects back on us."

Rory stopped and rubbed her face. "A few weeks ago I was a man with a wife and son. I was an American, a federal employee, and an FBI Special Agent. My life made sense. I don't understand any of this. Why am I a woman? Why are you and dad so young? I keep expecting to wake up and find out all of this was some weird dream."

"Your father and I have the benefit of time. I remember 50 years ago when Salvia invaded. I was terrified, but your father stayed calm. Not only did he survive, but he thrived under pressure. He forced aside his political enemies and made himself invaluable to the king."

The word "king" reverberated in Rory's mind like the clarion ring of a bell; it stirred her thoughts, provoking the imagination. That word repulsed her. Power belonged in the hands of the people, not with a single man and certainly not a tyrant; even the youngest schoolboy knew it.

Meredith resumed walking with her daughter, keeping a measured pace. "You're right. Your father and I have grown younger. That is unusual, even for Eden. I wanted to see a doctor, but your father would not allow it. He said, 'If they find out that we are not one of them, it might cause the king to remove me from power. There is a cause and effect for every action. I'm in good health and so are you: leave it at that.'"

They climbed the stairs, arm in arm. "After about 30 years, I thought it would be safe to look into the matter … but then I heard about Lord Nyman. He went to see the royal physician for a stomach problem; he had eaten some tainted meat. Anyway, they discovered that he was a halfling, his grandmother being a water sprite. They stripped him of his title and seized his lands."

"Why?" Rory blurted and furrowed her brows.

"It's a matter of law. I won't pretend to understand the intricacies of royal law, but the basic idea is that he lied on his 'Writ of Nobility.' When he officially registered as a noble, he never declared his association to the water sprites, an alliance that could affect his loyalty. It might have been an oversight, but his enemies would use it against him. They pushed him out of power and took everything. The last I heard, his entire family fled the region with just the clothes on their back. They are destitute. The King is brilliant that way; by forcing the nobles to keep their wealth in Salvia, he maintains his control. At any time and for any reason, he can take it away."

"Your father filed a Writ of Nobility for our family with the royal court. That way we protect our lands. If they find out that we are something other than what we claimed, then we will lose everything."

Rory said, "Tell me those girls aren't slaves."

"Ah … well … they are more than just slaves," Meredith replied. The bluntness of Rory's question startled her. *When did all this become normal to me?* It had been decades since she questioned the practice, and she realized how far she fell from her once dear virtues. "You're right. It is shocking."

"How long have you owned slaves?" Rory asked.

The Seventh Age

Meredith rolled her eyes upward and searched her memory. "We bought our first slaves 49 years ago. The king punished families by seizing their children. Martha Stein begged me to buy her daughter. Her father drank three beers and criticized the King. The judge seized his daughter, Tanya, and sold her at auction. As Americans, we criticized the president all the time; we never gave it a second thought. Anyway, I bought Tanya at auction. I wanted to free her, but Walter would not allow it. The king viewed freeing slaves as an act of treason."

"I remember Tanya. She played the violin," Rory replied. "Is she still here?"

"No. Five years later, a nobleman pled with us to sell her. He adored Mozart." Meredith gazed through a window and off into the distance. "I remember when she left. She had such a forlorn look on her face. I never saw her again."

Four men clad in silver armor, helmets upon their heads, and swords dangling from their hips marched past them, their heavy steps beating out a steady thump. They had a machine-like quality that sent a shiver up Rory's spine, and her right hand reached to her right hip, where she formerly wore her sidearm. She craned her neck and watched the march through the hallway. "They work for you? I hope."

"We employ them," Meredith replied, "but their loyalty is another matter. Living in Salvia is like the proverb of climbing a mountain. '… The higher one climbs, the more treacherous the footing ….'" She escorted Rory to her bedroom door. "Even one's closest friend may betray them."

Meredith waved to the five chambermaids. "They will assist you in preparing for the day." She turned to one of the girls, Amelia, and said, "I want her to wear the sky blue gown, the one with the sweetheart neckline. We need to see that she is made presentable as a member of the royal court."

"Yes, Mistress," the girl replied. Rory shuffle stepped backward as the girls entered the room. She raised her hand and opened her mouth to object as her mother closed the door.

Chapter 18

Walter slid up his suit sleeve and glanced at his gold wristwatch, a stark anachronism to the new world. This vestigial appliance subdivided life into measured segments, making it digestible by the industrial machine. It might as well have been a part of his body; he could not imagine life without it. Digital watches, like most technology, shorted out electrically, becoming junk after the Cataclysm. Walter's watch, however, was a product of Swiss craftsmanship, a mechanical triumph: gears, hands, and a mainspring. It would run for another 500 years – he was beginning to wonder if it would take that long for his daughter to get dressed for the day.

Heaviness overshadowed him like dark storm clouds rolling in from a distant horizon. He slipped down into a red leather chair and pondered Rory. Walter sank into the darkness, the driving winds and pouring rain of bittersweet memories raged in his imagination. He remembered his son's first baseball game, running the bases while still holding the bat. It shifted to Rory's first time on a horse. Peanut, the horse, walked under a low hanging branch, knocking his son to the ground, Walter struggling not to laugh. Then there was the senior prom; Rory appeared so dapper in his tuxedo and so thrilled to have Christy on his arm: love lit up his eyes. Could he actually be gone?

A serving girl approached him carrying a silver tray. As she poured a cup of coffee, wisps of steam danced in the air. She stole a furtive glance at him as she handed him the cup and saucer.

She was an adorable blonde, one of the countless young people looking to improve their station in a society with limited career options. Every day, at least three desperate people sought employment, and black necklace with a silver setting bore their family crest, indicated that the girl had sold herself into slavery. No matter how grinding the poverty, he could never imagine selling his freedom.

Slavery, the word still made him ill. He took a sip of coffee and tried to assuage his guilt. He knew all the arguments, the aristocrats reciting them like religious dogma, and he tried, in a measured way, to restrain the institution. However, his efforts were largely wasted. For all their protestations, the people embraced slavery with a speed that astonished him. Many times he considered fleeing Salvia for Asgard, but slavery, like some ancient enemy, infiltrated even the free lands.

Salvia aristocrats often slept with their male and female staff, and other aristocrats were required to reciprocate in kind, in many cases by law. Since Walter was Viceroy of Gleason, nobles and the king's official often visited, staying for months at a time, a fact that perturbed him; as such, he was expected to have a large staff of top quality servants and the best accommodations.

Walter was supposed to remember her name. They all wanted him to think of them as special. *What is her name? Damn it, not another one.* There were too many of them and more showed up every day. His estate was the dying ember of America, a link to the treasured past and an opportunity for future advancement.

He sipped the coffee and forced a pleasant reply. "Thank you. It's wonderful."

"I'm glad you like it. I bought the beans from the market myself. The coffee bean harvest on the southern slopes must be doing well."

"Anyone can be a farmer these days. Just throw a seed into the ground, and it shoots up a month later." He took another sip. "Don't mind me. I'm just a bit grumpy."

"Yes, sir." She primped her honey blonde locks, a hair clip pinning them behind her head, flowing down her back. She lingered for a moment, her mind groping. "The girl's dormitory down in the canyon, next to Riverside, is overcrowded. I was wondering; do you need more help in the main facility. Monica said that there are plenty of servant's quarters left in the basement."

Walter would have described them as mere closets rather than rooms, which included a single door, no windows, a small chifferobe, and a half-bath. The lack of natural light cast a pall over the room, leaving one feeling entombed. The occupant's sole source of comfort was a steel frame cot, and the mattresses, smelling of mildew, defined lumpiness. The toilet and shower were combined into one unit, and a corner sink allowed one to wash one's hands. Times had indeed become hard for such a room to be a bonus, and most of the town's people lived in nothing better than shanties. He felt her eyes gazing upon him, as only young women can, a complete enigma to the male mind, waiting for a reply.

"How many rooms are available?"

"There are 126 rooms, 51 of them are still empty," she replied.

"What's your name again?" asked Walter.

"Amy," she replied, appearing a bit deflated.

"The original architect designed them with single people in mind. He was German and loved the idea of youth hostels. Resorts, even when this building was erected, struggled to find help. He reasoned that he could attract more young people to work at the resort if they had free room and board." The young girl listened to him with interest but appeared pensive. "That's a long answer to a short question. Yes. You may move into one of the basement dormitories. Talk to Monica and have her issue you linens and a towel."

All the people who worked for him received food, living accommodations, and medical benefits – he also paid them a small wage and made sure they had free time, an accommodation so that his soul did not ache quite so bad. Also, he supplied them with cloth and thread to sew their leisure time clothing. One day he hoped to set them free, remembered as a liberator rather than an enslaver, a collaborator. The footsteps of doom seemed close behind him, and his heart felt like lead within his chest.

Walter picked up an oracle scroll from off a nearby lamp stand, trying to fend off the gloomy contemplation. *The Guardian News*, once a free press and now a propaganda arm of the throne, it still had pertinent facts that the skilled reader could glean. He took a sip and read about additions to the new textile mill. They were using soybean, corn silk, and milkweed to create synthetic fibers. Fortunately, a local chapter of the Future Farmers of America had several sample varieties of cotton plants. Like all the other plants in the valley, they thrived once planted.

The price of diesel fuel oil rose by two percent, speculators driving up future trading, anticipating a cold winter and high heating costs. The local utility consortium invested in the manufacturing of rhunite based heating technology. But taxes, importation duties on components, and shipping costs limited production. This put modern technology beyond the reach of most residents, preventing industrial investments and a consumer based economy. It was short-sighted on the part of the Royal Economic Council, but the members were greedy, not wise.

Walter mused about the contents of Rory's home. She owned a diesel, four-wheel drive pickup truck, with oversized, knobby tires and a lift kit. He always criticized Rory's choice in vehicles; an executive should drive a respectable car. Now he was glad for Rory's automotive quirks – the truck was worth its weight in gold. Gleason had seen the end of the motor vehicle age, gasoline based automobiles exploded with grim regularity, inevitably driving over hidden rhunite deposits. Thus, diesel powered trucks were the only reasonable option for off-road use, since few roads remained for passenger vehicles, and the maintained roads were for official use only. In addition, there were no new vehicles available at any price.

Jake hurried across the lobby, his toenails clicking and clacking on the marble floor. He wandered over to the large hearth in the middle of the lobby. A small fire dispelled the morning chill. He made three circles on a carpet and laid down for a morning nap.

Walter looked over his oracle scroll and eyed the dog. He was never a much of an animal person, but as long as the dog relieved himself outside and stayed out of the way, he supposed it was all right. He returned to the "Solva Tribune." He scanned the production figures for the fabrication plant. They recycled materials in rather ingenious ways.

"… Electricity, provided by the geothermal power plant, powered their industries. Valuable metals were re-forged and recast. Much of the metal found their way into wagon construction and other household products …."

They combined rhunite, electricity, and metal to construct weapons. Gunpowder was both difficult to make and outrageously dangerous to transport. As with gasoline, rhunite caused volatile chemicals to explode. Those who carried such firearms were suicidal, most often killed or crippled when their ammunition combusted. As a result, swords and armor manufacturing was the backbone of defense. He made a mental note to petition the king for updated armaments: swords, spears, crossbows, and bows.

He slid his finger across the scroll, turning the page, and a headline caught his eye. "FUGITIVE ARRESTED: Moyer Trimble, chief of staff for Governor Henrik Alexander Sanderson, was arrested today onboard a cargo ship, *Toffler*, bound for the Western Isle of Fairport. A coastal watch ship, the *Gallant*, was conducting routine inspections for contraband; they were tasked with stemming the flow of weapons and narcotics into Asgard. They stopped the *Toffler* and inspected their cargo. When they determined that the ship also carried passengers, they checked the visas. It was then that they encountered irregularities in one passenger's documents, Mr. Lewis Abraham. Upon closer examination, they determined that Sir William Blum's, 'The Crown's Secretary,' signature was forged. They arrested Mr. Abraham and transported him back to Solva. Once in custody, officials determined that he was Moyer Trimble, the most wanted man in all of Asgard ...."

"Are you finished with your coffee cup?" asked Amy.

"Hmm ... oh yes. I only have one cup a day. Otherwise, I can't sleep at night." She moved near to him and leaned forward. He traced the outline of her black satin pushup bra and the compression of a waist cincher, sculpting her youthful figure into an hourglass ideal. He may have been married, but he was still a man. She picked up the cup and stood a bit too close.

Her head bowed, gaze lowered, back arched, hands clasped behind her, her floral perfume teasing him, Amy said with girlish sincerity, "You're very important to the community. I want to make you happy. Is there anything I can do for you?"

"No," he said and cleared his throat, trying to purge his imaginings. "I'm fine for now. Perhaps you can help me with something when I return." As soon as the words left his mouth, he wished he could take them back.

Never had so many women been interested in him. He knew that women appreciated a powerful man, and women considered him attractive, but no physical attribute could explain their interest. Yet if questioned, women always indicated their sole criterion was love – a response that perturbed Walter since there were clearly other criteria.

When he voiced his observations and theories to Meredith, she rolled her eyes and said, "You think like a man." Yet Walter remained resolute in his observations. Women never said what they were really thinking, and women, as a rule, were enigmatic; but it was clear that Amy wanted something, and avarice burned behind her sparkling blue eyes.

"Anytime you need something you can come down to my room and wake me. I won't mind." Amy curtsied, a practice mandated by the king. Subordinate men and women had to show their respect for their superiors. It all became rather complicated, and lots of debate raged over the topic. Who bowed to who and when?

When the girl turned to leave, Walter reminded himself that he was married and tried to steady his nerves. His eyes followed the girl as she departed, noting her legs sheathed in black nylons. A war raged in his soul as he contemplated her. His flesh wanted to take her, but his intellect warned him that she was trouble. Women always made love with an ulterior motive: what was hers?

Amy's grandparents were among the thousands of tourists stranded in Gleason after the Cataclysm. Their family languished in a rented hotel room for the first few months. The hotel owner's hospitality and patience were soon exhausted. Her grandparents and the other stranded families, although no longer paid, continued to demanded services, assuming that they were entitled to lodging and food. The hotel owners acted with unanimity, ejecting the stunned guests – amid tears, protest, and consternation – but there was no reprieve. Her family found themselves without a home, without employment, and without food.

Amy grew up in post-Cataclysm Gleason. When she was a little girl, she spent hours on her grandpa's lap. His stories of Earth and the abundance of America enthralled her. She imagined royal palaces, overflowing food, and endless closets filled with elegant gowns. Luxuries as common as grain in a summer harvest, too wonderful and exciting a place for her to imagine, the recipients reveling in the great abundance, the people of Earth traveled the world in opulence, owned assorted automobiles, and lived in dozens of homes.

Reality for her, however, arrived every day at dawn and filled her days with endless toil. Her family labored as tenant farmers, working for long hours in the farmer's fields, and when they finished that, they worked in their small farming plot. In addition, they had to chop wood, feed the animals, cook meals, sew clothing, make furniture, creating household goods, and build their home: the work was wearisome and perpetual. She was sick of it, and she would do anything to change her life.

Chapter 19

Walter began to pace, which was never a good sign, and when he stopped pacing, he slid up his left coat sleeve, glanced at his watch – five minutes passed since he last checked – and muttered to himself about women. *What is taking them so long?* He rubbed the back of his neck and resumed pacing, uttering a string of unintelligible grumbles.

Meredith stood at the head of the stairs with a beaming smile on her face. "I would like to present your daughter, Rory Ann Vakhal." Walter glanced at his wife and then at the stairs leading up to the second story. Seeing nothing, he cocked his head and furrowed his brow. Meredith turned, and seeing the empty stairs, rushed up three steps. "Come on. Your father is waiting."

"I feel like an idiot," Rory huffed. Emerging from the darkness, holding up the front of her dress, descending the stairs, Rory emerged from the twilight, chewing on her crimson lower lips and cringing. "Here I am."

Sculpted and seamless perfection, the cobalt blue gown was a work of art, worthy of display in any gallery. A sweetheart neckline and sky blue satin molded around her perfect breasts, and the skirt flared out forming an A-line gown, extending back into a short train. A hundred tiny diamonds glittered like stars in a clear blue sky, embroidered on the bodice and skirt; resembling scrolling fleur-de-lis, the top fleur-de-lis pointed down while the bottom pointed up. Satin opera gloves, shoulder length, and oh-so-elegant, matched the gown, and her red locks were fixed up in an elegant coiffure, intertwined with silver thread. However, the coup-de-gras was a dazzling diamond tiara, earrings, and a necklace.

Rory's cheeks burned bright red, almost matching her hair. When she reached the bottom, Meredith jumped and clapped her hands; "Doesn't she look marvelous?"

The Seventh Age

"She's astonishing," Walter said.

"I knew we were the same size ... well ... she is built like my mother; her lingerie helped me get the right proportions. The wardrobe fits her like a glove." Meredith hurried down the steps.

"I was kind of surprised by all the clothes," Rory said.

"Most of it just showed up after the Cataclysm," Walter said. He turned away and pointed up to Rory's portrait hung on the wall. "When we went into your bedroom, we found a girl's wardrobe and all the rest. It even had boxes of memorabilia from when you grew up. Um ... your mother read your diary. I tried to stop her, but there was no holding her back."

"I just wanted to get to know my daughter." Meredith wrung her hands and leaned forward a bit. "She's my baby."

"I'll have to read it sometime. I have no idea what is in it. My memory includes my normal life before the Cataclysm," Rory said.

"Maybe you'll remember your other life in time," Meredith said. "You never know."

"I suppose," Rory said.

"Perhaps she will." Walter checked his watch. "Many of our guests are lingering in the foyer to greet Rory. News of her emergence spread faster than I anticipated. I had them set up a casual brunch on the veranda outside the ballroom. Monica set up an impromptu brunch, and Michael set up tables. You had better go make sure that you approve of everything."

"You're right." Meredith wrung her hands and angst marred her beautiful face. "I'll check on them right away."

After Meredith had left the room, Rory said, "Mom's gone nuts. She and five chambermaids attacked me. Before I knew what was happening, they squeezed, pinched, and perfumed me. It was like getting mugged by a group of cheerleaders."

"You're mother has worried about you for 50 years. Every morning I would find her in the chapel, praying for you. You have to give her time, and you have to give yourself time."

"I suppose." She tugged up her left glove and sighed. "It's just that ... well, I feel like I'm in drag. But I'm not, am I?"

Walter turned away from her. He saw the traces of his son's face in her, and it broke his heart. He rubbed his eyes, fighting off the tears and let his heart turn to stone. "We need to head toward the ballroom. Your mother will be waiting."

Rory watched her father walk away, an icy gulf between them, so much to say and so little said. Anger blazed through her like magma in a volcano, turning her face red, causing her emerald eyes to flash. She wanted to rip off the gown and march back up to her room, throw on her blue jeans and scream.

Walter stood at the head of the stairs, staring off at some distant horizon; he bowed his head and sighed, "We're already late." Rory moved to her father's side, hoping for some recognition, some words of comfort. He had none to offer and extended his right elbow saying, "I suppose you should take my arm. We don't want you to make your grand entrance by tumbling down the stairs. Just keep your chin up and keep smiling. We'll get through this."

Rory looped her arm through her father's arm, and after hiking up her gown in front, they descended the stairs. The curved stairway passed into darkness, the doorway light just up ahead, and they could already see the legs of the gathered guests. Rory struggled to repress her emotions; her father's rejection caused sorrow and despair to intertwine within her soul. She was a prisoner, a burden, an impediment – he did not want her: it would have been better if she had stayed asleep in the gray zone, forever lost. She looked up to her father, but his steel gray eyes remained straight ahead of him, his body rigid and his expression without compassion.

Although Walter said nothing, she could feel his accusations radiating from his icy façade; she was weak and pathetic: it would never have happened to a real man. When they reached the bottom of the stairs and saw the guests gathered just beyond the doors, Rory faltered. She stopped walking and struggled to fight off the tears. Her entire world was gone, destroyed, leaving her aching for yesterday when she was loved. Tears burst forth from her eyes like a summer rain. She jerked her arm away from her father and fled up the stairs, great heaves thundering and tears showering.

Meredith passed through the door and into the foyer, just in time to see her daughter flee and hear her soulful sobs. "What did you say to her? All you had to do was escort her downstairs." She chased after Rory, leaving Walter behind.

His lips parted in surprise, and then his face froze as if made of stone, and he strolled to the end of the stairs and gazed up at his wife. He said nothing. The accusation was untrue and unfair – yet it was both true and fair: his heart was a rock, having no safe cleft for his daughter. He sat down on the steps, craving a cigarette and wishing things were the way they used to be.

Chapter 20

The open carriage rolled at a leisurely pace, perfect for a warm afternoon. Walter sat on one side of the bench, a great gap between them, and Rory was on the far side. Walter looked to the left and Rory to the right. Only the clip-clop of the horse's hooves disturbed the silence – both of them lost in their thoughts.

Harvesters lay ladders against the apple trees, soiled canvas bags slung over their shoulders. Men and women picked juicy red apples until their bags became heavy. Children scampered around the base of the trees, playing a quick game of tag, their squeals and laughter music to their parent's ears.

"We get a nearly continuous harvest. Geothermal heat keeps the ground soft all through winter. We supply most of the other kingdoms with food," Walter said, his gaze fixed on the passing trees.

His words passed through Rory's mind and dissipated, like a whisper in the wind. She thought of Christy and their wedding day. It was a beautiful day like this one; Christy was as radiant as her gown, taking his breath away, everything he dared dream possible looked upon him with love. When she walked the aisle, a white veil covering her face, he wanted to shout for joy and weep all at the same time. His father's hand on his shoulder steadied him, love and strength communicated through a single touch.

Walter glanced at his watch and broke the spell. The icy winds of isolation and disapproval swept over her. She was a failure in the worst possible way, a failure as a man. Upon seeing the approaching cliffs, she contemplated suicide; one leap, a quick flight through the air, and all her troubles would end – the world and its pain would fall away as she winged to the eternal shores.

The Seventh Age

"I'm sorry," Walter mumbled.

Rory looked upon him with melancholy eyes. "I never asked for any of this."

"I see," Walter replied with all the warmth of a psychotherapist.

"No. You don't see." She gazed down at her body. "My life … no, my world was turned upside down."

"All of our lives were thrown into chaos." Walter's icy façade melted as his rage burned through. "While you were frozen in time, I was fighting to survive. Every day your mother and I hung by a thread. King Leopold struts around like a cock of the roost. He takes all that he wishes and gives nothing back. The man is self-aggrandizing, and he regards all those around him as an inferior species. He arrests citizens without trial and kills children at a whim. The only way I had to survive was to sell my soul and make myself indispensable to him. I am going to hell for the things I did for him. So don't lecture me on how hard life can be."

The furious exchange passed, and silence resumed, each one pondering the other's words. Rory slipped into a daydream and gazed at the rolling fields of produce. She imagined herself back in time, somewhere beyond the distant horizon. Christy was burning breakfast, and Michael played in his room. It was a perfect moment, one that would never come again.

The carriage rolled to the canyon's edge and passed down the road skirting the wall. Rory scooted over the seat and sat next to Walter. She leaned over the side and gaped in awe. The road formed a crisp right angle, and straight down a rock wall, she saw the distant river, a thin blue line, snaking through the bottom. "I had no idea we were so high up," Rory said.

"The valley came to rest like pancakes lying on lumpy sausage. The fissure ripped up toward the north; it almost destroyed the resort but passed us by at the last moment. That is the Cougar River way down there. It's fed by Prophets Mountain."

"My God, it's so deep. It's like having the Grand Canyon in our back yard." She gazed across the vast expanse, seeing other canyons and buttes. Horizontal layers of strata showed the age of the land. She tried to imagine how long they took to form. "I always loved geology, but I wanted a job after I got done with college. Now I wish that I studied it, everything is so amazing."

She jumped up and crossed to the front of the carriage. Kneeling on the front seat, she peered over the far corner, watching the cliff face pass by their left. "If you spit, I wonder how long it would take to hit bottom."

"Let's not do that," Walter chuckled. "There may be someone fishing down there."

The carriage tilted down at a steep angle, the team of horses slowing rather than pulling. Rory climbed back up to the rear seat. Every so often, she craned her neck, anxious to see what new wonder would appear. When they rounded the bend, they arrived at the end of a town.

This was the far outskirts of the town; Wood-framed homes, boxes with crude root-cellars, lined both sides of the streets. The stores of the business district pressed together as if jostling for business, brilliantly painted facades adorning their faces and covered wooden walkways sheltering shoppers from the noonday sun. They passed down the middle of the dirt street, Rory feeling as though she stepped back into the Wild West. Stores abounded: dry goods, clothiers, tools, furniture stories were filled with goods, dazzling store windows tempting shoppers.

Women in gowns as colorful as spring blossoms milled from shop to shop. Boys carried pails of beer to men for their noonday lunch break. Raucous music spilled out of a saloon, and a never-ending party filled the interior; men stood arm in arm, gathered around the piano and sang. Brazen whores clad in lingerie lounged on second-floor balconies, heavy breasts displayed like ripe fruit, tempting men to spend their hard-earned pay. The town had a city hall, a sheriff's office, an apothecary, a post office, a dentist's office, and doctor's office. The voices of a children's choir spilled out of a one-room schoolhouse. Men and women paused from their labors to wave and crowds gathered. When Walter waved, a cheer broke out from the crowd – he waved like a conquering hero home from war.

"They really love you," Rory said, feeling a little confused.

"I suppose they do. I have built towns like this all over Gleason Valley. We produce a variety of finished goods. Our main exports are high-quality wood furnishings, produce packaged in reusable glass containers, ground wheat, and refined rhunite ore. We ship everything down Cougar River to the ports on Hope Lake. From there, we ship them down the Ambling River to the Arner Sea. The merchant ships head north and south to the various trading ports. If I had my way, we would double or triple our manufacturing base. Industrial jobs bring wealth and prosperity."

The driver slowed the carriage and pulled up to the boardwalk next to the courthouse. After exiting, Walter extended his hand to assist Rory to exit the carriage, a practice that made them both feel uncomfortable; but long gowns and high heels required concentration, and she appreciated the help. Rory strolled down the boardwalk and up to a dress shop, admiring a deep emerald green gown. Its shimmery tones and fitted contours dazzled the eye.

"Do you like it?" asked Walter.

"Well, yes. It's beautiful." Her breath fogged the glass. She wondered how some people had the talent to create such clothing. The shop door opened and a bell tinkled. An elva appeared, the first Rory had ever seen, and she asked, "Do you like it? I made it not knowing who would wear it, but I think it would be perfect for you. You must try it on."

"I don't really think …." Rory stammered.

"Go ahead," Walter urged. "I have some business at the courthouse. Have the tailor adjust it for her and then deliver it up to the main house."

Scott Marcy

"Of course," the elva replied. Rory shuffle-stepped as the elva ushered her into the shop. The spiced aroma of burning incense and the soft pastel interior created a warm, peaceful ambiance. "I have a few gowns held in reserve in the stockroom. I will be back in a moment."

A cobalt lace gown caught Rory's attention. She picked the gown from off the display and held it up to the light. When a figure passed by the plate-glass window, she spotted Brent McClain. She set down the garment and hurriedly moved to the door. Standing on the threshold, she said, "Brent, is that you?"

Brent stopped walking and turned around. He gazed at Rory for a moment and cocked his head. "I'm sorry miss. Have we met before?"

"Yes, you lived across the street from me on Maple Ave. I was married to Christy. I'm Rory Vakhal."

"Rory ... I heard about what happened to you. I cannot believe it. So you finally escaped the gray zone." Brent scratched his head. "It sure is hard to believe it's you."

"It's even harder for me to believe." Rory did not quite know where to put her hands, and then she gazed down at her body. "But it is me."

"Do your parents know that you're back?" asked Brent.

"Sure, my dad is across the street." Rory stepped out of the shop and let the door close. "What happened to all the others?"

Brent twitched his nose and asked, "Others?"

"You know ... from our neighborhood," asked Rory.

"Oh," Brent said and rubbed the back of his neck. "Well, Rick Barnes and his crew made it to a Waypoint Town along the Great Mountain Way, but they had to turn back. Waypoints cost a small fortune, and that is just to stand in the courtyard. Ten years later, he joined the merchant

172

fleet and sailed away." He gazed up at the sky and thought a moment. "Tom Reynolds and Greta were killed by haugrs on the road; we never found their bodies, just their belongings covered in blood. Mary Strauss survived, but Richard and the boys died in a daemia attack."

"Um … Kurt Ripley managed to talk Pierce and Jeanie to come and stay with him. Their son Jeff lived in town and became a cobbler. Jessica works down on the docks." Brent whispered, "She's an escort at a brothel."

"Most of the others died in the mountains. The rest died of starvation or exposure over the next few years." Brent pulled open his black wool coat. A tin star was pinned to his vest. "I'm the law enforcer around here. When I retired from the New York City Police Department, this is not what I had in mind. I keep expecting to grow old, but I keep getting younger. I wish I'd moved to Florida; my sister lives … lived in Tampa."

The conversation lapsed into silence. Rory could see 50 years of painful memories in Brent's eyes. The door opened behind Rory with a chime of the bells. "I have those dresses ready for you," the elva said.

"Well, I have to go." Rory moved through the open door. "I suppose I'll be seeing you around."

"I'm here anytime you want to see me." Brent turned and walked away with a backhand wave. Rory paused for a moment and then entered the shop. It was hard to believe they were all gone.

———

Walter waited for a passing wagon and then crossed the street. The courthouse was one of the few structures made of stone, its fortress-like walls and barred windows served as a warning, as did the permanent gallows, which was visible from most windows in town. Too often, those in power ended up on their own gallows, a fact that Walter tried to ignore.

He jogged up the steps, and at his approach, the armed guards snapped to attention and saluted him with a fist bump to their breastplate. A female slave opened the door and hurried to keep up with him. "It's good to see you, Viceroy Vakhal. Would you like some coffee or something to eat?"

Walter stopped in the middle of the lobby and glanced at the pensive girl. "No thank you. I already ate."

Mayor Larry Stein, the local regent, strode across the lobby, his hand extended to greet Walter. "I had no idea that you would come to visit us today. I would have arranged for a luncheon."

"There's no need. I'm just taking my daughter shopping. Rory doesn't know it yet, but her mother is coming down to join her; Meredith has several days of mother-daughter time planned. I thought we could use the time go over our production quota and tax revenues. The topic is sure to come up next time I see the king."

"There's another topic sure to come up," Ben Stallman said. Walter turned and saw the judge walking toward him. Ben reminded Walter of an owl or perhaps a penguin: round glasses, balding, goatee, bullet shaped body, and a long-tail suit.

"And what would that be?" Walter asked, knowing the answer.

"Word of your daughter's emergence has already reached the king's ears. He is sure to send you an invitation to 'The Debutant Ball' taking place in two weeks." He then added what they both already knew. "There will be many who seek her hand in marriage, but the king will have to approve the final selection."

Chapter 21

"Time to wake up," Meredith said. "You and I have to go shopping." She whisked aside the curtains, flooding the room with early morning light.

"I just got to sleep," Rory whined.

"You've been asleep for 7 hours; your father and I need only 3 hours these days." Meredith strode into Rory's closet. She returned a minute later carrying a green satin dress, the one from the display window; it gleamed like fresh paint, seamless perfection, worthy of a princess, and perfectly tailored for Rory. "Go take a shower. I'll help you get dressed."

Rory swept the hair from her face and looked up at her mother. If this was a dream, she wanted it to stop. It had reoccurred every morning for the past week. Meredith searched Rory's underwear drawer, settled upon a black satin corset and panties, the corset having boning which created dramatic, hourglass lines, and then a pair of sheer black nylons that completed the set. Three questions formed in Rory's mind. First, why was her mother picking out her clothes? Second, why did her underwear matter? Third, who was going to see it?

Meredith held up the emerald green gown to the light. Where the sweetheart neckline ended, intricate green lace began, handmade and interwoven with glittering emeralds. The bodice sculpted to Rory's figure, emphasizing her hourglass shape, with a long slit up the right leg. Rory screwed up her face as she examined the dress. "I'd prefer to wear jeans."

"I'm sure you would," Meredith replied, "but you and your father are going to meet with the king at the ball. You have to look your best." She moved to her daughter's side and held up the dress for her to see, sure that a closer inspection would inspire her daughter.

"Mom, I really would prefer to wear something a little less girly." She looked at the corset and snarled. "I'm not really comfortable with all this."

Her mother's face tightened. "We need you to make a good impression. One misstep, one slip of the tongue could cost us everything. We would all wind up on the auction block or worse. Is that what you want?"

Her mother's aggressive attitude startled Rory. A questioning expression appeared on her face, and she uncrossed her arms. "No. But why …."

"No buts," Meredith said. "We need to make sure this dress fits. We are all counting on you." Meredith paused for a moment and collected herself. "We are members of the king's court. If you fail to present yourself, register, and take place in the debutant ball, it would be taken as a sign of treason."

"Treason! Why?" asked Rory.

"I know it has only been a short time, but democracy is dead; we live in a monarchy. The king permits only those in good standing with the court to own property or conduct business. There are protocols that govern our conduct, and it is by them that we maintain our relationship to those in power. The king can take our land and throw us in prison without a trial. It has happened."

Meredith sat down on the side of the bed and looked off into the distance. "I remember Linda Brewer screaming for mercy as she and her children were dragged away. Her husband, Karl, failed to register his children with the court and kept them from attending boarding school."

Rory said, "If you step out of line, they hold your children as a hostage?"

Meredith primped Rory's hair and said, "You don't know how hard it has been on all of us. We live day by day not knowing if the police will break down our door and drag us away. It is only because of your father that we still have all this. He knows how to deal with people in the royal

176

court. He told me that this was vital to our survival, and I believe him. Now I need you to take a shower and then get dressed."

"Okay, fine," Rory replied. "I'll go take a shower. At least we still have indoor plumbing. Not everybody does. Cougar Creek is a river of filth."

Meredith took a deep breath and let out a sigh. "I know this is hard for you. But, you know the old saying, 'Be yourself?' Well, don't be yourself: be as fake' as possible. Pretend you are on stage before an audience. When in doubt, look to your father or me. We will help you."

"Got it. Be fake," she replied. Rory wandered into the bathroom and muttered to herself. As she used the facilities, a knock came from the door. "What?" she asked with alarm and annoyance.

"I put a new scrubby, and a bottle of 'Floral Spring' body wash in the shower. I also put a fresh razor in the shower if you have stubble in your armpits or on your legs. Oh, and I gave you two different conditioners. Tell me which one you prefer, and I'll buy more."

"I have to do all that?" Rory replied.

"No one ever said being a girl was easy. Come on out when you get ready to do your hair. I'll help you dry and style it."

Rory stripped off her nightclothes and took a long, hot shower. After shampooing, conditioning, scrubbing, shaving both armpits and legs, she debated whether to shave her nether regions. She opted to use scissors and then used a razor to shave, cursed when she nicked herself where no one wishes it, rinsed out the shower gel, cursed again, wished she was a man, wondered why she was doing all this since no one would see her naked, worried that someone might see her naked, and fretted she had missed a spot. Soft, smooth, and hair free from the neck down, she exited the shower and felt relieved that the ordeal was finished.

She threw on a terrycloth robe and exited the shower where her mother waited for her. She clutched a hair dryer in her left hand and a round brush in her right; a crazed look gleamed in her eyes. Rory took a seat, and the hair operation began. Her mother heated, brushed, misted with conditioner, curled, and trimmed Rory's hair. When she finally escaped, she beheld her mother's handiwork. Her hair was fixed up behind her head in an elegant coiffure. She had to admit that it all looked amazing.

"I'm glad that's over with," she sighed. "I'll get dressed now." Her mother waited and gave her a knowing stare. "What now?" lamented Rory.

"We need to do your makeup before you get dressed," her mother replied.

"Fine," Rory said and flopped down again. Her mother grabbed a brush, jars, and tubes of cosmetics. As her mother applied the makeup, she lectured Rory on a proper beauty regimen. Men assumed beauty just happened, but women knew better. It took hours of preparation and great skill. If one did it correctly, it appeared seamless and natural.

When the long tutorial was complete, Rory cringed and asked, "Now can I get dressed?"

"Of course," Meredith said and handed Rory a pair of panties. "These were made in Solva. They're guaranteed not to leave panty lines." She then stood there and waited for Rory to try them on.

"Do you think I might have a little privacy?" asked Rory.

"Please, I've seen your bare bottom ever since you were a baby. The fact that you're a woman now makes no difference."

"I would just feel more comfortable if you would wait outside."

Meredith huffed, "Fine. However, I will be right outside. You might have trouble with your corset."

Rory sighed and slouched. "I appreciate that." When her mother left the room, she held out the panties and snarled. Somehow being home made the situation so real. With little other choice, she stepped into the thong and whisked it up her smooth legs.

The corset was a bit of a mystery. Rory held it out before her and turned it this way and that. Was she supposed to unlace the back? That seemed wrong. The laces appeared too long for that. Then she noticed a discreet set of hooks hidden on a right side seam. She loosened the laces and wrapped the garment around her torso. Even unlaced, it was encumbering. She hated to think what it would be like tight.

"How is it going?" Meredith called out through the door.

"Fine, I guess. Okay, not so fine, how do you tighten this thing?" asked Rory. Meredith rolled her eyes, shook her head, and marched into the room. "I'm not dressed."

"Hold onto the bed post," Meredith said, like a general taking charge.

Rory grasped one of the bedposts, dreading what was about to take place, wishing to exclude the compressive garment; and yet she knew better: she had to be perfect. Seeing Meredith take the laces in hand, feeling a knee planted on her back, holding on tight to the post, she took a deep breath and expelled the air from her lungs. After a sudden compression, a giant squeezed her abdomen, or so it seemed to Rory. She grimaced and groaned. The black satin garment grew tighter by the second, preventing her from taking a deep breath. The light danced on the black satin fabric as the fierce tugs and pulls drew the strings banjo tight. Her breasts slipped into the sculpted cups and began to bulge. Rory struggled to take a deep breath. Meredith mercilessly pulled, but she left a little slack in the corset, allowing for her daughter's inexperience with the garment.

Rory walked around with her bent elbows up in the air, her spine fused into a ramrod straight shaft. "I can barely breathe. It's too tight." She grimaced and tried to tug free some slack. "This thing feels awful."

"It's meant to look good, not feel good. Now sit down. I'll help you put on your nylons."

Bending her spine was impossible. Rory sat down on the edge of the bed, as though her back was fused, extended her right leg, and pointing the toe. Meredith dragged over a chair and sat down before her daughter. She rolled up a black nylon and picked up Rory's right leg. Rory watched in fascination as her foot was cocooned in the sheer nylon fabric. It unrolled up her calve and then up her thigh. "I would have preferred thigh-high nylons, but they fall down when you walk in them. Nothing is more embarrassing than walking around with your nylons down around your ankles."

Rory grimaced and tried to situate her breasts. The fleshy globes bulged upward and hung from her chest like a third person. "I always thought having your own set of breasts would be more fun than this."

"Men love big breasts, but they never give a second thought about lower back strain." Meredith stretched down each satin garter strap and clipped it to the dark nylon top. She then began to sheath the other leg. "Now be careful in these nylons. They are expensive, and they are shipped all the way from Solva."

"There we go," she said with satisfaction.

"Let me get your shoes while we are at it." Meredith hurried into the closet and returned with a pair of green, strappy high heels. She worked one onto Rory's left foot and said, "Good, they fit. You have small feet, like me. I thought, since you were my daughter, we would be about the same size. Your breasts are bigger than mine though, like your grandmother: she had a big chest."

This was the second reference Meredith made to Grandma Tabitha, and Rory wished she would stop. She remembered Nana Tabitha in her elder years. Her body curved like a pumpkin, her breasts sagging over her rotund belly, and she walked about as though on stilts. Rory scrunched up her nose and frowned; she never considered growing old as a woman. *I'll have to go through menopause. Wait a minute! I'll have to menstruate before that happens.* She glanced down at the black satin covering the junction of her thighs. Her lips curled into a pout. When would that happen? What would it be like?

As if reading her daughter's mind, Meredith asked, "Have you had your first period yet?"

"God no," Rory replied.

"It doesn't matter." She handed Rory a clear vial of blue liquid. "The blue halts the menstrual process and acts as a birth control. I'm told it also prevents sexually transmitted diseases; so I think it would be wise to take unless you want to experience a period as a woman."

Rory took the vial from her mother but paused a second. The blue liquid reminded her of ink. She prepared herself for the worst and poured the viscous liquid into her mouth. It surprised her. It tasted like a mixture of blueberry and raspberry syrup. "Not bad." She poured in the last drop. "How often do you need to take it?"

"Once a year, but some women swear it makes them look younger, so they take it once a month. It's up to you. It certainly won't hurt you." Meredith helped Rory stand and said, "All done."

Rory wobbled around and grabbed the bedpost. She used it for support as her mother retrieved the gown, drawing down the zipper. He held it over Rory's head. "Put your arm through the sleeves … be careful not to get your nails caught on the lace sleeves." Rory worked her arms and head through the garment, but they had a bit of trouble getting the garment over her breasts. Pulling and tugging, Meredith worked the gown down over Rory's cleavage, but once past them, it popped into place on her corset shaped torso. Rory held onto the post as her mother wrestled with the dress. She could feel it sliding over her bottom. All at once the waist slipped past the apex of her bottom and popped into place.

"Back on Earth, we had undergarment support built right into the dress. No one does that anymore. It's too expensive and a bit wasteful." The corset maintained her figure in the ideal hourglass proportion. Meredith drew up the side zipper. "Turn toward me. Let's take a look at you."

When Rory turned around, her mother tugged at the sweetheart neckline; where the green satin ended, the lace began. "There is a slit up the right thigh; it will allow you to walk more freely, and you can show off a bit of leg. Walk around the room for me."

Rory wobbled about as though she was on ice. Meredith took her daughter's hands and walked backward. "I know the heels are rather high, but you can do this. Don't walk on your heels; walk on the balls of your feet. Pretend that you're walking tiptoe." Rory did as her mother instructed. Soon she found her balance, though her strides were a bit mannish. "Now pretend you are walking a tightrope. That's good … one foot in front of the other." She released Rory's hands and held her breath.

Rory felt the sway, the undulation, of her hips, and the counter sway of her chest, her body assuming a graceful gait. "See, it's as though you've been doing it your whole life." This revelation felt more like an insult than a compliment.

When Rory turned, a redheaded beauty gazed back at her in the dressing mirror, like an ethereal beauty descended from the heavens. When she touched her face, the girl did likewise; until that moment, her body had been a costume, a temporary inconvenience. Life would right itself, and her male body would return; but when she drew in a shallow breath, her body sensed the weight of her breasts, the curve of her waist, the heart-shaped slopes of her bottom; the rise of her breasts, the elastic flex of her garter straps, and the cool caress of silk and satin – adornments for the quintessential female body – she was a woman: she was real. She felt light headed as this epiphany took root in her consciousness.

182

The Seventh Age

A broad smile appeared on her mom's face. "You look beautiful, like a movie star! The other girls will be so jealous." Rory cocked her head and raised an eyebrow. It was not what she wanted to hear.

"You need to take that dress off," Meredith said. Rory looked at her mother for an explanation. "We're saving that gown for the ball. Now we have to go shopping. You need more than one gown."

The outfit for this day awaited her near a three-way mirror. They debated the issue of whether a half-slip was necessary, but in the end, social convention and Meredith won. Rory stepped into the silk garment, feeling its cool caress through her nylons as she drew it up to her waist. The black, faux leather pencil skirt and matching bolero jacket were the latest fashion out of Solva. She stripped a chromed silver blouse from off a hanger and slid her arms into the sleeves, feeling the caress of cool silk and soft lace enveloping her. Her hands still fumbled with the buttons, at first trying to fasten the wrong facing buttons.

Even with the garment's elasticity, Rory struggled to zip up her skirt. The high-rise waist extended up her abdomen. Meredith sighed and shook her head. "Here, let me."

Rory turned her right side toward her mother. Meredith grabbed the zipper tab and pulled, but the zipper gap was too wide. "Your corset is loose."

"Too loose?" whined Rory. "It already feels like it's pinching me in half." Meredith stripped down the skirt, untucked the blouse, and pulled down the black silk half-slip. Pulling up the back of the blouse, Meredith dislodged the excess laces and untied them. Feeling her mother's knee in her back, Rory held onto the nearby wooden post again. "We need to get out that last bit of slack," Meredith said, her expression strained and arms pulling. Rory grimaced and arched her back as the corset constricted to its maximum compression, causing the closure to meet behind her.

"Can't breathe," she gasped.

"Don't be dramatic," Meredith huffed. She pulled and yanked until taking out every bit of slack. She then tied off the laces, tucked them in, and then tucked in the blouse. She pulled up the skirt, and this time the zipper glided up with ease. "That's much better."

"Sure, if you don't want to breathe," Rory said, her hands gliding over the treated leather material stretched around her hourglass figure, conforming to her curves.

Meredith handed Rory the black leather jacket and a set of matching gloves. Then she turned away and strolled through the room. "Have you given any thought about marriage after our discussion last night?"

"No," Rory said and avoided eye contact.

"You have to give it some thought." Meredith smoothed her skirt underneath her and sat at the makeup table. "A dozen different men have already contacted us. I know this is still new to you, but you have to get married."

"Why? I just woke up from that weird gray zone, and I'm happy being single." An ordinary pencil skirt restricts the wearer's gait, but the elastic leather allowed Rory to take adequate steps. The glossy material gleamed, flashed, and stretched as she walked around the room. She slid back on the bed and unzipped a knee-high boot. However, the corset made bending over impossible. "Although my whole life disappeared, I am still college educated. I could go back to school and study law." Rory grunted. Her arms were too short to get her foot into the boot.

"We discussed this last night before you went to bed." Meredith arose and moved to help her daughter. As Rory pointed her right toe, Meredith forced it into the pointed boot. "Women of your stature and rank don't practice law or hold down jobs. You get married and have babies. Practically every man in Parliament will want to marry you. A woman of your age, beauty, and wealth is required by law to get married, and the king will see that it happens." She zipped up the boot and moved to the other foot.

"That's ridiculous," Rory said.

"This isn't Earth. The law compelled young women to obey their parent's wishes. Your father could simply sign a contract and marry you off to whomever he sees fit. He doesn't need your permission." Meredith put her hands on her hips, feeling satisfaction at having sheathed Rory's leg with the tight boot.

Rory slid off the bed and found her balance on the stiletto heels. "This world is so backward. Why do men get to control women? It's not fair."

"You used to be a man so I would think you would know. Men do it because they can." Meredith circled around and inspected her daughter. "It's a man's world. You need to remember that."

"This is such a nightmare." Rory pulled on the jacket's lapels. The black leather garment barely covered her sides and focused the eye on her chest. "I feel like I'm back in the eighteenth century. What happened to women's rights?"

"It never happened here, and it never will." Meredith held Rory's hands and sighed. "You are the most beautiful woman in Salvia." Meredith primped her daughter's hair and sighed. "Just think about it, sweetheart. I know you want to get back together with Christy, but it is just not going to happen. She ... well, she wants a man to share her bed, not some girl, especially a girl pretty enough to be homecoming queen."

Rory's crimson lips formed a deep pout. Several witty remarks emerged into her consciousness, but she lapsed into silence. After a minute of silence, she swallowed and said in a quiet voice, "I know. However, you have to give me some time. It's been over fifty years to you, but to me, it was just weeks ago."

Meredith clasped Rory's left hand in her right as they exited the bedroom, and Rory picked up her black leather purse. "You also need to think about a direction for your life. There are only two paths for a young woman of rank: marriage or becoming a warrior – and you are not a warrior. I've known too many of them over the years. They are bawdy women who enjoy drinking, meaningless sex, and fighting."

As they passed down the long corridor, rectangles of light beaming through the windows and marking blocks on the floor, Rory pondered her mother's words. "I don't want to repeat my former life. It is in the past; I would like to leave it there. But I still think about Michael. What happened to him? How can someone just cease to exist?"

"It's been hard for your father and me, too. We lost our grandson." Meredith and Rory strolled through the lobby to the main door. When they exited the resort, they saw four platoons of mounted cavalry, two before and two behind, awaited them, ready to safeguard their passage. A gilded carriage, white with gold leaf trim and a blood red interior, awaited them in the center of the formation. The black top was down, and a team of four horses stood ready to draw it. The footman held open the carriage door. Meredith entered first and then Rory.

The driver cracked his whip above the horses head, and the column began to move. The sun beamed through vivid blue skies and warmed the crisp mountain air. It was a perfect September morning, but ruminations consumed mother and daughter: each one pondering their future.

The carriage passed underneath trees lifting their leafy hands toward the skies. Every so often an old truck cruised past them, belching clouds of oily smoke. The diesel engine's rugged design allowed for long-term use, but they represented a dying way of life. Soon there would be neither replacement parts nor people to repair them.

"Your father is trying to get shuttle service for our community," Meredith commented.

"That doesn't seem very practical considering all of the mountains in the way," Rory replied, idly watching the red brick buildings marking the outskirts of town.

"Well, there are other kingdoms to consider. Shuttle service is a temptation that might compel the King to join the National Parliament. The kingdoms that join Asgard get the shuttle passing through their lands. It means increased trade and investment. Land prices would double overnight. There are a great many city people who would value a country estate or a cabin."

"Sure, if you don't mind monsters," Rory said. Rory crossed her legs feeling nylon slide on nylon, the caress of her silk slip, and the flex of her garter straps. She tugged at the hem of her pencil skirt, trying to cover her black nylon sheathed legs. The peculiarity of the situation resurfaced in her mind like a forgotten appointment. When she looked past the mountainous slopes of her silver breasts, she saw black leather wrapped around wide hips and feminine legs – all of which belong to her. Her sense of normal shifted like Gleason to Eden. Women were "us, " and men were "them."

The town was alive with activity. Men and women paused from their activities to watch the procession pass. Teenage boys shared a private conversation and then laughed; teenage girls offered fashion critiques. Young boys climbed up on lampposts and half walls. Young girls viewed them with dreamy eyes, imagining themselves as a princess.

When they neared the center of town, they approached a banner stretched across the street: "Founder's Day Celebration." The swell of the crowds moved like a slow river through the center of town. It flowed into Circle Park, located in the center of town, and then broke up into eddy currents as revelers visited booths. The cedar smoke carried the aroma of cooking meat and baking corn. It soon mixed with the tantalizing aroma of funnel cakes frying in hot oil. Rory's stomach rumbled in anticipation, but it was far too early to eat.

No matter where Rory looked, someone was looking back at her with fascination. Meredith smiled and waved to friends. Others wishing to join the festivities mounted their carriages and followed behind them. Soon the procession was blocks long. The police struggled to keep spectators on the sidewalks.

They passed through Old Town and headed toward the Western Shopping District on Pearce Blvd. As they passed over the Ruben Goddard Truss Bridge, Rory gazed through the steel structure and down at the water. She sniffed and screwed up her face as the stench assaulted her nostrils.

Even the old Federal Building found new life. It now housed various Salvia government agencies. Men and women gathered behind the smoked glass windows and watched the procession. Rory gazed up at her old office and wondered who occupied it.

"It's getting warm," Rory said, gazing up at the round yellow sun.

"Don't worry. It will cool off fast. The west winds pick up in the afternoon. I have heavier coats packed away in the back if we need them." Meredith clasped Rory's hand and drew in a deep breath. "I'm so glad you decided to come with me. I'm so happy to have you back."

"Everyone is staring at me," Rory replied. "I feel like a new panda bear at the zoo. And then there are all the men leering at me. I know what they are thinking, and it makes me feel weird, knowing what they want."

"You're probably right. You are a girl now. You have a different part in sex. Men pursue women: it's a biological fact." Meredith turned toward her daughter and asked, "Is that what is bothering you about picking a husband? You're worried about sex?"

Rory's cheeks flushed, and she said, "I'm not worried about it. I was married. Christy and I slept together."

"Yes, but that was when you were a man. It is a far different experience for a woman. We receive the man inside our bodies, and the emotions are overpowering. At times you are singing with the angels, and on other occasions, you're languishing in purgatory." She sighed. "I really miss those days. Your father and I have drifted apart. We're just two strangers who seldom share the same bed."

"Too much information, Mom," Rory replied.

"Well, my point is that love is one of the most amazing experiences a woman can have."

"And if she ... if I love another woman, is God sitting in heaven condemning her ... me? Are all those preachers right? Am I a vessel created for destruction, a freak, an accident?" Rory looked off into the distance and saw the wind gust plumes of snow off the jagged mountain peaks.

Meredith turned toward her daughter and held her hands. "No. Sweetie, God loves you. You are not an accident or some kind of freak. He made you just as you are. He has a special life for you, and you have to be strong enough to embrace it. If you love another woman, your father and I will support you. Somehow, I think we are not talking about just any woman. Are we?" Rory shook her head. "Your marriage to Christy ended over 50 years ago. That is longer than you have been alive. Christy has a new life."

"Right, I remember, she's the dock supervisor," Rory said with a shrug.

"That's what she is now." When Meredith saw a curious look in Rory's eyes, she shook her head and sighed. "After she left you, she stayed with her boss, Tom Granger. Tom was a good man, but he had a weak heart. Just two weeks later, he died while chopping wood. One day Christy went to town looking for supplies, and when she made it home, strangers were squatting in Tom's home. They drove her away at gunpoint. The town was in shambles; she had nowhere to go, so she lived in a shanty downtown."

"A few days later, one of the king's officers, Captain Turnbolt, ordered his men to find girls for the brothels. The men raided the town and carried away terrified girls. They chased Christy for three blocks, and they finally cornered her in an alley. She tried to escape, but there were too many of them. After they had raped her, they tied her up and threw her on the back of a wagon with other captives. Christy and the others were each locked in a room at the Bonita Estrella Hotel."

Meredith paused and searched her thoughts. "What can I say? A person can resist for only so long. They broke her and turned her into a prostitute. She had to service all of the king's guards for years. When the docks opened, Christy and the girls moved. I went to the docks from time to time. They only provided the girls with lingerie, no clothes. I guess it kept them from running off."

"I spotted Christy on a second story balcony. She was wearing nothing but a cobalt blue panty set, the garter belt had black lace trim, and she wore real black stockings and high heels ... Well, anyway, she was holding a glass filled with red wine. She and the other girls were chatting and laughing with some merchants who just arrived in port." Meredith looked off into the distance. "We locked eyes for a moment. Then she turned away and hurried back into the brothel."

"Ten years passed before I saw her again, and she was still in the same brothel. It was just about then that Bill began to take over the docks. He made several smart investments and forced out a few scoundrels. I have to say, for a man who used to work for the FBI, he had quite a knack for organized crime. Many of his competitors just disappeared. After he had taken over, he offered Christy a position as a madam in charge of all the brothels. She did well, and he eventually made her responsible for all his brothels in town too. After another 20 years, she ran the whole dock in Bill's place." Meredith put her arm around Rory's shoulder and hugged her. "Even though Christy looks like a girl of 20, she's been through an awful lot. No one should judge her or Bill. He did what was right for the town and the girls."

190

The Seventh Age

"I wasn't judging." Rory gazed up at the overpass for Highway 24 as they passed underneath it. Like the Coliseum in Rome or the pyramids in Egypt, the concrete and steel structure was a monument to a bygone era, the last remembrance of a fallen civilization. "What about you and dad? Did you ever try and help Christy?"

"Your father forbade it." Meredith crossed her arms and tensed her lips. "He blamed her for your predicament. When you needed her the most, she abandoned you. She got out of the gray zone and left you behind."

"She had no idea that I would be trapped in a gray zone," Rory countered.

"I agree, and your father came to accept it … after a long time passed. But she might have been able to persuade you to join us at the resort. Anyway, it was over 30 years before he spoke to her, and even then, it was only about business. He wanted nothing to do with her on a personal level. About seven years ago, they reconciled. They both cried, and so did I. Ever since then things have been good between them." Meredith held up her hand and said, "Driver, stop here."

Chapter 22

A three story, stone-faced building, which had once been a brokerage, rose up before them with pompous self-importance. The guards dismounted and took up stations on the sidewalk and inside the store. When the area was secure, Meredith grabbed Rory's arm and dragged her daughter into the store. Potpourri overwhelmed Rory's sense of smell and nearly drove them back out to the street again. Meredith, however, insisted and forced Rory into the shop.

An eager shop girl approached them. "Hello, my name is Cindy. How may I assist you?" She interlaced her fingers and stared at them as though they would announce that she won a prize.

"Well, this gown is lovely." Meredith held a baby blue and white satin and lace gown up to Rory. "Oh yes, you'll look amazing in this." Rory twitched her nose and looked down at the gown pressed up against her. There was enough silk and lace to make her feel engulfed by femininity. "My daughter will try this on," she said and handed the dress to Cindy.

Rory was contemplating the first dress as Meredith selected three more. "Have her try on these too." She picked up a silver gown, gleaming as though made of liquid metal. It had a sweetheart neckline and a slight train. "Give her this too."

Rory pouted and asked, "Don't you think this is a bit much? I'll never get a chance to wear it."

"Nonsense, the gala can last for weeks, perhaps even a month or more. You will need gowns for every occasion. I love this princess cut bodice. Have her try it on."

Cindy carried the gown into a private fitting room, and Rory reluctantly followed her. Rory glanced over her shoulder and saw three more sales associates and a seamstress with a tape measure draped around her neck.

The Seventh Age

After hanging up the dresses, Cindy said, "Step up on the platform, please."

Rory complied, stretching her pencil skirt to the limit, and moved into the center. "I'm not sure if we need to try on all those gowns. Perhaps I could try on just one," she said. Then three more women entered with piles of skirts, blouses, and lingerie. "Wait … um … whoa," Rory said, arching her back. The associates converged on her like the defensive line of a football team and began stripping off Rory's clothes.

When Rory was down to her lingerie, she said, "I can't try on everything in the store."

Meredith disagreed. She swept through the store like a tornado, selecting most of the inventory. It was the first time in 50 years she had a chance to splurge on her daughter, and she was going to make the most of it. Scores of salesgirls formed a beeline and shuttled clothing to the changing area, throwing the store into chaos.

Each new outfit required its own lingerie, but Rory refused to put on new underwear every time she tried on a dress. They used her measurements for the lingerie. Cindy dutifully scanned Rory in each gown. She downloaded the images into an oracle scroll so that Meredith could peruse the collection.

Six and a half hours passed, and Rory's patience grew thin. A clerk slid Rory's arms into a pair of black satin opera gloves, extending all the way to her shoulders. "We need to take a break. I have to use the restroom," Rory said, moving off the platform.

"Certainly, Daphne and Rose, assist her," Cindy ordered.

"What? No. I've been doing that by myself for years."

"The public restrooms are across the store."

"Across the store?" asked Rory and worriedly surveyed the spacious sales floor.

"There is an employee restroom on the second floor, in the back of the stockroom. You may use it, or I could help you dress and then assist you in the restroom."

Rory was neither able nor willing to have another woman help her to use the toilet. She hurried from the room as fast as the pair of stiletto high heels permitted. Although wandering around in her lingerie seemed like a bad idea, staying and trying on more gowns seemed like a worse idea. She pushed open the swinging doors and made a break for freedom.

Unlike the sales floor, the stockroom was gray, dusty, and bare boned. Wooden crates, bolts of cloth, and display rack filled towering shelves. More cobbler's workstations occupied the far wall. After crossing the warehouse, Rory climbed the stairs, mindful of the stairs each creak and groan. When she arrived at the second level, she rounded the banister. There were several unmarked doors, but except for an open freight elevator, the second level was much like the first.

Fabric remnants and design illustrations lay strewed over a desk located in an office. The lighting was poor and the room plain. Piles of clothing covered scattered desks, and six sewing machines lay idle. She tiptoed across the room, fearing discovery at any moment, wishing she had worn something other than lingerie while going to the restroom. She made her way across the room and saw three doors, none were labeled.

The sound of voices echoed down a narrow hallway. Rory panicked and grabbed the doorknob nearest her. The voices grew louder, and the clatter of high heels on hardwood joined them. Rory stepped through the door and found herself on the sales floor in the lingerie department. When the knob slipped out of her satin-gloved hand, she heard a mechanical click. She spun around and yanked on the knob. Once again, her gloved hands slipped off the knob, and she stumbled backward.

The Seventh Age

"I think this gown is the one, but I want to try it with a different veil ... oh." Christy grabbed a young woman from behind and stopped her from falling. "Are you okay?"

Rory turned around, and her heart skipped a beat. Her hands fell limp, and she gaped at Christy. Her cheeks burned hot, turning as bright red as her hair. Clad in a pristine white wedding gown, Christy looked as radiant as the day they were married. In fact, she was younger and more beautiful.

"Rory, how are you?" Christy brushed a blonde lock from her face and struggled to keep a smile on her face. Her head cocked; she surveyed the young woman clad in a black satin corset, panties, garter straps, black stockings, and high heels – and nothing else. "Um ... are you here trying on clothes?"

"I can't believe this." Rory looked for something cover up with, but there was nothing but bridal lingerie all around her. She held out her gloved hands and said, "I've had nightmares about this."

"You look beautiful," Christy replied.

"That's just what every man wants to hear." Then Rory saw Christy raise an eyebrow and stare at the swells of Rory's breasts. "Right, I'm not a man. I'm a woman. I keep forgetting that."

"There's a mirror right over there," Christy said pointing.

Rory cocked her head and glanced at the mirror. A moment later, her face lit up with comprehension. "Right, just look in a mirror," she said, smoothing her panties over her bottom. The fact that Christy wore a wedding gown penetrated her consciousness.

"I'm getting married," Christy said. Rory felt the blood drain from her face, and her body became weak. Her field of vision narrowed, and Christy's voice became distant, as though at the opposite end of a tunnel. "... His name is Benjamin Cross. He's a dry goods merchant."

195

Rory could not breathe, and her mind went blank. "Congratulations," Rory blurted. Her thoughts spun into a death spiral, and she struggled to contain her emotions. "When is the date?"

"Next June," Christy said. "It is nine months away, but we want time to plan. It's going to be a big wedding. It's his first time."

"Wow, I can't believe it. That's so … amazing." Rory's face grew red and pressure built up within her. "I have to … I just need to go." She hurried around Christy and fled through the lingerie department, tears streaming from her eyes.

"Are you all right?" asked Christy, chasing after her.

Rory held onto a T-rack filled with pink satin bras and turned around; rage and sorrow blazed in her eyes. "No. I'm not all right. The only woman I ever loved is getting married to another man — no, not another man — a man! I'm a woman." She palmed her breasts. "I loved you from the first day we met in the seventh grade. I could never think of anyone but you. When you dated Brad Carson in high school, it crushed me, but at the very least, I could dream that you would be mine one day. Then a miracle happened, and you loved me. Now it is all gone. The day you left … it was like someone reached into my chest and ripped out my heart." She took a deep breath. "Fantastic, you're getting married. Don't send me an invitation, and don't invite me to your housewarming. I'm not happy you're getting married."

Christy crossed her arms and tears flowed down her cheeks. "You're not the only one who suffered. I lost my husband and my baby."

A couple passed through the room and gawked at them. The woman lingered behind, wanting to hear the rest of the conversation, but the man ushered her toward the door. Both women languished in silence until the couple exited the room.

The Seventh Age

"I lost my baby too," Rory said. "Michael's gone, and I'll never father another child." She gazed up at the sparkling glass high above her. "Christy, how did life get so messed up?"

Christy chuckled and said, "You could always have a baby now."

A laugh burst from Rory's lips, and she wiped away her tears. "Like that's going to happen. That would mean having sex with a man."

Christy walked toward Rory and said, "Oh I see, you're a lesbian."

"No. Yes. I don't know." Rory shrugged. "When I was a man, I used to wonder why all women weren't lesbians. Nothing about a man interested me. Now, life is different; this body is different. It has a definite interest in men. That sounds so weird coming out of my mouth." She rolled her eyes and sat down on a nearby by a chair. Christy then sat cattycorner to Rory.

Rory closed her eyes and sighed. "For you, it was 50 years ago, but it has only been only a few short weeks for me. I wake up every day without you, and it hurts. I still remember making love to you. You know I never had sex with anyone else."

"Yes, you did. You had sex with Mary Drew in college." Christy angled her body toward Rory. "It was your first time. We all celebrated."

"Never happened," Rory replied. She winced and clenched her hands in her lap. "She drank too much and passed out. When I kissed her, she vomited all over herself. It was a real mood killer. I washed the vomit off her dress and let her sleep in my bed. When I got up in the morning, everyone was waiting. I had to lie."

"I never knew that," Christy said. "So you were a virgin our first night together."

"Yes," Rory sighed.

"That explains a lot. You were really awful in bed. It worried me." Christy laughed. "You got better though." She thought for a moment. "You got to be a virgin twice. Not many people can claim that."

"I'm still a virgin." Rory laughed and wiped her face with a tissue. She looked at Christy and sighed. "You were so beautiful it took my breath away. I couldn't believe you wanted to marry me."

Christy primped her blonde locks and then crossed her arms. "You need to take a better look at me. I will be 82-years-old this September. My body may seem younger than ever, and I may look like a teenage girl, but I feel old on the inside." Christy crossed her legs and lingered deep in thought. "Ben wants to have a baby. I told him that I can't. I had a rare and permanent reaction to the blue. It is irreversible. It makes me sad – to know that I'll never have life growing inside me again."

"Okay, that's one of the things I still don't understand about women. The idea of a baby growing inside me is weird. I am so not ready for that."

"Well," Christy chuckled and patted Rory's bottom through her black silk panties, "if you keep running around in lingerie, you're going to find out. If you're not on the blue, then babies can and will happen."

Rory closed her eyes and grimaced. "I can still see you walking out the door. I can actually feel my soul ache."

"I can't remember it." Christy shook her head and sighed. "The whole year is gone. I have tried to remember it, but it is a blank. I remember the last Saturday we were together. You and I were working out on the lawn. The next thing I remember, chains bound me to a bed in a strange hotel room. When a man came in, I did not understand what was happening. When Turnbolt came to me, I tried to push him away, but he forced himself on top of me. He …" her words trailed off into silence. Her expression turned poker-faced. "He raped me."

The Seventh Age

"I'm so sorry," Rory said and cringed.

Christy smirked. "It took me seventeen years, but I managed to get even. I lured Captain Turnbolt to my brothel and drugged him. I gave him the serum while he was still asleep and dressed him like one of my girls. Bill shredded the captain's uniform, covered it in blood, as though a daemia got him, and he left it in the mountains where it would be found."

"We dressed Turnbolt up in some lingerie and sold her to the merchant. One of the crew threw her over his shoulder and gave her bottom a smack; that woke her. I remember her looking around in confusion, trying to free her hands, kicking her bound legs, and shouting into her gag. I still remember the rage in her eyes as he carried her into the ship. Her protests were cut off by the slam of the ship's hatch."

"That's disturbing," Rory replied.

"Really, I felt fantastic, as though a burden had rolled off my shoulders. The ship returned a year later. The merchant sold Turnbolt as a slave girl in the Western Islands. I hear a brothel bought her." Christy rose to her feet and brushed away the unpleasant memory. "Why don't I change, and you put on some street clothes? We can go for a walk."

Chapter 23

Christy and Rory exited the store and strolled down the stairs. They turned to the left and walked across the intersection. Horses, carriages, and pedestrians replaced much of automobile traffic in the city, but a few diesel automobiles remained. Some suggested reviving steam-powered trains, and it remained an option. However, the cost of construction and maintenance put the system out of reach.

When Meredith heard whom Rory was with, she gave her daughter a temporary reprieve. However, eight guards, four behind and four ahead, escorted them. The guards cleared a path for the ladies, which caused spectators to gawk at them.

Christy walked at a brisk pace: she always had, even as a girl. But Rory wore a leather pencil skirt, and the elastic material still required short strides. She scurried trying to keep up with Christy. "Do you think we can slow down? This skirt and these heels aren't made for jogging."

"Oh, sure. I'm just used to walking fast down at the docks." Christy smoothed her white sundress and adjusted her pink angora sweater. This combined with sandals made her appear modest, perhaps even innocent. Most working girls dressed modestly when not entertaining men. They relished the chance to wear street clothes, and the last thing they wanted was more male attention.

When Rory caught up to Christy, she noted that Christy was staring at a wedding ring in a jewelry shop window. "Have you and Ben picked one out? I assume you're wearing the submissive ring."

Christy twitched her nose. "We talked about it, but I don't like it. I still prefer a plain wedding ring, but he wants a traditional Asgard wedding, and it is his first time." She crossed her arms and strolled at a leisurely pace. "He wants me to quit my job. I worked fifty years to get where I am. I earn twice his wage. He should quit his job and stay at home. He should wear my ring … but that is not the Asgard way. Once I wear his ring, I will not have any choice. I'll have to do what he says."

"I had no idea the Asgard rings were so controlling," Rory replied. "My mom made them sound great. They protect women from monsters and evil spells. But she may have been trying to convince me to get married."

"Married?" asked Christy.

"Yeah, according to my mom, it's a matter of national importance that I marry and have babies," Rory remarked.

"I understand: nobles are like that. Anyway, how the rings affect wears depends upon the man and the magical enchantments. They can range from benign to draconian. I guess giving that kind of power to someone else frightens me a little. Don't get me wrong; Ben is a good man, but — "

"But you never know what someone is like until you live with them," Rory said. "Sonja Miller had that problem. He was fine when they were dating, but once they were married … well, he tried to control her life. He took away her checkbook and credit cards. Then he gave her an allowance. Oh, and she had to drive straight home from work. When she complained, he slapped her."

"I remember." Christy crossed her arms and gazed at the sidewalk. "Sonja divorced Lou, but very few people do that here. Men will not allow it, and the courts will not approve it. For better or worse, marriage is forever in Asgard."

Rory smelled popcorn and roasting nuts on the breeze; it made her stomach rumble, but she wore a black satin corset; and it compressed her abdomen, which made her stomach too small to accommodate more than a handful of seeds. "Our marriage had problems too. You traveled all over the globe, and I barely got to see you."

"These days my commute is much shorter. I live in the city, and I commute down to the docks," Christy replied.

"Which part of the city?"

"The east side of town: we're renting a house on Pine Avenue, not far from where we used to live," Christy said with a distant look in her eyes. "Ever since the gray zone collapsed in that area, there's been a land rush. Everyone wants a real Earth home. We're going to have to take out a huge mortgage to buy the house."

"Why don't you live in our old home? Your name is still on the deed. I'm not going back there. There are too many memories," Rory said with downcast eyes.

"For me too," Christy said.

They crossed another intersection. Above the three-story buildings, they saw the gray zone, which enveloped the Oak Park Shopping Mall. The shopping mall became somewhat of a legend. Stories about the vast riches contained within grew larger with each passing year. Children imagined piles of gold and silver lying about; their parents imagined royal gowns and lavish furnishing worthy of a king.

The din of conflicting music flowing out of taverns, drunken revelers wandering about the street, scantily clad women in lingerie calling out to pedestrians from second floor balconies, carnival hucksters bellowing the name and virtues of their snake oil, casino signs flashing, criminal predators hunting, constables accepting bribes, dogs barking, the insane laughing, drunks vomiting, urine-reeking, death stalking, they reached the red light district.

Christy strolled as though in the park, the sights and sounds relaxing her. Every so often she waved at a prostitute on a second-floor balcony. Rory, on the other hand, looked about with anxious eyes, glad for the guards. She heard sordid stories about the West Glenn Shopping District. Once a slice of Americana, now it was the home for every vice one could imagine and a few beyond imagining. There were so many sights and sounds that they dizzied her.

The Mayfair Casino across the street attracted Rory's attention. Whistles, beeps, and sirens escaped the yawning mouth of the club. Girls clad in costumes worthy of a Las Vegas showgirl languished inside tall brass cages, suspended overhead, as though they were canaries. "What's going on with those girls?" asked Rory.

"Hmm ... oh, they are prizes to lure in the suckers," Christy remarked as if discussing the weather. "It's the standard pitch. 'Gamble with us, and you can win a slave girl.' Of course, few ever do. Most people lose all their money."

"I can't imagine why a girl would do such a thing, sell herself as a slave," Rory said.

"They usually don't. Sailors, miners, and travelers pile into the casinos and lose all their money; and then they gamble on credit – and lose. When they can't pay the bill, the casino owners seize their assets. It could be their wives or themselves, and in many cases, it is both. After transforming the males to females, they make them work in the casino with paying a wage. If a girl tries to escape, they give her away as a prize. It's all perfectly legal."

It did not sound legal or moral to Rory. "If this was Earth, they would all be arrested. I don't know why they put up with it."

"Eden doesn't have a prison population. Crime is very low. In fact, if you were to set your purse down on the sidewalk, no one would pick it up or even look at it. Children can play without fear of child molesters, and there are no drive-by shootings. Most of the social elite see these places as a necessary purge for society." Christy paused in thought and said, "I suppose I do too. People are free to do as they wish. Who are we to judge?"

Rory wanted to argue the point, but she recalled Christy's biography. After 50 years at the docks, anyone would be jaded, and Christy did have some good points. "It's just hard to see such human tragedy. At least the children are safe."

"To a point," Christy replied. "Once they reach their Ascension Day, at 19, they can do as they wish. I have seen young people reach their nineteenth birthday, go straight to a casino, and lose their freedom. Most others stay clear; its survival of the fittest."

Rory doubted Christy would have such a cavalier attitude if their son Michael was still alive, but she remained silent again. She had just reconciled with Christy; she did not want to start a new conflict. Yet she felt the need to say something. "I don't think the Christy of 50 years ago would agree to any of this."

Christy paused and reflected on the comment. "I suppose you're right. Suffering has a way of changing people."

Rory and Christy reached the outskirts of the red-light district and stood on the curb across the street. The pair looked up in unison. Grey fog boiled and swirled as if stirred by some unseen winds. These clouds flowed around the mall, which turned it into an ethereal specter, a ghost of bygone days.

Christy sighed if only she could go back to those days, to be the woman she once was. Her gaze fell to the cracked pavement, and the wheels of a wagon rolled past her. She recalled her life with Rory, and the son ripped from her arms. How she wished she could go back to just one of those days and spend it with her family.

"We should be getting back," Meredith said. The footman opened the carriage door, and Rory climbed into the wagon. The whip snapped above the horses head, and the carriage lurched. As they rolled away, Rory spun around in her seat and gazed back at Christy. They locked eyes

The Seventh Age

for a moment, and then Christy returned to the red light district – the only life she now knew.

Chapter 24

A week passed, and it was time for Walter to present Rory to the royal court. A vintage Mercedes-Benz waited in the carport, and Walter sat behind the wheel. He stared straight ahead, not acknowledging Rory as she exited the lodge. However, all other heads turned toward her. She looked like a princess in a shimmering emerald green gown. A footman held open the passenger side door and waited for her. Rory performed a maneuver that so many women take for granted. She sat down, smoothed her dress, swung her legs into the car, and held her clutch bag in her lap. She cocked her head and asked, "I thought cars blew up?"

"Gasoline-powered automobiles explode 78% of the time, but diesel automobiles are fine 80% of the time; the other 19% they burn, and 1% of the time they vaporize, immolating the passengers. There is no need to worry though. This car is diesel, and the roads we will be traveling are clear." Walter started the car, the engine offering a quiet whisper. They swept through the resort with quiet grace, and a tap of the accelerator shoved Rory into the seat. They swept down the road and then passed through the gate. Walter turned right onto Highway 191 and headed toward downtown.

The vintage car swept along the road without a sound, only adding to the tension, the silence becoming deafening. Walter stared straight ahead, refusing even to look at his daughter, and every so often he released a heavy sigh. Rory wanted to say something, but her mind was blank, so she languished in silence, watching the scenery pass.

The top of Rory's head began to itch. She wished that she refused to wear the tiara; it struck her as being way too much. While it kept her thick locks in place, it dug into her scalp. She wanted to rip it off and march away. She brooded in anger as they neared the edge of town.

A brick building passed by on their right, Mason's Market, and then Dawson's Laundry passed on their left. They rushed past an array of two-story red brick buildings and then crossed a bridge; downtown Gleason surrounded them on every side: men and women pausing from their labor as if something important was happening. As they circled around Center Park, Rory saw yet another auction, and leaning over, she looked past her father.

"Slave sales are a primary source of revenue. Debtors and lawbreakers are imported from all the surrounding kingdoms. Most of the major lot sales take place down at the ports. That way they can be shipped all around Asgard," Walter said with cold indifference. Perceiving his daughter's revulsion, he added, "You need to hide your true feelings. The people of Asgard don't view slavery as we do."

"Monica told me that these lands used to be free," Rory said and crossed her arms.

Walter made a right turn on Pearce Boulevard. "That's true from what I understand. A lot of the old timers tell me things used to be very different. It's like someone, or something has been slowly eroding Asgard's freedoms. Anyway, we can't change all of that. We need to survive."

Rory pouted and stared at her knee. Survival was not enough; she needed more, and yet it was all beyond her ability to reform. She watched the town pass her by and recalled fragments of her former life. The place of their first date, the pizza parlor, made Rory smile. After they had passed over the steel trestle bridge, they traveled through West Gleason. Rory spotted the burned out hulk of a building. It was the old armory.

"That's where freedom died." Walter rubbed his face. "The US Army Reserves used the old armory as their headquarters. They held off the Salvia Guard for a month, but it was no use – there was no help coming. Eventually, they ran out of ammunition, and the Saliva Guard used trebuchets to lob energized globes. The globes exploded with blue flame; we could see the building burning for miles – no one survived."

"The king left the ruins as a lesson to all who would revolt. Every year they hold a parade. It passes through town and ends at the ruins, and then they hold a victory celebration: everyone has to participate."

They passed through the shopping district and took the on-ramp for US Highway 24. Once on the highway, Rory had a prime view of Western Gleason and the West Glenn Shopping District. From the highway, she could see the entire district stretched out before them. 50 years washed away the cosmopolitan community like a sandcastle on the beach, and what took its place was a stranger to Rory: worn masonry structures, wooden buildings, and an endless street bazaar, stretching out as far as the eye could see.

Walter lowered his window a bit and then clenched a cigar between his lips. After lighting it, he said, "This is one of the busiest cities west of Midway City, in Central Asgard, and it's one of the most treacherous; anything can be had for a price, and I mean anything. It's a dangerous place: every day hundreds of people go missing. 'Caveat Emptor' applies to all purchases. The smart merchant or traveler hires armed guards to see them safely around the city."

"Mom and I had a guard when we went shopping," Rory commented.

"Yes ... well, your mother knows of the many dangers in Gleason these days. If you get in trouble, you can forget about the police; they only take care of the king's business or if you have the cash to pay them."

"You can buy anything?" asked Rory.

"Slaves, drugs, magical potions, arms, assassination, and armor – you can get anything. There are more brothels, casinos, and saloons than I can count. I wrote up a law banning child prostitution, and the king signed it, but it is never enforced unless the violator is someone out of political favor." Walter took a long draft of his cigar and jetted the plume out the window. "I've had 50 years of trying to hold back the darkness, and I'm sick of it. Sometimes I feel like I'm another species; nobody else sees things the way I do. I enjoy a quiet life of family and spirituality. There are too many drunks if you ask me."

Rory's eyes were sharper than most, and she searched the shopping district for something familiar. Her gaze wandered to the gray cloud that enveloped the shopping mall. Will the gray zone ever lift from the mall?"

"What?" Walter glanced over her left shoulder. "No one knows when the gray zone will lift from the Oak Park Shopping Mall, or if it will ever lift. Sometimes I think the people frozen in time inside the mall are better off. At least they don't have to see what Gleason became."

They soon rushed along at 60 mph, which seemed surreal compared to the leisurely pace of the city roads. For some strange reason, it made her feel safe, as though they could keep on going, arriving back in the Kansas. The harsh truth, however, towered over the land to her right and left. The proud Wolf's Maw Mountains, white capped and majestic, assured her that she lived in Asgard, extinguishing her fantasy. One mountain reminded her of Mount Fuji, standing like a mighty sentinel directly in their path, and flanking it on either side were its fellow Titans. Even if one defeated these mountains, others would rise up to take their place. They were truly stranded on Eden.

Walter slipped a CD into the player and played Vivaldi's "Four Seasons." He recognized only two forms of music, classical and Jazz. All other forms were crude, bastard children and without merit. He let the dulcet melody wash over him and eased his mind. When she tried to engage him in small talk, he retorted, "I'm trying to listen to the music."

Rory was far less enthralled, and she crossed her arms, her right foot beginning to bounce. Anger exploded out of her saying, "I never asked to become a girl, and I sure as hell don't deserve your contempt. If you're so unhappy with me, you can drop me off anywhere." Walter ignored her and continued listening to his music.

They raced past lodgepole pines, but they were far larger than Rory imagined possible. On the other side of the car, she saw parallel rows of corn. Their green stalks stretched up toward the warm sun, worthy of a tropical rainforest. "We get two harvests a year," Walter said. "For some crops, we get three. No, it doesn't belong to me: I manage it for the King. If I fall out of favor, he will give it to someone else."

"I thought the Benhaus family owned it?" asked Rory.

"They did. The petition for lesser noble status and obtained it. Everything was well enough for them until they hosted a private meeting for concerned citizens. They wanted to petition the royal court for land reforms. Spies reported it to the king, and he found them guilty of sedition. The court executed Herb, and it threw Judith out of her house during the middle of winter. The king barred from giving her shelter or aid. We had to watch as she starved and freeze to death."

"What about their children, Peter and Stacy?"

"Stacy works for Bill down at the docks in one of the many brothels. Peter joined the Black Dragon Guild and never returned. I can't say I blame him. I would leave if I could." He paused and then added, "Bill took a real chance helping them. Without him, they would have died." Bill took more of a chance than Walter knew: he saved Judith and smuggled her out of Gleason on a cargo ship bound for Solva.

"So no Christmas cards for the Benhaus'?" Rory quipped.

"The king found Christmas wasteful and heretical. He decreed that all loyal citizens participate in the true state religion. They worship Antha, goddess of the mountains; Salvia religion is banal, full of platitudes and empty philosophy. We pretend to be inspired by it, and we participate in the mandated festivals."

"King Leopold is a monster," Rory said.

"Yes, and a dangerous one," Walter said, and his face returned to stone a moment later. "You have to imagine yourself in Berlin 1938, and you have been summoned to meet Hitler. Be paranoid, because everyone is out to get you."

Chapter 25

The fertile green valley dwindled to crusted earth and then gave way to rock, the boulders starting small but growing larger by the minute, growing to the size of houses, forming a maze through the craggy hills. Likewise, the smooth highway soon gave way to paving stones, the rough road circling around the base of the mountain, weaving across the mountain's face, and then disappearing from sight. Several stone towers, sheer walls, and armed guards ensured that only those with permits traveled to the castle.

The city of Fairview lay at the northern foot of the mountain, a community that sprawled through the twisted plateau, constructed on the edge of the fertile green valley. The builders used fieldstones to construct the walls, dark timbers for framing, tan stucco to fill the gaps, and slate to cover the roofs. Chimneys belched out suffocating black soot, blanketing the town in a murky haze, irritating the lungs and watering the eyes.

The commercial district lay on the in the center of town. Men and women were jammed into a three-block district selling their wares: providing alcoholic concoctions, women carrying bolts of cloths, priests wafting incense, girls praying at shrines for a price, and children stealing coin purses. Men operated street booths – selling tableware, furniture, glass wear, hats, shoes, linens, and other household items. Tradesman sold specialized weapons, such as swords, knives, armor, archery, and such the like. Sex workers roaming the street and a bazaar of greed bathed one in a cacophony and dizzied the senses. But the most profitable trade took place behind closed doors: wizards enhanced items with magical power — talismans, potions, staffs, weapons, and even jewelry could be imbued with magic.

A streetwalker strutted along the avenue and propositioned a man. Almost out of sight but with quick access, a pimp observed his girls, which both assured prompt payment and protected his workers. When she spotted a teenage girl sitting on the railing of a second-floor balcony, Rory moved to the edge of her seat. The girl raised a wine glass to her lips, and she brushed aside her wheat blonde locks, exposing a slave choker necklace, leaving little doubt as to her profession; and she was not alone – most of the girls appeared far too young to be prostitutes. It was wrong; it was cruel; it was life.

Rory kept her window raised and the door locked. The car served as a protecting vessel to pass through the chaos about her, a ship sailing troubled waters. They passed a boy and a girl, sitting on the ground, their faces smudged and their clothing dirty. Their mother hurried out a door and ushered them into the house, the front door slamming shut a moment later.

They cruised by a man in rags. He lay upon the side of the road with his face down in the sewer drain. When she took a closer look at him, she realized that he was dead. No one even took the time to bury him.

Inns and taverns stretched out as far as the eye could see. Whether highborn or lowborn, anything was available for a price, but most of the businesses offered professional services – lawyers provided legal counsel, specializing in petitions submitted to the royal court. Many desperate people sought to escape the legal ruin that threatened their lives.

Rory felt misplaced relief when they exited the town and arrived at the foot of the mountains. A black gate and two watchtowers blocked their path, armed guards moving toward them. Walter slowed and approached the gate, lowering his window; when he stopped, the guard captain asked, "Who is your guest, Mr. Vakhal?"

"My daughter, Rory Vakhal, and I are here for the Debutant Ball." He surveyed the man with an icy stare. "I'm sure the king would prefer us to be on time, and please refer to me as Viceroy Vakhal."

"Yes, Viceroy Vakhal. I meant no offense." He stepped aside and waved to the other men. "Open the gates. Let them pass" The guards heaved open the heavy black gate. "Sorry for the delay."

Walter raised the window, leaving the man's plea for forgiveness
unanswered, and cruised forward, ignoring the guard's salutes. As a last
act of mercy, he offered them an idle wave. Rory turned in the seat and
looked over her shoulder. Watching the gate close, she felt
claustrophobic and trapped.

The roads, if one could call them that, skirted through many mountains
and were always under repair. Teams of men labored year round through
ice, sleet, and snow, using chisels, hammers, and brute force to keep the
roads open – the work weathered the men like the surrounding
mountains, but men, unlike stone, perished under the brutal conditions.

"You see that one over there?" asked Walter.

"The one with the scraggly beard?" asked Rory.

"No. The balding man, with the craggy face," Walter replied. "He's
wearing the gray and blue rags."

"Yes," said Rory. "I see him."

"He used to be a royal steward, but then he made a joke about the king.
It seemed harmless enough to me at the time, but I knew better than to
laugh. The judge sentenced him to 10 years at hard labor. The man next
to him laughed at the joke."

As they cruised by, Rory observed the men at work. She smiled at first. It
had to a joke, but her father's expression assured her that he was deadly
serious. "Every action, every word will be scrutinized." When they
rounded three swaybacks, the guards opened the next gate at their
approach, and Walter continued Rory's education. "… If asked for an
opinion, defer; if cornered, default to vague flattery; if pressed, find me,
but say nothing. Never offer more information than what is requested,
and expect chauvinism. Women are beautiful decorations whose sole
existence is to bear children and keep one's home. Beautiful women are a
commodity to be bought and sold; wealthy women bring prosperity to

their husbands, and marriage to a noble woman is the key to power: you are all three. Expect men to compete for you, but never believe anyone's profession of love. These people don't know the meaning of the word."

"They will test you to see if you acknowledge male superiority. It was decreed by edict, so to disagree with it is to commit treason. You are a woman and therefore subservient unless the king declares you to be a man, which he has not. I know you are a redhead, but pretend to be a dumb blonde."

"I wish I had more time to coach you, but your awakening came at an unfortunate time. The King's Gala is tonight; all young women of social standing are required to attend. We dare not miss it."

Rory said, "I feel like a Christmas present, all wrapped in satin and lace."

"In a way you are, the king will decide who you will marry tonight," Walter said.

"Marry?" she blurted. "I don't want to get married. I'm not gay."

"Gay?" asked Walter and eyed Rory. "You're a woman: women marry men. The daughters of officials marry whomever the king requires. I am a wealthy man and Viceroy; that makes you choice property. When they see how beautiful you are, you will be every man's desire and a prime prospect of a wife."

"I don't want to marry a man." Rage swelled up within Rory again. "I think I'm a lesbian. In fact, I'm sure of it."

"It doesn't matter. Homosexual men marry women in Salvia – they maintain their male lovers with discretion. You can do the same. Straight men will want to have sex more often, but they will also have many concubines. The more you get for him, the less you will have to share his bed."

"So let me get this straight. I might marry a gay man and have a baby, all the while he is going to run around with the boys?"

"It's possible," Walter replied. "It is more likely that you will marry a heterosexual man. I don't wish to be crude, but they don't expect you to be a virgin for the wedding day. If you get pregnant, then they will know that you are fertile and capable of bearing an heir."

"I am not getting pregnant to prove I'm 'fertile.' I'm not having sex with a man. I'll play this game and pretend to go along with it. But I am not getting married."

"Then you condemn all three of us. The court will sell you as a slave. Your mother and the court will executed us if we are lucky. I think I have enough friends to see to that. A quick death by the ax is best."

"You're being dramatic," Rory snapped.

"No. I am not. If you are serious, I will send word to your mother. I supplied her with a vial of cyanide; it is fast and efficient. The castle has messengers. I will send a message with a code word. She will be dead before they can get their hands on her. I won't have that luxury."

"I cannot believe this. This is impossible. A few weeks ago I was a married man." She frowned and crossed her arms. "Fine, I'll marry someone. But make sure he's gay, I don't want to have sex with him any more than necessary."

"I can work with that. The parents of such sons are eager to obtain obliging women. Considering our status, it would work out well. You would still have to bear them an heir."

"Just perfect," she huffed. "Okay, I'll have a baby, but only one. It better be a boy."

"We can only hope," Walter replied.

The Seventh Age

One road intersected with another, and they crossed a bridge that spanned a high gorge. When they passed over it, Rory looked down over the side and saw a river, appearing like a black thread, which weaved through a deep gorge – vertigo made her head swim, and gravity wooed her to destruction. She fixed her gaze on the road, ignoring the looming doom to her right, and she observed the curved face of the sheer wall, still bearing the scars of chisel and hammers, as they passed around it. They traveled around the side of another mountain and saw more impediments: iron gates, towers, and more guards than she could count.

The Mercedes-Benz crept up to the guard post, and Rory sank low in the seat, the smooth leather and luxurious interior comforting her. After a brief exchange, the guard waved Walter through the next of several barriers ahead of them – each barrier making her feel a little more trapped and suffocated.

The air grew thin, forcing her to take deep breaths, and they passed up into a cloud, everything turning white, allowing them to see only a precious few meters of the road ahead. Rory leaned to her right and gazed at the sharp road edge, knowing that veiled destruction was a misstep away. The clouds came to an abrupt halt, and they broke through to crystal-clear skies. Far to her right, she saw the last vestiges of the green valley surrounded by jagged rock spires.

An epiphany emerged in Rory's consciousness: Bill was trying to protect her. He knew about all the chaos: the arrests, the secret police, the tyrannical government, and the human rights violations. If she had only listened to him, she might have escaped on a ship, sailing away to freedom. That path was forever lost; she was destined for whatever fate lay at the end of the rough mountain road.

Chapter 26

The sun sank behind the western mountains, long shadows stretched across the jagged peaks, countless sundials marking the end of the day, dusk stealing away the warmth. The castle's spires jabbed into the sky like needles, its gray walls, gates, and battlements blending into the aged, craggy face of Spire Mountain. The cold edifice loomed like a prison, devoid of beauty or warmth. She wondered if her fate would be a life sentence behind cold stonewalls and was her last view of the outside world.

The monolith grew ever larger, foreboding and cruel. Sentries patrolled its towering curtain walls, and a crisp northern wind snapped the pennants like the crack of a whip, each one bearing white flowers and a sword, placed on a coat of arms and then set on an azure field.

The car crept toward the wooden drawbridge, as though fearful of an attack by some mountain beast. Guards clad in silver armor and blue uniforms blocked their path, the elite Salvia Guard, loyal to the king and his crushing right hand. The Captain stood tall and strong, his chin raised, eyes narrowed, fixed in a contemplative gaze.

"Stay in the car," Walter said as he opened the door. The driver's side door closed before she could reply. Men gathered around the car until she could see nothing but armor and swords. She held her breath, certain the guards would arrest them and thrown them into a dank dungeon. The trunk popped open, and the men moved to the rear of the car. Looking in the review mirror, she saw her father handing out bottles of whiskey and wooden boxes. The guards laughed and joked with one another as they returned to the tower gate. The captain signaled the keeper, and the portcullis began to rise into the structure.

The door opened, and Walter took a seat. "I make a regular practice of giving gifts to the castle guard. I want them glad to see me. They looked the other way on many occasions, hiding some noble's indiscretion. I try to clean up the messes before the king hears about them, but when I can't, people die."

They cruised over the thick planks, each rattle and groan sending a shiver through Rory. She slid forward and looked out the windshield, and upon seeing the yawning ravine beneath the drawbridge, she was sure that the bridge would give way; and after several minutes of falling and screaming, they would hit bottom, exploding into a ball of flames.

Rory sighed after she and her father passed through the outer gate; the last step in an unnerving trip was complete. They crossed a short span and entered through the inner gate. Across an expansive courtyard, Rory saw classic cars, worthy of an automobile museum, parked in neat rows. Walter cruised through toward the main reception hall and passed underneath a red awning, red carpet covering a flight of stairs and flowing into the entryway. Walter stopped, and a valet rushed to take charge of the vehicle.

Getting out of the car was almost as complicated as getting into it. Rory swung out her legs, keeping them together, doubled over, adjusting her balance, rose to her feet, and smoothed her emerald gown. She caught one of the young men leering at her chest. His interest was so intent that he never noticed her looking back at him. A chilly gust urged her to enter the unwelcoming building, and as they approached, a pair of guards opened heavy wooden doors, heat washing over them, dispelling the chilled evening air.

A pair of grand staircases curved around the side of the foyer and rose up to a walkway that skirted the perimeter. Beyond a row of great arches, Rory saw a gilded hall, bright white walls supporting a gold and silver adorned ceiling; the stunning hall took her breath away, and she crossed the inlaid marble floor like a child lost in heaven, overwhelmed by the grandeur of it all. Paintings two stories tall depicted legendary battles, long faded from living memory but eternally memorialized. The most striking element was a statue – a hero stood upon a pedestal, clutching a sword in his right and a shield in his left, the shield bearing the Salvia crest. He focused on an invisible horizon, a menacing expression upon his face.

"I bet he's the head valet and the last customer didn't give him a tip," quipped Rory.

Anger and fear flashed in Walter's eyes. "Remember what I said. No jokes. If the king heard that, we would both be thrown into prison."

They passed through one of the arches and found themselves in the rectangular reception hall. Windows, at least two stories tall, lined the eastern and western walls. Scores of petitioners milled about the hall; some were dress in the fashionable garb of the court, but others wore traditional attire. When they spotted Walter, they mobbed him.

"Mr. Vakhal, can you look at my proposal," asked a Robert Anson, manager of the Healing Herb Pharmacy. "If we add recreational products to our shelves, we can double our revenue."

"Recreational products" was a euphemism for narcotics.

Walter raised an eyebrow and said, "I will consider it."

"Thank you, sir," Robert replied. At hearing Robert's success, the others spoke at the same time. They shouted in a growing frenzy and fought for him to hear them. They passed through the chaos, and Walter said, "Arrange for an interview with my assistant, Hayley. I will be meeting with petitioners for the next few days. You need to control yourselves – the king will not tolerate this commotion." This warning deflated the crowd and caused an uneasy silence. "As always, see my secretary in the administrative building for an appointment. She will hear your request and then advise me. Impress her."

Many people fled the reception hall, but a few remained. "Please," begged a woman. "They've taken my daughter. She never hurt anyone. She is loyal to the king. Why did they take her?"

The Seventh Age

The nobles harvested attractive young women like agricultural crops. After training as household slaves, the nobles shipped the girl to foreign markets. The more attractive the girl, the better the price the owner received. They presented a few of the women to other nobles as gifts. His unsympathetic eyes gazed down at her. "Your daughter now serves the state. You should feel honored."

"Honored?" she echoed. "She is my only child, and my husband died two years ago. What will I do now? It took both of our incomes to pay for our home."

Walter looked away and kept walking. Rory's eyes welled up with tears. She watched the woman stare at the floor and languish in sorrow. She then turned and walked away.

A pair of guards snapped to attention. They each wore a gleaming silver cuirass, helmet, and pantaloons. The men clutched a halberd in their right hands, and they wore a sword around their waists. Rory felt like she was passing back into the eighteenth century. After they had passed, the men resumed their at ease stance.

When they were well away from the guards, Walter said, "That grieving mother is a member of the secret police. I have seen her deceive and arrest entire families. Remember, danger lurks in the hearts of everyone you meet."

They passed through an arched hallway toward a menacing door, which was guarded by a pair of sentries, and at their approach, the guards snapped to attention; and a page hurriedly opened the door. Brilliant white light flooded the hallway, which was so vibrant that it hurt Rory's eyes.

They emerged from the corridor and stood between brown marble pillars, a walkway extended to their right and left, skirting the room; and a grand staircase led down to the central court where an expansive white marble floor, inlaid with a striking brown marble pattern, stretched out before them, casting an ethereal glow upon the entire hall.

221

Scott Marcy

Walter drew an invitation from his jacket pocket and handed it to the attendant at the head of the stairs. The man opened the invitation and read the gold embossed lettering. After he had a quiet exchange with Walter, he declared, "The Honorable Viceroy and Defender of the Realm Walter Vakhal and his daughter Miss Rory Anne Vakhal."

Walter held out his right elbow. Rory glanced at it and then at Walter. It was a clear signal for her to take it. She repressed her resentment and clasped his arm. The entire assembly paused from their conversations to watch them descend the stairs. As they passed through a gauntlet of spectators, Rory felt like a prized panda bear that just arrived at the zoo.

Rory noticed something peculiar. Many of the women wore rings; some were stainless steel; others were silver, and a few were gold, one having platinum inlay. Rory sensed men and women looking at her, but they fixed their gaze on her left hand; out of instinct, she covered it with her right hand, shielding it from their lecherous gaze.

Anticipating her question, Walter said, "Married women magical wedding rings. Your mother refuses to wear one … which causes me no end of difficulties."

The crowd parted and bowed. King Leopold passed through the midst of them like a god visiting mere mortals. He wore a military uniform, or his interpretation of it: a golden jacket – festooned with medals and rope braid looped around his shoulders – black trousers, black boots, white gloves, and a golden ceremonial sword hung from his left hip. He moved with his chin held high, looking down his equine nose at the assembled guests. At the wave of his hand, the guests arose from their prone position.

The king stood before Walter with his right fist on his hip, as if posing for a portrait. Walter bowed. *If dad bowed, should I bow? He said something about it being required. Women don't bow. Do they? No. They curtsy. Are they kidding? I have to curtsy? This is ridiculous. I guess I have to do it.* Rory curtsied, which greatly embarrassed her, and only when the king waved his hand

222

did Walter and Rory arise. Walter said, "Thank you for inviting us to this wonderful gala. It is the highlight of the season."

"You are quite welcome," King Leopold said. "And this lovely creature must be your daughter."

The King lifted Rory's chin as if inspecting some work of art. His face reflected a grudging admiration. "Her eyes gleam like emeralds. She is a beauty that could inspire a thousand artists and make ten thousand poets dream. She is perfection."

The king gestured with a limp wrist. "This is my son Gregory. He will be your escort this evening." Gregory was handsome and tall, what one expected of a prince. Like his father, he wore a uniform: a red jacket festooned medals, a silver ceremonial sword, and black trousers. Walter released his daughter's arm; Gregory moved to her side, and taking her arm, he led her through a long procession.

Leopold drew close to Walter's side. When a waiter passed by, he picked up a glass of champagne. He took a sip and said, "Your daughter's portrait doesn't do her justice; she is so beautiful. I can see why you kept her hidden."

"She was trapped in a gray zone your majesty," Walter said. "As soon as she was freed, I sent word to the court."

"Yes of course," Leopold replied, "as any loyal citizen would. We should speak in private. Let's retire to my study."

"Of course, your majesty," Walter replied.

Rory's heart sank when she saw her father leave; a moment later fear seized control, leaving her feeling like a small child abandoned in a crowd. Gregory took her by the hand and led her into a magnificent ballroom, reminding her of a glass cathedral. Lead crystals formed a high dome ceiling, having no visible means of support, and a white marble with gold inlay floor bid them to dance upon it; and a crystal chandelier cast a wondrous rainbow of light upon them; and a host of people lingered around the peripheral, gazing down upon them for a high walkway that skirted the room, eager to see the royal couple dance.

When they reached the center of the hall, the prince took her by the hand and placed his other hand on her side; he looked upon her with a steadfast gaze and waited, and when the orchestra began to play a symphony, he started off slow and then moved faster, whirling around the room with her in his arms.

Rory worried at first, but she recognized the three-step beat. Of course, women have to perform the same dance steps as men — backward. But the dance felt natural and flowing, and they swept around the ballroom as if floating on a cloud. Others emerged from the crowd and joined them. Soon the dancers circled the room as if caught up in a great current. She flowed around and around, losing herself in the revelry.

When the music stopped, the prince led her to the side of the hall. Other women rushed up to him and barged in between them. Rory was all too glad for the interference. She used the opportunity to slip away and disappear into the crowd. Servers carried silver trays filled with champagne and hors d'oeuvres. She took two glasses and gulped down both of them.

If the prince danced with her, other men would also wish to, and she hoped to avoid that at all costs, something about it reminded her of sex, which she profoundly wished to avoid with a man. If she found a hiding place, she might be able to avoid the many amorous suitors. She passed through the crowd and hurried up the carpeted stairs to the upper walkway. It was an upward battle and against the flow of traffic. When she reached the top of the stairs, she saw crystal French doors that led out to a garden balcony.

A few couples strolled about and enjoyed the warm night air. Torches lit up walkways and cast a gentle glow upon the well-kept garden. She hurried down the steps and entered a garden, fleeing unseen pursuers, flying from one path to another. She passed over a footbridge that spanned a gentle creek.

A white gazebo lay in the center of the garden, covered with white and pink roses. She hiked up her dress and hurried up the steps, and standing in the center, she lingered in the darkness.

"Hello," said a male voice. Rory yelped and spun around. A man emerged from the shadows. "I'm sorry. I did not mean to startle you. I was just enjoying the night air."

"You sound Spanish," she replied.

"I am Antonio De Madera. I am from New Spain. My family resides on the island of Madera in the south. Perhaps you have heard of it?" asked Antonio.

"The only Spain I know of is the old one; I mean regular Spain." When he took a step toward her, she stepped backward. "Just plain Spain … it's the one that exists back on Earth."

"Spain," he said with some disbelief. "My ancestors were swept through a terrible storm one night. Lightning flashed all around them, and their ship rode over great waves the size of mountains. They passed through a brilliant white ball of light, a winking gate, and a moment later it vanished. They found themselves in calm seas, and the sun was high in the sky. They searched for Spain but never found it, and after a time, they founded my homeland, New Spain. But you say you know of Spain. This is remarkable."

"I guess," she replied. "I went there once when I was in college, but I live in Gleason. It is the valley to the west. It was in the United Stated, across the Atlantic Ocean from Spain." He kept walking toward her, and she kept backing away from him. "We went as a part of cross-cultural studies. The food was nice, and I enjoyed the flamingo dancing." Her back bumped into one of the roof supports and brought her to a halt. Antonia stood so close to her she could feel his hot breath on her skin.

"What a wondrous journey. I came here on a mission of good will and commerce. There are certain resources which we wish to acquire." He reached out and picked a rose. He held it to his nose and drank in its aroma. "A rose smells as sweet no matter in which world it grows."

"Right," she said. "I'm glad you like the flowers. Maybe you could take a step back."

He placed his left hand upon the pillar and leaned in close. "Do I make you uncomfortable? I do not wish to."

"There you are," said Prince Gregory. "I see you've met the Spanish Ambassador. He has become well acquainted with the ladies of the royal court."

"You insult me, sir," Antonio replied.

"Such was not my intent. I was merely pointing out that you must appreciate the female form since you have seen so many naked women. You must be an expert on the female anatomy, like a gynecologist," the prince replied.

"If you were not of royal blood, I would demand satisfaction," Antonio replied.

"I will have my man fetch sabers. We can settle this matter tonight," the prince retorted.

"Your grace, the ambassador has been granted protection by the King of Asgard." The elder man, Thomas, stood by Prince Gregory's left side. "It would be an act of war to harm him."

"I see. Once again, you hide behind your mother's skirts. You are nothing but an errant child pretending to be a man," the prince replied.

"Don't let my family's title dissuade you. I am quite capable of dealing with you." The men moved between the two combatants and separated them. Rory slipped out the other side of the gazebo and bumped into her father and the king.

"What's all this then?" asked the king.

"Just some high spirits, your Majesty. The prince and Ambassador De Madera were in dispute over the affections of the young lady," Thomas said. "I informed them that a duel was quite out of the question."

"Yes. It is most certainly out of the question. Cooler heads must prevail. Let us return to the ball and set our differences aside," the King said.

Antonio bowed and said, "Of course, as your Majesty wishes." He then handed the rose to Rory. "Until later, my lady," he said and passed through the crowd.

Before Walter could speak, the prince put his right arm around Rory's side and rested his hand on her hip. "By your leave, I will escort the lady back to the ballroom."

"Yes. That will be all right," King Leopold said.

Rory looked to her father for help as the prince led her away. As they passed over the bridge, the prince's hand slid down to the small of her back. When it slipped over the swell of her bottom, she arched her back and scurried forward. He gave her bottom a squeeze and led her toward the bright lights of the ballroom.

"The prince seems quite enamored with your daughter. She is most striking, a flower that stands out above her peers. Is she betrothed?" asked the king.

"Her hand is available," Walter replied. "Before her transformation, she was married to a woman though."

"Oh yes, I remember you telling me the story. After changing from man to maid, she fell into a deep sleep in a gray zone. The story has a mythical

227

air about it. Of course, her change in gender annulled the marriage. A woman can only be married to a man in my kingdom."

The king crossed his arms and raised his chin. "I had thought to have him marry Princess Luna of Pyrolace. Her father controls much of the shipping routes to the south. Before the appearance of the valley, we relied upon Pyrolace for most of our food stores. Now the alliance is unnecessary and perhaps redundant. Our minerals pass through Hope Lake and then out to sea. But the question remains what to do with her."

"Yes, your majesty," Walter replied. Walter held his breath and waited. If it was unfavorable, he worked out a signal with a court page. He would drop his handkerchief, and the page would then dispatch a messenger. Meredith would receive a sealed message the next day, and in it was a code word. If she read it, then she would use the poison. Walter would have to die as the king decided.

Walter stiffened and braced himself. He clutched the white handkerchief in his right trouser pocket. Out of the corner of his eye, he watched on the page stationed on the veranda next to the ballroom.

"If I were to take your daughter as my ward, she would have royal standing." The King squinted and looked off into the distance. "She could then marry someone of royal personage, such as my son."

———

The people of Asgard completed the Hargal Wall in 1000 CE, supposedly heralding a new era of human achievement, but what ensued were bloody wars that raged all over the Wolf's Head Peninsula. One by one, each kingdom joined the combat, spreading like a contagion; kingdoms rose up overnight, only to topple the next day. Royal families, aristocrats, and entire communities, the slaughter consumed all. After 192 years of war, Great King Langar wished to put a stop to the violence; so he called for a council of all the kingdoms. "The Ordinances and Succession of Kingdoms" were the result – it established rule law for the transfer of governmental power. If a kingdom defied the rules, then all other kingdoms were obliged to sever diplomatic relations and trade. This proved to be an effective peace measure, which ultimately led to the establishment of Parliament in 1203 CE, and after 2005 years of consideration, the Kingdom of Salvia had yet to ratify the Articles of Parliament.

The ordinances included complicated rules for succession and acquisition. Walter was a talented lawyer, and before Salvia's invasion, he acquired the ten volume set of ordinances from a traveling merchant; he filed a petition with Parliament that the Vakhal family was of royal Scandinavian lineage; and he registered with the Asgard Royal Court, claiming "Minorem Regiam Provisionem" (lesser royal rank). While his station did not allow him to rule, it protected his lands from unlawful acquisition by higher royal families – only a legal heir could lay claim to his lands.

Walter obeyed the law and presented Rory as his legal heir, as mandated by the ordinances, and anyone who married her would inherit his property. If Walter and Meredith objected to the marriage, the king would have them murdered, declare Rory mentally incompetent, and appoint her a ward of the king; then he would marry her to whomever he wished. Many kingdoms used intrigue and criminals to achieve their goals, often resulting in assassinations.

––––––

"The alliance would be beneficial. Your family holds title to most of the valley and my family rules. It would be a good match," the king said and turned his back toward Walter. "You are willing?"

"Yes, your majesty," Walter replied.

"And the girl is willing?" asked the king.

"Yes, your majesty. My daughter is obedient to the King's will and will marry whomever the king desires." Walter stuffed the handkerchief back into his pocket.

The king turned toward Walter and smiled. "Excellent, then the matter is settled. Your daughter will marry the prince. This will cement our families and form a legal bond between us."

"Yes, your majesty," Walter said. His body relaxed, and he finally took a breath. He straightened his necktie, a sign that all was well. The page left the veranda and returned to the party.

"We must discuss our children's pending nuptials. I think a spring wedding would be best. It is in fashion among the royal families. We will have it here at the castle of course …." The pair strolled through the garden.

Chapter 27

Prince Gregory's spies informed him of the decision, but he guessed the news long before his father announced it - he raged, knocking pots and pans off the kitchen counter, hurtling glass jars at the wall, and then grabbing a bottle of wine, he gulped it as though he was dying of thirst.

Wine dribbling over his neck, he used his shirtsleeve to wipe it away. He leaned over the counter and closed his eyes. Rage exploded within him again, and he hurled the bottle at the wall, shattering upon impact, leaving behind a purple stain. He grabbed another bottle and slid down onto the floor. He took a swig and pondered the situation.

The union would cement his father's hold on the territory. If the girl produced an heir, then all would be well. If not, he would have her assassinated, and the royal family would still control Walter's lands. Even so, Gregory hated his father and the unceasing control he had over Gregory's life.

Asgard law allowed up to four spouses: Rory would be the prince's first wife but not his last. The prince would certainly marry three more wives, none of whom he loved, cementing the king's political alliances with other kingdoms, and even if Rory did produce an heir, his father might still murder Rory – the king would have a grandchild, and the prince would have a fourth marriage option.

Prince Gregory would oblige his father: even sons could die by the King's order, and it had already happened. When his older brother, Thomas, escaped one night, his father sent men to hunt him down and take his head. They returned with it in a box. Gregory bided his time. One day it would be his turn to rule, and he would do so with an iron hand: everyone would bend to his will.

Gregory rose to his feet and took another swig, not caring about the red stain it left on his white shirt. He stormed through the kitchen and hurtled open a door. A girl in a pink and white gown happened to past him. He grabbed her from the ball and dragged her into the kitchen.

The girl pled with him to release her, resisting him as he dragged her into the room. The kitchen doors opened, and a pair of concubines entered; the King tasked these girls with satisfying the prince and protecting the assembled guests. He flung away the struggling girl, and she landed with a bone jarring impact. After recovering her wits, she scrambled to her feet and fled the kitchen, tears streaming down her cheeks.

"We could entertain your Majesty if he has the strength," said a brunette, Sienna.

Gregory snatched a bottle of wine from off the countertop. He took a long swig and let out noisy gulps. The wine flowed down his neck and stained his white cotton shirt. "What happened to that other whore?"

"She was the king's guest and has returned to the ball," said Sienna. "Can we satisfy my lord's need?" Her hand slid down his stomach and between his thighs.

"I suppose, but I will have a need for both of you." The girls wrapped his arms around their shoulders and helped him walk. He staggered through the hallway. Their names were unimportant to the prince; all that mattered to him was sex.

He grabbed both of them and laughed: "I shall use both of you all night."

"Certainly my lord," said Sienna. "We live to serve."

The trip through the castle was full of curses and singing, out of tune and at the top of his lungs. The guards snapped to attention as they passed and clutched their halberds tight. The trip finally ended. They opened the royal bedroom and closed the door behind them.

A fire burned in the hearth to the right. An enormous four-poster bed lay in the center of the room, and leather furniture set lay to the right. A terrified young woman, clad only in her lingerie, gazed up at them with large eyes. She was bound and lying on the sofa.

Sienna dropped Gregory onto the bed and rolled him onto his back. She crawled up his body, kissing and stroking him. Hayley, the blonde, hurried over to the bound girl and released her. "The Prince changed his mind. Return to the party." The terrified young woman scooped up her clothes and fled the room, eager for the safety of the crowd.

They worked together as a team and stripped off Gregory's outer garments. When he was clad in his briefs and T-shirt, Sienna lay atop Gregory's stomach and stretched his arms above his head; then kissing him, she distracted the prince as Haley bound the prince's wrists with a pair of leather cuffs, securing them to the headboard.

Sienna raised the bottle to the prince's lips and gave another taste of spice wine, but this wine had an addition beyond the common herbs and peppers: it contained a muscle relaxant. When the drug took effect, Hayley pressed down Gregory's jaw, working a ball gag into his mouth. When it popped into place, a string of garbled objections came from the prince, and after she had cinched the gag, his protests were reduced to stifled moans.

Sienna reached around behind her back and tried to loosen her corset. "Here, let me help you," said Hayley. Sienna turned her back toward Hayley and sat on her feet. Hayley untied the knot and then loosened the laces. The glossy cobalt blue satin corset became slack enough for Sienna to release the hooks on the right side. After releasing her garter straps, she stripped off her nylons and high heels. The girl then stood up on the bed and stripped off her panties.

Three knocks came from the door – the girls froze. A few seconds passed, and two more knocks followed, and relief replaced fear. Hayley scrambled off the bed and hurried to the door. She released the lock and peered out into the hallway. Bill hid in the space afforded by the wide doorjamb. "Open the door already. Everyone can see me."

"Get in," Hayley said. She opened the door wide, and Bill rushed past her. She scanned the hallway, and seeing no one, she hurried him into the room. She then closed and bolted the heavy door. Hayley reached behind her neck and removed a ruby, diamond choker, and the moment it left her flesh, her face ripped like waters, shifting and contorting; and as the waters stilled, Christy appeared. The real concubine Hayley consumed a drugged meal and slept in a closet. "You took your time."

"You think it is easy getting in here?" Bill groused. "Do you have any idea how many coins I spent getting into the castle? And there are drunken aristocrats everywhere."

"Never mind that," Christy hissed. "Just get busy. We don't have much time."

"Yeah right," Bill replied. He stripped off his backpack and set it down on a table. After untying the cover flap, he pulled out a branding rod. The crystal tip glowed brightly as a naked spotlight. "That thing is bright," he said and shielded his eyes.

Christy retrieved a small vial and a funnel from the backpack. She ran back to the bed and scrambled up to the prince. By this time Sienna secured Gregory's ankles to the floor board. Christy wrapped the medallion that she once wore around the prince's neck. Sienna then pricked her finger placing a drop of her blood in a vial, and a drop of the prince's blood was put in another vial. The vials were then filled with a gray liquid, but as the blood mixed with the potion, they began to glow like bright points of light. Christy worked the funnel into a hole in the center of the gag. "This had better work." She opened the stopper of Sienna's vial and poured the contents into the funnel. Gregory choked and coughed, but then he then gulped down the mixture.

"How long does it take," asked Bill.

"Minutes to hours," Sienna said. "It all depends."

The Seventh Age

"I vote for minutes," Bill replied.

As they waited, Sienna's mind began to drift back in time, to a time when her life was very different. She remembered the journey to Salvia and the carriage ride. It rocked like a ship on the sea ....

———

Sienna played with her favorite doll, brushing its hair and primping its clothes. Her father ceaselessly read his oracle scroll, and her mother idly watched the rugged. When the carriage came to an unexpected stop, her father removed his reading glasses and exited the carriage. As the minutes passed, her mother grew impatient. What was the delay?

"RUN!" her father screamed and then let out a cry like that of a dying animal. Her mother launched off the bench and looked out the window. She gasped. "We have to run." She grabbed Sienna and hurried her out the other door.

"What's happening mommy," Sienna whimpered as they ran. Her mother never answered. She kept looking back over her shoulder in terror. They hurried over the rocky terrain and around enormous boulders. When they arrived at the edge of a cliff, her mother looked down at a swiftly moving river. Without warning, she shoved the girl, and Sienna plummeted into the river.

The frigid water engulfed the girl, stabbing her with a million needles, stealing her warmth. She burst up from the swift waters and drew in a desperate gasp. When she looked up at the cliff, she saw her mother: her back arched, a bloody arrow jutted out of her chest. A second later her body shuddered as another arrow joined the first. She tumbled forward and collapsed into the river. Men sprinted up to the edge of the cliff, armed with bows and arrows. They fired at the girl, but the swift current carried her around a bend, saving her life.

When the river slowed, Sienna crawled onto a small sandy beach. Even though the sun scorched the land, she shivered in her wet clothes. It was then that she saw her mother's body. She floated face down in the river, two arrows jutting out of her back. Sienna never heard the slave girls approach her or their questioning voices. Hands grabbed the dumbstruck girl and dragged her away. Though she was a mere child, it made no difference to the slave auctioneer. He kidnapped and sold her.

———

Gregory contorted in agony and thrashed about as convulsions tossed him like a ragdoll, all the while screaming. His eyes shot wide open; garbled curses came from his lips, and his body arched like a bow. When the convulsions resumed, the bed rattled beneath him. Gregory's powerful arms began to wither, as the reaction consumed him, and at the same time, the black curly hair on his chest and legs retreated into him. A pair of breasts engorged on his chest; his manhood receded into his body, sinking deep into his pelvis, leaving behind a smooth arc between his thighs; snaps and crunches coming from his hips, his entire body began to shrink, withering to a fraction of its former mass. The prince bucked about as if possessed by a demon, straining his limbs and bouncing upon the bed.

Bill gaped at the scene before him and asked, "Are you sure that wasn't poisoned?"

"I'm sure," Christy said. "Help me hold him down."

The three of them piled onto Gregory, but he still tossed them about like a bucking bronco. His brown eyes turned blue, and his black, curly hair flowed out from his head. His face began to contort, and his muffled cries rose to soprano, and his face changed into Sienna's doppelganger. Her breasts grew full, and his body assumed the classic female form. Somewhere during the process, Gregory passed out.

"Let's get him … her dressed." Christy untied Gregory's ankles and stripped the newly created woman. She then fed his feet through Sienna's panties and worked them up his body. Sienna rolled Gregory onto his right side, placed the corset underneath him, and rolled him onto his left side. She then secured the corset hooks down his right side. "Pull his laces tight," Sienna ordered Bill.

"Yeah, okay," he said. He grabbed the laces and planted his knee in Gregory's back. He pulled with all his might. The laces grew tight, and the corset constricted, squeezing Gregory's torso. Gregory's breasts slipped into the cups, and the shiny material compressed his body into an ideal, hourglass shape.

Christy rolled up a pair of nylons and then cocooned Gregory's right foot in the sheer black material. She unrolled the stocking up his leg, all the way to the top of his thigh, and Sienna took over and clipped the garter strap to it. After the other leg had been sheathed, Christy shod Gregory's feet with the strappy high heels.

"It's time for me." The three of them moved Gregory's transformed body over to the sofa. After Sienna had dressed in the prince's underwear, she said, "You two will have to hold me down." She worked the ball gag into her mouth.

"Got it," Bill said.

Sienna lay on the bed with her arms by her sides and nodded. Christy inserted the funnel and poured the liquid. Sienna swallowed the prince's glowing mixture. "Wits wawwul," she said, a scream ripping from her mouth.

Bill lay across Sienna's chest and shouted, "Help me." Christy threw herself across Sienna's thrashing legs. Sienna's thin arms and legs grew thick with muscles. Male genitalia took shape and filled out the prince's briefs. Sienna transformed into a male, a perfect copy of the prince, and her new male body tossed them about like children. Her blue eyes turned brown; her nose grew broad; her jaw grew square, and her voice boomed like thunder.

"I hope this ends soon," Bill said. He bounced around atop Sienna. "This guy is strong."

Sienna grew still, like the forest after a sudden storm. Bill and Christy lingered on top of Sienna, a baritone groan coming from her. "I think it's finished." Bill sat up and gazed at the man lying on the bed. Except for the long hair, he was an exact duplicate of Prince Gregory. "I can't believe that worked. It's the weirdest thing that I've ever seen."

"Yeah, it is," Christy agreed.

Bill glanced at Christy clad only in lingerie and leered for a moment. She was an exceptionally beautiful woman. "I never noticed it before, but you have a really hot body."

"In your dreams," Christy replied.

Sienna moaned and reached behind her head. When she fumbled with the gag strap, Christy helped Sienna release it. She pulled the ball from her mouth and rumbled with a deep voice, "That hurts."

"Well you did just get a full body makeover," Bill said. "Everything looks good but the hair. It's too long."

"Easily solved," Sienna groaned and sat upright. "I can shave and have Christy give me a haircut." She, now a "he," rose to his feet and rubbed his back. "We need to get busy before someone comes to check on him … me."

The Seventh Age

Chapter 28

Rory hid in her room, the wedding hitting like a punch to the gut. She paced back and forth; every so often, she paused. The sound penetrated the sturdy oak door. She stared at the door, paralyzed with fear as if a monster would enter. The voices grew louder by the moment but fell into the distance.

Rory reminded herself to breathe, taking in as much as the corset allowed. She released a tremulous breath and grasped the bedpost. "Okay, calm down. Getting married isn't so bad. Marrying Christy was fun. I was the groom, not the bride. Do I have to wear some sort of white poofy dress?"

She sat on the side of the bed, her gown constricted around her thighs. She placed her hands on her lap and watched the flames dance in the hearth, mesmerized by the ballet. A flame danced atop a log like a prima ballerina, rejoicing in the few seconds of its existence. She mused about her former life, and in her mind's eye, she saw Michael, playing with his plastic dinosaur, a plastic soldier riding upon it, jam smeared on his face smiling face.

More voices penetrated the door, and her spirits collapsed: sorrow dispelled fear. She rose to her feet and gazed at the woman in the mirror – *Am I really her?* Ethereal beauty incarnate: *How can it be?* She understood why everyone wanted this beauty, everyone but Christy.

A knock at the door made her jump. She stared at the door. The knock returned. Her lungs released a quiver as she unbolted the door and opened it. A man held a silver vase filled with a beautiful bouquet of flowers. "A gift from his Majesty, the King," the servant said.

She opened the door wide and said, "You can put them on the table over there." The man carried the roses over to a small, round mahogany table.

He set them on the table and exited without a word. She closed the door and leaned her head against it. Her thoughts returned to Christy: her heart ached for one last smile.

I'm living like a victim. I need to do something. The question was what?

She could think of but one thing; she needed to talk about her feelings with Gregory. Perhaps a human being lingered beneath his arrogant, regal façade. Whatever the cost, she needed relief from the ache of her soul.

She exited her bedroom and steeled her mind. They would have to reach some sort of agreement. What, she was not sure. Perhaps she just needed to see that a human being lay beneath the surface. The guards snapped to attention at her approach; news travels fast in a castle. Everyone knew of the king's decision. She was to be a princess and then the queen.

After a few wrong turns, she arrived at Gregory's bedroom. She stood before the door with her hand poised. *What am I doing?* It was a poignant question, but one without an answer. All that she knew was that she needed to speak with him.

She was about to knock when she heard voices penetrate the door. Curious for some hidden insight into the man, she gripped the knob and opened the door a crack. She saw Antonio. He restrained a struggling brunette girl, both gagging and binding her. When she saw Rory, she let out a series of frantic mews.

The door snapped open and sent her tumbling forward. Hands grabbed her and slammed her into a wall, a moment later sensing a sharp knife at her throat. When her vision focused, she saw Prince Gregory. His lips were curled into a fierce snarl and hate radiated from his eyes. She glanced past him and saw Bill. When Christy stepped into view, Rory's heart leaped within her.

Bill took a step forward and asked, "I need to know. Are you with them or us?"

The Seventh Age

"Them? Who is 'them'?" asked Rory. "I've been your friend since we were kids. I've seen you drunk, angry, and crying when your dog, Misty, got cancer. Life may have changed us both, but I am still your best friend. If I'm not with you, then no one is!"

Bill nodded and rubbed his chin. "Yeah, I guess you're right. I don't have many friends like that. Let her go." Gregory relaxed his grip on her neck a little and moved the razor sharp blade from her flesh. "Let her go. She'll be fine."

"Would someone tell me what is going on?" Rory crossed her arms and walked over to Bill, ignoring Christy. "You have to admit this is kind of weird." Bill recounted the abbreviated version of the tale. She especially paid interest when he explained how Sienna turned into Gregory. "Do you think that potion would work for me? Could I return to my old self?"

Antonio shook his head. "The potion is very expensive and only works with the amulet. It's more than just a reversal of one's DNA: it infuses the old spirit with the new flesh. Given your story, I doubt very much it would work for you."

Chapter 29

The king strolled through the castle at a leisurely pace, his dominion now certain and power absolute. Walter was a tool he used for a while, but it was time to dispose of him. He was the unquestioned monarch of all he surveyed. The day was bright and the air warm, and he said, "Perhaps I will go for a ride or a hunt."

When he entered the dining hall, he spotted his son and Walter enjoying breakfast. If only the King knew that his fate hinged upon the next decision, he would have considered it more thoroughly, but men never do – they assume what has been will continue to be.

As he strolled through the hall, all those present rose to their feet and bowed. With a rolling wave of his hand, he bid them resume their meal. When you are king, there is always room at the table. He took a seat next to Walter, and a serving girl rushed to his side, setting a steaming mug of coffee before him. She then set down a plate of food before the king and placed a napkin on his lap. After taking a step back, she waited to meet his every need.

"So what is the topic this morning? Arrangements for the wedding I suppose." King Leopold took a sip of coffee and took a bite of pastry. "Will it be a spring wedding?"

"Yes, your majesty," replied the prince. The king smiled and nodded, pleased with his son's agreeable attitude. "We are both looking forward to it."

The king paused and arched an eyebrow. "I am surprised to hear you say that. You were so adamantly opposed last night. What changed your mind?"

"The morning and sobriety," Gregory replied. "Ale and the night stir up many passions. The light of day brings them into proper focus."

"Well said," the king replied. "You will still have three other wives available for marriage."

Gregory and Walter shared a knowing glance. When Walter nodded, Gregory said, "I agree. I was thinking of proposing to Princess Alisha of the Stonecrop. Her father is well situated with the Asgard Parliament. His influence would be helpful when negotiating trade treaties," Gregory said.

"An intriguing thought," the King tapped his index finger against his lips. "Yes. It is very intriguing."

The Spanish Ambassador, Antonio, entered the hall. He was dressed in his best black velvet suit and silver cravat. When he spotted the king, he crossed the hall, gripping a leash in his left hand, leading a beautiful brunette girl. The brunette's curls spilled over her shoulder, flowing down her back, and a black leather gag covered her mouth, jaw, and neck, a Y-strap stretched across the bridge of her nose, merging into a single strap that traversed the top of her head, emphasizing her vivid blue eyes.

The choker necklace worn by slaves offered levels of control, mostly binding the wearer to a location. However, only a wizard could erase her memory, not that Antonio wished this. He savored the thought of reshaping the prince's mind: the prince would be transformed into the perfect slave, a fate that befell many of Antonio's political opponents. Prince Gregory, Sienna's doppelganger, would have to obey the slave choker necklace, but she would still be able to speak her mind, thus the need for the gag.

The new Sienna wore an ultramarine blue satin corset, highlighting her new curves, over top of a full body stocking. A black satin skirt wrapped around her hips and crossed over her pelvis, forming a "V" across her thighs. Two pairs of leather cuffs, placed on her ankles and above the knees, connected by short chains, and hobbled her. Antonio was not taking any chances.

Antonio snapped his heels together and bowed. "I wish to apologize for my ill-tempered outburst last night. Also, I most humbly thank you for this gracious gift." He pulled Sienna to his side and put his arm around her waist.

The king looked to Walter for some explanation. "I met with the king's council last night. We sought some way to comfort the ambassador on his long journey home. We took the liberty, your Majesty, and presented this slave girl as a gift."

"Ah, I see. Quite right," the king said and rose to his feet. "Traveling over long distances can be so … wearisome. I am glad the gift is well received. Won't you join us?"

"Yes, your majesty. It would be my pleasure." He sat down next to the king. Sienna resisted the necklace's control at first but then succumbed to it. She sank down and knelt by Antonio's side. He turned toward the king and said, "I selected the girl myself. I like a wild filly. It makes the training process so much more enjoyable." zx

"Yes. I understand," the king replied and crossed his legs. "I was married eight times."

"Eight times, your majesty?" asked Antonio.

"Yes. This is a hard country, and it can be wearying on those of royal blood. Unfortunately, all of my wives passed away. These days I satisfy my needs with my many concubines and handmaids. The trauma of losing another wife is too great for me to bear."

"And you Mr. Vakhal, how many wives do you have?" asked Antonio.

"Just the one," he replied. "I am told that this is common among the lesser nobles."

"Quite so," Antonio replied. "Their duties preclude such luxuries."

"Very true," Walter replied. "Which reminds me, with your permission your majesty, I must see to my daughter. We must discuss the wedding details."

"Yes. That is fine," the King said. Walter arose from his chair and left the table. He spoke with a pair of chambermaids and exited the hall.

Sienna strained against the necklace's control. She bit down on the fluid filled sack inside her mouth and strained against the taut kid-leather sculpted around her lips. The gag reduced her protests to quiet whimpers.

She stared at the king, hoping to offend him. He might remove her gag and let her speak. Antonio pressed on the back of her head and whispered, "Lower your eyes." The girl grimaced and fought the command. It was as though a powerful force pulled down on her head. She had no choice but to comply. She wanted to cut Antonio's throat with a table knife and watch him bleed, but the restraints left her impotent.

Chapter 30

Walter paced in his bedroom, and every so often, he glanced at his watch. The royal guard assembled in the courtyard outside his window. They wore their blue and gold tabards. Their polished silver armor gleamed in the sunlight. He tried to count them and lost track. The King scheduled a military assembly as a show of force. It impressed upon the nobles that any attempt at treachery would meet with swift and violent retribution.

A double knock came from his bedroom door. Walter walked around the foot of his bed and hurried to the door. When he opened it, he saw the maid who served breakfast to the king. He ushered her into the room and closed the door.

"Well, did you do it?" asked Walter.

"Yes, I did it. You think I go around like this for fun?" She removed a bandana from her neck and revealed the magic pendant. She reached around behind her neck and fumbled with the clasp. "Can you help me? I can never get these things."

Walter put on his reading glasses and examined the clasp. He flipped a latch and removed a ring from a hook. A second later, the choker slipped from around the girl's neck. Her entire body shimmered and face warped. A second later Bill appeared.

"I'm never going to be the same. You know a couple of guys actually looked at me as I walked past them." His expression became stern. "No one, and I mean no one, can ever know about this."

"Of course," Walter said. "Now change clothes. You look ridiculous."

"Yeah, you don't have to tell me twice." He stripped off the apron and drew the dress over his head. Walter returned the ruby choker to a velvet lined case. Another knock came from the door, and they froze. Walter signaled with his hands for Bill to hide. Bill scooped up the clothes and ducked into the closet.

Walter checked the room and then walked to the door. Another quiet tap came from the door. Walter opened it a little and saw Antonio, holding Sienna's leash. "Come in," Walter said and opened the door wide. Antonio entered and led Sienna in after him. Walter closed and locked the door.

"Is it finished?" asked Antonio.

"Yes. I just got it back." Walter handed the case to Antonio. "It worked perfectly."

Antonio opened the case and inspected the pendant. "This has passed from one woman to the next in my family. Even though it appears common enough, it is beyond price."

"It worked well for us. The king ingested the first half of the binary poison. All that is left is to administer the second dose." They both turned toward the closet as Bill exited it.

"What's she doing here?" asked Bill.

"I want her to witness the end of her wretched family line. They have been a scourge upon these lands for a millennium, and they killed more members of my family than I can number. Today, at long last, we have our revenge." At hearing this, Sienna began to struggle. She twisted her wrists and let out unintelligible threats. Antonio smirked. "I see someone has not learned her place yet." He grabbed her chin and looked into her eyes. "Don't worry. You will. Year by year I will transform you into an ideal concubine. Not a shred of your royal personage will remain."

"I suppose the moral of the story is – never kill a Spaniard's mother," Bill said.

"Nor any other member of his family," Antonio replied. "You will fulfill our agreement. We will by the Rhunite dust at wholesale prices, and we will have exclusive distribution?"

"Of course," Walter replied, "all we want is our freedom and a representative democracy. Having our man on the throne will ensure that."

"Excellent," Antonio said. "This is a day I have longed for."

Rhunite dust was essential in the manufacture of weapons and high technology. The finer and more energetic the dust used, the great the resulting power. The De Madera family owned the only other mine capable of producing such dust. The Salvia and the De Madera family were competitors. The Salvia family tried many times to eliminate the competition by killing their competitors, and Antonio saw many members of his family die at the hands of Salvia assassins.

When Sienna began to struggle, Antonio grabbed her. "Today the last of your wretched family will die." He jerked Sienna's leash and led her from the room. Walter followed them. Bill headed the other way and slipped down a stairwell, bound for the servant's quarters.

———

The next morning, the king lay in bed, snug under the duvet, with two young women by his side. His eyes opened, and he drew in a deep breath. "Time to rise," he said jostling the concubines.

"Yes my king," the girls said with a yawn. They rose up from the bed, clad only in nightgowns, and each one put on a white silk robe. They hurried and prepared for the king's day to begin.

Not waiting for his attendants to dress him, he rose up from bed. "I shall dine in this morning," he announced. When the morning chill penetrated his white silk pajamas, he donned a royal blue robe that had a black collar. It was thick and warm, able to fend off the deepest chill. After putting on his slippers, he shuffled over to the circular breakfast table, set in the far corner of the room, near a wall of two story windows; overlooking his castle, the other wall, and the valley beyond, he saw his kingdom: the greatest in the Wolf's Maw Mountains.

Rose hurried across the room carrying a silver tray and Deborah placed serving trays filled with breakfast food before the king. The girls waited on his right and left, eager to meet his every need. "Eggs, pancakes, sausage … and orange juice," he declared. The girls hurried to fill his plate.

When a knock came from the chamber doors, he said, "Enter."

Two massive doors opened, and Prince Gregory entered. The king glanced up at his son and raised an eyebrow. Gregory wore riding garb. Perceiving the king's curiosity, Gregory said, "With your permission your Majesty, I would like to take Ambassador De Madera on a hunt in the valley before his ship departs."

"Yes, I suppose that would be fine." The King scanned the parchment in Gregory's hand. "Hand it here." Deborah retrieved the king's writing table and set it beside him. The king then scrawled his signature on the document. "It's good to see you assume your proper role. I have to say, I thought this day would never arrive." The king searched his son's face for a reaction.

"The notion of marriage has changed me. It has matured me," the prince replied.

"Yes, I suppose." The king cleared his throat, not believing the frail reasoning. He was sure Gregory was up to something. He made a mental note to have his security police keep a watchful eye on the prince. The security police employed wizards in their duties. This ensured the royal family's safety against dark magic. If a wizard scanned the prince, he would know in seconds that this man was an imposter: Gregory knew his time was short.

The prince sat across from the king, and his right hand patted his jacket pocket. He felt the vial containing the second half of the binary poison. Somehow, by means he had not yet divined, he had to get the poison into the king's orange juice. Walter planned for him to arrive before the king and supervise the king's breakfast, slipping in the poison unaware. However, that opportunity was lost with the king's early and unexpected rising.

The king sipped his morning coffee and glanced at his son. "I have engaged the best wedding planners in all of Asgard. It should be quite an extravagant affair …." Gregory feigned listening to the king, but his mind was on the poison. The girls exited the room, seizing the opportunity to draw the king's bath. "… Of course, the Vakhal family will have to die: the parents killed by thieves, and your wife will die by poison. We will have to wait a year before carrying this out …."

Primal rage ignited within Gregory. His hands began to tremble; his stomach quivered; his heart raced; his breathing quickened; the king's voice became muffled, and his vision began to narrow. Everything became "rose-tinted" as he literally began to see red.

"… Their deaths will consolidate my power and my hold upon the valley," the King said. "I've contemplated killing them many times in the past, but the occasion never presented itself …."

Gregory's right hand moved to his throat. Although it was long gone, he swore he could still feel the presence of a slave necklace around his throat, and he remembered the countless rapes. His anger ignited into a blazing inferno. He slammed down his fist, rattling the dishes. The king looked up at him with startled eyes. Gregory leaped to his feet and grabbed a knife from off the table. Grabbing the king by his throat, he hauled the man to his feet. He plunged in the knife, and a bloody bubbling gasp came from the king's lips. In a crazed flurry, Gregory repeatedly stabbed the king. Arterial spurts splattered his clothing and face. zx

The Seventh Age

When at last Gregory came to his senses, the king lay on the floor, blood pooling around him. "That is for my family. Burn in hell!" He spat on the king and threw the knife onto the floor. Eyes fixed upon his son, ashen like the grave, the King released a tremulous gasp and died.

Gregory wiped his bloody hands on his jacket. Dread fell upon him, and he began to tremble. He would suffer the worst, most painful death for this crime. He had to cover the blood. How? Then he spotted a decanter of red wine on a table near a tall window. He hurried over to it and snatched it off the sterling silver tray. After removing the stopper, he poured the wine down the front of his chest, covering the bloodstains.

Almost as an afterthought, he grabbed the pass to leave the castle and left the room. The guards, standing at attention outside the king's chamber, eyed the prince but failed to act. The prince drank in the morning, and red wine often stained the prince's clothes.

Back in the prince's chamber, Walter, Christy, Bill, and Antonio waited for news. If the plan failed, they had poison of their own to take. It would be a merciful and quick death. "Do you suppose it's done?" asked Bill as he wrung his hands.

"There's no telling," Walter replied. "But we should know shortly."

Christy gripped the vial of poison in her sweaty right hand. She rehearsed opening the lid and swallowing it before the guards could take her. When she glanced at Antonio, he was placid like a cat basking in the noonday sun. He appeared sleepy and disinterested, as though requiring a nap.

The chamber doors burst open, and Gregory charged into the room. "I couldn't control myself – he's dead." He looked down at his bloody clothes, and a wet spot appeared in his trousers where he urinated himself.

"Quick, tell me what happened," Walter said. "Now!" Gregory gave them a brief recounting of the encounter. "Then you're sure the king is dead?" When Gregory nodded, he asked again, "You're sure."

"Yes, he's dead. His blood was everywhere. It's all over me."

"What are we going to do?" asked Christy.

Antonio said, "The king is dead, and the prince killed him. We must get him out of the castle."

"He's right. We'll have to use our backup plan. Christy, help Gregory change his clothes. Leave the bloody clothes on the floor. Don't try and hide it. Give Gregory a shot of whiskey and send him down to the river. The 'Gypsy Spirit' is waiting for him in the river port. It will transport you to the Western Islands." He slapped a vial into Gregory's right hand. "Take the potion after you are out at sea. It will provide you with a new identity. It's safer for you if we don't know what it is." Looking at Antonio, he said, "We have to go. We still have our parts to play."

They strolled through the castle, chatting about the day's activities. When they entered the King's wing, they spotted Devon, captain of the king's bodyguard. She was a brunette beauty and lethal. Rumor had it that she was a Valkyrie candidate and soon to leave Salvia. She wore typical garb for a female warrior: an ornate silver cuirass, various supplemental armor, a glossy black slip-suit, a maiden's belt, and thigh high boots. One might have been tempted to leer at her, but her stern disposition precluded it.

When she concluded a conversation with a pair of guards, she turned and walked toward them. Walter said, "Devon, I have a matter which might require your attention." She turned toward them and put her right hand on her hip. "Ambassador De Madera is scheduled to depart the castle today."

"Yes. I am aware of that," she replied and scanned Antonio.

"Well, I was informed that the prince just departed the castle. When I questioned why, his aid informed me that the prince was going hunting with the ambassador." Walter stroked his chin and furrowed his brow. "It makes no sense. The prince left without his game wardens and dogs.

The Seventh Age

He rode from the castle as if being chased. Is there some emergency of which I am not aware?"

"None I know of," Devon replied. "We should speak with the king."

"We were just on our way to do that very thing," Walter said.

They strolled and chatted about the pending wedding and the security arrangements. When they approached the king's quarters, the king's chief aide intercepted them. "The prince gave strict orders that the king not be disturbed."

The king's attendants, Rose and Deborah, stood upon the fringes of the conversation. "Yes, but what about the king's bath? He hasn't dressed for the day. It's not like him."

Devon looked toward the king's bedroom doors and said, "Open the doors, at once!" The guards jerked open the doors and followed her into the room. "Quick, summon the king's physician!" She ran to the king's side and knelt beside him. Feeling his neck, she checked for a pulse. A heavy sigh escaped her lips. "The king is dead." She stood to her feet and questioned the attendants. "Who was the last person to see the king?"

"Prince Gregory," Deborah replied. "It was he who ordered us not to disturb the king."

The captain surveyed the crime scene. Arterial spray and droplets formed around a void. She drew out a hand scanner from her utility belt and flipped it open. She scanned the footprints and recorded the infrared heat signature. She then scanned the bloody knife for DNA. The king's blood, the prince's fingerprints, and the prince's epithelial cells were present. She ordered, "Search the prince's chambers." The guards ran from the room, their footfalls echoing in the hallway beyond. Devon then said to Walter and Antonio, "Return to your private chambers. It is not safe for you to be about. I will have guards posted for your protection." She then ran from the room and alerted the guard.

When they were alone, Walter looked down his nose at the king's corpse and whispered, "Sic Semper Tyrannis." *Thus, always, to tyrants.*

Chapter 31

Christy joined the gawking crowd assembled outside the king's chambers. Pounding heart and parched throat, she scanned the assembled crowd. Did they see her? Would they recognize her and drag her away. After that, an ax would chop her neck, or the whip would slice her flesh. The possibilities ground away at her calm. The evidence of their crime was so near.

When Walter exited the chambers, he never looked at her. When a few people exited the room, she seized her opportunity and made her escape. She steeled her mind, pushed down her fear, and fixed her eyes straight ahead. Every sound became thunder, the drumming of her heart within her ears, and she fixed her eyes on the doorway and cringed at the guard's fierce visage. The guards remained still, as though made of stone. She passed between them, the weight crushing her.

Breathe! Don't look at them. Chin up. Glide, don't walk. God, my hands are wet. Keep calm!

She joined the end of the crowd, desperate to look as though she belonged. The king's bedroom fell behind her, and at long last, she took a deep breath. A nobleman said, "I hope we have fair weather for the funeral. I loathe standing in the rain."

"I suppose we must attend, although my aching feet would think better of it," a noblewoman replied. When they turned right, Christy went left, every footstep carrying her from danger. The urge to run quickened her pace. *Slow down. Take it easy. Don't blow it now.*

Agonized sobs arose from a group of women. Christy smirked. Their grief was so hollow and self-serving. Then fear seized her once again. Did anyone see her? The weight of the past 50 years pressed down upon her, crushing her soul, nausea swept through her, pain gripped her skull, and sorrow spilled out of her. So many people died waiting for this day, and it was finally here. *He is dead, he is really dead. I cannot believe it.* She fought for each breath and kept moving.

Christy descended a set of stairs and exited near the stables. The warm, fresh air greeted her like freedom. The sunshine, which beamed down upon the parade ground, dispelled the chill from her heart. She scanned the compound, eager to make her escape.

Bill slung the last rope over the gray tarp which covered the cargo wagon. He looped the rope around a hook and tied it off. Christy scanned the mountain of goods that bulged underneath the tarp. It weighed down the wagon, made it heavy, preventing quick escape if they were chased. "What's all this?" she asked with a tone of indictment.

"This is valuable merchandise. I don't get to the castle very often. I wanted to make the most of the trip. Besides, the guards would think it was strange if we left empty-handed. No one does that. Just relax. We're okay."

Christy wrung her hands; "Did you get the pass to leave the castle?"

"It would be a short trip if I didn't. The king's secretary signed our pass just before the fun started. If anyone asks, we are returning to the docks with supplies. Some of the nobles wish to use our services, but they want better decor. That's what we are hauling."

The pair climbed onto the wagon. Bill's relaxed attitude proved contagious. Her shoulders sagged, lungs took in a deep breath, and her mind grew still. A chuckle escaped her lips. "I really wish I could have seen you in a dress. That would be priceless."

Bill released the handbrake and said, "Never going to happen. That was the one and only time I'm going to wear a skirt." Christy laughed and gave him a hug. He slapped the reins, and the team of horses started the wagon rolling. They passed across the courtyard and stopped at the gate. When requested, he handed the guard the pass to leave the castle.

The Seventh Age

The guard sniffed and handed back the papers. "Very well, be on your way," he said. He waved his hand, and the portcullis rose up before them. Every inch of space meant freedom and escape. When it came to a stop high above them, Christy took in a breath. Bill slapped the reins, and the wagon lurched forward. They rolled past the guard, but Christy kept her gaze fixed on the open road, the clear blue sky, and the towering mountains. Even Bill sighed as they rounded the turn and put the castle behind them. It would be a trip without rest or sleep: nothing would stop him until he reached the harbor and safety.

Their hearts leaped in their throats at the sound of thundering hooves. "Out of the way," Devon shouted. They pulled over to the side of the road, hugging the sheer cliff wall. A hundred mounted guards sped past them and around the first swayback. They were soon out of sight and even the sound of their horses faded.

"Well, that was exciting," Bill said and slapped the reins. Christy sighed and rubbed her face. Bill gave her a sideways glance and said, "Try and relax. Enjoy the trip. We don't get out enough."

Back in the castle, Walter and the king's secretary prepared for the king's funeral. Cremation was common practice on Eden, and without means to preserve a corpse, funerals took place soon after death. The guards carried the king's body to his bed. The chambermaids stripped him and washed his body. The Secretary selected the king's finest clothes and laid them on the bed. The maids then dressed his body.

Walter lingered a moment. He gazed, with an icy heart, at the king's dead body. He thought of all the dead, all the blood on his hands, all the cries of anguish, and wished he could kill the king again.

Chapter 32

One month later, Walter and Rory rose early. He exited his chambers and walked at his usual brisk pace. Anxious nobles waited in the royal library. Seldom read books soared up three stories, and rolling ladders provided access to them. His finger traced along the binding of "Torrey's Legal Journal Volume 14-28" and removed the book from off the shelf. He carried it through the room, all eyes upon him. It reminded Rory of a gladiatorial pit, with her in the center. The most senior nobles within the king's court stood at the center of the gathering. The further back one stood, the lesser one's power, and the higher up one stood, perched around brass and wood railings, the lesser one's wealth.

Walter entered the room, an air of confidence about him, a gleam of victory in his eyes, causing the murmuring to grow quiet, opening a path to the center of the room, and forcing a downcast gaze by lesser men. Although no one knew the details, they all sensed the shift in power and were determined to align with it. When Walter sat at the head of the table, the noble leadership gathered around the table and took a seat, leaving the lesser nobles to watch in quiet expectancy.

Alistair, the king's treasurer, wrung his hands and broke the silence. "Did they capture the prince? Do you know the mind of the last testament? Who will take the throne? Will it be you or someone else?"

Rory stood behind her father and to the right, a symbol of rank and influences. Walter gazed back at his daughter, and she saw a smile in his eyes. He looked back at the assembled group and took a cleansing breath, a little ritual of his before sparing in verbal combat. "The Prince is still at large. Devon informed me that the prince's ship escaped our lands and is sailing west on the Arner Sea. She doubts that we will be able to capture him."

"Prior to his death, the king was determined to make sweeping changes. He wished to institute a parliamentary form of government, such as those which are common throughout the Wolf's Head Peninsula. This institution will be permanent. A formal declaration will establish a 'House of Lords' and a 'House of Commons.' The king intended to appoint 30 nobles to the House of Lords, which extends for the individual's lifetime. Those serving in the House of Commons will be elected from community leaders. Both houses will then vote together and elect a prime minister. Once the prime minister is established, he will appoint ambassadors to negotiate our inclusion in the Asgard Parliament and sign the charter."

"And you will be a member of this House of Lords?" asked Alistair.

"The king professed a desire that I serve in such a role. Five of the seats are reserved for the priests, and three for the generals. That will still leave 22 seats to fill. The leaders among the nobles will be given first opportunity to serve. I would think those seated around this table would qualify. Thus 15 seats would remain. Those who wish to fill them should write a petition to my office and describe their desire for service."

"The king was wise," Alistair said and interlaced the fingers of both hands. "I lobbied the king for such an institution for years." The ranking nobles settled back and basked in their newfound power. The lesser nobles shifted about and began to murmur. One glance from Walter returned the room to quiet.

Cosmia, an elder female noble, crossed her arms and asked, "What of our progeny? Will they inherit our seats?"

"'Rules of Ascension and Lineage' will be observed. Descendants, in good standing with the royal court, will be eligible. Typically, that privilege passes on to the eldest child. If he or she is unable or unwilling to serve, then it will fall to the next eldest and so forth. In this way, the kingdom will have continuity of leadership."

259

"Yes, that is for the best," Cosmia replied. The elderly woman may have appeared like a withered raisin, wearing a white wig, but her mind was sharp. "It does maintain the continuity leadership. But what of the commoners, will their offspring inherit their seats?"

"No. Each generation of commoners must prove themselves. I am sure, you as leaders of your provinces, will have some influence over that process …."

Rory basked in her father's aura. He served on many boards of directors and trustees, and it took up much of his time. He often brought Rory along with him and let her color with her crayons as they discussed business. She was always impressed by his ability to manipulate those in power. Few could match his abilities and none who could best him.

Chapter 33

The rising sun, a ball of crimson fire, crept over the Wolf's Maw Mountains. It cast long shadows across the jagged spires. Red rivers, colored by algae, began to glow, making the mountains appear to be teeth drenched in blood.

The morning light stripped away the gray, making the Royal Salvia Castle appear white, and clean, a brilliant beacon in a barren wilderness. It sat atop Spire Mountain, its big brother Iron Mountain looking down upon it. Both loomed high above the clouds and looked down upon the great valley spreading out before them. Cold north winds from the West blasted the castle's spires, battlements, and outer walls like some implacable foe.

The night watch sentries lingered upon its exterior walls: aching and tired, but alert – sleeping at one's post meant a terrible death. The biting wind swept over the gray stone, through parapet, and blasted the guards with a wet, frigid slap. A lone guard, Geth, stamped his feet and milled about, groping for a few fragments of warmth. His halberd jostled about in the wind as his tired right arm struggled to steady it. Growing restless and bored, Geth leaned over the stonewall, cold radiating from the rock that penetrated his clothes, and he peered down into down the sheer wall. The valley, the village, and the rivers lay far below the castle, appearing like a tiny diorama. At that moment, he wished he was still at home, sleeping in his warm bed, the aroma of breakfast rousing him from his slumber.

The doors of peasant homes opened and workers set about their chores. Mothers and daughters carried bundles of laundry down to the river, babies slung on their backs. Men and boys were too preoccupied with their work to notice the women. There were chickens to feed, eggs to collect, pigs to slop, and cows to milk; and when the chores ended, the real work began.

Scott Marcy

The village of Heather Vale lay at the cross-junction of the Silvery and Jade Rivers. Smoke arose from chimneys and shop doors opened for business. Some merchants swept sidewalks while others wheeled merchandise onto the sidewalk for display.

A barge floated down the Jade River, thus named for the high copper content that turned the river walls green. The crew used their staffs and punted up to the quay. Men threw them lines and tied the barge to the dock. The tiny figure of the captain strolled across the dock and stopped by the port authority; there were ready to transport another load of ore for processing. Carts wheeled up to the edge of the dock and dumped quarried rock into the center of the barge. The deckhands then used shovels to distribute the load within the barge.

Men and boys left their homes and joined their comrades in the long trek up the mountain. These sparse parties soon joined into streams and then formed rivers of men. Miners dressed in rough leather garb, wearing heavy gloves, protected by a crude steel plate, made their way to the mines. Rhunite was just one of many stones quarried from the heart of the mountain. Semi-precious gems and other ores had industrial applications, and the extraction and processing paid a good wage.

Geth leaned back and returned to his duties. The aroma of cooking bacon and baking bread made his stomach rumble. At the same time, his weary limbs and heavy eyes cried out for sleep. Neither would occur until the day watch relieved him from the 12-hour shift.

The main entry doors swung open wide, and a host of armed men exited the dining hall. They plodded across the parade ground with the speed of a glacier, or so it seemed to the night watch. Six guards entered the tower, and a minute later, they emerged onto the wall. As he transferred the halberd to the day watch, his arm glad for the relief, Geth complained to his replacement: "You took your own sweet time." He walked through the tower, and he plodded toward the wardroom; laughter echoed through the structure. Officers lounged around wooden tables, mugs of coffee in hand, warmed by the fire in a metal stove. Geth removed his

262

sword and armor, each piece placed upon a wooden frame; but his dagger remained on his person. Too tired to complain, he trudged down the stone stairs, cold radiating from the rough block walls.

When Geth exited the tower, a blast of frigid air shoved him backward. He leaned into the wind and pressed toward his destination. The dining hall, the barracks, and blissful sleep lay across the courtyard. The other night watch guards greeted him with weary nods or rumbling grunts. When they reached the dining hall, the aroma of hot food wooed them back to life. Male and female guards gathered around rough wooden tables. Plates filled with food and steaming mugs of coffee lay before them. The guards closed the doors behind them, glad that the night and work were finished.

Another guard, Jerome, pulled Geth aside and said, "Trouble is brewing. Rumor has it that the Prime Minster is in deep trouble."

"How do you mean?" asked Geth.

"The nobles are conspiring against him." Jerome looked both ways and moved close. "Word is that they are planning to overthrow the provisional government. If it comes down to it, can we count on you?"

"Of course," he said, anger and fear in his eyes. "We've been friends since we were boys. You know I'm on your side. But open revolt –"

"Hush! We don't speak of it." He put his arm around Geth's shoulders and led him toward the serving line. "You just keep your eyes open and mouth shut."

The entire castle buzzed with activity. The cooks in well-equipped kitchens prepared breakfast for the royal family and honored guests. The serving staff hurried through a maze of hallways underneath the castle, each to his or her appointed task. Oracle scrolls required updating; chairs were arranged; curtains were opened; the tables were set; the hearths received fresh firewood and were then rekindled, and countless others tasks were performed.

Scott Marcy

The door to Walter's suite opened, and blue eyes scanned the hallway. Amy hurried out from Walter's bedroom, smoothing her black maid uniform. She adjusted her white lace and black satin hairpiece in her long blonde locks. It was quite an honor for her to serve the Vakhal family in the royal court – and sleeping with the Prime Minister ensured a place of prominence for her.

Meredith, Walter's wife, slept in a separate suite just down the hall. The official reason given to the royal court was Walter's snoring. Quiet whispers, however, perceived the truth. The husband and wife slept apart, and each night found a new lover in their beds.

A chandelier hung over the expansive white bed, the matching furniture placed with care about the room. Everywhere one looked, opulence abounded: from the hand-weaved area rug to the exquisite décor, to the private bath, to the walk-in closet, and to the dressing chamber, surrounded by fitting mirrors. Rory's suite was fit for a princess.

Rory threw aside the pillow. She sat up in bed and let the covers collapse into her lap. Russet brown locks spilled over her shoulders and cascaded down her chest. She yawned and stretched. The peculiar weight and swollen sensation of her breasts barged into her consciousness. She pressed her chin to her chest and once again contemplated these strange appendages. Her breasts filled out the cups of a black silk nightgown and rose up with her next breath. The hardness of her nipples from the cold air, the prominence upon her chest, the strain on her back, the jiggling sway when she moved, she wondered how women ever got used to breasts – in somber moments, she tried to imagine a nursing infant.

Through framed glass doors and beyond her private balcony, she saw the Wolf's Maw Mountains. Their snow-capped peaks stabbed the sky, casting long shadows on the valleys. The room and the vista were both impressive, the stuff of every girl's dream. Yet reality never measures up to one's fantasies, and the rigor of court life wore upon her: the life of a politician. What she craved was a simple life.

The Seventh Age

It had been six months since her father's victory over the king, and life settled into a dull routine. Prince Gregory, having once been Justine, was a fugitive on the run, and the real prince was now a beautiful woman, a prisoner in New Spain.

Rory dismissed magical rings as a perverse instrument of control foisted upon women and some men. She was no trophy wife, no prize for powerful. She remembered her life back in the United States, and she would have given anything return home, hop in a car, and drive to the nearest restaurant. She longed to be just another person, a woman among equals.

This was not possible. As the daughter of the Prime Minster of The Kingdom of Salvia, she had responsibilities, duties befitting a woman of her rank. There were endless court intrigues and affairs of state. The women only let the men think they were in charge because it suited them; they set events in motion and negotiated with adversaries; they moved their husbands and servants around like pieces upon a chessboard. A misspoken word and careless gesture could harm her family and the people she loved. The responsibility pressed down upon Rory.

I'm a CPA damn it! Not a princess, she brooded.

Every day she walked to the balcony doors and hoped to see the fertile planes of Gleason and nothing else. She longed to see Earth and the life she loved. She made a bargain with God. She would stay a woman and be happy in it if she could just go home. That was all she wanted, to go home and live in the United States – anywhere in the U.S.A.

She collapsed and sat on the edge of her bed, her feet dangling over the side. Thanks to her reduced height, they no longer touched the floor. She rubbed her face and drew in a deep breath. Another day of this new life arrived and brought with it fresh challenges. She slid off the bed and rose to her feet. Arms up stretched, she threw off the stiffness of the previous night. In the midst of a groan, she felt the caress of her silk nightgown on her wide hips.

Scott Marcy

Mornings required greater effort these days, and it was best to get started. Rory hurried to the bathroom and grabbed between her legs. Her right hand felt silk panties stretched over the smooth arc of her new sex, and her labia sensed fingers touch them. A curse escaped her lips. How many times would she repeat that mistake? She was a woman, and there was nothing between her legs to grab. Yet the phantom aches of her missing male genitalia persisted long after their disappearance. She wished for her male equipment to return, but failing that, she longed for the annoying aches to stop.

She stripped down her panties, squatted on the toilet seat and rested her elbows on her knees – this fact of her new biology more than any other vexed her – she relaxed her bladder and urinated. She remembered standing to pee and longed for the simplicity. Urinating as a woman was so complicated; if she sat up to piss, the urine would dribble; if she wiped it the wrong way, she would get an infection; if she used the wrong toilet, she might catch something. It never occurred to her that women could be unsanitary.

Public toilets, like those used by commoners, were worse. They were equipped with porcelain bowls set low on the floor. It required her to squat, hold up her gown, and struggle not to tip. To make things worse, the urine splashed her legs, which disgusted her and necessitated washing her legs with a hand towel. In the middle of this uncomfortable maneuver, some woman would invariably use the toilet right next to her. Why? All the other booths were empty. Use one of them.

She relaxed and let the urine dump from her body. Her gaze wandered to the panties gathered around her knees. Black silk panties wrapped around her feminine knees, causing her thoughts to drift back to a simpler time, a time before panties and squatting.

With a flush of the toilet, she arose and stripped off her clothes. The shower was larger than most. Its square footage was the size of most walk-in closets and was beset with an array of sixteen showerheads that created a maelstrom when activated.

266

The Seventh Age

Caring for a female body required time and patience. She exfoliated, applied skins creams, shampooed, repeated, conditioned her hair with two separate products, perfumed her entire body, and then applied more creams. While this might be tedious, failure to do so yielded a tsunami of criticism and a host of unrequested beauty tips. After this morning ritual, she exited the shower and wiped the condensation from the mirror.

Vibrant blue eyes stared back at her. She touched her cheek, leaned close to the mirror, and a stranger gazed back at her. Rory's petite right hand glided over her face. Her sun-kissed skin was creamy smooth, the flower of perpetual youth.

Before her transformation, she celebrated her 33 birthday, but now she appeared no more than 18, a mere youth. Even by Eden standards, this was peculiar. Some friends politely guessed that she was twenty-five, but most changed the conversation to safer topics, offending those in power could be lethal. After all, she was the Prime Minister's daughter, heir to his vast fortune, and her displeasure could ruin them financially or worse.

Rory accumulated a host of superficial new friends. They hung upon her and showered her with praise, whether earned or not. In private, unguarded moments, she overheard their true feelings. The universal cry was, "It isn't fair." It was hard to blame them. Her ethereal qualities were beyond the grasp of mortal woman: perpetual youth, supreme beauty, and maximum health – furthermore, she was wealthy and powerful. What person would not look upon her with covetous eyes?

Marriage amongst the nobles and the privileged class were a more akin to a business merger. Brokers matched clients and garnered a handsome commission. The concept of romantic love was childish and laughable. The Vakhal family disagreed, but they were in the minority.

Every day new male and female suitors showed up at the castle. They arrived with noble titles, certificates of land holdings, portfolios of stocks, and expectations of marriage. By day, they presented their marriage offer, but by night, they had liaisons with the serving staff.

Scott Marcy

Many hoped to persuade Walter with bribes. Although her parents were patient and understanding, every day came with greater pressure, most of it focused on her. She had to make a decision. Who would she marry?

Sorrow welled up within her. Her tears flowed, and her breasts heaved — that made things worse. Yet another weary day came upon her with indifferent cruelty. Another day of empty friendships and pointless activity, it was too great a burden to bear.

The first month she refused to accept or acknowledge her new gender. Others did though. Strangers and friends often commented about her lack personal care and hygiene. They typically comments were, "I see you didn't have time to put on your face, or are you going with the natural look?" The only way to silence them was to comply with culture and embrace her new status as a female.

She pushed repressed the tears and set about her preparations. An array of cosmetics lay before her. Picasso never had to deal with so many colors, and she often appeared like one of his paintings, yet practice yielded results. She opened the various cosmetics and set right to work. Foundation, blush, lipstick, lip gloss, eye shadow, mascara, and eyeliner were applied with skill gleaned from endless repetition. To her great relief, it took little to highlight her great beauty.

As she traced eyeliner across her eyelid, she remembered Christy performing the very same task, and it fascinated her. She made it appear so easy and natural. Of course, Christy knew nothing else, having grown up female. Rory assured herself that this would someday seem normal, yet it was a hollow comfort, more feared than anticipated.

She screwed on the eyeliner cap and picked up a tube of lip-gloss. She parted her lips and applied a smooth coat. Passionate Rose made her lips shimmer, Christy's favorite color.

The news of the court's decision regarding her marriage to Christy arrived by courier. He hurried into the castle and handed her father an official proclamation by the court. Her marriage to Christy was annulled, a misstep of a previous timeline. Rory saw Bill from time to time but never Christy. Christy ran the docks with ruthless efficiency. If ever there was ever a woman that would have made an outstanding queen, it was Christy.

Satisfied with her appearance, Rory strolled into the bedroom. Opening her top dresser drawer, she scanned the assortment of panties. She grabbed a pair of simple white cotton panties and snarled at the various corsets. Wearing a corset was yet another accommodation to her new gender. Going without it caused stares and snickers.

She stabbed her feet into the panties and whisked them up her legs. With a tug and a wiggle of her hips, the cool cotton panties covered her. She snapped the elastic band around her waist they were in place.

The door opened, and Amy entered. "You should have waited for me, Mistress Rory. I am your maid. I am my charged with your care, and it is my duty to dress you – if I fail … I can be imprisoned." Amy selected a pair of silver panties. They almost appeared chromed, decorated with embroidered red flowers. "Your mother wants you to appear presentable for your many suitors."

"Why? Are they going to see me in my underwear?" asked Rory, still unable to say the word panties aloud. She knew it was no use to argue. Amy would simply race down the hallway and tattletale to Meredith. Rory stripped off the cotton panties and snatched the silver panties from Amy. She stabbed her feet into them and whisked them up her legs. The panties sculpted to her new, curvy form in ways that vexed her.

Amy selected the matching corset and released the hooks. Rory held up her arms and blew away her red bangs. The maid wrapped the corset around Rory and secured it. Rory then grabbed the lacing post and held on tight; a few seconds later a knee pressed into her back, and the laces began to tighten. Rory winced as the steel boned corset compressed her abdomen, causing every breath to come with greater effort and a little bit shallower. When the ends met, Amy tied off the excess and tucked it underneath the laces. She gave Rory's bottom a playful pat; "Now you look like a lady of the Royal Court. Let's put on your stockings."

"By the way," asked Rory. "What am I wearing today?"

Chapter 34

Rory emerged from her bedroom with Amy in hot pursuit. "You forgot your handbag." Amy scurried to catch up with Rory, bag in hand. Rory sighed and snatched the purse from her. "You look breathtaking," Amy cooed – and Rory did, much to her annoyance. A gleaming silver gown and shoulder length gloved made her appear ethereal, a goddess just descended from heaven. Rory held out her arms, sheathed in long satin gloves, and gazed down at the twin peaks of her breasts – she swore they were larger.

The gown was floor length with a short train. It highlighted Rory's, wide hips, perfect bottom, and a wisp of a waist – all testifying to her fertility and readiness for impregnation. A sweetheart neckline presented generous breasts, bulging from her chest like ripe fruit. They were an impressive pair – firm, round, and a tight cleft between them. They moved like counterweights to her hips when she moved.

The family crest set in the middle of a ring. It signified that she was a woman of royal status but unmarried, a fact that made her stomach twist into a knot. She examined her ring. She fretted over the day when a permanent ring would fuse to her hand, binding her body and soul to her spouse.

Tamara emerged from Meredith's bedroom still zipping up the back of her maid uniform. The girl blushed and hurried on her way. They never talked about her parent's many liaisons. What was the use? If her parents were satisfied with the arrangement, what could Rory do? However, she did wish her parents would be a little more discreet.

Unwilling to wait for her mother, Rory turned up her heels and strode down the hallway, as much as the tight gown permitted. Amy hesitated

271

for a second and then chased after her mistress. Rory became used to an entourage. Sometimes two or three women followed her around the castle. If she sat, they fixed her gown. If her cup emptied, they filled it. If a gentleman requested a walk, they walked ahead and behind them. To the royal court, servants were things, like a pair of shoes, were used and discarded. She started to feel the same way. There were too many of them to remember their names or care about them as persons. Only Amy remained her constant shadow, and she slept with her father. Although no one admitted it, she also slept with her mother.

Rory descended the circular stairs, the red carpet padding her steps. When she emerged in the yellow great-room, all eyes turned toward her. Women curtsied, and men bowed. Quite whispered arose from those banished to the outer areas. Male and female suitors looked upon her with avarice.

A mature but sexually potent woman declared a man by the court, Countess Julianne Hasford was the lead contender. Formidable was the word most people used when describing her; her blue eyes hid a depraved mind and dark soul. She always dressed in black, a symbol of her widowhood, yet her gowns were provocative, crafted with low necklines and tailored to display her body; and like Rory, she was a redhead. Many a fool lusted after her body and ignored the evil in her heart.

After the death of Julianne's husband, Marcus Hasford, she petitioned the court, and it granted the status as a man, no mean feat for a woman, becoming dominant and able to take a wife. Thus, she inherited his title and wealth. Julianne stared at Rory's hand: it would soon wear her ring. Rumor had it that Julianne already had a magical ring crafted. She and Walter were in the final stages of negotiation. If they struck a deal, Rory would wed to Julianne regardless of Rory's feelings. zx

Julianne stepped out of the crowd. She smiled at the young woman with an air of condescension. "You look radiant this morning."

The Seventh Age

"Thank you," Rory replied.

The Countess assumed a nonchalant tone saying, "Your father and I spoke last night. He assured me that you are fertile." Her gaze shifted to Rory's breasts. "How many children do you suppose you will bear?"

Rory was dumbstruck. What could she say to such a thing? "Yes." "No." "Go to hell!" In the end, she remained silent and moved away from Julianne.

Gilla intercepted Rory and offered an unsolicited observation. "I understand that Prince Richard of Stone Crop has decided to remain a bachelor." Gilla shared the prince's bed that night and knew of his plans to avoid marriage to Rory, but somehow she concluded that she was an exception: the prince would marry her. She had no way of knowing that this news pleased Rory and that her own status was far more tenuous than she imagined.

"Yes," Rory replied. "The prince is in no hurry to marry. He is a young man and has plenty of time to start a family."

Prince Richard hated the royal court, his parents, and the women who courted him. Their flattery was insincere; their love was false, and their desire was avarice. He was alone, and the loneliness ate at his soul, twisting his desire into something dark and festering, a septic wound that would not heal. The Prince hired a dominatrix, set aside private residences, and bent the women to his will.

Gilla had no idea what awaited her, that her life was about to alter in such a profound way, that she would never escape it. She would spend the rest of her days as a courtesan, a kept woman by the wealthy and powerful, a woman held in literal bondage, for the prince developed a taste for it.

"If you will excuse me, I must attend to a personal matter," Gilla said, very pleased with her achievement; she smugly turned away before receiving a reply, treating Rory as if she was beneath her. She gathered up her lilac satin gown as she ascended the stairs, and she faded into the shadows, never to be seen again.

Julia watched this drama, bemused, and a smirk appeared on her face. He was her chief competitor for Rory. She introduced the prince to the dark delights. She corrupted him, diverting his attention from the consolidation of his power, preventing him from ever taking the throne; and she was responsible for Gilla's fate, and that pleased her. The thought of the girl's abasement and suffering satisfied a deep yearning within her.

"I found somebody who wants to see you," said a woman near the glass white framed doors. The crowd parted, and Christy stepped forward, she was a golden hair goddess, a rare beauty clad in white gown that sparkled with diamonds: a work of art, strapless, seductive, having a sweetheart neckline, and tailored with a slit up the right side; and her accessories were a pair matching opera gloves, stockings, and stiletto high heels. The radiant beauty stole Rory's breath away.

Christy's right hand released a leash. Jake, her border collie, charged about and yapped with delight. He jumped about and danced with unvarnished joy. Rory squatted down, stretching her gown over her round bottom, and stroked his head. The dog melted into her hand and tried to lick her face. Julianne looked upon the display with disgust and made a mental note to have the creature dispatched after the wedding.

"It's good to see you." Christy crossed her arms and sashayed up to Rory. Christy said to Julianne, "Why don't you fetch me a cup of coffee?" Before Julianne could reply, Christy said, "I'm sorry. That black dress made me think you were part of the serving staff." A titter arose from the other guests. Julianne stuck up her nose and marched away in a huff. Christy called out, "I like my coffee with cream." This yielded outright laughter. Her glossy crimson lips curled into a smirk, and she said, "Hello Rory, it's good to see you."

Chapter 35

"Have you lost your mind?" shouted Christy, her face red with anger. Before Walter could reply, she continued her tirade. "I remember a time when Walter Vakhal had box seats for the Colorado Rockies. He bought everyone beers and hotdogs. I don't know you. You're walking around this palace like you were king."

"'We the People …' put you here. For fifty years –" her eyes welled up with tears, and she could not speak. "– We suffered under King Leopold's law. He took away our freedoms, threw us in prison, killed us for going to church, and starved people to death … what was our crime? Someone made a joke about the king, or they campaigned for a democratic election."

"I spent the last fifty years … fifty years of my life as a madam. I did it so we would be free. I fed information to the resistance and killed people. I killed our own people: those who collaborated with the king's secret police. After all that, we won." She closed her eyes and sighed. "I had that monster inside me to get information about his security forces … but it was worth it. He is dead."

She leaned over in Walter's face. "Now you are screwing it all up. There are over 68,371 Americans back in Gleason who won't stand for it."

"I still don't understand why you are angry about," Walter said.

"You don't understand? Have you become so dulled by wine and whores that you can't think? Those pretenders looking for Rory's hand in marriage are all destitute aristocrats. Asgard is a representative democracy, a republic. One wins a seat House of Commons by popular vote, but one achieved a seat in the House of Lords by merit; the nobles of merit expelled these worthless aristocrats.

Once upon a time, they grew fat off tax money and bribes, but now all that is gone. Oh sure, they have a title and posh estates, but they are broke. No. They are worse than broke. They are over their heads in debt and desperate. They need your cash to keep them afloat, and they will do anything to get it. If they fail, they will become debtor slaves."

"The day after the wedding, they will plot your death. When you are dead, Rory will be your only heir. As your heir, the groom will inherit all of your lands, and, more importantly, he will inherit your title. That means he will become the new Prime Minister. Once he is the Prime Minster, he can block our admission into the Asgard National Parliament. That would leave them one step away from becoming king and abolishing the Salvia Parliament. Then these leeches will take our land and our freedom."

"We would lose everything!" She put her hands on her hips and scowled. "They have another thing coming if they think we will just roll over and go back to feudal life. We have enough arms and troops to fight. But that would cost a lot of lives."

"Now get your ass in gear and get with the program," she shouted, her fists clenched in rage.

"It's not as dire as you say," Walter said and crossed his legs. "I have many loyal supporters in Parliament and my personal bodyguard."

"Your bodyguard is not loyal to you. I may live 90 miles and a world away, but we still get news. They meet with aristocrats every night behind closed doors and auction off their services. They are holding a lottery to see who gets to kill you."

She pulled over a chair and sat next to him. "The Council sent me up here to try and get you to see reason. Your detractors were one vote away from getting a 'no confidence vote.' That's it, just one vote, mine. We know about your tryst with Amy. Hell, she told everyone that she is going to be your second wife. Then she will give birth to a baby, and, if it is male, he will inherit your title and lands. Then these leeches can kill you, Meredith, and Rory. Your heir will be ideal for their plans. They can rule by proxy and take away our freedoms."

"You have one option," she said and held up her index finger. "You stall for time. The wolves will behave themselves only as long as they think they have a chance to take over Salvia. If word of this gets out that you changed your mind about the wedding or if they find out that Amy is pregnant, then your supposed supporters and quiet friends in the Salvia Parliament will stage a coup."

Walter leaned back in the chair. He rubbed his face and sighed. "I've been such an idiot. The trappings of the royal court are so seductive. I convinced myself that I deserved them. I was so much more clever than them. I was convinced that there was nothing they do a thing to oppose me. I've been a fool."

"They planned their countermove the day you formed the Salvia Parliament. They do not intend to join Asgard. The idea of democratic elections terrifies them, and it should. They are a bunch of leeches, but they are not idiots. You need to let them think that they are winning. Keep them guessing," Christy said. "Let them believe that you are still playing their game. When you are hanging by a thread, don't pull on it," she replied.

"I know what I need to do. You can count on me." Walter rose to his feet. "For what it's worth, I'm sorry."

"Apology accepted, just get your head back in the game," she said. "All of us are counting on you."

Chapter 36

Walter stood on the walls, his hands, and feet numb. The icy wind cut through his cloak and shoved him backward. He warmed his hands by a fire and kept watch, as though a sentry. It was a common sight these days – sleep came in fragments and ended with panic attacks. He stole away from his private chambers as though a thief and skulked from shadow to shadow. He arrived at the same wall and stood upon the same spot, his eyes searching for Gleason Valley and home.

Home. It made his spirit heavy and mind overwrought. The men of Gleason raised the call to arms. The ragtag volunteer army assembled: peaceful men now brandished blades. Was it a comedy or a tragedy? Nevertheless, they were all Gleason had to offer. Christy sent a warning that they were on the move. They would take the castle by force and win their freedom.

It was an empty gesture. The castle was perched high upon Spire Mountain. Only the great eagles soared up and reached its outer walls. How would an army reach it? Guards watched the road at every turn, and the valley floor lay far below him, at the bottom of a sheer cliff. Even if they were mountaineers with long ropes and climbing gear, the guards would cut down invaders before they made it halfway.

They could cut off the castle, he reasoned. It was a frail plan. The surrounding kingdoms would send armies and rush to the aid of their fellow aristocrats. Then what would they do? They would be scattered and killed as they fled.

Think Walter, think! Damn it, man, this is your fault.

The Seventh Age

He grabbed the icy stone wall and leaned over through the parapet. Yellow lights began to dot the windows in Heather Vale. By the first rays of dawn, he saw them. Tents dotted every available spot, and men filled the taverns. An advance party, he reasoned. Perhaps they would try to take the castle by surprise, another pathetic option. The guards were too numerous and wary at night. They would discover the attackers and then execute them.

Walter shivered and turned to the east. The first rays of dawn broke over the Wolf's Maw Mountains. The yellow shafts of gold caressed his cheeks like the hands of a lover and soothed away the cold sting. "God, I don't pray very much, and I'm not a religious man, but I need your help. This is beyond me. I'm at the end of my tether … and everyone I love will die. I need your help. Save us, please save us."

Chapter 37

Yellow light illumined windows as the castle arose from its slumber. The smell of breakfast hung in the air. Servants cleaned, cooked, and set places in the dining hall. Chambermaids hurried to wake their Masters and Mistresses, dressing and caring for them like they were little children.

Countess Julianne Hasford departed her quarters and departed before the chambermaids arrived. Rather than go to breakfast, she made her way to the king's keep and then his private residence. The building afforded a panoramic view of the mountains and of the entire castle. The king's study, constructed on the roof, a glass dome, offered a 360-degree view. The Countess strolled through the study, glided her fingers along the mahogany desk, and admired its rich texture. She crossed her arms and sighed. Just a few more strategic moves and everything would be hers.

The headings of the compass were set in the middle of the hardwood floor. She followed the line southwest and stood before the curved glass. Although in the distance, she saw a fertile green valley. Gleason, it was a rare gem, located in the middle of a harsh wilderness. It would make her the envy of all other monarchs in the region.

The Countess turned toward the south and saw the triple peaks of the Talon Mountains. Their summits were bereft life: harsh, jagged, and raw. Their spiked digits reminded her of Count Hadrian Hasford, her deceased husband.

For a moment, she drifted back in time – back to a time when she was a young and innocent. Her wedding day was regal, as one might expect. Well-wishers and hangers-on attended from kingdoms everywhere. It was magical, everything she dreamed of as a girl. Then the crowds departed, and her honeymoon began.

Nothing prepared her for his cruelty. He shoved her face first into the bed, jerked up her gown, and ripped off her lingerie. What came next made her sob in agony and left blood stains on the bed. This act would come to symbolize their entire marriage. Year after year, decade after decade, his cruelty twisted her soul, like a gnarled scrub oak on the side of a windswept mountain. The enraged woman consumed the kind-hearted girl of her youth.

The Count murdered each of their three daughters when they turned 18-years-old, fearful that they would usurp him. Their murder broke her, and her tentative grip on love gave way to hate.

It was either her life or his. She purchased a talisman from a daemia shaman and placed it in the count's bedchambers. He seldom slept alone, but never with her. The talisman tormented the count with recurrent nightmares, and although he slept, it prevented true rest. In the end, he went insane and threw himself off the chapel tower.

No one mourned his passing. Julianne burned his body, and rather than place his ashes in the royal mausoleum, she flushed them down the toilet. The next day she assumed management of the late count's estate. Like most nobles, the count was destitute. He sold or borrowed against his ancestral lands. This left her deep in debt without the means to repay. At best, they would eject her from the estate and be left a pauper. For although she was 250-year-old, she still appeared in the prime of life, a beautiful woman by anyone's standard. The more likely fate was that a slave, her mind erased, or worse yet, she would be a whore, her mind intact.

Life had been too cruel and the fates too harsh. They would never allow that to happen. She would seize this opportunity or die in the attempt.

The lights illuminated in Rory's bedchamber. Through the white gauze curtains, she saw the rare beauty pass by the window. The girl would be hers or no ones. After they were married, she might even let the girl live, if she behaved herself. The girl's death, however, seemed inevitable.

The Countess recalled a recent visit. She requested a private audience with Rory and Walter agreed. It was lesser-known practice but still valid. It gave the dominant spouse a chance to survey the bride. Matrons, legal staff, and many staff supervised such encounters. Rory objected, but she had little choice in the matter. Her father agreed, and she had to perform. Failure to do so would have resulted in her death and that of her family.

Rory stood in the center of the room. Three maids removed her clothes and attended her. Julianne raised her eyebrow and tapped her chin. The girl had magnificent breasts and curves to match. *Her ring would break the girl and adjust her attitude,* she pondered.

As she strolled through the office, a better idea occurred to her. The black arts, her expertise, offered many options. She could steal the girl's body: switch places with Rory and assume her identity. Although she was still a young woman by Eden standards, a return to the flower of her youth appealed to her. Yes. That was a much better idea. Her lips curled into a predatory smile.

The Countess exited the King's keep and returned to the main complex. The final details of her plan were in motion. She crossed the compound with a spring in her step. She felt lighter and happier than she had in years.

The dining hall was octagonal and three stories tall, a choice place to dine. The middle wall was lemon yellow, and a ring of lead crystal glass ringed the wall just underneath the roof. Bleached hardwood comprised the floors, and the furnishings were white.

When Julianne entered the dining hall, all eyes turned to her. She saw fear in their eyes. *So this is what it is like to be king. I'm going to enjoy it.* As she scanned the vast dining hall, she saw Christy seated on the opposite side.

The Seventh Age

The defiant blonde paid her little note. *My first act as king will be to put that whore to death. Slow and filled with screams, I think.*

Cosmia, an elder female noble and Salvia Lord, said, "Julianne, you must join us for breakfast." A chair remained empty between her and the treasurer, Alistair. The other lords and ladies looked up at her with hopeful eyes.

"Of course," Julianne said. The Countess smoothed her dress underneath her and took a seat. A servant assisted her and slid her chair up to the table. A cart then rolled over, and she selected her breakfast.

Cosmia said, "I told everyone what marvelous plans you have for Salvia."

Anger flashed in Julianne's eyes, but she snuffed it out a moment later. "Well yes, I do have many plans. I think our union with Asgard is ill-considered, too hasty. We need time to grow as a people and accustom ourselves to local parliamentary government. We can always join Asgard later. 'Haste is the vice of the ill prepared.'"

"I couldn't agree more," Cosmia replied. The elderly woman sipped her tea. "But you would honor the title and land holdings of nobles. Would you not?"

"Oh my yes," Julianne said. "We must respect tradition, even if others do not. The aristocracy provides sound and sophisticated leadership. The simple masses have no idea what is good for them or the kingdom. I'm sure we can convince Prime Minister Vakhal of this."

"I totally agree," Cosmia said and set down her cup. A servant refilled it with hot tea and removed her empty plate. "We must be circumspect in our actions."

Julianne detected the hint of warning in Cosmia's words. To solidify her position, she had to make concessions to the other suitors. Thus, when she made her play, no one would oppose her. However, many of those concessions involved title to lands, lands that belonged to others.

The truth of her plans would have shocked them. The day of her wedding to Rory, she would kill them all. One by one, the prince first, then Walter, and then the nobles, they would be dragged out into the courtyard and then beheaded. The guards would cast the bodies off the castle wall, and then mount the head on pikes. They would line the road leading up to the castle. There would be neither revolts nor intrigues, all assassination attempts preempted. She would reign as sovereign without challenge, without mercy, and without pity. It was the way of the world: a lesson she learned from bitter experience.

Chapter 38

Rory had had enough: enough doubt, enough self-loathing, and enough fear. It was time to act. She saw her father's distress and heard of the pending battle. Everyone in the castle spoke of it in whispers. She would strike out against their enemies if she could avoid her parents.

The squeak of the door hinges sounded like thunder. Rory opened the door a crack and peered into the hallway. Amy, her father's watchdog, was gone. She slipped from the room and hurried down the hallway. The clack of her high heels and the rustle of fabric broke the silence. Her breathing quickened, and her skin flushed; but her heart remained silent – strange, as though it slept.

Armories, distributed throughout the castle, prevented aggressors from isolating them from their arms. Thus, guards and citizens could defend themselves. From what little Rory witnessed, the captain of the guard stocked them with armor and weapons, many of them designed for females.

She hurried down a blue and white marble tiled hallway and came to a stop at a T-intersection. All the tan hallways and fixtures blended into one another, which created a maze. Her composure failing, she rushed down a hallway to her right and broke into a run. The blue and silver gown flew behind her as she fled.

The armory placard hung over a white door. Rory grabbed the knob, hurried into the closet, and closed the door with a quiet click. Silver swords hung on a wooden rack and across the aisle were javelins. Rory turned to her left and traversed the cross aisle. Ornate armor hung beside battle-scarred armor, helmets on the rack above the corresponding set.

The male armor would hang loose upon her, like a child wearing a parent's clothes. She passed down the row, used across the aisle, and came to a stop. Sunlight beamed through a high window and gleamed on silver female armor. As if in a trance, her fingertips traced the scrollwork and embellishments that adorned the breastplate. The silvery twin peaks appeared large enough to accommodate her breasts.

Taking off a gown and all the accouterments took time. A pile of clothing accumulated on the floor at Rory's feet. Finally, she was naked. While donning a slip-suit, a glossy black catsuit, she danced about and then sat on a bench. She drew the garment up her torso, worked her arms into the sleeves and pulled up the banded jacket collar. The battle harness, resembling a corset, came next.

Unfamiliar with Asgard armor, the maiden's belt took her a while to understand. It wrapped around her abdomen and a metallic thong cleaved between her cheeks, a V-panel covering her crotch. The silver chainmail tunic reminded her of a silver mini-dress with long sleeves and left her upper thighs, allowing one to see the silver glint of her maiden's belt in her crotch. The chest plate and pauldrons made her feel safe for some reason, almost invulnerable. Greaves, gauntlets, and gloves completed the armor set. In a strange sort of way, it felt like she was going to a grand gala.

In her former life as a man, Rory served in the military and had an interest in fencing. He qualified for the state championships, but a groin injury during a track meet put an end to it. She strapped a pair of swords to her back, X-fashion, and knives to her lower back, handles pointing down at an angle.

Helmet in hand, she felt ready for battle. All she had to do was avoid her parents, escape the castle, and join the resistance. She twitched her nose and pondered the matter. *I'll just say that I'm going for a ride. That is a stupid idea. They would tell dad, and he would stop me. I can hide in the back of a wagon.* She had no idea what wagons were leaving the castle. *I could bribe a guard.* However, she had no money. *Damn it, there has to be way out of the castle.* In the end, she decided to bluff her way into a mounted patrol and escape if the opportunity presented itself.

After grabbing a rucksack and helmet, she opened the door a little and peered into the hallway. She rushed from the room and scurried down a corridor. A door flung open behind her and hands grabbed her. A yelp ripped from her lips as she stumbled backward.

Christy slammed the door and put her hands on her hips. "What do you think you're doing? This isn't a game."

Rory cocked her head and twitched her nose. Christy wore a silver breastplate over a brown leather tunic. With it, she wore black tights, boots, and had a sword strapped to her left hip. Rory asked, "What are you doing?"

"I asked first."

"I'm joining the resistance. If everyone I care about is going to war, so am I." Rory crossed her arms and hardened her expression. However, it made her appear like an angry little girl. "You can't stop me."

"I have an important assignment. I don't need you upsetting everyone. Go back to your room and wait." Christy glared at Rory.

"No. I'm helping. You have only two choices, get out of my way or let me help you."

"There is a third: I could tie you up and gag you."

"The guards would hear you. Besides, I can help. I know how to use a sword, and I am the Prime Minister's daughter." Rory held Christy's hands and looked into her eyes. "I failed Michael, and I failed you. When my community needed me, I was frozen in time. I have to do this."

Christy's hard edge melted. "It wasn't your fault. The universe blinked and took him away from us. I forgave you a long time ago." She took a deep breath and released it. "Okay, you can come, but you do as I say."

287

"This should be fun," Rory said, wrinkling her nose with a smile.

"It's not fun," Christy said, repressing a smile. "It's serious."

"Very serious," Rory said with a somber expression. "You won't be sorry."

"I already am." Christy opened the door and peered into the hallway. She waved to Rory and left cover. The pair hurried from hallway to hallway, leaving Rory turned around.

"Where are we going? Do you have a secret way out of the castle?" asked Rory.

"Shh," Christy replied. "No talking."

After they had descended four flights of stairs, the castle's interior transitioned from expensive decor to rough stone and flaming torches. At the sound of voices, they ducked into a closet filled with empty wine casks. Christy listened at the door as the voices neared. The sour wine made Rory's nose itch, and she struggled to stop a sneeze.

"ACHOO," she sneezed.

The voices stopped. Christy waved at Rory, and they hid behind a stack of barrels. The door opened, and a guard entered. Christy gripped her knife as the man rummaged about the room. "Let's get going. I'm hungry." The other man mumbled something, and they exited. The sound of voices and footsteps faded.

Christy exhaled. "Don't do that. You nearly got us caught."

"It's not my fault. It stinks in here. They could mop the place out once in a while."

Christy clucked her tongue and rolled her eyes. They left their hiding place and exited another door. The service tunnels formed a maze underneath the castle. Servants used them to transport food, wine, and other goods. They would just pop up in an area and depart without anyone seeing them. However, the tunnels ended with the building. It would force them to climb up to the parade grounds and wait for an opportunity to rush the main gate.

Chapter 39

Walter strolled along the outer wall, the hand of fate clenched around his throat. His footsteps tapped out a staccato beat on the walkway. The morning sun warmed the curtain wall and drew the chill from the air. He passed another pair of guards and nodded. They watched him pass and spoke in whispers. The chessboard was set, and the pieces were in motion. He stood alone and watched the ravine for an approaching army.

He walked down the steps to the courtyard and devised a desperate plan. He would concoct some excuse to leave the castle, and then could escape and join them. Rory and Meredith would be safe. Julianne would need his permission and blessing to wed Rory. Then he saw the malice in the guard's eyes. They would never allow it; it would be their heads if he escaped. It trapped him in a prison of his own design.

Walter was about to walk back to the dining hall and meet his fate when a glint of silver metal caught his attention. He saw Rory and Christy, and they wore armor and weapons. They skulked about a doorway on the far side of the compound. *What are they doing?*

When they made a mad dash for the gatehouse, his hands clenched the wall and muscles tensed. "Guards," he called out. "Are there any more guests to arrive?" The captain of the watch turned away from the compound and faced Walter.

He checked some documents and said, "A few more guests are due to arrive. Are you expecting someone special?"

"Oh … ah … no, I just like to be prepared. The castle is full. We barely have an empty room remaining."

The Seventh Age

"I see. Well, a few more noble families are due to arrive. I will inform housekeeping to make provisions for them." When he saw that the coast was clear, he excused himself and went to the gatehouse.

———

Christy climbed the stone stairs, her hand feeling the rough walls. The smell of smoke meant the watch-fires burned. Hot oil, boiling in cast iron cauldrons, awaited any trespassers in the gate below them. Once tipped, the oil flowed through tubes and spewed from the mouths of grimacing gargoyles. After the coating the attackers, flaming arrows set them ablaze.

She removed her weapons and handed them to Rory. After primping her hair, she strutted into the gatehouse. The guards lingered at the windows, their hands near the gate release mechanism. One released, it would take three strong men to hoist the counter weight. "The captain says that you men need some entertainment." She primped her golden locks and wore her best smile. "Anyone here need some relief?"

"The captain sent you?" asked the sergeant. "That doesn't sound like him." The men all moved toward her and inspected her.

"What harm would it do?" asked one man.

Another said, "It's been months since I had a woman, and this whore is a real beauty."

"I am a gift from the Prime Minster. His daughter's engagement is near. He wishes all to celebrate." Christy turned around, bent over at the hips, and drew up her tunic. Leather tights sculpted to her ass cheeks and shapely legs. "Who's first?"

All the men moved toward her. "Back off you lot," barked the sergeant. "I go first. I'll not catch any diseases from the likes of you."

291

Rory crept up to the circular stairs and peered around the wall. Christy stood still, bent at the hips, her tights down around her knees, and a man behind her. She lurched forward, and the man drew her back to meet another thrust. They locked eyes for a moment and then Rory withdrew. Sickness twisted her stomach, and her soul ached as if bleeding. Her eyes welled up with tears and trickled down her cheeks. She tried to reason it away. *She has been doing this for fifty years. It is nothing new to her.* All these rationalizations failed to bring comfort or soothe the ache of her soul.

———

Walter had his foot on the first step to the gatehouse when a commotion caught his attention. "I Joash Edward Faroe, and my father is King Olaf Erickson III, the high king of Asgard. You will open the gates for me. I have a right to contend for the daughter of the Prime Minister. To refuse me is to invite war."

Walter hurried around the wall and through the gate. "Are you a fool?" said Walter. "Open the gate. Let him pass."

"But the Countess Hasford gave him strict orders that no one was to enter or exit the castle, except by her permission." The gate commander rubbed his face and searched his mind for an answer. He leafed through the various registered guests. "I'm sorry, but he's not on the list Prime Minster. He may not enter."

Joash was a giant of a man encased in steel. He drew his sword and cut off the gate commander's head with one swipe. His men drew their weapons and attacked. "SHUT THE GATE!" shouted a guard. "Hurry!"

Up in the gatehouse, Christy leaped into action. "Now! Throw me my sword." Rory scrambled up the stairs and threw the sheathed sword to Christy. She jumped forward, snatched the sword from the air, drew it, and swept through the air. The blade cut through the front of the sergeant's neck. Blood spurted from the wound and coated his men. He grabbed his neck and gurgled. Blood sprayed through his fingers, and he staggered.

Christy lunged at an unarmed man, running her blade through his chest until it jutted out the back. She planted her foot on his chest and pulled the blade out, letting the mortally wounded man drop to the ground. The other guards rushed for their weapons.

Rory drew her blades and attacked the men. A guard grabbed a sword and turned around. Rory's blade cut through his right elbow, and it hung only by a few strands of muscle. He grimaced in agony and clutched his wounded limb. Another guard lunged at Rory, she easily sidestepped and deflected his blow. She brought her blade down on the back of his neck. The spinal cord severed, the man dropped to the ground, and his eyes wide with terror, he tried to swallow air like a fish out of water.

When a man reached for the gate release, Christ cut off his hand. The man screamed and clutched the bloody stump. "You bitch!" he shouted. She thrust through his heart and jerked around her sword. The man staggered and fell out of the window and onto combatants in the gateway.

Mounted cavalry thundered around the swayback and charged around the road. Arrows flew at them from the archers stationed on the wall, but they bounced off the warrior's shields and armor. Hooves beat, weapons brandished, and war cries screamed, the cavalry charged at the gate.

Joash swung his sword, cutting a man in two. Both halves hit the ground with a wet splat and tried to crawl away from the battle. "HOLD THE GATE!" Joash shouted.

Bill threw off his cloak and sprinted up the stairs. Seven dead bodies littered the floor. He saw Christy, and to his great surprise, he saw Rory. "Fantastic job," he said. The cavalry thundered through the gate and entered the castle.

"Now for that Countess bitch," Christy growled. Rory faltered for a second, unsure what to do. Then she hurried after Christy and scrambled down the winding stairs.

———

Walter hurried away from the fighting. Cavalry charged past him, and combatants spilled into the courtyard. Joash was the largest man Walter had ever seen. He sat on a knight's charger and led a platoon of grim-faced warriors. They were all well-armed and armored, having the look of veterans.

Walter devised a quick plan. Whoever this man was, he would offer him Rory's hand. He had only a platoon, but it might be enough to take the castle. Some of the guards would join them. Steel met steel as the fighting raged through the castle. When a soldier ran to him, Walter recoiled in fear. Bill removed his helmet and said, "It's good to be back. Now the fun begins."

"What is all this?" Walter shouted above the noise.

Before Bill could reply, a warrior blew a small, trumpet. The clarion call cut through the morning air and echoed off the mountains. Seconds later, the thunder of hooves came from the road. Walter strained to see who approached by his line of sight was cut off by the bend around Iron Mountain. A column of mounted cavalry and men charged down the road and flooded the castle.

Joash rode into the center of the courtyard, and his charger reared onto its hind legs. He roared, "I am Joash, son of King Olaf. I am taking charge of this castle in the name of Asgard. Those who oppose me will die."

The chaos Joash caused lasted only a few minutes, but it was long enough. An army charged into the courtyard. Warriors leaped from wagons and rushed up to the walls. They disarmed the guards and ushered them off the wall. They fixed arrows in their bows and kept them at the ready. Other warriors rushed into the guard's barracks and mess hall. They drove half-dressed men and women out into the open air.

The doors to the royal dining hall flew open. The nobles emerged and gaped at the carnage. The bodies of the castle guards lay scattered across the courtyard, and the victors glared at them with hateful eyes. The Countess pushed her way through their midst and strode up to Joash. "How dare you barge in like a thief? I have a prior claim on the girl."

"And I have claim upon these lands. The Asgard Parliament held an emergency session. They approved the inclusion of Salvia, and I am authorized to take charge over these lands. So marry the maiden if you wish, but these lands are now under Asgard rule."

Joash dismounted his horse and approached the Julianne. He drew out his massive blade and wielded it as if it was a twig. He stared her down and then scanned the crowd. She uncrossed her arms and cringed before the massive man. "Let me assure you, anyone attempting a violent rebellion against the King of Asgard will be met with swift justice."

Christy emerged from the crowd and sashayed up to Julianne. She handed the Countess a chessboard king and said, "Checkmate." She then said to Walter, "I'm going up to my room to read. Let me know how it all turns out."

Chapter 40

Two days later Christy lingered before her bedroom window. She saw The Countess Julianne Hasford step into her carriage, and her bags were loaded onto a separate wagon. Without a second look, she told her driver to leave. Rumor had it that she hired a ship to ferry her to the Western Isles, one step ahead of her creditors.

The other nobles who laid claim to Rory left the prior day. Joash refused to provide them with funds for their transportation. Most of them were so impoverished that they had to leave the castle by foot. It did Christy's heart good to see it.

A knock came from her bedroom door. "Come in," she said. The door opened. Walter and Bill entered. "Ah, just the pair I wanted to see. How did it go?" She sat down in a private breakfast nook and poured a cup of tea.

The men sat, and Walter placed papers on the table. "This is the last of the court rulings. All of the land stolen from our people over the past fifty years has been returned, and compensation paid for their unjust seizure. Cosmia is livid. She lost all of her land and wealth. I hear that she is going to stay with family on the Western Isles. As for the countess, she is fleeing her creditors."

"Nasty bitch," Bill added. "Her husband probably committed suicide to get away from her."

"I was told that she had a very hard life," Walter said.

"I'm surprised to hear you defending her. She is a witch, and all three of her daughters were witches. They performed every dark art and ritual they could learn. They wandered around the countryside at night: terrifying people, kidnapping children, and murdering anyone who opposed them. When they tried to have the dark spirits kill their father and take his place, he killed them first. Their entire family is a nightmare. I'm glad she's gone. I wish she was dead."

"Back to business." Walter sorted through the papers. "Alistair is going to prison for embezzlement of the Salvia treasury. He's been siphoning off money for years. They caught him at the lesser gate on Table Mountain with a chest full of gold. I hear they are selling him as punishment. I can't imagine him bringing a very high price."

"I have to admit, the Asgard Parliament really knows how to clean house," Christy said. "It's more than I hoped for. What about Prince Gregory?"

"Still missing," Bill replied, "fled to the Western Isles."

Christy leaned back and crossed her legs. "Smile Walter: you don't know how to win. We're free."

"Don't make my mistake, Christy," Walter replied and removed his reading glasses. "The Elven priests are coming here on some important business. When I asked Joash, he evaded my question and dismissed me. But I heard whispers. Some of the warriors were saying that there is a 'Great Gate.' This gate controls all the gates to Earth. As far as I can tell, they need to take some sort of measurements in Gleason. I suppose it's because we are from Earth."

"I had no idea the gates to Earth were open," Christy replied with a smile.

"They're not open yet," Walter sighed. "It will be a disaster when they are."

"What? Why?" asked Christy.

"You know about all the creatures in this world. There are more evil things than I can count. Imagine a gate opening and all of those evil monstrosities rushing to Earth. They would have no defense against

297

them. It would be a massacre." Walter crossed his right arm and covered his mouth. He shook his head and gazed out the window. "If the enemy finds it first, Earth is lost."

Bill rose to his feet and walked to the window. He stared out for a second and turned back toward them. "I remember the first year before King Leopold took control. Shit, I wish we hadn't been so sucked in by him. Anyway, I was part of a crew that sailed out of Safe Harbor."

"I remember," Walter said. "You encountered something."

"Yeah, we encountered the shit out of something," Bill said. "Tentacles shot out from a calm sea. It ripped apart our sails and circled around our boat. It was like some sort of giant squid. It had razor blades on its tentacles. I saw it cut Bob Kelly in two with just a slap; the man looked up from the deck as blood gushed out from his severed body – it was like a chainsaw ripped him apart. I ran to the stern and jumped into the sea. When I came up, I saw our ship pulled under the water and disappear from sight."

"I never knew," Christy said.

"It's not something I'm proud of. Everyone else was fighting that damn thing. I ran. Don't bother telling me, 'It wasn't your fault. You made the right choice.' I told myself those things a million times. They never make me feel any better."

"How did you get home again?" asked Walter.

"I used some rope and lashed together some debris. The currents carried me back into the Wolf's Maw Mountains. It took me three months of climbing over every damn rock between the coast and Gleason to get home. I ate some things … well, let's just say no one should have to eat."

"My point is that this planet is a death trap to the uninitiated. Hell, rhunite alone could devastate a city and destroy all of Earth's technology. Imagine an army of haugr or daemia, armed with rhunite weapons, loose on Earth. It makes my gut twist into knots." Bill sat down at the table again. "We have to warn them."

Chapter 41

Rory lounged in front of the fireplace, and the light flickered on the room around her, casting long shadows across the floor. The hearth warmed a damp and frigid night – comforting both body and soul. She sipped a glass of merlot and leafed through a yearbook. It and a few other precious mementos arrived the previous day in a shipment from home. The soothing sounds of Dobie Gray came from a vinyl record. He sang "Drift Away." She closed her eyes and wandered the landscape of her life.

She remembered joining the wrestling team and a rather unsuccessful season. Even so, the day of the photograph was the proudest day of her life. Her fingers glided over the glossy color page. The team photo remained, but she was gone; or rather, the photo of her as a teenage boy vanished.

On the next page, she saw a picture of the cheerleading squad. A russet hair beauty stood in the right center of the front row of the portrait, beauty blazing above her peers like a torch in the night. Her rosy cheeks, ruby lips, and sparkling blue eyes captivated the eye. Her lips curled in an irrepressible smile, the trials of life far away and unsuspected. A pleated white miniskirt danced around her upper thighs, and a white sleeveless top had a blue lightning bolt with GHS embroidered on it. She read the list of names to identify the girl, "Sarah Adams, Grace Tabbot, Erin Louis, Rory Vakhal …."

She flipped the page in the book. The next photo was one of her kissing a boy. They were seated at a table and decorations hung from the ceiling. A slice of cake lay in the foreground. The caption read "Rory's Sweet 16 Kiss." She turned the book this way and that, but she could not see the boy's face. It was probably a good thing.

She had no memory of it or any of the other details of her life. In this reality, she attended Brown University, was an English literature major, and worked as a cocktail waitress. She posed in swimsuits, dresses, and gowns for fashion magazines. Someone had saved magazine ads, bearing her image, in a scrapbook.

Jake, her border collie, groaned and stretched his legs. The soft rug and the warm fire wooed him to slumber. He looked up at his mistress for approval. Rory was brooding again. There was no dissuading her from it – even a game of fetch failed to lift her spirits. Jake closed his eyes and let blissful sleep engulf him.

Rory released a heavy sigh and set aside the yearbook. A voice cut through the silence. "I'm going to my room now." Monica rose from a chair. She had arrived with the belongings and spent the night comforting Rory.

"Bye," Rory replied.

Amy cinched down her robe and slipped her feet into her slippers. "How did the meeting go?" asked Amy with a yawn. "Are we joining 'The Asgard Republic'?"

The corners of Rory's lips curled into a smile. "Yes. My dad signed the charter this morning. It's all settled. We're free."

"Good," Amy nodded and yawned again. "I'll let Javier know. He's been pestering me about it."

A gust of wind rattled the window, and driving rain turned it opaque. Rory rose to her feet and strolled over to it. Thick, gray clouds hung low in the sky and cast a dark hue over the mountains. Every so often, the moon peeked out from the clouds and bathed the mountains in a gentle glow.

Sheets of rain flowed down the side of the castle and formed a pool in the courtyard. It then passed through drains and spewed out in powerful jets from drainpipes. This waterfall cascaded off the rocks and crashed into the river.

A commotion arose from the gate, and guards clad in rain slickers run over to it. They drew the gate open and stood at attention. She had seen many warriors arrive over the past few days. None of them compared to the Elva who just entered. She was a vision, a Valkyrie in armor with black wings.

A helmet obscured Sabrina's face, and a few soaked clumps of hair lay upon her shoulders. The rainwater flowed over her armor and black slip-suit. She kept her raven wings tight to her body, her overlaid feathers repelling the rain. The Maige warrior scanned the courtyard. The warriors all stood at attention and greeted her with their right fists pressed to their chests. She returned the salute, and they stood at ease.

A pair of warrior women sat upon horses behind her. One wore armor like Sabrina, but a pair of wings – as white as new snow – silhouetted her body. The other woman was a sorceress. Although her face remained hidden beneath a hood, it glowed ever so slightly. The rain flowed over their slip-suits, washed over their horses, and splashed into great pools. It was an ominous trio, and Rory doubted she would ever see their equal again. It was as if she saw a legend incarnate, an image drawn in pen and ink upon some page of lore.

They dismounted, and Marla and Alexandra moved to their Mistress. They shared some private conversation, and when Marla, departed a legion of soldiers followed after her. Rory wondered where they would all sleep.

For a moment, Rory thought Joash rode with them, but then Joash walked out to greet them. Father and son shared the same square jaw, strong nose, and powerful body. However, the father was gray, and his skin weathered. Kelvin had the look of a young man just entering his prime, a bull charging into the storm.

Kelvin dismounted and spoke with his father. He then strode toward the wall. Cody jumped down from her horse and chased after him. The pair strode up the stairs and marched across the curtain wall. They disappeared into a watchtower.

Rory wondered at the meaning of these new strangers. They were familiar but not familiar at the same time. It was as if old friends had arrived and warm greetings would ensue. Another peculiarity struck her. The courtyard was far away, longer than three football fields. Yet she could see them with perfect clarity. Her eyes could make out the subtle lines in Sabrina's chest plate. When she looked at Sabrina's face, they locked eyes.

Rory gasped and pulled the curtains closed. Her heart raced and pounded in her throat. Every instinct told her to run and never look back. It was as if a great beast focused upon her and contemplated her fate. She wrung her hands and returned to her chair. Jake roused for a second and returned to sleep.

It was too early to go to bed, since she required less and less sleep, but Rory did not intend to leave her chambers. There were too many faces and too many questions, and she had precious few answers. Quite a few men still negotiated with Walter for her hand in marriage. She was, after all, a wealthy heiress and of noble status. Nevertheless, Walter's patience grew thin when she rejected each suitor.

"You will have to marry someone. Women of your station cannot remain unattached. Pick someone," he chided her.

Rory looked at her mother for aid, but she provided little. Meredith's passion for Tamara consumed her. They spent every day and most nights together. Rory tried not to think about it. No one wishes to think about a parent's sexuality.

It appeared as though Walter would soon get a second and a third wife, Tamara, and Amy, whether he wanted them or not. Meredith hired a sire to impregnate Tamara, and the trio spent most nights together. Rory wished her parents would divorce and marry their lovers. To remain together, stuck in a loveless marriage discouraged her, but wealth, land,

and title trapped them both in a loveless marriage. It almost seemed to be a race to see who could bear the first male child. Although a mere infant, he would inherit the bulk of their lands and the family title. Time and tide would sweep her aside.

Rory lingered long in doubt as night engulfed the castle. The firelight reflected off the blackened glass, multiplying the flames. She rose up from her chair and wandered toward the hearth. She picked up a log and tossed it onto the fire. Sparks leaped from the logs and soared up the chimney, the smell of burning wood and lingering in the air. Her fingers glided over stylish silver and glass containers. They held vanilla and other scents to pour on the flame.

A knock came from her bedroom door and took her by surprise. "Did you forget something," she said to Amy. When she opened the door, she saw Sabrina. She leaped back and gasped. "I'm sorry. I thought it was my handmaid. Please," she said and stepped aside, "come in."

Sabrina no longer wore her armor but wore a long antique white silk gown. It contrasted her raven hair and wings, making her appear angelic. The Maige strolled into the room. "I like your chambers. They feel like a comfortable cottage set out in the woods. May I sit?"

"Of course," Rory replied. She hurried to the hearth and said, "I can make us a cup of tea if you would like. I have some chamomile."

"That would be nice," Sabrina said. Rory set the kettle on an iron armature and swung it into the flames. She then opened a small chest. "I have some sugar cookies too." She placed eight of them onto the plate and carried it over to a small, round table set between the chairs. The kettle began to whistle. Rory used a potholder and removed it. After filling a tea-cozy, she carried a serving tray back to the table.

Rory smoothed her silk gown and robe underneath her. Sabrina waited in silence as Rory poured two cups of tea. She handed a cup to Sabrina and took the other. Sabrina took a sip and pondered a moment. "It's very comforting, like this room."

"Thank you," Rory replied. However, she sensed a greater depth to Sabrina's words. They felt like a stinging rebuke.

"Joash told me of your narrow escape at the altar. It surprises me how some traditions linger. They live on well past their usefulness. I am sorry to hear of your ordeal." Sabrina set down her cup. "It may surprise you to learn that we share a common origin." Rory looked up from her tea and cocked her head.

"I too was born of other lives, some male and others female. I suppose most of them were male though. I remember what it is like to be a man, to love a woman and father children. It is so much different from my life now, as a female. There are many times I wake up disoriented by my body."

Sabrina crossed her legs and nibbled a cookie. "Unlike you, I can transform myself and change back into a man." Rory perked up at this news, and for a moment she let herself hope. "It's never the same. I am a woman playing at being a man. My feminine gender is like gravity pulling back toward my true form."

"I can only give you this advice. Allow others to share your feelings of awkwardness and self-doubt. It allows them to connect with you and know that you are genuine," Sabrina said.

It was not the news Rory wished to hear. Christy flashed in her mind, and then she felt the rise of her breasts. One day, a child would come from her body, and an infant would suckle at her breasts. It was a strange and disturbing destination. "But you could change me back."

"No. I'm sorry. That is beyond my ability. There is a power at work within you that has not completed its task. You are no longer human. But I'm sure you sensed this," Sabrina said.

Rory nodded and shivered, "What am I?"

"You're an elva, an Elven female. Time will draw your entire family to your new people. All of this is a phantom of your past." Seeing Rory's glassy eyes, she said, "I did not come here to upset you. I wish only to tell you that I know above anyone else what you are going through. You are not alone."

Sabrina took a sip of tea. "I also wish to impart some advice. When one is on a journey, one will happen upon places of rest and repose. They are so sweet and joyous that one may be tempted to linger. This is a mistake. For what was once a reward may soon become a burden. As each day passes, the journey ahead grows longer with the delay. If one lingers too long, one may perish without reaching one's goals."

"You cannot remain here, looking backward at what was. Let go. The sooner you do, your burden will lighten."

"I know what you said makes sense, but I want to go back. I want my life back. I want to go home," Rory said.

Sabrina rose to her feet. "Thank you for the tea. I know I just arrived, but I will be leaving soon. I only stopped by to make sure that the Elven priests had the provisions that they required."

Rory lingered in silence as Sabrina strolled across the room. Sabrina's wings framed angelic body, and her round bottom draped in silk. The Maige lingered in the doorway and turned back to Rory. "Consider my words. Remember, they come from experience."

The door lock clicked as it shut. Rory picked up the scrapbook and thumbed through the book. Memories of a life she never experience lay before her. She set down the book and rose to her feet. Sabrina's words reverberated in her mind like the pure clarion call of a trumpet.

Rory awoke several times during the night. Sleep came to her in fragmented bits. When she turned on the light, Jake would his head and pry open his eyes. Jake watched Rory stand before the window and stare off into the darkness. Far off in the distance, she could see the Gleason City lights blazing in the darkness.

She smoothed her silk gown underneath her and lounged on her favorite brown leather recliner. After she had swung out the leg support, she drew a blue blanket over her for warmth. A copy of "The Deep" by Mickey Spillane provided a much-needed distraction. She put on a pair of reading glasses and opened the book. She read a few paragraphs and noticed something peculiar. The text appeared too large and out of focus. She removed her glasses and again read the passage. "Hmm, that's weird." She needed reading glasses since her sophomore year in college. Yet she could read the text just fine without them.

Jake grunted and lay down his head. He dozed off to sleep, intent on finally catching that rabbit that sprinted through his dreams. A few minutes later, he was fast asleep, and the hunt resumed.

Rory read a few paragraphs. She then read the same paragraphs again. After the third attempt, she set down the book and sighed. Her gaze drifted off to the darkness just beyond her window. Her thoughts turned toward Sabrina's departure. She replayed the conversation and her reaction. The prosecuting attorney of guilt and shame leveled its accusations.

Once upon a time, she craved action and adventure. That was when she was a young man before her life and gender changed. He joined the army. After six weeks of training, he was overseas driving a truck. Every bit of desert looked like every other bit. The featureless landscape swept by in endless repetition. When insurgents attacked their convoy, it came as a shock. The crack of automatic weapons fire mixed with explosions and screams. He grabbed his rifle and leaped from the truck. Okay, it was a water truck, but it seemed the right thing to do.

A man wearing old clothes and a red-checkered scarf wrapped around his face scrambled over a dusty hill. He carried a dirty AK47 and a satchel charge. Rory raised his rifle and took aim at the man's chest – the rifle leaped in his hands. Blood spurted from the attacker's neck, and unlike in the movies, the man dropped to the ground like a sack of rocks. He writhed, clutching his neck, and blood squirted through his fingers. He cried out in terrified agony, words without translation but understood – the mortal cry of a dying man. The man's hands slipped from his neck, and his body went limp. Rory sat by the truck tire, his mind numb. The ringing in his ears drowned out the combat.

Everyone complimented him on the kill. They baptized him in beer that night, a unit tradition. He lost his combat virginity and was now a warrior. Rory smiled and accepted the compliments. However, even as they patted him on the shoulder, accepting him as one of their own, the man's death throes and cries replayed in his thoughts. As the alcohol permeated his body, he forced the memory into a secret place inside his mind, present but out of sight, a phantom in the shadows.

This first kill led to more. It is hard to get an exact tally because of the fierce combat: bombs fell; tanks charged; jets soared, and men died – enemy combatants and men he loved like brothers. His platoon killed 16 killed insurgents. This led to a citation and a medal, which he levied in civilian life for admission to the FBI.

A strange thought occurred to Rory. If her male life vanished, what happened to the enemy soldiers? Since she was never there, she never killed them. They might be alive. It was redemptive and disturbing. If she was not there to kill them, what violence might the terrorists have visited upon her comrades? Who died because of her?

Rory rose to her feet and shuffled to her dresser. She picked up a framed photo. She stared at the image of her spring break in Cozumel. She and other teens played in aqua green waters and lay upon golden beaches. It looked all so wonderful and happy. She wished she had that memory instead of the war.

The Seventh Age

Rory put on a white silk bathrobe and released a heavy sigh. She opened her bedroom door and wandered through the castle. Jake followed her, his claws clacking on the marble floor.

Like a restless wraith, Rory wandered through the castle. She trudged up the stairs and entered the bar. Jake hurried past her, eager to explore the labyrinth of interesting smells. She exited through a set of double doors and walked into the night. She strolled along the parapet wall. Puddles of water reflected the torchlight, and a spray of cool mist blasted over the wall. She stood at the wall, her hands touching the rough, wet stone. The darkness hung like a black curtain over the valley and the mountains beyond. She considered leaping from the wall and letting the darkness engulf her.

"Is everything well, Mistress?" asked Geth, the guard on the wall.

"Yes. I had trouble sleeping," Rory replied. "I thought a walk would clear my head."

"I never have trouble with that," the guard chuckled. "By the time morning arrives, I am exhausted. I sleep like the dead, and from what my barrack mates tell me, I snore like an old boar. That's their problem, though, not mine."

She crossed her arms and shivered a bit. A silk nightgown was meager protection from the cold. "Do you ever wonder what your life would be like if you left the castle and did something else?"

"Well, my brother wants me to join with him and buy a farm in Gleason. It would be a lot of work, but I would see my wife and children more often. She favors that. Still, the castle guard pays well. I suppose I think about it more and more lately. Nothing lasts forever. My father always said, 'Life is like a great river. It flows where it wishes and carries us along on its mighty course.'" The guard leaned upon his halberd and sighed. "I do think my time here is short. The season has changed, and it's time to move along. I guess I just linger here hoping for one last glimpse of the good days. But too many of my friends are gone, and the distant shores of my life will never come again."

"I suppose so," she replied and rubbed her arms.

"Say, would you like to come into the guard tower? We have a warm fire and a hot brew. It would warm you down to your toes," he said.

"No thank you. I think I will return to my chambers and try to sleep. It's been good talking to you," she replied. "Come on Jake." The dog chased after her and ran toward the building.

"It's been good speaking to you, Mistress," he replied with a wave.

As Rory walked away, she remembered that she never asked the guard's name. The man disappeared into the night on his appointed rounds. A frigid gust of wind carried icy rain upon it. She hurried up the stairs and reentered the building. The guard was right. She had lingered too long looking for shores that would never come again. Resolve took shape within her, and she set her mind to move forward to new shores.

Chapter 42

Rory moved through the castle like a ghost. She hurried through one hallway to the next, taking the time to peer around corners. Her many suitors were gone, but Christy remained – and that terrified her.

She hurried down three flights of stairs thanks in part to blue jeans and tennis shoes. It felt so wonderful to wear jeans again. As far as she was concerned, the women of Salvia were idiots. Blue jeans were much more practical and comfortable. Their obsession with fine clothing — skirts, corsetry, silks, satin, and lace — bordered on the pathological. The bra, however, was both practical and comfortable, when compared to jiggling boobs.

The empty dining hall was empty; the lunch crowd was not yet arrived. She searched for activity and saw no one. She surged from her hiding place and rushed through the hall, circling around tables and dancing around chairs. The kitchen doors approached. She pushed through them and hurried inside the kitchen. Christy was never a good cook, and Rory was certain that Christy would avoid it.

Rows of stainless steel racks, counters, and stoves lay before her. The dual upright refrigerators lay far down to her left. After circling around the counter, she made her way through the kitchen. She grabbed the handles and opened the dual doors. Glorious food: clusters of grapes, roast beef, ham, chicken, bread, vegetables, and beverages filled the shelves.

She grabbed some sliced ham, cheese, mustard, and rye bread. A sandwich soon filled her hands. She took a bite and purred. The wonder of food to a hungry stomach filled her imaginings. She poured a glass of iced tea and swallowed a gulp. If only they had potato chips, the meal would be perfect. She made a mental note to ask the chef make some.

She took a sip of tea. She felt the weight of eyes upon her. "Hello Rory," Christy said. Rory yelped and jumped. The sandwich flew from her hand, and the glass tea splashed onto the counter. "I'm sorry. I didn't mean to frighten you." Christy grabbed a towel and wiped up the spilled tea.

"It's good to see you." Rory flicked a russet tress over her shoulder and crossed her arms. "I heard you were back in the castle. It is so weird to say that like it is normal. Who lives in a castle anyway? What's wrong with a home? No one needs more than a nice home. True, people with children require more space ...."

"Where are you going?" asked Christy.

"I spoke with Sabrina. She offered me a position in the Valkyrie. They are a group of warrior women. I never really thought of myself as a warrior, but I can't stay here. There are too many memories."

"Does Walter know?"

"No. He would try to stop me. I need some time and space to think," she hitched the pack up her shoulders. "I've arranged for a caravan to take me southeast to Midway City."

Christy hung her head and then embraced Rory saying, "I will miss you."

"I'll miss you too," Rory said.

Bill emerged from the kitchen doors. "Are you two done? The entire kitchen staff is cowering in the back. They need to get lunch ready, and I'm hungry."

"Yes," Christy said, rising to her feet. "We're done."

The Seventh Age

"Bye," Rory said with a wave and jogged out of the kitchen. Christy leaned upon the counter and hung her head. Bill knew he was supposed to comfort Christy, but he had no idea how. "Listen, I'm sure she will be fine. It's just going to take time. Look at you, you got over her 40 years ago."

Fire flashed in Christy's eyes, but it died away. "I suppose. It's like they always say, 'Time heals all wounds.' I have a new life, and I'm happy now."

Her tone, however, led Bill to believe otherwise. "Ben is a good man, a little boring, but a good man. No one stacks a grocery shelf like Ben. He even won awards for it," Bill said. "Or so I hear."

Christy laughed. "You're really terrible at the whole comforting thing." She lapsed back into silence. "When she was in the gray zone, it was like Rory was dead. I had to get over her and go on with my life. I never looked back; I had to be strong. Now all I do is look back."

Chapter 43

A caravan of horses drew merchant wagons over the rough terrain. Armed men kept watch for daemia attacks. They had to reach the next refuge point before nightfall. Rory rode the crest of a rocky hill and pushed back her hood. Wild rolling terrain stretched out before her, and the majestic mountains looked down at her in approval. She was an elva and a warrior. The path to the future lay ahead of her, and it caused a shiver of excitement within her. Her entire life seemed like a dream, but now she was awake, and she was excited to see where the next road led.

She tapped her spurs and rode down the hill. Endless plains of golden wheat stretched out before her. She joined the wagons that snaked along the dirt floor and greeted new friends. The crowd of men, women, dogs, children, and horses soon engulfed her. They pressed on to Midway City, leaving the Wolf's Maw Mountains and Gleason behind them.

The Seventh Age

Epilogue

Tarina closed the scroll and released a weary sigh. The warm fire, the soft pillows, and her melodic voice wooed many young Elvens to sleep. The remainder struggled to keep their eyes open and fought the soft caress of slumber. "That is enough for tonight. We shall resume our tale another time."

This news roused Analee. She yawned and stretched. "But what about the baby?"

"What?" asked Tarina. "What baby?"

"Michael, Rory and Christy's baby," the girl said, "he can't just disappear. He has to be somewhere. They never found him. They can't just leave that poor baby all alone with no one to take care of him. We need to know what happened!"

"The hour is late, and it is not the time to discuss temporal and dimensional mechanics. That story will have to wait for another time." Tarina rose up to her feet and smoothed her gown down her legs. "Now it is time for bed."

"But I want to know about Rory and Christy. Did the new Salvia Parliament government succeed? Are the people of Gleason free?" asked Telgilbor.

"Once again, these are questions for another night. You must have patience. Such stories take time, and great learning takes more than a single day." She rose up and weaved her way through the midst of the sleeping youths. "Lay your heads down and rest. I will tell you another story soon, and then all your questions will be answered."

Tarina lingered in the doorway and watched the young people lay down upon the pillows. Within seconds, their eyes shut, and they fell into a deep slumber. The morning and chores would come in a few hours. The simple tasks would afford them time to meditate on the stories she told and prepare their minds for the ones yet to be told.

She closed the door ever so quietly and lingered on the stairs upper landing. The roar of the waterfalls thundered in the darkness, creating a cool mist that caressed her skin. The city climbed the sides of the hills and lights in the windows twinkled like stars on the land. By them, she saw the lofty towers and resplendent structures of her home.

A pair of night-watch guards strolled past her on the pathway below her. After they had shared a greeting, she strolled onto the upper patio and sat upon a soft lounge. Her elva eyes gazed up at the stars and gave thanks for the worshipful night. Unlike the youths, which required six hours of sleep, she required only three. She opened the scroll and found her favorite story. Each line met her as if it was a letter written by the hand of a friend. Images took shape in her mind, and she imagined herself in the Golden Age of Man: she imagined herself walking the streets of New York City amidst the bustle of the crowd and the perpetual traffic. It must have been so magnificent – a paragon of human achievement – but there was no going back to those days. She and all those who survived were citizens of the "Seventh Age."

The End

www.ingramcontent.com/pod-product-compliance
Lightning Source LLC
Chambersburg PA
CBHW021305250626
47155CB00002B/393